A Good Place

Curt Iles

"Now I don't mind choppin' wood,
And I don't care that the money's no good.
You take what you need and leave the rest,
But they should never have taken the very best."
— Robbie Robertson
"The Night They Drove Old Dixie Down."

A Good Place

Curt Iles

Author of

The Wayfaring Stranger

Creekbank Stories

www.creekbank.net

Also by Curt Iles

The Wayfaring Stranger
The Mockingbird's Song
Hearts across the Water
Wind in the Pines
The Old House
Stories from the Creekbank

To learn more, visit www.creekbank.net

Curt is represented by Terry Burns of Hartline Agency.
www.hartlineliterary.com

A Good Place
©2009 Creekbank Stories
ISBN 978-0-9705236-9-3
Library of Congress Number 2009909012
Library of Congress Cataloguing in Publication Data available upon request.

Contact Information
Creekbank Stories
PO Box 332
Dry Creek, LA 70637
1 866 520 1947

For Book Discussion Guide, Author Notes, and more,
visit www.creekbank.net

Cover design by Chad Smith
Interior design by Marty Bee
Cover painting by Bill Iles "Upper Field Pines"

Acknowledgements

In spite of the fact that my name is on the cover, closer inspection would probably reveal hundreds of fingerprints all over this work. I've been so fortunate being blessed with friends, encouragers, fellow storytellers, and editors who've guided this book along.

After seven books as an independent author, I know how important a team is. In the back of this book, I've attempted to acknowledge those who have made major contributions toward *A Good Place*.

As you enjoy this novel, remember that many others helped. Any deficiencies in the book are all mine, not theirs. By the way, for corrections, improvements and additions in future editions, please email us at **curtiles@aol.com**. Your involvement will make *you* part of our team.

Thanks to all who've put their fingerprints on this book, on my writing, as well as my life and heart.

Curt Iles
November 2009

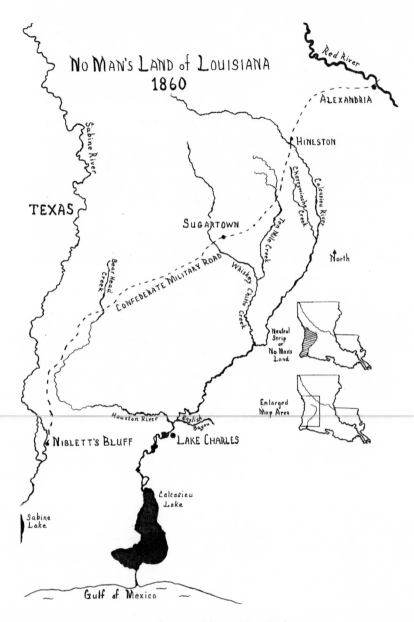

Map designed by Debra Tyler

Dedication

In memory of my great grandparents, Frank and Theodosia Iles.

During the short decade that we shared life, "Pa" and "Doten" connected me to the beauty and wonder of Louisiana's 19th century "No Man's Land."

Pa was the grandson of Joe and Eliza Moore, the fictionalized heroes of this story. Doten's family homesteaded the land I grew up on. They both gave me a precious legacy—one that I attempt to pass on in my writing.

Although long gone, Pa and Doten live on in my heart. I thank God for this couple who instilled deep roots, a love of the woods, and a strong sense of connection in our family.

Westport

There are two villages named Westport, both
connected in this story.

One sits along the mountainous Atlantic coast of Ireland.
The other is a rural crossroads deep in the rolling
piney woods of Louisiana.

Both are good places.
Two good places connected by this story.
The story of an unlikely couple named Joe and Eliza.

Part I

THE STORM

Chapter 1

WHEN Daddy shoved me under the table, I knew this wasn't just *any* storm.

As the crow flies, our Louisiana log cabin was a hundred miles from the Gulf of Mexico. When this day had quietly begun, no one had any idea a hurricane was churning ashore. Here we were less than twelve hours later, however, riding it out under our kitchen table.

Watching Momma trying in vain to keep the lantern lit, a knot of fear as big as a turnip formed in my throat. Giving up on the lantern, she turned to Daddy. "This ain't no normal thunderstorm. Do you think . . .?"

She couldn't, or wouldn't, say the word. In her eyes was something I'd never seen before—raw fear. Her hand trembled as she placed it on my knee. Momma's obvious alarm moved Daddy into action, and he said the word she'd couldn't. "*Hurricane*—this has to be a *hurricane*."

Crawling from under the table, he said to her, "Eliza, get the windows covered best you can." Then he grabbed me. "Mayo, come with me to get the animals in."

On that August evening in 1862, I was nearly 12 and didn't have enough sense to realize the danger, so I eagerly joined him.

As soon as we cleared the lee of the house, the wind whipped us, tearing Daddy's hat right off his head. He ran toward the barn, not even looking back as the lightning outlined his silhouette with each strike. Reaching the building and pulling me inside, he said, "Pen the animals, and throw some hay in their troughs."

He hurried out, leaving me alone in the building's growing darkness with only whimpering animals. I found our horse, Dallas, and began stroking his mane. He was snorting, pawing, and shaking as bad as Momma, sensing some kind of evil blowing in that howling wind.

Daddy stuck his head back in, "Hurry, it ain't safe. Let's git." Hunkered down, we ran by our outbuildings, stopping only to bolt the smokehouse and adjacent kitchen.

I cowered under the walkway that connected our kitchen and house, holding onto a post. With my other hand, I covered my head as debris whizzed by.

A flying object struck Daddy square in the back, causing him to stumble. He turned and shouted, "Whoa! Let's go." Scampering onto the porch, I heard the first tree crash, causing both the house and my heart to shudder.

As we went through the door, my dog, Bo, brushed straight past me and hunkered down under the table with my mother and sister, Colleen. Momma, who was in the family way, squatted on the dirt floor, still fiddling with the flickering lantern.

"There ain't no use fooling with that thing," Daddy said, "There's too much wind blowing through the cracks for it to stay lit."

Holding out the cypress shingle that'd struck him in the back, he knelt by Momma. Frowning and rubbing the whelp on his back, he whispered, "It's real bad out there."

"Honey, are—are you all right?" she asked.

Before he could answer, another crashing tree jarred our house and Colleen cried, "Daddy, wh—what's happening? Is this the war?" Colleen, half my age, had a fear that the ongoing War Between the States was coming to kill us. The noise outside assured her that its cannons had finally reached Western Louisiana.

Another crashing tree, this one even closer, caused her to scream, "It's a big gun."

"No, Child, that was a tree falling." Momma said as she watched Daddy at the window peering out. I was watching him too, and knew *one* thing for sure, my father would get us through this.

"Eliza, kids, listen to me," Daddy said in a steady voice. With the howling wind outside, we had to lean in real close, but when he spoke, his words seemed to drown out the storm. "Now, this has gotta be a hurricane. I don't know how long it'll last, but we're gonna be all right 'cause we're together. We'll trust the Lord to get us through. This may've caught us flat-footed, but we'll get through it together."

We'll get through it together. That was all I wanted to hear, and it was what I needed to hear: Together.

"Daddy, are we gonna blow away?" Colleen asked. I glanced up at our creaking roof, wondering the same thing.

Before he could answer, Momma pulled my sister closer, "Baby, this house was built 'horse high, bull tough, and pig tight,' by your daddy and it'll stand up to anything any storm throws at it."

Colleen nervously burst out giggling at Momma's saying, causing us all to laugh in spite of our fear. However, our smiles soon faded as the storm intensified and the rafters lifted and shuddered with every strong gust.

"I feel—I feel so helpless," Momma said, holding Colleen closer.

Daddy repeated, "We will get through this. Together, we can do it."

At that moment, I hoped he was right.

Sitting under the table as the wind howled, it was hard to believe this day had started so quietly. Looking back over it, we'd missed several signs—omens of the approaching storm.

The coming storm's first clue had occurred earlier that morning when Daddy had met me at the barn for chores. "Listen, Mayo."

"To what?"

"It's too quiet—even the crickets have stopped chirping." Daddy was almost whispering.

Later, as daylight appeared, he'd nodded toward the rising sun before saying, *Chomh deargle le fuil.*

"What?" I asked.

"It's Irish for 'Red as blood.' Look at the sun—where I grew up along the Irish coast, the sailors always said, 'Red sun at night, sailor's delight. Red sun at mornin', sailor take warnin'.'"

Shrugging his shoulders, he sniffed the air and added, "Air even smells funny. Gives me the doggone willies."

As we'd returned to the house for breakfast, I'd noticed Bo under the steps and called him out. He wouldn't budge, even when I whistled and hollered, "Hunt 'em up, Bo."

Another omen missed.

By midday, the morning's clear weather was long gone—replaced by dark clouds rolling northward on a gusty wind. Darkness came early, seemingly snuffed out by the rising wind, which began driving the rain through the cracks in the walls.

So, less than twelve hours after a clear sunrise and promising day, we were huddled under the table as our whole lives were being blown away.

From time to time, Daddy crawled out and peered out the window. Flashes of lightning lit the worry on his face as he whispered, "Well, this ain't my first storm."

I knew he was right. He'd come to Louisiana fourteen years ago as a lonely teenager at the end of a long journey, from another land of storms—Ireland.

Here in this area called "No Man's Land," he'd grown into a man, met and married my part-Indian mother, and made these piney woods his home. He even named the hill where he built our house "Westport" after his hometown in Ireland, laughingly saying, "This spot's the closest thing I've seen to a mountain in Louisiana."

Daddy loved Louisiana's clear creeks, tall trees, and the freedom it offered—and, until the day he died, referred to it as "a good place to be."

Watching him made me wonder if he thought of it as a good place at this moment. Another crash outside jolted the whole house, prompting Momma's warning, "Joe Moore, get back under here."

He hadn't been back under the table ten seconds, when a huge oak tree smashed through the cabin wall right where he'd stood. As wood splintered and contents of the shelves crashed to the floor, we hunkered tighter under the table.

"Lord, have mercy! It's the end of the world," Momma said.

Reaching out in the dark, I grasped onto a dripping wet limb, thinking It may not be the end of the world, but it's sure gonna be a long night.

Chapter 2

DADDY crawled out to examine the wreckage in the room. Peering through the gaping hole left by the tree, he said, "It took down our whole kitchen!"

I followed, peeking around his elbow. What if that tree would've fallen on the middle of the house?

What we saw next chilled us to the marrow—the coals from our stove, scattered by the crash, had caught the remains of our kitchen on fire. Watching the sputtering fire spread, I said, "Hard to believe anything could burn in this much rain."

"Well, it is." Daddy said. The heat intensified, pushing us back from the hole. The fire lit up the dark room as we watched our entire world collapsing around us. My mind spun as I wondered what could—or would—happen next.

"Will it burn down our house, Daddy?"

"I don't think so—the walls are soaked and the wind's blowing away." Matter-of-factly, he added, "That's why we built the kitchen separate—to prevent fires from spreading."

Momma crawled from under the table, stood by Daddy, before saying, "That table wouldn't have done much good, if that oak had fallen on us."

The fire's reflection lit up their faces and highlighted the great difference in their appearances. My mother was a Redbone, an isolated No Man's Land group that lived in a section called "Ten Mile." She carried all of the strong Indian features that identify the Ten Mile Redbones—bronzed skin, long black hair, and high cheekbones framed in a wide face set off by deep dark eyes. Those dark eyes, now shimmering with tears, could always mystically delve into a person's soul—especially mine when I was in trouble.

My father stood beside her. It was difficult even to describe *his*

7

eyes—Momma called them 'fierce green,' and their hue changed according to his mood.

The glow of the kitchen fire highlighted everything Irish about him—those eyes, sandy hair, freckled fair skin, and ruddy cheeks. Like an old faithful hat, Daddy always wore a faint trace of a grin that seemed to say, *Go ahead, Life. Throw your best shot at me.* Even in spite of this storm, I still could glimpse the glint of that smile.

Sensing my stare, he turned and winked, "Lad, this too shall pass. It'll pass and we'll be all right. Remember—*together.*"

"Together." I repeated the word as if it was the magic password out of this nightmare. Despite the comfort of this word, the storm continued to rage even as the fire ebbed, and we returned to safety under the table. I eased in between Bo and my sister Colleen. Amazingly, she'd slept right through the big oak's crash and the kitchen fire.

Breathing softly, now cradled in Momma's arms, she was a tiny female version of Daddy. Everything about her was "Pure Irish," including her name, which meant "girl" in Irish.

Her fair skin made her stick out in Ten Mile like a new saddle on an old pig. My grandma once remarked, while watching Colleen playing among her dark friends, "Child, you look like a lost grain of salt in a pepper shaker."

Looking down at my own brown arms, as dark as any Redbone in our neck of the woods, I knew exactly *what* I was: a dark grain of pepper—a child of these piney woods and creek bottoms.

Daddy often reminded me as he rubbed my arm, "Just remember that under that dark skin is an Irishman, stuffed into a Redbone body."

I did have one trait from Daddy, my green eyes. There were no other Redbones with green eyes; so, I took lots of ribbing. I was just as proud of my eye color, as I was of my dark skin.

Those green eyes of mine watched the smoldering remnant of the kitchen fire, as the rain finally put it out and darkness returned. I wondered what time it was. Our mantel clock lay shattered on the floor.

With or without the clock, the night seemed endless. Darkness, and the uncertainty about whatever was happening outside, made the hurricane seem even more sinister.

Colleen startled awake and began crying. To calm her—as well as pass the hours—my parents took turns telling stories. Daddy, who loved telling of his childhood years in Ireland, began: "Once when a spring storm blew in off the Atlantic, the wind was so fierce it overturned my wagon. I crawled under it, hiding with the four pigs I was taking to market."

He poked Momma. "Here I am again—stuck in a storm—this time with three pigs."

"And one smelly dog," Momma added.

Daddy had a weak spot Momma could always exploit—he was some kind of ticklish, so she goosed him good, saying, *"Four* pigs and a dog."

"Did the pigs smell bad?" Colleen asked.

"Do pigs smell any way *but* bad?"

We giggled as Daddy sniffed. "It smells a little like pigs under this table."

"It's that wet dog." Momma grabbed her brush broom and swatted at Bo, who quickly scurried out from under the table.

Daddy grinned. "No. It's worse than that ol' dog. I believe someone must of messed in their britches when that tree fell."

"Well, it ain't me," Momma said.

"Or me," Colleen added. "I was asleep."

"Well, it must be Mayo or me."

"It ain't me neither," I quickly said. "But it scared me bad enough to."

"Sure enough, Son. I agree."

We all laughed, and he returned to his story. With the hurricane howling outside, his tale took on a new nature. Huddled under our table, we were back in Ireland under that wagon with him.

Then my mother, with her deep roots in these Louisiana woods, told about a tornado she remembered from her childhood.

I loved the way she said it, as in "that 'tornader' drove pine straw plumb into the bark of trees. I seen it with my own two eyes."

You'd have thought these stories would terrify two children in a hurricane, but the fact that my parents had survived these storms strengthened my faith that we would, too.

Colleen jumped with each lightning flash, so Momma began stroking her hair, telling of Jesus calming the sea after being asleep in the boat with his disciples.

My mother, in spite of little book learning, was a marvelous storyteller. "Child, those disciples thought they were goners on the raging Sea of Gal'lee that night, but you ain't never in danger when Jesus is in the boat with you."

"Even if he's asleep?" Colleen asked.

"Yep."

"Is Jesus in this storm with us, Momma?"

"Child, he's been with us through thick 'n thin, and he promised never to leave us."

This reassurance calmed my sister as well as did a whole lot of good for me, too. I had begun to be kind of a "doubting Thomas" in the midst of the hurricane, but her soothing faith calmed me.

However, I knew exactly how those disciples had felt in the tossing boat and silently prayed, Jesus, if you don't keep this house together, it's gonna fall on top of us all.

Daddy, a little more reserved on spiritual topics, cleared his throat, "Well, there's one thing for sure—life's right full of storms." He paused, nodding toward the huge gash in our wall. "A fella's in one of three places in his life: In a storm, coming from a storm, or headed right into a storm."

"Where are we?" My sister asked.

"If it's possible, we're in all three right now." Even in the darkness, I could see his smile; like the earlier flames, it seemed to light up the room. I knew that if he could smile in the middle of this storm, so could I.

That stormy night was one of the worst of my life. I'd always been scared of the dark, and a terror-filled night during a hurricane didn't help my fears.

Looking back a lifetime later, it was a memorable night in another way—I was under the table with my family, and all we really had was each other. Now, as then, I realize that was enough.

The hours crept by as Colleen, wedged between our parents, fell asleep again. We shivered as the rain blew into the pitch-black house, soaking our clothes, and making our cabin's dirt floor a muddy mess.

Finally, light grudgingly came while the wind slackened. To call it sunrise would have been a great exaggeration as only faint streaks of daylight timidly showed themselves above the horizon.

As the storm ebbed, we ventured out onto the front porch. The sight that met us was stunning—trees snapped off in every direction, leaving a foot-deep carpet of pine limbs, wet leaves, and debris covering the ground. The roof of our barn was gone, as well as the adjacent rail fence, with no sign of our animals anywhere.

A heavy wet fog hung as testimony to the storm's deluge even as the sky cleared in the south. Our attention turned to the house along with the destruction from the fallen tree. The huge pin oak had actually split, leaving one-half still standing, while the other half smashed our kitchen and house. The split clearly revealed that the heart of the oak was rotten and nearly hollow.

"I sure thought it was the strongest tree on this place, but all that time, it was purt'near hollow," Momma said.

On top of the kitchen damage plus the hole in our wall, the oak's limbs had knocked loose a whole section of cypress shingles from the roof.

Daddy surveyed the wreckage and debris in every direction. "Well, it's *still* a good place."

Momma scanned the fallen trees. "One good thing about it—we'll have plenty of firewood this winter."

Soberly, Daddy added, "Shame we can't eat pine cones and tree limbs, 'cause it'd be easy pickings." He poked a hoe handle in the smoking rubble of the kitchen, where most of our foodstuff and seed corn had been lost in the fire. He pulled two cast iron cooking pots and a skillet out of the ashes before shaking his head. "Ain't nothing else worth saving in this mess."

Momma joined us as we headed toward the barn, stepping lightly on the wet debris that squished with every step. "It's like walking on a wet quilt."

We worked our way toward the barn fearing the worst. Sure enough, there were several dead pigs and sheep, and Dallas was nowhere in sight. The chicken coops were all busted up and none of our chickens, geese, or guineas were around. Daddy scanned the woods. "I don't know how any of our range cows or woods hogs could survive something like this."

"Daddy, are we gonna be all right?" I asked.

He looked me squarely in the eye after picking up a broken fence railing. "Sure we will. This is just one of them storms we talked about during the night." Standing the railing against the fence, he said, "We'll get up, build back, and keep on." I didn't see as much of the glinting smile—it seemingly had been replaced by resolve visible in his tightened jaw.

Just then, we heard barking in the distance. Thinking Bo might have found Dallas or any of our other animals, I ran toward the sound. Climbing through piles of fallen trees, I was soon a good quarter of a mile from the house. The storm's aftermath shocked me—the world as we knew it had been destroyed. Hundreds of large longleaf pines had been snapped off like matchsticks. Their twisted trunks and mangled tops all pointed northwest, bowing as if in respect to the night's strong winds.

Hardwood trees—oaks, sweet gums, even hickories—had given way in an entirely different manner. They'd fallen whole— "clay-rooted" with tops, trunks, and tangled limbs lying on the ground. The mud along with red clay covering their exposed root systems showed the sheer power of the storm.

Walking in heavy fog among the fallen trees and dangling roots, I wandered further from the house, the blue sky reassuring me the worst was over. Feeling a little cocky, I hopped up on a fallen pine and yelled to the north at the fading storm's clouds, "Bring it on—we can take it."

That's when I heard yelling, but it wasn't my echo. Turning

toward the house from my high perch, I saw Daddy gesturing frantically. I could only make out two words. "*Storm . . . run!*"

Looking behind him to the south, I saw it—angry low clouds rushing toward the house. As if in a dream, I watched the trailing wall of the storm swallow him.

Well, run *I did*. I sprinted for my life toward the house, dodging branches and clambering over roots. Cold panic quickly replaced my cockiness. A night with this storm convinced me I didn't want to wrestle this monster alone.

The hurricane erupted with sudden fury before I made it halfway to the house. Blinded by driving walls of rain and the fog, I stumbled through the maze of fallen trees unsure of my direction. Tripping over a limb, followed by a face-first fall into the mud, I struggled to rise, thinking this storm has returned with one evil purpose—to kill me.

Suddenly I felt a movement beside me—it was Bo. He sniffed me and began barking. Getting to my feet, I put my hand on his back as he, still barking, picked his way through the downed trees and debris. After a few long minutes of following Bo in the biting rain, I fell again. Before I could rise, a strong hand grabbed me.

"This ain't no good—let's git to the house." Daddy's shout over the wailing storm was music to my ears. In his strong grip, we struggled onto the porch and back into the house under our sturdy table. Once again, Bo pushed through the cracked door, and I hugged his wet body close, knowing he'd saved my life.

On the other side of me was my mom, who was hugging me as tightly as I held Bo. She said, "Mayo Joseph Moore, don't you wander off again like that. You hear me?"

"Yes Ma'am." She was a dangerous woman when she was scared or mad, and right then she was some of both.

The winds on the backside of the hurricane were from the opposite direction, seemingly not as strong. Daddy later laughed. "Oh yeah, the second half of the storm was just as strong—it just didn't seem so because it was daylight. Besides there weren't too many trees left to blow down."

We didn't understand about a hurricane's calm eye until that day, but we learned a lesson not easily forgotten.

After many more hours, the wind and rain gradually eased. This time, we waited a long time before venturing off the porch, our experience with the temporary blue sky having taught us a lesson. Daddy, pointing at the now clear sky, remarked, "Fool me once, shame on you. Fool me twice, shame on me."

I agreed, "I ain't going back out there until I'm sure this time."

Finally, convinced that the storm was truly over, we did the only thing we knew to do— we got up, dusted off, and went to work.

'Cause that's what you do when you live in a good place.

Chapter 3

IF someone asked me when I became a man, I'd reply that I *started* becoming one the day after the hurricane. It began when Daddy called for me. "Come over here, Mayo. It's time you became friends with a crosscut saw."

I'd watched men use a six-foot crosscut, and they made using the saw seem easy. I excitedly gripped the wooden handle while my father took the other end. It took only a few pulls for me to realize it wasn't as easy as it looked.

By the end of the day, my hands were covered with blisters. I realized this two-man operation wasn't easy to learn or do. Daddy showed me how to push then pull in rhythm to keep from working ourselves to death, saying, "Any two people can cut with a crosscut saw, but knowing how to do it well is an art.

"Mayo, you find out what a man is made out of when you're on the other end of a saw with him. If he's lazy or quits easily, you'll know it soon."

Now, I was a long way from being a man, but I was determined that no one, *especially* my father, would ever say that about me. However, in spite of my desire, I probably wasn't much help. It seemed he pulled both the saw and me on each stroke.

That day was busy—repairing the roof, working on the fence, plus rounding up animals scattered through the woods. Most of all, it was a day of cutting an endless line of limbs and treetops. The best news of the day came when our horse Dallas, still looking unnerved as well as skittish, showed up right before sunset.

As we returned to the house in the lengthening shadows, I felt as whipped as Dallas looked.

"Come help me with one more thing," Daddy said as I

shuffled across the yard.

He cupped his hands and hollered in a series of loud yells mimicking an owl. I stood by him, waiting for the answer from the next homestead south, the Tyler family. Ben and Bessie Tyler were my parents' best friends. Ben's evening holler specialty was his hog call, which he'd repeat six times in a row.

We waited in the dusky stillness to hear his reply but none came.

Daddy repeated his hoot owl call, a realistic version of the barred owl's eight-note song. "Hoo hoo-hoo hoo, hoo hoo-hoo hoawww."

Momma came up behind us and tickled him as she whispered the owl's call in his ear, "Who cooks for you? Who cooks for you-allll?"

Daddy tried to ignore her as he listened for a reply. Repeating his call with still no answer, he said, "If they don't answer this time, I'm riding over there."

He hooted again then waited. There was a long silence before we heard it. I can't describe Ben Tyler's hog call—it was high-pitched carrying a long distance through the woods. It was similar to what folks later called "a rebel yell."

As it was repeated six times, we knew all was well at the Tyler household.

I asked, "How'd this evening holler thing get started?"

"I'm not sure. They were doing it long before I came to these woods."

"It's been part of our Ten Mile ways forever and a day," Momma said.

Then I asked, "What about other neighbors, the Merkle family? Why don't they do the evening holler?" Daddy scowled at the mention of these new neighbors to the north.

"I've tried to be neighborly to those folks, but they ain't interested."

Momma frowned too—at my daddy. "Joe, you need to be nice to those folks. They've had a hard time."

"But they don't want to be neighborly—that Merkle fellow

told me right out loud."

"Yep, but they're *still* our neighbors. In the morning, we're going to check on 'em."

The story of how the Merkle family settled in our area was a sad one. The previous spring, they'd been part of a seven-team wagon train passing through on their way to Texas. While they camped here, their two-month-old baby died. They'd buried the child beside the road. The following day when the wagon train moved on west, Mrs. Merkle had refused to leave. She told her husband this was where they were staying—they wouldn't be "leaving her child." So she, her husband, their ten-year-old twins, and three-year-old daughter stayed behind, seemingly chosen by fate to put their roots down in Ten Mile.

Since then, all kinds of stories spread about their background. One of the twins told a wild story of them being run out of Mississippi, changing their names, and traveling west to start a new life. This tale took on a life of its own making neighbors wary of them.

When Daddy reminded her of these stories, Momma said, "It don't matter what stories we've heard. They're our neighbors, and we're gonna check on them."

"But honey—."

She clapped her hands. "Those folks ain't got a pot to pee in, nor a window to throw it out. They need our help, and we're gonna go help 'em."

That settled it. When my strong-willed mother put her foot down, it was just a matter of time before we all fell in line. We'd learned long ago that resistance was useless.

The next morning, my daddy tried again to talk her out of going to check on them. He pointed at her bulging belly, "Honey, don't you think you're a little far along to be riding over there?"

"I'll be just fine."

So, by mid-morning, Daddy saddled Dallas, helped Momma on, and our family made our way through the downed timber to the Merkle homestead.

He and I walked together.

"Daddy, you're not too happy going over there, are you?"

"Not really."

"I think Momma's wrong to make us all go."

He stopped in his tracks, grabbing me by the shoulder. "Son, your momma ain't *always* right, but she ain't *never wrong*." His wink let me know this was said half in jest. We both laughed as he nodded toward her. "Son, don't you forget it. She's *never* been wrong in all the years I been with her."

Arriving at the Merkle place, we found damage everywhere. A big pine had smashed their wagon to pieces, but their rickety lean-to had barely survived.

The destroyed wagon caused Daddy to say under his breath, "Well, there goes any hope of them moving along."

A smoky fire under a black kettle in the yard showed some life. Nearing the house, an awful odor caught my attention. Daddy noticed it too, saying, "Whew, that smell would gag a maggot."

"Joe Moore, hush your mouth and behave yourself. These are our neighbors, so we'll be nice to them—smelly or not," Momma said through clenched teeth.

Sarah Merkle came out of the shelter holding the dirty three-year-old girl.

My momma spoke first, "Mornin' Mrs. Merkle. How'd y'all fare?"

The woman looked as if the storm had sucked both the breath and life out of her. "Survived it. That's 'bout all—jes' survived it."

Daddy helped Momma off the horse, and she took the baby from Mrs. Merkle, asking, "Where are Mr. Merkle and the boys?"

She hesitated. "He… he's, uh, gone off huntin', hoping to shoot some game. The boys are…" Before she could finish, the twins ran out of the lean-to.

Festus and Felix Merkle, identical twins about two years younger than I was, were the worst two boys I'd ever known. After first meeting them in the spring, Daddy said, "I know why the Merkles got run out of Mississippi, as well as any other place they lived—it was on account of those boys. They are *some* kind of bad."

He called them the "Sons of Thunder," adding, "No wonder they're bad. Any boys named Felix and Festus are bound to be rascals."

Momma had corrected him, "But they're Bible names—right from the book of Acts."

"But they ain't *good* Bible names," Daddy said. "Those two fellas were bad guys—you don't name your boys after bad fellows—unless you want them to be bad, too."

The twins had already achieved a rowdy reputation in their few months here. They'd burned down their own smokehouse as well as tearing up several homes where their family visited. Also, they'd earned a well-deserved name for meanness to animals and little kids.

The boys came out in the yard, staring at us as if they'd never seen other humans. Then they went straight to Dallas to harass both the horse and Colleen. While one brother poked Dallas in the withers with a stick, the other twin pulled off Colleen's shoe, then threw it towards the woods.

Momma didn't see what the twins were doing as she again asked. "Mrs. Merkle, how did y'all fare in the storm?"

"We did all right. When you ain't got nothin' to lose, a storm can't do you too much harm," Mrs. Merkle said, her voice trailing off.

"But you're all alive and you've got hope."

Gesturing weakly, she said, "I ain't got much hope, if any."

"Anything we can do to help?" Momma asked.

"Oh, we be jes' fine." Saying this, she gazed blankly off into the woods toward where her husband was, as if she was afraid to speak without his permission.

19

She stood stiffly as Momma talked. When she turned, I saw her black eye and swollen nose. This wasn't the first time she'd shown the marks of her husband's fists since they'd arrived.

I'd only seen her husband, Silas Merkle, twice—and he didn't make a good impression either time. If Mrs. Merkle showed signs of hopelessness, her husband gave off a sense of smoldering hostility.

His looks matched his personality—a long scar ran the length of his right arm, the result of his catching it in a wagon wheel, according to his sons.

However, it was one of his ears that really got my attention—the lobe was gone. Felix had supplied the story. "He got it bit off in a fight." Then he proudly added, "But the fellow that bit it off got a lot more than a mouth full of ear—he caught the business end of my daddy's bowie knife."

The twins lied so badly that it was hard knowing if this story was true or just another one of their tall tales. Having observed their daddy, I could fully believe it was true—Silas Merkle just looked mean. He'd made it clear he didn't cotton to neighbors snooping around, and wanted to be left alone.

As the women visited, Daddy shooed the boys away from both my sister and Dallas. Momma went to the horse, took down a bag of flour along with some roasting ears, handing it to Mrs. Merkle. At first, she resisted, but then as if some rope holding her back had snapped, she greedily grasped it. Her reaction revealed two things: how badly she needed the food as well as how hesitant she was to take it.

She then walked to the lean-to, speaking back over her shoulder, "Thank you—thank you for coming." She went back inside, followed by her children as she hurriedly closed the rickety door.

My parents stood there for a few moments, finally shrugging at each other as if not sure whether to leave or follow her. Then, they returned to the horse, and we headed home.

The trip home was quiet. Finally, Momma said, "Joe, those poor people need our help."

"It's hard to help folks who won't let you. Them's queer folk there. There's a feeling that worries me every time I go there. Did you see her face?" Daddy said.

"Yep, it was hard to miss, weren't it?"

"A grown man that hits a woman ought to be—" He stopped, realizing that I was listening.

He took the saw to cut a limb, and I trotted ahead with him.

"Daddy, will those people make it?"

"What do you mean, 'make it'?"

"Will they survive this time after the storm?"

"I reckon they will." He threw the limb out of the way for the horse to pass. Catching his breath, Daddy pointed back toward the Merkle homestead. "Son, a storm—or any difficulty in life—reveals a lot about people."

"What do you mean?"

"I learned that in the years 'fore I came to America, during our Potato Famine. It destroyed nearly everything good about Ireland as people starved, died, or left by the thousands. In the midst of all this, I saw how hard times reveal a lot about people. I once heard that hard times *build* character, but I don't really agree. Rather, hard times *reveal* character."

"What do you mean—reveal?"

"Mayo, character is who you really are—on the inside, down in your heart. All hard times do, whether it's a famine, hurricane, or whatever, is show the world *who* you are, as well as *what* you're made of.

"Let me give you an example—you noticed how our big oak that fell was rotten inside?"

"Yes, sir. That surprised me."

"Me, too. It seemed the hardiest tree on our place." He wiped his brow. "But that hurricane *revealed*—showed us—what was truly inside. It was dead, rotten, and hollow. It'd been like that all along. It just took a big storm to show us. It's no different with people.

"In Ireland, I saw mean folks get *meaner* . . . and good folks get *better*. Often people acted much different from how

I'd thought they would. Often in bad ways, but sometimes in amazing good ways."

I couldn't get our neighbors off my mind, so I asked, "How will those Merkle people react to the storm?"

"Can't say yet. Only time'll tell. They've taken some hard licks, and I believe that man is as crooked as a dog's hind leg."

"What about us?" I asked.

"What?"

"Will *we* make it?"

He grinned as he leaned on the crosscut saw. "With the help of the Lord, we'll get through this. We'll get better, not bitter. We'll come out of this stronger—stronger and better."

We resumed sawing and each stroke seemed to repeat, *stronger, better.*

Yes, stronger, better; stronger, better; stronger, better.

Neither of us knew it, but there were plenty of storms waiting to give us chances to get stronger and better.

Chances for both: stronger *and* better.

Chapter 4

THE day after our visit at the Merkle homestead, we made another journey—a four-mile trip along a narrow trail to the home of Momma's parents, Willard and Virginia Clark.

PaPaw and MaMaw, as I called them, lived on a homestead not far from Cherry Winche Creek. Momma had worried as to how they'd fared in the storm. In addition, she wanted to bring MaMaw home with us before the baby arrived.

So, Daddy helped my mother onto Dallas, and we set out on the trip. Normally, it would only have taken a few hours, but there was nothing normal about the time after the hurricane. Pine tops as well as debris littered the trail, so we had to cut and pick our way through the mess.

Daddy walked ahead, followed by me with Colleen in my footsteps. I couldn't resist turning to her, "Remember about snakes: 'First person scares it; second one makes it mad; third one gets bit.'"

She squealed, running forward for Daddy to carry her. Scowling, he looked back, "Quit tormenting your sister like that."

"But Momma's the one who taught it to me," I shrugged innocently.

Later, he put Colleen down, making me walk last. She taunted, "You walk third so the mean old snake'll get you."

To get revenge, I pulled a locust shell off a tree, stuck it on my nose, and came up behind her. "Boo."

She screamed which made Daddy turn, "Son, I'm gonna whup you good if you keep aggravating your sister." I knew he meant it, so I fell back.

Soon we reached a tangle of fallen pines, so we cut the twisted tops of three trees blocking the road, pulling them free to make room for the horse. Just ahead was Oakland Graveyard, a small family graveyard west of the trail. This is where Momma's people were buried, and she wanted to see how it'd fared.

The six small grave houses had all lost shingles, with one leaning badly. The graves though, seemed fine. As Daddy and I worked on the leaning building, Colleen turned to Momma. "Momma, why do they build these little houses?"

"It's respect for the dead. The roof keeps the weather off, while the wooden fence keeps livestock or wolves from bothering the grave."

Colleen picked up a white shell from one of the graves. "What's this?"

"Our people have always covered graves with white shells. It goes back to our Indian roots."

"But why?"

"Don't nobody rightly know."

With the building straightened, we looked at the lone cedar tree in the center of the graveyard. It had lost several limbs, which we began sawing up. Momma and Colleen straightened up some of the wooden grave markers knocked over by the limbs.

Momma turned to Colleen. "This cedar tree was planted when they put the first grave here. With its year-round green leaves, it represents eternal life."

"What's 'eternal'?"

"It means forever—without end."

I watched Momma break off a cedar twig and discreetly put it in her dress pocket. Near the big tree were two fresh graves—a large grave beside a smaller one.

"Why's this red dirt on these?" Colleen asked, tugging on Momma's skirt.

Momma stood upright.

Daddy quit sawing.

They stared at each other, as my mother said, "Honey, in these woods, sometimes little babies get sick and die. A baby's buried in that little grave, but it's not really here—that baby's safe with Jesus."

She whispered, repeating to herself, "*Safe with Jesus.*"

I held my breath hoping Colleen wouldn't ask anymore—especially not ask about the larger grave.

I looked at both graves—the grave of a mother with her baby buried beside, covered by piney woods red dirt. I knew the story well. Late last year, a pioneer family was traveling through our area when the mother went into labor. Both she and her newborn died in the wagon during childbirth.

As soon as we'd gotten word about these deaths, Momma immediately said, "We're going over to help that poor man bury his dead."

"But we don't even know them," I had said, showing my frustration.

"It don't matter. They deserve for folks to be there out of respect." So on the coldest day of that winter, our family had traveled to stand by these strangers. When we arrived at the graveyard, I watched the broken-hearted husband standing with his four small children, all of them weeping loudly.

I never took my eyes off him, and never saw him say a word. Two open graves, dug earlier by several local men, lay in front of the silent husband. As the bodies of his wife and child, wrapped in sheets, were carefully lowered into the holes, I thought he might jump in after them. Like the cold wind, you could actually feel the grief blowing around the whole graveyard.

My PaPaw Clark stepped forward, hat in hand, to say a few words and then to pray. When he said "Amen," the men began covering the graves. Each shovelful of dirt brought shrieks from the children. Everyone, except the men with the shovels, stared at the ground as if averting their gaze would block out the horrible sounds.

When the shoveling stopped, no one knew what to say or do, as the father silently loaded his sobbing children into the wagon. Their crying for their mother was so painful that two couples bolted away, and several of the remaining onlookers put their hands over their ears.

The stone-faced father climbed up on his wagon, turned it

westward, and continued his journey. It was a long time before the cries of the children faded. No one standing at the graveside said a word as everyone left in family groups.

We were the last to leave. "I ain't sure I'll ever get the cries of those poor children out of my mind," Momma said. "Saddest thing I ever seen."

Turning to go, I'd said to Daddy, "That sure was cold how the man just up and left without a word."

He placed his hand on my shoulder. "Son, cut that fellow a little slack on the plow rope. Grief and pain are hard traveling companions. Folks often choose to move on, trying to escape it, but it goes with you—jes' follows you along."

Pointing up the trail where the wagon had disappeared into the pines, he'd repeated, "Jes' follows you along."

He spoke it as a man who well knew what he was talking about.

I was jarred back from my recollection by Daddy's elbow. "Wake up boy, and move that last cedar limb."

Dragging it away from the graveyard, I thought about how grief affects people so differently—one *woman*, Mrs. Merkle buries a baby, vows never to leave, and changes a family's destiny. Then, a *man* buries his wife and baby, not able to leave quick enough. Neither choice is right or wrong—just different ways of dealing with the same thing—sorrow.

I thought about how my mother broke off that twig, wondering what it meant.

Daddy called to my sister, "Colleen, come over here and help me on my end of this saw." She ran over, and he told her, "Back in Ireland, where there aren't many trees, graves are made of stone."

Colleen asked, "What's stone?"

He laughed. "I guess you've never seen rock or stone, have you?"

As Daddy tried to explain, I could only think, *Imagine living somewhere where there aren't trees.*

Finished with our cleaning, I walked over to a lone grave in the corner of the graveyard where Barzille Bryant was buried. When Barzille, or "Old Bar" as he was known, had neared the end of his life, he'd made two requests. First, he requested burial under the nearby oaks so that "the chinquapin acorns could fall on his grave."

His second request was even more unusual—Bar was the head foxhunter in our neck of the woods and told his sons, "Boys, hang a cow horn on my grave, so whenever you fellas go hunting, come by, blow it, and I'll wake up and go with y'all."

Sure enough, an old horn hung from his grave marker. I asked Daddy if I could blow it. "Go ahead, son, but if you wake ol' Bar up, you're gonna hafta take him hunting."

Blowing a cow horn is not as easy as it looks. I puffed my cheeks and tried hard, but only a pitiful bleating came out. "Son, you're gonna have to do better than that. Barzille never did hear too good anyway, so I don't think that'll do it."

"Daddy, I wanna hear you blow it," Colleen said.

He took the horn, blowing a loud series of blasts that made my sister cover her ears. In my young mind, I fully expected Barzille Bryant, shotgun in hand, to break right out of the ground hollering, "Hunt 'em up, Boys, let's hunt 'em up."

"That's enough of this foolishness," Momma said. "Let's get on our way."

As always, we obeyed. Daddy loaded the womenfolk on the horse, and we continued our journey. As we turned to go, I asked, "What was the name of the woman and baby buried back there?"

My parents looked at each other. "I believe their name was Vincent," Momma answered.

"No, I think it started with a B—something like Benjamin or Benson. I'm not sure."

"Neither am I," said Momma, as she stared back at the two

graves, clutching her swollen belly, absentmindedly twirling the
cedar twig with her free hand.

It seemed as if we would never get to PaPaw's house as we
cut treetops off the narrow trail. Colleen was tired of riding with
Momma, so she walked hand in hand with Daddy.

Walking beside Dallas, I took the reins so Momma could get
comfortable. I could tell she wasn't feeling well, so I kept up the
conversation. "That was some kind of bad storm, wasn't it?"

"It sure was, child."

I always liked the way she said "child." It was a Redbone term
that could be used toward a sixty-year-old as well as someone who
was six.

"Child, it's the worst storm I ever seen."

"Was it the worst thing that's ever happened in Ten Mile?"

She looked at me with her dark eyes turning my question over
in her mind. She must have turned it a while 'cause it was a spell
before she spoke.

"It's hard judging what's good or bad right when it happens."

"What do you mean?"

"What seems good *can be* bad, and what seems to be *worst*
may one day turn out to be good."

She could tell I didn't understand, so she continued, "During
my growing-up years at Occupy Church, Joseph Willis was
my preacher. He told a story from his Carolina days during
the Revolution—it was a tale about a farmer's best plow horse
jumping the fence and disappearing. A neighbor of the farmer
kindly commented, 'That's bad luck' to which the farmer's simple
reply was, 'We'll see.'

"A week later, the plow horse reappeared, with five other fine mares following. The neighbor said, 'You sure are a fortunate man,' to which the farmer responded, 'We'll see.'

"That week, the farmer's oldest son decided to ride one of the new horses and got thrown, breaking his leg. The neighbor shook his head, 'That's sure bad about your boy's leg.' The farmer quietly answered, 'We'll see.'"

Momma had me in her grasp with the story; I walked closer so as not miss a word. "The week after the boy's broken leg, the British came through taking all of the young men for their army. They didn't take the farmer's son because of his leg.

"When the good fortune of this was mentioned to the farmer, he said—" Momma paused and winked at me as I finished the sentence for her, "*We'll see.*"

We both laughed, as I asked, "What happened next?"

"I don't know. You'll have to fill that in for yourself, but Preacher Willis made a good point, didn't he? It's one I've never forgotten."

"Yes, Ma'am. I guess it's hard to tell what's gonna work out when it happens."

"That's right, Child. We'll see if this hurricane's the worst thing ever to happen. For all I know, it might turn out as the *best* thing. We'll just have to wait and see. I do know God takes all things and uses them for his good."

I cleared my throat, "Momma, uh—back at the graveyard, I saw you break off that cedar twig and put it in your pocket. Why did you—"

"Mayo, hurry up here and help me." Daddy's call stopped my question as well as her response. Handing the reins back to her, I ran forward.

A huge red oak completely blocked the path. We sawed out a section and then rolled it aside for the horse to pass. Catching my breath, I asked, "How do you think ol' Silas Merkle would be on the other end of a crosscut saw?"

Daddy's green eyes seemed to look right through me. "It's hard to say 'til you've been there with a man—but I suspect he—"

He never finished because Momma yelled out in pain. We turned and saw her bent over the horse's neck moaning, grasping her stomach. Running to her side, we heard her say, "I be—I believe it's time."

It seemed that baby was ready to come whether we were ready or not. If this was a good or bad thing, only time would tell. I leaned down picking up the small cedar twig that'd fallen from her pocket, thinking *we'll just have to see.*

Chapter 5

MOMMA thought the baby wasn't coming for a few weeks, but babies are born when *they're* ready. This one evidently was. She moaned, laying her head across the horse as Daddy led them toward my grandparents' around the fallen trees and through the pine tops.

He sent me ahead to warn PaPaw and MaMaw of Momma's situation. My grandpa was outside chopping limbs when I rounded the path to tell him the news. He said, "Mayo, you go through the swamp and git Miz Girlie to help us—I'll run to the house and tell your MaMaw."

I raced around the treetops, along the path to the home of Miz Girlie Perkins, the local midwife. Miz Girlie was a larger-than-life Ten Mile legend. A widow for nearly fifty years, she lived by herself. She was tough, gruff, and stubborn to a fault. In spite of her ornery personality, Miz Girlie shared a special friendship with my family, especially my mother. They shared a mutual love for birds, the outdoors, *and* my dad.

Miz Girlie was the first person my father met when he first came to these woods. She befriended the lonely Irishman and loved him like a son. Daddy said her friendship was one of the main reasons he'd eventually been welcomed in Ten Mile.

Nearing her place, the shrill yipping of her watchdogs greeted me. Her cabin door opened, with the first thing out the door being her big white goat, Fred. He ran out onto the porch sniffing and snorting as if he was one of the dogs. Right behind him was Miz Girlie cradling an old musket.

I hollered across the field, "Miz Girlie, come quick. Momma's hurting—the baby's comin', and we need your he'p."

Hearing this, she laid down the gun and disappeared into the

house. She came out with an armload of bottles. I continued my
story as we hurried along through the swamp. We arrived at the
house just as Daddy and Papaw were helping my momma down
from the horse.

Miz Girlie followed them straight into the cabin, slamming
the door behind her. Daddy and PaPaw sat on the porch edge,
with Colleen between them. I went toward the door, but PaPaw
grabbed me, "Hold it, boy. It's just women folk in there. Sit here
with us."

A long day and night followed as Momma suffered what they
called "a hard labor." From time to time, MaMaw exited and I
knew from her strained face revealed things weren't going well.
When Miz Girlie came out she said, "My soul, that girl's having a
bad time."

It killed *my soul* to be out on the porch not able to do one
thing for the person I loved best in the world. I could hear her
moaning as I hung my head helplessly, doing the only thing I
could—praying.

The two men didn't say much. Daddy whittled on stick after
stick as if this would help with the struggle going on inside the
cabin. I asked why he didn't go in there; he shrugged. "That ain't
how it's done here. It's the women in charge, and they don't want
any men around."

By now, more neighbor women had arrived to help. They
went in and out, shaking their heads each time. I knew things
were serious, not from what anyone said, but from what they
didn't say, as they glanced sadly at Colleen and me.

As darkness fell, PaPaw said, "A baby comin' is a happy, yet
worrisome, time. It can be a wonderful event—or a terrible one—
and you never know ahead which it'll be."

I stared off into the dusk and thought of Momma's "We'll see"
story. I pictured her backwards look at the fresh dirt of the two
graves—the small one next to the larger one.

PaPaw continued, "You jes' don't never know how this is
gonna come out. It may be a healthy new baby brought into this
world, or it can be—"

He couldn't finish—and I was glad he didn't.

It was then that my favorite person in the world arrived, my Uncle Nathan Dial. Uncle Nathan, or as nearly everyone called him, "Unk," was actually my great uncle—the brother of my grandmother. He'd been named "Unk" by my mom as a little girl and the name had stuck.

My father was one of the few people who refused to call him that, once remarking, "Unk sounds like a name for a pig, not a person."

But to me, Nathan Dial was "Unk" and, on this terrible day, I was glad to see him. He took his place on the porch as Colleen climbed up on his lap. He listened grimly as the men filled him in on the situation, pulling me over by him on the porch.

Now Unk was described by folks as "not quite right." When he was born forty years ago, his navel cord was tangled around his neck causing brain damage. This was evidenced by a slight limp, speech impediment, and a silly grin always on his face.

I'd been in numerous fights due to boys making fun of him. To me, Unk was the wisest and kindest man that'd ever lived. During this crisis as my momma lay near death in childbirth, he was the person I wanted beside me.

After sitting there to hear the full story, Unk stood and went into the house. No other men were allowed in—not even Daddy, but no one ran Unk out. He just had a way that folks wanted him around in a crisis.

Miz Girlie soon came out, nodding her head, saying, "My soul, my soul." There were two things I noticed immediately: she was crying and her hands were bloody.

PaPaw turned to me, trying to take my mind off the events inside the house, "Have you ever noticed how often Girlie says, 'My soul?' Listen and see. I bet 'Bell Cow' Girlie says it every third sentence."

That was PaPaw's name for her—Bell Cow Girlie. He was the only one brave enough to call her that to her face. In our woods, the bell cow was the leader of the herd—the one all the other cows followed into the barn. Farmers put a bell on this cow, so they'd know the herd's location. Calling a person a "bell cow" meant they were in charge, or at least, *thought* they were.

However, there was no disputing that when it was child-birthing time, Miz Girlie was the bell cow, and her every decision as a midwife was respected and obeyed.

Miz Girlie pulled my daddy to the side, talking with him in a whisper. Then she brushed past us back into the house. From inside, I heard her frantic words, "My soul, let me take a look."

I'd sat as long as I could and leapt off the porch. Even though I was deathly afraid of the dark, I ran into the woods, Bo loping beside me. I tripped over a limb tumbling headfirst down the path. Getting up, I ran on. *Anywhere* was better than the porch of that house listening to my momma dying.

The night was clear and moonless, the hurricane having sucked all of the clouds northward, leaving a beautiful star-lit sky, seemingly as an apology for its earlier trouble. In spite of the cloudless sky, my heart was overcast as I hurried down the dim path. In the privacy of the swamp, my tears flowed freely as I asked God to spare my momma's life.

I reached nearby Cherry Winche Creek and sat on a log, torn between wanting to be back at the house yet needing to be alone. Bo, sensing my anguish, nuzzled up under my elbow. I began praying to the Lord—then talking to Bo. Back and forth I went, but don't believe God minded that I split time between Him and Bo. I believe God is man's best friend, while dogs are one of his gifts to comfort us. Right then, I needed God's presence, but I also needed something—or someone—I could touch.

Finally, I lay my head on the moss-covered bank, closed my eyes, and drifted off to sleep. I'm not sure how long I slept, but awoke realizing from the movement of the stars, that it'd been a good while.

Jumping up, I hurried back to the house by starlight. I was in as much of a hurry to get back to the house as when I'd left it. Coming up the path, nearing the house, all was silent. No one was on the porch. The only light came from the lantern in the corner of the room where they'd placed Momma.

The silence unnerved me.

No moaning.

No crying.

Nobody around.

Entering the yard, I heard the first sound—a baby crying, but that wasn't what I wanted most to hear—I longed to hear my mother's voice. More than anything I wanted to have those dark eyes look into mine and hear her speak my name.

I leapt onto the porch, shoving open the door. Over by the lamp, my grandmother sat holding the crying baby. In the dim light, I saw the form of my mother laid out on the bed. Her face was ghostly pale, with her arms folded just as I'd seen in death.

I could hardly stand to look. Moving toward the bed, I said, "Momma."

There was no answer or movement, so I repeated louder, "Momma."

Her eyes blinked, and I heard the only thing that mattered as she weakly whispered, "Mayo—Child, it's gonna be all right."

I knew she was right.

They named my new little brother Patrick Moore. Like my sister, he had fair hair and light skin. Daddy said, "He looks Irish, so he needs a good Irish name, and it's hard to beat Patrick."

Momma was deathly ill; her life hung in the balance for the next two days. Others may have doubted her ability to pull through, but I didn't. She'd told me she'd be all right, and I believed her. She'd never told me anything that wasn't true, so I trusted her word on this, too.

In the days to come as Momma improved, she noticed I wouldn't have anything to do with baby Patrick. On the third day after his birth, she had finished nursing him when I entered the room. "Son, ain't you gonna hold your baby brother?"

I couldn't say it, but she sensed that I resented him. I felt he was the reason she'd nearly died, and I didn't want anything to do with him.

"Son, I know you worried yourself sick over me, but I'm gonna be fine. You can't be scared of him—or mad at him—

'cause of that."

She extended him to me. "He's your brother. Now take him and burp him."

I'd rather have cuddled a rattlesnake than take that baby, but I saw the hurt in her eyes when I hesitated. So I took him—the way he felt warm in my arms, coupled with his chubby face and little hands, melted my heart right there.

Momma said, "He's your brother—Patrick—and it was worth every bit of the pain and fear having him. Just like it was worth having you and Colleen."

Holding him, my thought was, *Well, if she loves him that much, I guess I'll have to, too.*

In the coming days as Momma got better, I was sent home on an errand. She wanted some clothes, and Daddy needed a saw file. He gave instructions on checking on our animals before I headed home.

"Keep your eyes peeled for snakes on the way home. Now, get on your way, so you'll be back 'fore dark."

Bo trotted beside me as we picked our way through the gaps in the debris. Coming up on our house, Bo growled as the hackles rose on his neck. I knew him well enough to know something was wrong, so I stopped to listen.

Studying the house and yard, everything seemed normal, but Bo, hackles raised, kept up his low rumbling as he watched the house. I eased around through the trees for a better look and saw our front door ajar.

Hearing movement inside, I knew someone—or something— was in our house. I squatted behind a tree to watch. Bo trotted over by me, and I told him, "Shh, quiet boy."

Soon, a man, followed by a woman, backed out onto the porch. The man had an armful of our things. The woman held a bag of flour just like you'd cuddle a child, but because of the angle, I couldn't see her face.

They next went to our smoke house where the man pried on the lock. With the door opened, they went inside. Bo continued growling and I whispered, "*You stay put.*" Running to our well, I crouched behind it waiting to get a clear view when they came out.

I could hear muffled conversation and thought I heard a female voice say "bacon." This was confirmed when they came out, the man carrying a slab of our bacon on his shoulder. He sat the loot down as he closed and relocked the smokehouse. Backing away, the woman used a pine limb to cover their tracks.

When they turned, I saw who they were—Silas and Sarah Merkle. My blood boiled as I thought of how hard my parents had worked fattening one of our woods hogs to supply this bacon—now here were these people stealing it right out of our smokehouse.

My dad's words echoed, "Son, a storm don't *create* character. It just *reveals* it." I looked at the nearby toppled oak with its hollow rotten heart thinking how our neighbors had the same kind of decay in them.

The character of these neighbors, or rather the lack of it, was being revealed right before my eyes. I wanted to jump up and scold them, but a glance at Silas Merkle's musket by the porch discouraged me. I'd just wait and report to Daddy. He'd know just what to do.

The woman asked, "They'll never miss any of this?"

Before the man could answer, Bo began a low growl that erupted into loud barking. This brought the Merkles' full attention toward us. In full bellow, Bo charged, having seen enough of the trespassers on his home turf.

Everything was happening too fast now—I saw Mr. Merkle drop the slab of bacon as he picked up his gun, taking aim at Bo.

Now I'd seen enough, too.

I jumped from behind the well, stepped out into the open, and whistled for Bo to stop. I ran in front of my dog, and then turned to see Silas Merkle sighting down the musket barrel at my chest. The hate-filled expression on his face was a look I've never forgotten. I braced for the blast of the gun but instead saw Sarah Merkle push the barrel down.

The three of us stood frozen as if a sudden icy blast had covered us leaving us motionless forever.

No one said a word. Even Bo stood motionless.

Finally, I spoke in a choked voice, "All you'd had to done *was ask*, and my folks would've shared anything we had."

They dropped their heads. The man laid his rifle down moving angrily toward me, fists balled. His face was contorted in deep animal-like rage—a rage born of shame and embarrassment. Shame at being found out—and worst of all—found out by a kid.

"Boy, where are your folks?"

"They're at my grandparents'. She—my momma—had the baby. Daddy sent me back to get—" I stopped and repeated, "If you'd have just *asked*. . . ."

I never finished my sentence. He grabbed me roughly by the throat. "What're you gonna do now, kid?"

I trembled knowing full well this man could easily kill me. I had no doubt he'd killed before—and this situation gave him all the reason he needed to kill again.

At that moment his wife stepped in, removing her husband's hand from my throat. She had a flour streak down her face that only partly hid the anger on her face. "Well, *Mister* Mayo Moore, what *are* you gonna do?"

She asked in a manner as serious as her husband, but not as if she would be any part of killing me. Her question clearly implied, *How this plays out is in your hands, not ours.*

Not willing to wait, the woman repeated, "Come on now—what are you gonna do?"

I rubbed my throat, gazing into their eyes. I don't rightly know where my next words came from. I guess that sometimes God puts words in your mouth to plant seeds. I walked to the smokehouse, stopped at the door and turned. "I'm gonna get you another side of bacon. Y'all are gonna need it, in the hard days to come."

Chapter 6

I watched the Merkles leave with their contraband—*our* food. Gathering the items I'd been sent to get, I left quickly, wanting to get as far away from that couple as possible.

Trotting toward my grandparents, I had no idea another encounter awaited me. Bo wandered off in pursuit of a squirrel, and a few minutes later, a noise came from the woods ahead. Figuring it was Bo, I whistled. However, what stepped out into the clearing was much bigger than a dog—it was a huge red bull, snorting and pawing the ground.

In our area, cattle roamed the woods. Most were gentle and grazed close to the homes of the settlers. Others, what we called range cows were truly wild and foraged in a wider area.

Some of these wild cattle, especially the bulls, were fierce and greatly feared. The most infamous one was a big red bull nicknamed "Roscoe." His normal area was West Bay Swamp, a good fifteen miles from where I stood.

This bull got his name from attacking a settler, Roscoe Goins, about ten years ago. It'd chased him for a spell before goring him right in the butt. Goins survived the attack, but his name was forever attached to the animal as in "Roscoe's Bull." It'd been shortened later just to "Roscoe."

I'd heard tales of this bull and had no doubt it was him standing fifty yards in front of me. *It's Roscoe.* That storm must have run him off from his usual stomping grounds.

Speaking of stomping grounds, that is exactly what Roscoe was doing. Upon spotting me, his front hoof began throwing clods of mud behind him angrily. He was the bull of the woods and well known for attacking other bulls, horses, and even humans—I fit in that last category and it was obvious this meant trouble for me.

Filled with fear, I looked around for a climbable tree, but saw only tall pines with no lower limbs. Only a fox squirrel was going to scale those trees, not a scared boy. My best shot at escape lay toward the swamp, where low-limbed climbable hardwood trees grew.

We both moved at the same time—I scampered like a scalded dog toward the swamp, with Roscoe chasing after me. Each time I'd glance back, he'd gained on me. Soon, I could easily hear his plodding steps closing the distance.

There was no way I'd make the swamp at this rate, so I decided to use the fallen trees to my advantage. Directly ahead of me was a pine top. I waded into it, pushing my way clear to the other side. Roscoe couldn't get through as quickly, and I gained some running room.

However, in the clearings, he'd shorten my lead. A panic filled my chest knowing I couldn't outrun him much further.

Climbing through another treetop, I broke off a small limb. When I came out of the top, Roscoe was already around the treetop, heading me off at the pass.

I immediately reversed direction—running right back into the treetop. Snorting with rage, he came back around, matching my every move. We danced a deadly dance, a terrified boy and an angry, two-thousand-pound bull.

Again, I retreated into the fallen treetop, waited, and when Roscoe came around, I sprinted out the backside. Running for my life, I saw my salvation ahead—a leaning pine lodged at a forty-five degree angle against another pine. It was climbable *if* I beat the bull there, so I dropped my bag and sprinted as hard as I could run.

However, beating Roscoe there was a big *if*. He emerged from the fallen pine in a rage—he'd had enough of being toyed with. I ran, arms pumping, hollering at the top of my voice as if yelling would propel me faster.

Neither Roscoe, nor I could have predicted what happened next.

Bo came hurtling out of nowhere, launching himself at the large patch of skin dangling below the bull's neck.

The enraged bull bellowed, slinging his head and spinning, attempting to shake Bo loose.

I forgot all about the leaning tree; this was a fight I had to see. My daddy always said that no Redbone worth his salt would ever willingly miss a good fight.

He was right—I wasn't going to miss this one and began hollering for my dog. "Hang on, Bo. Get him, boy!"

I'll never forget it—the bull turning savagely in circles churning large clods of dirt as Bo, tossed about like a limp rag doll, determinedly held on. It was a sight to behold, and better than any rodeo I've been to since.

"Come on, Bo—hang on, buddy. Show that bad bull what you're made of."

Finally, Bo slung loose, flying a good ways before hitting the ground hard. He lay dead still as the bull, ready for the kill, went after him.

Now, there was no way I was going to let that happen, especially after how Bo had saved me. What I did next wasn't very smart on my part, but loyalty and instinct clouded my better judgment.

I ran and poked the bull in the eye with my limb, blindsiding him since he was focused on Bo.

Being poked in the eye was all it took for him to turn after me. By then, I'd dropped my limb and was halfway to the leaning tree.

Like a fox chased by a pack of hounds, I scampered up the tree. Roscoe arrived just seconds after I did and actually got his forefeet up on the leaning trunk, scraping loose pieces of bark and shaking the entire tree.

He snorted with rage as he slipped off, hitting the ground hard. I climbed higher and held on for dear life, safely watching him pawing and snorting below. From my high perch, I hollered down, "Next time, I'll have my daddy's gun, and I'm gonna bust you with a load of buckshot."

As if in response to my threat, he butted the tree, and I heard a sickening sound above me—the unmistakable cracking of a limb. Looking up, I saw the splintered limb that'd caused the pine to lodge.

Each time Roscoe rammed his head against the trunk, the limb cracked a little more and the dead tree seemed ready to go down. Sensing victory, the bull backed off to get a running start at the tree.

Looking around desperately for any way out of this mess, I glanced over and saw Bo standing, wobbly shaking his head. He barked loudly, causing Roscoe to stop and turn. It was almost comical to see the big bull repeatedly staring up in the tree at me, then at the barking dog, trying to decide which one he hated most.

Bo's non-stop barking turned the bull's full attention toward him. Roscoe snorted and trotted after Bo, who seemed to make a game out of it, alternately running at the bull and then backing off.

I couldn't help laughing as I hollered, "Watch him, Bo. He's faster than he looks."

As Roscoe made a full charge, Bo took off for the swamp. They were off to the races again, the bull futilely chasing after Bo, as they went out of sight.

"Make it count, Son. Run that bull ragged." Then the barking and snorting faded and the woods became silent.

I waited a while before climbing down, retrieving my sack, and making tracks for my grandparents. I'd had just about as much excitement as one could stand for a day—first with the thieves, and then the "bull of the woods."

Daddy was sitting on a stump sharpening his ax when I trotted up. Out of breath, I handed him the saw file.

"What's the big hurry?"

"You wouldn't believe it if I told you."

"Try me."

I started telling him of my adventure with Roscoe. He stopped me and asked, "Are you sure it was Roscoe?"

I described all about his markings and behavior as he nodded. "That's Roscoe all right. The storm must've pushed him down our way."

I continued the story, adding a few additional details for dramatic effect. He knew my tendency to stretch a tale for all it's worth and said, "Whoa now. Are you sure it happened like that?"

I answered with, "Daddy, it all happened just like that. *If I'm a lying, I'm a dying.*"

He just shook his head, and returned to his filing. We heard a noise from the woods and looked up to see Bo coming—soaking wet, tongue hanging out, breathing hard. Daddy studied him before saying, "Why I believe he's got a smirk on his face."

Daddy, who normally didn't show much affection to animals, called him over, stroked his head, and spoke to him in Irish. When I asked what he'd said, he replied, "Dogs understand Irish. It was a private matter 'tween us." Setting his file aside, he went to the house and returned shortly with a large hambone.

Tossing the bone to Bo, he turned to me. "You know how that bull got his name?"

"I've heard—Roscoe Goins."

He laughed. "Once I was with 'Ol Roscoe when someone asked him about his wound. Before we could stop him, in mixed company, he dropped his overalls proudly to show off his war wound."

"Daddy, I thought I was goin' to get a scar just like it when that bull was breathing down my neck." It seemed funny now, but I would never forget how scared I'd been.

As Bo gnawed on the bone, Daddy resumed his filing and I held the ax in place. It was now time to tell him about the other part of my adventure—catching the Merkles stealing our food.

"Something else happened."

He looked up. "I bet it can't beat your bull chase."

"Well, actually, it might—"

His green eyes locked on mine—"What?"

I'll never know why I lied. "Uh, you see, two chicken hawks were chasing some of the hens around the yard. I got after them and ran them off, but I'm afraid they'll come back."

"Really?"

"Yes Sir."

The trouble with a lie is this: It's easy to tell *a* lie, but hard to tell just *one*. I knew sooner or later, *my chickens* would come home to roost, and I'd have to tell the truth about the Merkles. It just wasn't gonna be today.

Chapter 7

AFTER my encounter with Roscoe, I didn't make the trip home alone any more. Daddy went every other day to check on our place. Most of the time I went with him, secretly hoping that ol' Roscoe would show up so my father could shoot him.

One day as we headed out, Daddy, shouldering his rifle, said, "Son, we're 'loaded for bear' if that hookin' bull shows up."

I couldn't resist. "No, we ain't loaded for *bear*—we're loaded for *bull*."

He laughed. "No, I believe I'm loaded for *bear*, and you're just *full of bull*."

Each time we went, he commented on our missing chickens that'd disappeared during the storm. "Where are those chickens that you talked about?"

"I guess those chicken hawks got 'em."

A couple of weeks later, we returned home to stay. Momma and baby Patrick were doing well, and we were glad to get back to our house on Westport Hill. Coming home meant a busy time for everyone as October arrived with its welcomed cooler weather after our long, hot summer.

However, there was worry in the air in spite of the mild weather. The hurricane had destroyed everyone's crops and food was in short supply. Winter always meant times of want in our woods, but this winter was going to be even leaner. From listening in on my parent's conversations at night, I knew they were worried our foodstuffs wouldn't last until the spring crops came in. We'd lost food in the kitchen fire, and the storm had damaged our crops, so there was reason for concern.

One day I saw just how worried my folks were. Momma got Colleen and me to help spread all of our food and supplies out on the front porch. Daddy cleaned out the smokehouse, as I helped Momma bring out all of our canned items, seeds, and sweet potatoes.

Bringing out slabs of bacon, ham, and jars of meat from the smokehouse, we stacked it on the porch. Scanning it all, Daddy said, "Back in Ireland—where we seemed always one step from starvation—we always did this on the first day of May. Every home did an inventory of their foodstuffs and supplies as they tried to see if they had enough until the crops came in.

"We knew about having a 'hungry July' if the food ran out before the August crops came in."

The four of us looked over the food covering our porch. "I believe we'll make it if we're careful, but I'm not sure," Momma said. Her worried look taught me that my parents carried a great weight that I'd never fully understood until that day.

Daddy, always the optimist, said, "Honey, we'll make it. I'll hunt a little more, and pen up a few extra woods hogs. We'll be fine."

"I know we'll make it, but it sure don't look like enough to get us through the fall and the coming mean winter," Momma said.

Walking to where the smokehouse contents were laid out, Daddy said, "Eliza, I'd swear we had more slabs of bacon than what I've got laid out there."

"And I thought for sure we had another bag of flour under the bed," she added.

They both looked at me, and I quickly turned away, still visualizing the Merkles as they were carting off our food.

"It's..." I stammered.

They both turned to me.

"It's 'cause. . . ."

It seemed as if my tongue couldn't form the words needed to tell the story.

"Go ahead boy, and say your piece," Momma said.

"It's just... 'cause...."

What next came out surprised even me.

"It's gonna be all right 'cause the Lord done told me we'll be fine."

Daddy smiled. "See Eliza. I told you so. Even Mayo knows we gonna be all right."

Momma whispered, "Out of the mouth of babes. . . . "

Not sure what I might say next, I scampered off. I heard Momma's voice trailing off as I ran, "I swear that boy knows something we don't."

I'm not sure if she meant my uttered prophecy—or the missing bacon and flour. I didn't hang around to find out, heading toward the safety and silence of the woods.

We made it through that winter—everyone made it because all of the local families came together and helped each other out. Everyone pitched in, sharing what little they had. I'll never forget the generosity among our Ten Mile neighbors after the hurricane. Whenever neighbors butchered a cow or hog, everyone came to help, and the meat was shared among the families.

Neighbors came by to help if hay needed to be cut or a crop needed putting in. Of course, everyone helped by returning the favor. Even though the storm's aftermath was *a hard time*, it was also *a good time*.

One day, Daddy and I made the trip over to our nearest neighbors, Ben and Bessie Tyler. They'd been friends of my mother since childhood, and there was a special bond between them. I'd heard whisperings as to how years ago, during a feud between Ben and Bessie's families—the Tylers and Wilsons—Ben had rescued Bessie and my Momma from some kind of dangerous situation that was a hush-hush event in our community.

This secret event—a shooting of some kind—ended the feud between the families, and resulted in Ben and Bessie's marriage. I couldn't get much out of my parents on this story, as my questions were usually met by a stone wall of silence, followed by the classic Ten Mile put off, "I'll tell you more when your legs get long enough."

As Daddy and I walked, I tried again. "Now what ended that bad feud between Mr. Ben and Miss Bessie's families?"

"You'll have to ask your mother. She was there."

"I done asked her before, and she won't say."

"Then ask her again."

Some mysterious event had ended the feud, but no one would talk about it. I was determined to find out what'd happened... and I didn't plan to wait until "my legs got long enough."

We arrived to a warm welcome at the Tyler home. They had two daughters, Helen and Ellie, who were a little older than I was, and we always had a good time playing and visiting.

The reason for our visit was to "pay back" the Tylers for helping us the week before at our place. Bessie pointed toward the barn saying, "Ben's out there waiting for y'all."

Nearing the barn, I *smelled* today's job before I saw it. The strong unmistakable aroma of manure greeted us. Rounding the corner, we found Ben Tyler shoveling manure.

My least favorite farming job was going to be our "payback" chore for the day—we were going to be hauling "barnyard," which is what we called animal manure. Hauling barnyard to the garden for fertilizing was the nastiest farming job in the world.

We spent the day hauling wagonloads of the stuff to the fields. By the end of the day, I was covered in it and exhausted. As we started home, Daddy looked at me. "Son, you look worn out."

"I am."

"I guess you're *pooped out* from hauling manure all day, huh?"

I was so tired that I didn't catch his joke at first. Laughing, I asked, "Mr. Ben saved his worst job for us."

"It didn't hurt us, and he needed our help."

"Did I hear you say that in Ireland, y'all used seaweed for fertilizer?"

"Folks that lived close to the coast used it."

"Did it smell as bad as barnyard?"

"Nothing smells as bad as barnyard manure—your momma'll agree when we get home in these smelly clothes."

We both laughed, and I asked, "Tell me about how Mr. Ben fell in love with Mrs. Bessie."

"Later on I will, when your legs get longer, then I'll tell the whole story." He wasn't falling into my trap.

"But that's what you always say, 'when your legs get longer.'"

"Like I said earlier, ask your Momma."

Changing the subject, he said, "Son, you've seen how the storm has brought out the best in people. Folks are sharing their food and helping with work, and that's how it's supposed to be."

This was true about the sharing—it was a time of hospitality and kindness. The next week, we helped the Perkins family rebuild their barn and the week after that, we fixed fence for a widow woman over on Steep Gully.

There was a community feeling of sharing throughout Ten Mile. Everyone was part of it except one family—the Merkles. Even though they were the recipients of meat and food, they never showed any gratitude, shared, or took part in the "payback."

Of course, Momma reminded us, "They don't really have anything to share, and we need to go easy on 'em."

If anything, Silas Merkle seemed resentful of any help as if it had strings attached. Daddy and I took them a venison roast, but we still just got the cold shoulder. Mr. and Mrs. Merkle eyed me cautiously the entire visit, probably wondering if I'd told of our encounter.

Pulling me aside, Mrs. Merkle whispered, "You ain't told nobody about our little visit at your place?"

"No Ma'am."

"Are you going to?"

I shouldn't have said this, but I did. "I'm still thinking on it."

She gripped my arm. "It'd be *much* better—for you and us—if you didn't."

I wasn't sure if it was a threat or not.

Just then Daddy walked up, ready to leave. Sarah Merkle, patting my head, said, "Mayo sure is a fine boy, ain't he?"

I wanted to slap her.

As we rode off, Daddy said, "Boy, those are some odd birds. Did you notice how they watched us like a calf looking at a new gate?"

"Yes sir."

"Mayo, that man is the one I worry about—he ain't no good. We're trying to help him, but you can't make a good knife out of bad steel, and he's bad."

I grimaced when he said "steel," thinking he'd meant "*steal*."

I wondered how much longer I could keep my secret.

Two nights later, another secret event occurred.

We'd all gone to bed, and the house was quiet. I slipped out of bed to go take a leak and sat on the porch edge after I'd taken care of my business. A screech owl had been calling in our live oak tree, and I wanted to see if I could get him to answer.

Bo lay beside me, snoring softly. I called out in my best owl imitation: "Whooooooooo."

Screech owls have a completely different call than their bigger cousins. In fact, they have two calls. One's the eerie "woman screaming" screech from which they get their name. It is enough to scare even the bravest person when heard out in the loneliness of the woods. Their second and more common call, is a soft "whinny call." It goes "Whooooooooo." I "whinnied" several times and got an answer from the oak.

Just as I turned to go inside, I saw a dark form coming out of the woods. Someone was creeping along toward our barn. I bumped Bo, and he sniffed the air, growled, and then lay his head back down. His reaction surprised me, as he was a good watchdog. Normally, he'd been howling and raising his hackles. The person had to be someone he was familiar with.

The figure went to the barn, and I watched until finally it shuffled away. Bo never barked or raised his hackles.

Watching the person disappear into the woods, I thought that it had to be Unk—my own Uncle Nathan, who had a similar limp and was about the same size. But why would he be slipping up to our house in the dark? And what was he doing at the barn?

I slipped carefully to the barn and in the moonlight saw a small sack hanging down from the barn opening. Taking it down, I hurried inside the house.

Slipping to the fireplace, I opened the bag to see four gold coins glowing in the light. Other than a couple of pennies, I'd never held money before and couldn't believe what I saw.

Kneeling by the fire, I glanced over to be sure my parents were asleep. Then I turned one of the coins over in my hands. Its bright finish featured a woman's head on one side with the date 1844 beneath. The other side had an eagle with outstretched wings. Scripted across the top was "United States of America," and beneath the eagle was inscribed, "Ten D."

I blurted "Ten dollars," then turned to see if I'd awakened my parents and was relieved to see them still sleeping—dead to the world.

I softly repeated. "Ten American dollars." I picked up the other three coins. "Forty American dollars. I'm rich." Then remembering that they didn't belong to me, I said, "No, *we're* rich."

Gripping the coins, I crawled back in bed, but sleep was replaced by dreams of what I'd found and I examined the night's events from every angle. My Uncle Nathan was a poor sheepherder with no house, horse, or property. He had no way I knew about for getting hold of this kind of money.

This was a mystery I had to solve, and daylight came with me still awake, wondering how to do it.

On cold mornings, Momma stoked the fireplace with rich-lighter and draped our clothes on a nearby chair. When the clothes were toasty, she'd call us for breakfast with a cheerful, "Mayo, Colleen, get up and come get warm."

We'd jump out of bed, sprint to the blazing fire, quickly donning our warm clothes. On this morning, once I'd gotten warm, I held Patrick while Momma cooked. We talked as the crackling fire warmed the room. Laying my sleeping brother down, I took out the coins. "Momma, what do you know about these?"

She nearly dropped the pot of grits she held with a potholder. "Child, where'd you get those?"

"I found them last night. Found them—out by the barn—in a bag somebody left."

"Somebody left?"

I told her my story, ending it with, "I know it was Unk. Don't anybody else walk just like him."

She stirred the grits, went over to cover Patrick before speaking. "I'm sure it was your Uncle Nathan. He's done stuff like that before."

"But why would he sneak up to leave money here? He's in and out of our house all of the time."

"Son, there's something about him that don't nobody know but me and your daddy. You see—"

She stopped as I peered into her eyes. When Momma got excited, her eyes darkened. Daddy called them her "Indian Eyes" adding, "They get like that when she's either real happy *or* on the warpath."

"You see something happened years ago—"

Right then, my sister Colleen bounded into the room. She'd never kept a secret in her life, and Momma's wink assured me she wouldn't be hearing this one.

"Son, it's a long story that I'll tell you another time."

"I want to know now."

She nodded at my nosey sister. "Your daddy has an Irish saying, 'If three people know something, it's no longer a secret.'"

I was determined to learn what was going on but knew she wouldn't tell now. As Colleen ate her breakfast, Momma reached out and I reluctantly placed the four coins in her hand. She whispered, "Those are American eagles."

"They're worth ten dollars each?" I asked.

"Sure are."

As the day went on, some pieces of the puzzle began to fit in place. Though we lived isolated lives, news traveled quickly when something happened. When Ten Mile residents began finding small bags of money on their porches, hanging in their barns, or tied to a tree in the yard, news spread quickly. The nearby settlers reported their bags contained two coins.

Mother made me promise to say that we also got two, instead of the actual four. No one knew the source of the good fortune, but all manner of theories abounded. Families who'd wondered how they would make it through this mean winter, now had money to get food and supplies at the general store in Sugartown or Hineston.

Even the Merkles received two coins. Mrs. Merkle came over that day, and told Momma, "Some angel must've come and helped us. I just can't believe it. I've been thinking all day about what to buy with this money. For the first time in a long while, I feel a little hope for the future."

However, her tone turned dark when she said, "My husband says it's some kind of trick and somebody'll expect somethin' back in return, or that's it's blood money from some shameful act."

I saw Momma wipe a quick tear from her eye, and I wondered if it was because of this sad woman's plight or Unk's generosity.

She put her hand on Sarah Merkle's shoulder. "Just accept it and thank the good Lord. We got two coins too, and I'm some kind of thankful." I was standing behind Mrs. Merkle when Momma said this and held up four fingers, mouthing with a grin, "Liar."

She gave me a glare that'd peel paint off a barn door, so I scampered out just as Mrs. Merkle said, "Well, I guess you don't look a gift horse in the mouth. I'm just thankful for that angel, whoever he or she might be."

My only thought was how 'her angel' had a limp and usually smelled like sheep.

It was followed by a promise I made to myself to find out where, and how, that "angel" got enough gold coins to give two to every family in Ten Mile.

Chapter 8

TRY as I might, I couldn't get a word out of my momma on how Unk got those gold coins. All she'd say is, "When the time's right, I'll tell you." However, I didn't have time to wait, so I came up with a plan to find out—a plan that needed the right time and place.

As our excitement over the coins faded, the hard work of rebuilding from the hurricane continued. Life kind of got back to normal with the only dark cloud being more bad news from the war. Any information we got was usually old and couldn't always be trusted, but we knew our state capital of Baton Rouge had fallen and the Union had next occupied New Orleans. Most of the big battles were still far away in Virginia or Tennessee, but it seemed as if the war was slowly moving our way, and everyone was worried, especially my daddy.

I overheard him talking to Momma one night. "That war is gonna come to us whether we want it to or not."

She said, "Joe, those Yankees won't find anything useful in these piney woods. They want cotton, cities, and slaves to set free. We don't have any of that here."

"Eliza, my ancestors thought the same thing in western Ireland. Everyone thought the British would leave rocky and bare County Mayo alone. No one believed they'd come, but they did.

That was the end of their conversation, but it was a long time before I heard the soft breathing of sleep. I knew they were lying in their bed, mulling the future.

Like my dad, I had a gut feeling that this war was surely going to come our way. Just like the hurricane, we couldn't do anything about it. The only difference was that the storm surprised us, while this war came much slower. We knew it was coming just the same.

I fell asleep to the sound of distant thunder far off to the north. A cold front was moving through, and geese flying south in the night woke me. As the storm neared, the lightning flashes became brighter, and the accompanying thunder drowned out the sound of the geese.

I slept fitfully and dreamed of that far off war, I guess it was due to the sound of that distant thunder.

Late November was time for one of the men's favorite things: foxhunting. No hurricane or war could stop the Ten Milers from planning a hunt.

Everything we did in those days had a bona fide reason for taking place—we work to produce food; went to church to grow closer to God, and hunted to supply meat for the table. *Nothing* was done without a reason, and wasting *anything*, whether it was food, sweat, bullets, or time, was inexcusable. We worked hard, and all of our work had a reason—to help us survive.

After a full day of work, we'd always take an afternoon coffee break about four o'clock. Momma would ring the triangle on the porch, and we'd gladly come in from the fieldwork to the back porch for coffee. On this day, "Pistol" Perkins and his son Dan were helping us with a hog we'd butchered. They were returning the favor from the week before when Daddy'd helped them rebuild a rail fence at their place.

As the men sat along our porch, Momma brought out the steaming coffeepot with fresh sugar cookies. Pistol said to Daddy, "Joe, I think it's about time we took a foxhunt. The weather's been cooler and the ticks, skeeters, and snakes are gone. I'm ready to hear Ol' Trailer barking down in the swamp."

They agreed to meet up the next night after dark. Daddy and Pistol divided the chore of contacting the other hunters.

I'd never been allowed on a foxhunt because the men drank whiskey and stayed up all night. Momma prohibited me from going saying, "It just ain't the place for a child."

The men's excitement about the hunt only deepened my sorrow at not going. However, it all changed at supper that night when Daddy said, "Eliza, I'm thinking about taking Mayo along for the hunt."

I was thrilled but glanced at the *real* decision-maker in the Moore house—my mother. Her approval would be needed.

She looked at the two of us as if she were going to whip us, before winking at me. "Mayo, you been working like a man since the storm. I believe you've earned the right to go."

I started to shout, but her stern words stopped me as she turned to Daddy, "Joe Moore, if that boy gets even near that whiskey jug, I'll *kill* both of you. And if you let him get snake bit, just let that serpent get you too, 'cause otherwise, *I will kill you.*" She said, "kill you" in that high voice that Redbones use when making a point.

Even as a grown man, I've never been able to sleep on the night before a hunt, and I'm not sure I slept a wink that night. We worked hard the next day, hours dragging like pouring syrup on a cold morning. All I could think of was the upcoming night's hunt.

Late that afternoon, Unk and PaPaw showed up with their foxhounds and were joined shortly by Pistol and Dan. The excitement could be felt in the clear evening air as we rode out toward West Bay Swamp.

I've been around dogs all of my life, and there's nothing like watching hunting dogs before they're turned loose. They're shaking with excitement, just aching to get to the woods and do what they were born and trained to do.

The men were just as worked up as the dogs, especially Pistol. He was a wiry, nervous kind of fellow anyhow, and this hunt had him keyed up, talking a mile a minute. He was always interested in my dad's Irish stories and asked, "Joe Moore, did y'all hunt foxes in Ireland?"

"Well, if you owned land, you could hunt it. But only the rich, mainly Englishfolk, owned land."

Pistol leaned in, "*What*? You mean to tell me a fellow can't just go hunt whatever he wants anytime and anyplace?"

"Nope, where I came from, you couldn't walk a hundred yards without having to climb someone's stone wall. Most folks don't even own the land they live and work on. It all belonged to a landlord."

"What's a *landlord*?" Dan asked.

"It's the person, normally rich, who actually owns the land. He rents it out to people who pay yearly rent for the privilege of farming it and living on it. The landlord, who often doesn't even live in Ireland, gets his pound of flesh or you get evicted."

PaPaw, who was riding close to me said, "The only *landlord* we got in Ten Mile is the *Lord* God *Himself*. He created it and allows us to live off it. Where we're heading tonight, there ain't nary a man or woman claiming it, saying it's theirs."

He continued, "That's why we call it *open range*. It's open for everyone to use—whether it's hunting or running cattle or sheep. "It don't belong to *none* of us—it belongs to *all* of us."

I nodded. "PaPaw, I like what you just said. Say it again."

"It don't belong to none of us—it belongs to all of us."

Every man nodded silently at the wisdom of his words.

We soon passed an area where the huge pines were still blackened twenty or thirty feet high. PaPaw turned to me, "Mayo, right about here is where your daddy became a hero during the Big Fire."

I'd heard stories about this fire but never from my father. He wouldn't talk about it. PaPaw turned to him, "Joe, you ain't never told this boy about your part in the big fire?"

"I've never had a chance. Everybody else keeps telling it. Besides, they make a lot more of it than it really was."

PaPaw said, "Well, I guess I'll have to tell it again—Mayo, there was land trouble back when your daddy first came to these woods. Some timber company from up North decided they were going to evict all of the settlers and cut our forests.

"It was a bad time for folks in these woods. Those timber people were willing to do about anything to run us out."

"Babe, but we're still here," Pistol Perkins added as an aside.

His son Dan, on cue, added, "And the timber people ain't."

Pistol used the word "Babe" in about two-thirds of his conversations. It was a trademark phrase among Redbones, but he had the patent on it.

PaPaw said, "Now, you boys be quiet—this here's my story.

"As I was asaying, the trouble went back and forth until one winter day when matters were at their worst, the timber people set the whole woods on fire. It was dry. Lots of tinder and limbs were down because of a recent ice storm and —"

"Say babe, it was the strongest and rawest north wind you'd ever seen," Pistol said.

"Sure was," Dan added.

PaPaw feigned anger, "Y'all be quiet. This here's *my* story."

"As I was fixin' to say, the whole woods were ablaze and the fire seemed to build on itself. It wasn't just running along the ground but caught up in the tops of the pines, whipped along by the wind.

"Everyone was gathered up at Ten Mile Creek trying to figure out what was happening. It was then we realized Aunt Mollie Weeks was missing. She had just lost her husband and lived right near where we're riding.

"Then we realized that Aunt Mollie, who was in her eighties and lived alone, was in the fire's path. Because the fire was between us and her place, there wasn't nothing we could do."

PaPaw took a breath and Pistol shot in, "If it hadn't been for that crazy Irishman..."; his son concluded, "She'd been a goner."

My grandpa balled up his fist as if he was ready to fight. "Shut your mouth—this here's my story—now if it hadn't been for that crazy Irishman, Joe Moore, she would've burned up. But no, he jumped on his horse and rode off toward the fire to rescue Aunt Mollie.

"He was riding Dallas who was then a young horse. When they disappeared into the smoke and fire, we never expected to see them again."

"But we did," Pistol said.

Before Dan could add his two cents, PaPaw held up his hand. "If 'Pete' here, and his son 'Repeat,' will hush, I'll finish my story. Your daddy burst back through the smoking woods with Aunt Mollie sitting behind him. The horse and riders were all covered in black soot, and the old woman was whooping loudly, holding on for dear life.

"Nobody that seen it ever forgot it, and on that day, your daddy became one of us."

I'd heard the story many times but still wanted to know more, so I asked, "What happened to the timber people after that?"

Every man became silent. No one—Pistol, Dan, or even talkative Unk—said a word. This was always the case when the story of the timber people and the Big Fire came up. Everyone talked all about the fire, but the subject of what happened next was something the men knew about but wouldn't talk about.

I wanted to know more but knew it wouldn't come now.

Pistol Perkins finally spoke, "Babe, we're still here." Dan dutifully added, "And they ain't."

PaPaw spurred his horse, and our pace quickened. The story was over, and it was more likely that the blackened pines we rode under would tell what had happened next, rather than the men I was riding along with.

It was late evening when we arrived at the foxhunting site. Three unsaddled horses were tied to a hitching rope, and an empty wagon sat near a roaring campfire. Several men, their backs to us, sat on logs around the fire.

We tied our horses, except for Dallas, beside the others. When Dallas saw the fire, he began fidgeting. Ever since the Big Fire and the horse's heroic run through the flames, Dallas got skittish near a fire, so Daddy tied him away from the others.

There were happy greetings and backslapping among the men. Daddy whispered, "That there is Barney Bryant. He's the hunt master in charge. Remember when I told you about ol' Barzille Bryant and the blowing horn on the grave? Well, Barney is one of his sons."

Then he pointed at the other two men. "Over there is Fred Wilson, and the shorter one is his brother, Gideon. I know you've probably seen them before. They're our neighbor Bessie's brothers."

Barney came over, shook each man's hand, and after meeting me, tousled my hair. "Boy, are you ready to hunt?"

"Yes, sir."

"Dis' evening gonna be your first foxhunt?"

"Yes sir."

"Bet it won't be your last."

"I sure hope not."

Barney turned to Daddy, "Do y'all hunt foxes back in Eye-land?" I always liked how some of the Redbones always called his home country "Eye-land."

Daddy winked at me. "Well, in Ireland, or Eye-land, foxhunting's for the rich folks. The landowners get all dressed up fancy and hunt on horses. Poor folks like me would be hired just to walk along to take care of the hounds."

Barney looked flabbergasted. "Who ever heard of hunting foxes from a horse? That'd defeat the whole purpose. We're gonna show your boy the *Ten Mile* way of foxhunting." Spitting a dark stream of tobacco juice into the fire, he snorted, "Who ever heard of getting dressed up and riding a horse to hunt foxes."

As the sun set and darkness fell, two other men rode up. Each had a dog, and this now made six hunting dogs tied up and ready to go.

Our neighbor, Ben Tyler, stood by the fire, and beside him was a man named Caleb Johnson. He was a quiet man who didn't say much, and I'd always been a little scared of him 'cause of his stony silence. I'm not sure he said ten words that whole night, but he didn't need to because with Barney as hunt master, the conversation never dragged.

Barney took it upon himself to keep up a steady stream on the fine points of foxhunting, and I'd been selected as his star pupil.

Even though I entered this night with little knowledge of the sport, by night's end, I knew more than I ever wanted to know.

Gideon was in charge of the fire. Taking his ax, he split several strips of pine kindling and threw them on. As the fire crackled and hissed, his brother Fred said, "There ain't any better smell on God's green earth than pine sap."

As if in agreement, the fire blazed up. Thick black smoke curled up through the trees until the night breeze turned and blew it in Barney's direction. Hopping up, he coughed and fanned the smoke with his hat. "They say smoke follows beauty. I've always had that trouble."

This brought a round of hoots from the men, because you could say many things about Mr. Barney, but being "beautiful" was not one of them. Glancing around the fire at their faces, I knew there was no place on this round earth I'd rather be.

My thoughts were broken when the breeze shifted, blowing smoke in my face. I was determined to be tough and not move until Unk jabbed me in the ribs. "You better move. If you let smoke get in your eyes, you'll wet the bed."

This brought on a long discussion of various folktales about smoke, nighttime, campfires, hoot owls, and goblins. I knew they were trying to scare me, so I acted disinterested by poking a long stick in the fire.

Mr. Barney stopped the tales by standing up. "We didn't come out here for a lying contest. We came to hunt. Now you boys hush up."

He turned to me, once again assuming his role of patient teacher. "Now, Son—we'll turn our dogs loose in a few minutes. This is our favorite hunting spot and here's why—high on this hill, we can get a fair view of the whole area. With the leaves off the trees, hopefully we'll see the fox and dogs pass by."

Mr. Barney punched Caleb on the shoulder. "Caleb here'll

agree with me—the real reason we hunt here is because it's the home of Topper."

Caleb, moving the coffeepot, laughed as Barney continued, "Topper is the finest red fox in these woods. We been hunting him for about four, five seasons hand-running."

"You mean you haven't caught him in five years of hunting?" I asked.

"Caught him? We ain't trying to *kitch* him. We just love to hear the dogs run him."

Barney, in the excitement of the night, kept talking. When he finally drew a breath, I asked. "Are you Irish, Mr. Barney?"

He looked at my father, then me. "No, why do you ask?"

"Daddy says that the motto of every Irishman is, 'How can I know what I'm thinking, if I don't say it out loud?'"

Everyone roared except my daddy, but Barney laughed enough for both of them. "Son, are you saying I talk too much?"

"Well. . . ." Daddy stomped my foot hard with his boot.

"Ouch, that hurts."

Barney, trying to help me out, turned to Daddy. "Joe Moore, in I-land do they kitch the fox?"

"Yes sir, that's the whole aim of the hunt—catch the fox and kill it. The sheepherders want those foxes killed."

Barney stood up as if he couldn't believe it. "Boys, y'all come over here and listen. Pistol, Ben, stop what you doin' and come listen."

It was obvious that when the hunt master spoke, the others obeyed.

"Now, Mr. Joe Moore, tell these guys that they kill the fox in Eye-land."

Daddy repeated his story of the hunt's aim—to kill the fox. Then he added, "Because the land is posted, the average fellow can't go on it for hunting or anything else.

Pistol asked, "You mean to tell me, a normal fellow couldn't go out and hunt a fox on his own in any way he wanted?"

"No sir, to hunt anything on the landowner's acreage is poaching, and there's a big price to pay if you're caught."

"You mean you can't shoot a squirrel, a deer, or even a bobwhite quail."

"The answer is no. I tell you, no. *Everything* is considered trespassing, and that includes fishing."

The men mumbled among themselves. Barney spat before asking, "You mean to tell me I couldn't fish out of any creek or river?"

Daddy hesitantly looked around the circle of men until one of them said, "Go ahead."

"Let me give you an example: during the salmon running season, a fellow could catch fish by the fistful. But the rivers belong to the landowner, and salmon poaching is handled severely and roughly."

Every man was listening closely as Daddy asked, "Any of you ever seen a man trap?"

"A what?"

"A man trap. It's a huge spring trap similar to the 'layovers' you use around here to trap coons or varmints. The difference is the size—it's big enough to trap a man. The landowners in Ireland, especially during the salmon run, place them in prime spots along their streams or hunting trails. It's big enough that if you step on it, the teeth will get you about mid-calf.

"Once a neighbor got caught in one. First, it broke his leg bone, and then left a terrible wound from the teeth. It's an ugly tool used to keep poachers away."

"That's hard to believe, Son," Barney said.

"But it's true. I saw the fellow everyday for all of my growing up years. He limped the rest of his life.

"I also saw one of the traps displayed in town as a warning to stay off property."

This was almost too much for Barney. "Setting a trap to catch *a man*. I can't believe it. Then, the idea that a man claims he owns a river and can't nobody fish in it 'cept him. If a man said he owned the Calcasieu or Cherry Winche, we'd smoke his sausage and cure him of that *real* quick."

All of the other men agreed and added all kinds of country

terms of what'd they do to someone who tried to bar them from hunting or fishing wherever they wanted.

Thoughtful silence then ensued, broken only by the crackling fire and a few crickets brave enough to chirp in the cool night air.

I halted this quietness with a question. "Y'all just mentioned Cherry Winche Creek. How'd it get its name?"

I'd heard the stories numerous times but wanted to hear them again. Daddy kicked my foot as a reminder that children were expected to be quiet around a campfire, but his prompt was too late.

Of course, this was all the excuse Dan and Pistol needed to start another argument. It began with Pistol's version. "I was always told by my granddaddy that a man with a Cherokee wife lived along the Creek. He died in a hunting accident, and she lived alone for the rest of her years.

"Because of that, they began calling it the 'Cherokee Wench's Creek.'"

"Did you say 'Cherokee witch,' Mr. Pistol?" I asked.

"No, it's *wench*, not witch." Winking at my daddy, he added, "You can git your poppa here to explain what 'wench' means later. It ain't a real nice word."

Dan Perkins got his word in edgewise when *his* poppa paused for a breath. "Mayo, don't pay no attention to that old man's tall tale there. My mother's people, the Perrys, had a different story."

As if this disproved the story just told by his own father, Dan said, "Daddy always swore he was told the man married to the Cherokee woman was a Negro, and ya'll all know we ain't never let those kind on our side of the Calcasieu."

There were several grunts of assent from the men around the campfire as Dan continued. "My momma always said it was 'cause of the tall cherry bark oaks growing along the creek. That's how it became Cherry Winche Creek."

"Son, your momma—my wife—don't know which way is up most of the time, and her people have always been the worst—," Pistol said.

Dan Perkins flew back, and I wasn't sure if it was partly in jest or not. "I'll clean any man's plow who says—"

His threat was interrupted by the furious barking of the dogs followed by the sound of a horse's hooves. Everyone instinctively backed away from the fire into the shadows. I saw Ben and Caleb reach for their rifles—Redbone men have always been touchy about anyone coming up on them in the dark.

Daddy pulled me away from the fire. "Stay low and listen."

One of the hunters said, "Hey, who goes there?"

The ingrained fear of "bushwhacking" was why the men melted away from the fire's light. I heard one of them whisper, "We ain't expecting no more hunters, are we?"

"I don't believe."

Hearing the sound of a gun cocking to my right, I huddled lower against a pine.

There was no answer from the direction of the horse.

"Who goes there? Speak up."

Daddy knelt by me. "The men are scared of bushwhacking."

"What's that?"

"It's a night ambush where a person's shot from the dark."

Daddy continued, scanning the woods. "Don't ever go up to a Redbone house at night. It's a right good way to get shot."

Just then, a loud blast came from a cow horn. I could see a white-dressed figure on the horse who shouted, "This is ol' Barzille, and I've come *back* to hunt with y'all."

Another blast followed on the cow horn, which set the dogs to howling. My jaw gaped as I recalled the story of ol' Barzille Bryant's grave, the cow horn, and his vow to come back. I didn't believe in haints or ghosts, but right then I wasn't so sure.

Daddy stepped out from behind his hiding tree, saying, "Hold your fire, boys. It's just Eli, my crazy brother-in-law."

Sure enough, riding out of the dark came Eli Clark, Momma's younger brother.

He laughed when he saw Barney's gun. "Whoa, looks like I got you good. You thought a ghost got you, Mr. Barney? Thought your old daddy done come back from the grave?"

Barney didn't see much humor in it. "Son, you just about

become a ghost yerself." Nodding at my PaPaw, he said, "Willard, didn't you teach your boy better than to sneak up on a man like that? It's a good way to get shot."

PaPaw just shook his head. "I purt'near gave up on taking the foolishness out of that boy a long time ago."

Unk stepped out. "Rattler, you just about scared us to death and got shot." He always called Eli "Rattler," after he nearly died from a rattlesnake bite at age ten.

Eli Clark was now twenty-one and worked at a sawmill up the river near Hineston. Always fun and full of life, he was everyone's favorite. He was the greatest prankster I've ever known, and he delighted in scaring other folks. To top it off, he was stubborn to a fault. PaPaw always said, "My boy Eli would argue with a fence post."

Eli shot back at Uncle Nathan, "Unk, I believe you wet your britches when I blew that horn."

"I did *not*."

"Believe you did."

Before the argument could go further, Barney said, "Well, Boy, did you come to hunt or just scare folks?"

Eli knew he was in Barney's area of authority and straightened up. "I came to hunt, Mr. Barney. I just had to help initiate my nephew Mayo into the West Bay Hunting Club."

He turned to me. "Did I scare you, Mayo?"

Standing safely beside Daddy, I answered confidently, "Not a bit, Uncle Eli."

Everyone knew I was lying and laughed. I smiled too, knowing the others had been just as scared.

Barney got everyone's attention by clearing his throat. "Listen boys, that's enough of this foolishness. We've come to hunt—so let's hunt. I hear old Topper barking for us to turn the dogs loose and get after it."

It was time for my first foxhunt to begin.

Chapter 9

ALL conversation ceased when Barney blew his horn. It echoed off the trees and excited everyone present, men and dogs alike. The other men joined in with a chorus of horns as the dogs howled and pulled at their ropes. It echoed off the trees, sending a chill through me.

I knew that a special night lay ahead.

Hunt master Barney got everyone's attention. "Boys, let's bow our heads and ask the Lord's blessing on our hunt." The men doffed their hats, and even the hounds quietened down as Barney prayed.

"Lord, we thank ye for letting us be out in these beautiful woods tonight and ask for your blessings on our hunt, and Lord, I thank ye that we live where we can hunt, without trespassing, on nobody's property except yours.

"May it always be so in our Ten Mile country.

"In Jesus' name. Amen."

Each man gave a hearty amen as they turned their dogs loose. The dogs raced off, noses to the ground, barking excitedly.

"They're doing what they were born to do. Yep, what they were born to do," Barney said.

As the dogs disappeared into the darkness, each man's face seemed to glow in the firelight. I'm not sure if it was the heat of the fire, the excitement of the hunt, or maybe a little of both.

Caught up in the moment, I said my own simple prayer, *Lord, thanks for letting me live in this good place—these woods I love. Amen.*

The barking of the dogs faded, and each man took his place around the fire. Caleb poured everyone a cup of dark black coffee. The smell of the coffee in the crisp night air was one of the things

I'll always associate with my first foxhunt. Although it was a little strong for my taste, I felt like one of the men—trying not to burn my mouth as I sipped from an old tin cup.

"There ain't nothing better than a cup of hot Louisiana coffee on a cool Louisiana night. It's why I don't plan to live nowhere else," Barney said as the other men all heartily agreed.

Then everyone got quiet as the attention of each man was on the wind, listening carefully for the dogs. Barney, seated by me, leaned over, "When they pick up a trail on ol' Topper or one of his family, they'll really cut loose. You'll see what I mean directly."

The old man continued, "Topper's a fine, red fox and our favorite to hunt—he's a crafty old animal that probably looks forward to these hunts as much as we do.

"We gave him his name from the fact that his tail stands a little higher than other foxes. It's kind of frayed on the top."

All at once, we heard the far-off baying of the dogs. Even from a distance, the barking suddenly took on a deep, full volume that instantly affected every man around the fire.

"They're on him. They're on him." Barney stood. "Hunt 'em boys, Hunt 'em up."

I've always loved the passion of my Redbone kin. Whatever they do, they do with whole hearts. Whether worshipping, fighting, living, or laughing, they get after it with every ounce of their being. Foxhunting was no different.

The men stood listening to the sound echoing through the trees. Sound travels differently through the woods at night and has an eerie ring to it. The baying of the hounds coupled with the normal nighttime echoes of crickets and frogs created a magical glow as we stood around the fire.

Due to my excitement, I began shivering. I tried to hide it, but couldn't. PaPaw put his arm around me and whispered, "Don't worry, Mayo. I've got goose bumps, too." I felt his arm trembling as he added, "I hope I don't ever get where a night in the woods don't cause me to shiver a little."

PaPaw pointed into the darkness. "I call all of this 'swamp music.' There ain't no fiddle, guitar, or voice can match the music of hounds running a fox through the swamp."

As the dogs neared with their desperate baying, Barney hollered, "Bring 'em around. Topper, bring 'em here, Baby." Waving his hat in excitement, he seemed to be pulling as much for the fox as our dogs.

His voice had risen as the dogs neared. Turning to me, he said, "You see, Topper's a red fox and'll lead the dogs in a circle—just like a rabbit. We'll get to hear the dogs as they circle through this area over and over."

The baying dogs neared, and the men peered into the darkness for a glimpse of the passing fox. This jostling for position resulted in PaPaw spilling his coffee all over Unk.

The men's shouting blended into a chorus.

"Push 'im, Trailer, push 'im."

"Hunt 'em up."

Get 'im, Boys."

"Come on, Susie Baby, run 'im by here."

Mixed in, I could still hear Mr. Barney, "Come on, Topper. Come by here—we wanna see your bushy tail."

Each man tried to catch a glimpse of the fox or the dogs. In the dark, it was difficult to see much, but we all heard the crashing of the dogs through the underbrush as they went by.

As the barking faded, the arguing began. "I know that was my dog, Big Boy out front," Pistol proudly said.

"There ain't no way on God's green earth, Pistol. That was Trailer. I know his voice like my own wife's," Gideon replied.

The arguing was good-natured but intense. The two men went back and forth on whose dog was out front. Finally, Barney cleared his throat, and the arguments ceased. "You're both wrong. That was my dog—Lady."

Everyone laughed, which puzzled me, so PaPaw filled me in. "Lady was Barney's favorite foxhound, and been dead for three years, but he always mentions her in any hunt."

Barney gave his judgment on the lead dog. "Seriously, I'm giving the lead dog to Trailer."

Pistol reacted as if he'd been shot. "Ain't no way, Cuz."

"I'm sure it was Trailer."

"Babe, that weren't Trailer," Pistol said in mock anger.

"I said it—I'm the hunt master—and that settles it."

Barney's word was final. The men knew from decades of hunting that Barney was uncanny on distinguishing each dog's tone, rhythm, and pitch of its barking.

As bantering continued, we returned to the warmth of the fire. More pine knots were piled and the coffee cups refilled. Several of the men got pipes out and began puffing away. Barney told me, "We got us a rule around here—no smoking until the dogs make their first circle.

"Mr. Barney, how long will this go on?"

"It might go on 'til daybreak—that's kind of up to the fox. If the fox tires of the chase, he'll 'go to earth' in one of his holes, or the dogs might lose the scent as he crisscrosses through the area.

"If either of these happens, the dogs may pick up a fresh scent from another fox and the fun starts again."

"Why does Topper do this over and over instead of leaving from here?"

"Now, I can't get inside the mind of a fox, but I believe he enjoys the thrill of the hunt as much we do." He turned to Pistol. "Tell this boy about Topper's snack."

"Once on a daylight hunt, I saw him stop to catch a mouse. It was as if he was waiting for the dogs to catch up."

"The fox ain't our enemy. We can't do it without him," Barney added.

"What's the part of the hunt you enjoy most, Mr. Pistol?" I asked.

"Oh, that's hard to say—the woods at night, a pine knot fire with my friends, the sound of the dogs, and the freedom of the land. It kind of all blends together for me."

Mr. Barney asked me, "What about you? This here's your first foxhunt. What do you like about it?"

"Well, Mr. Barney—there's several things. The freedom of being out in the woods is good. Then there's something hard to describe I like—I've seen it in y'all's faces—it's the thrill of friends being together doing what they enjoy."

My daddy, who'd been quiet, said, "It's the *craic* he likes, Barney."

"Joe, did you say '*crack*?'"

"Yes, that's the way we say it in Ireland—*crack*, but it's spelled c-r-a-i-c."

"What does it mean?"

"It's hard to explain, but here's an example—Irish winter days are short and the weather is often bad for days at a time. The cold rain and wind keep people indoors, so neighbors often gather around the warm hearth of a cabin. They eat hot Irish stew, and the laughter spills out from the stories and jokes. Someone pulls out a fiddle or guitar and begins singing folk songs, and then one of the men starts dancing a jig or reel.

"The men pass around a jug of potato whiskey—while the women sit in a corner laughing and gossiping.

"In the midst of this visiting, in spite of the weather and sparseness of food, every face glows, and it's not due to just the fire or drink. It's the glow of fellowship—people enjoying being together. That's what craic is—and I've seen it around this campfire tonight."

"That's a good word, Joe. 'Craic.' I'll remember it," Barney said.

I watched Daddy's face as he talked. His cheeks were a healthy red as they always got when he was hot, mad, or excited. I also noticed how he spoke of Ireland in the present tense as if he were still there.

Then Daddy added, "But I think what gets me about this hunt is the total impracticality of it."

"Now what do you mean by that?" Barney asked.

"I mean it as a compliment. In Ireland, every action and thought was, 'How am I going to survive this famine?' Every action, idea, or word was motivated by the looming shadow of starvation. I've seen people—and done it myself—do desperate things to keep from starving. To think that someone would be able just to spend the night out in the woods around a fire listening to dogs chasing a fox and not feel the hunt had to provide food is something I can't get over. I like it."

Barney and Daddy had the stage as every man listened attentively. Stirring the fire with a stick, the older man replied, "A fellow can't appreciate what he's got until he's lost it. I hope we never lose this freedom of the woods."

Mr. Barney spat into the fire, then turned our talk from the future to the past. "Joe, tell us again about your run to freedom from them British."

Daddy scanned the faces. "You've all heard it before."

"But we want to hear it again. Go ahead."

He began with what he always called "me famous wild Irish potato run." Even though he'd lost some of his brogue, he reverted to it as he told this story.

"A pack of dogs attacked our sheep, and I killed the most aggressive one with my shovel. My bad luck was that it was the prize-hunting dog of an English landowner. Word got out about it, and the Englishman sent a threat, 'I'm going to do to you what you did to my dog.'

"Sure enough, they came after me, and as he and the British soldiers neared our house, I ran for my life and hid. Using tracking dogs, they finally flushed me out from behind a stone wall.

"I ran across the potato field, and he helped speed me along by peppering me with several shotgun blasts."

That night I swam out to a ship in Westport Harbor, and hid aboard it. It eventually made land in New Orleans. From there I came up the rivers to Alexandria, before crossing into this No Man's Land."

Daddy gazed into the fire before finishing. "And I'm *still* running, I guess."

"And then he ran right into my baby girl's arms," PaPaw said.

Daddy's story brought all kinds of comments from around the fire—some that I probably shouldn't have heard, before Pistol said, "Our No Man's Land is a good place for a fellow to run to. You ain't the first one to end up here running from the law. 'Cept most are running from the Texas Rangers or the Sheriff of Rapides Parish."

"Babe, a man running from somethin' is in good company here," Barney said.

I wanted to hear more of Daddy's story, but the baying of the returning dogs jolted us back to West Bay Swamp.

Chapter 10

THE dogs thundered by in the darkness, soon passing out of earshot. As quietness returned to West Bay Swamp, the idea of the log float came up.

It started with a recap of the hurricane. Pistol and Dan Perkins, being father and son, loved to argue and outdo each other in tall tales. Pistol's first recollection of the storm began, "It blew so hard, it blowed our well right out of the ground."

Not to be outdone, Dan said, "It blowed a crooked country road straight."

Pistol was quick on the draw. "No—that hurricane scattered the days so bad, we didn't get around to Sunday 'til late Tuesday morning."

"Pop, I can't top that one. You win round one," Dan said.

Next, the men discussed the hard times since the hurricane, and how the war was affecting the availability of supplies as well as the prices.

At that time, most Ten Milers didn't use a cash economy. They grew or made nearly everything and used bartering to get additional items. A man would trade a horse, pig, or a load of corn for something he needed. There's still a local term for making a living this way—"Redboning for a living."

Most of the men sitting around the fire had seen little cash money in their lives, which is why the gold coins had been such a big deal.

Pistol was the one who hatched the idea. If the men around the fire had known what this idea would lead to, they'd probably have shot him right there and been done with it.

No one knew it that night, but this log float would be a crossroads for every man sitting around the fire. We had no way of knowing that when Pistol said, "Boys, when I lived over along the Sabine River, I floated pine and cypress log rafts down the river. We'd cut them and drag them alongside the smaller streams, lash them together into rafts. When the June rise came, we'd ride 'em downstream to the sawmills in Orange, Texas.

"When we got there, we'd deliver our logs and get paid in hard cash. It was a good way to make money for the supplies we'd buy."

"How much money'd you make?" one of the men asked.

"On one float, I made a hundred and twenty-five dollars."

Several men whistled appreciatively. It was more than any of them could scratch together in several years of working around home.

"Are you talking about U.S. dollars or Confederate ones?"

"They were U.S. dollars—it was before the war."

"But we're miles from the Sabine," Daddy said.

"I know, but they've opened a new sawmill in Lake Charles, downriver on the Calcasieu. We could start our float ten miles from here. It'd be a long river ride down and a good five-day walk back, but we could all make some sorely needed cash."

"Can you buy salt in Lake Charles?" PaPaw asked, there being a shortage of salt since the war started.

"There's plenty of it at any of the larger river towns. Word is they're digging it out of the salt domes south of Vermilionville." Pistol had seen more of the world than anyone sitting there, except my daddy, so no one knew enough to question his word.

"How would we get the supplies back here?" Ben asked.

"We'd buy pack mules or horses, maybe even a wagon. When we got home, we could sell them as well as any extra goods—or keep 'em."

The men all nodded their heads in agreement. I knew each one was calculating what they could do with a hundred and twenty-five dollars.

Like a storm hovering over us, the subject of the war came up repeatedly that night. Men from outside our area had enlisted in the Confederate Army, but few Ten Milers had.

Ben Tyler spoke for everyone around the fire when he said, "I ain't interested in fighting no rich man's war for their cotton and slaves. I'm gonna sit this one out in the pines and let them settle it. I ain't got no dog in this fight."

"It's Abe Lincoln's War, not ours," Barney added.

Word had spread from Alexandria that conscription laws were in place requiring every man from eighteen to thirty-eight to join. Ben said, "If they want me, they'll have to come git me."

"Word is there are conscript bounty hunters fanning out from Alexandria. They'll take a man back dead or alive. It don't matter to them," Barney said.

The men looked into the fire wordlessly. Finally, Ben said, "If they cross the Calcasieu into our part of the country, we'll send *them* back dead or alive."

No one said another word, but several of the men stared off toward the east. I wasn't sure if they were listening for the dogs or approaching bounty hunters.

Pistol, who had a wealth of stored sayings, said, "The South can't win a war against the strength of them Northerners. All we've got is cotton, donkeys, and jackasses." He poked Barney. "Especially plenty of jackasses."

"Speak for yourself, Fella," Barney replied.

Only Daddy and my Uncle Eli had refrained from commenting on the war. I noticed this as I studied their faces. They were both what PaPaw always called "wild cards," meaning you couldn't figure them out that easily.

Daddy wasn't a "real American," at least not yet, while his brother-in-law Eli was a mystery to everyone, including his own family. Eli spent his whole life paddling upstream—never being content to do anything just because others did it. PaPaw described him as "wild as the wind and crazy as a loon."

Barney noticed both of their silence on the war. "Joe, you and Eli both been mighty quiet. What do you think?"

Immediately I thought of the term used for newcomers like Daddy: "Come-over-heres." In Ten Mile jargon, it meant you were considered an outsider. Dad's status as a come-over-here caused him to be quiet in a crowd of locals, so he hesitated before speaking.

"The way I see it—" Daddy started, but stopped as the barking of the dogs echoed in the cool night air.

I'll always wonder what he was ready to say, and if whatever it was would have changed anything if he'd said it.

The hound's deep-throated howl took everyone's mind off the war and log floats.

As the dogs passed, fierce argument again broke out about whose dog was leading the chase. Four men claimed *their* dog was the leader.

Dan Perkins, who owned a dog named "Susie," got agitated when, after claiming his dog was in the lead, the other men laughed at him. He got right in Caleb's face, balling up his fists. "I don't take to no man making fun of me."

Before the argument got out of hand, Mr. Barney slipped up beside him, and led Dan away by the elbow. "Son, don't get all riled up. It ain't nothing but a hunt."

Then the hunt master pointed under the wagon. "Look, Dan—there's little Susie right there." Sure enough, Susie was asleep under the wagon, snoring contentedly, sleeping off the excitement of the hunt.

Dan was some kind of embarrassed, and what he said to Susie wasn't repeatable in mixed company. For the rest of the night, every approach of the dogs was greeted by one of the men shouting, "It's Susie out front. I know it."

By the fourth or fifth round, Dan at least smiled about the teasing. After that night, Susie's story passed into Ten Mile hunting lore and is still called out around foxhunt campfires.

It's amazing how time flies when you're enjoying yourself, and the hunters seemed never to grow tired of the baying, circling, and excitement.

There was a long lull, and then Uncle Eli dropped his bombshell.

"Fellas, we been talking about that war all night, so I reckon now's as good a time as any to tell you something."

Every man looked up from the fire at Eli.

"I'm going to go sign up and join the Rebels."

I glanced at my PaPaw, Eli's dad. He was stone-faced, but soon the firelight clearly reflected tears in his eyes. A deep silence covered the swamp that no barking dogs could break.

Unk, who loved Eli like a son, finally spoke. "Rattler—Eli Clark, why would you go and do something stupid like that for?" I'd never heard Unk call him by his real name, so I knew he was upset.

"'Cause I feel in my heart it's what I ought to do. It's my duty."

Barney, whose job as hunt master extended to guiding campfire conversation, said, "Well, I heard up in Alexandria those rich cotton farmers will pay a man good money to take his place and be a 'substitute' in the fighting."

Eli stared into the fire before speaking. "No sir. I ain't goin' to take no man's place or his money. I'm going to stand in *my* place. It's *my* duty."

Barney poked the fire with his boot. "A man's gotta do what a man's gotta do."

Several of the hunters nodded their heads in agreement, but no one spoke a word.

I was sitting by my dad, hoping he'd say something, but he kept his peace. Daddy, though respected inside the Redbone culture, was still kind of an outsider. He knew this was neither the time nor place for his input—that could come later.

My PaPaw, Willard Clark, was the next one who spoke, and as he began, tears coursed down his cheeks.

"Son, I'd rather them cut off my right arm than see you go off to that war. It ain't our war, and it won't be nothing like what you think. But you're a full-growed man. It's like Barney just said, a man's got to set his own sail. I ain't got but one question: Is your mind made up?"

"Yes sir, it's made up. I've thought 'bout it for a while."

PaPaw grimaced. "Well, I sure ain't gonna be the one to tell your momma. In fact, I jes' believe I'll stay down in the swamp a couple of days while *you* tell her."

Barney whistled. "She won't take it good, Eli. You know how our women folk are."

Even as a boy, I understood about Redbone women. Later as a man, I learned the word that best describes them. It's matriarchal. It's pronounced 'may-tree-ar-kal,' and means the women are really in charge.

A Redbone man'll fight you over joking that he's not running his household, but everyone knows the old saying that if 'Momma ain't happy, ain't nobody happy.'"

It was plain that even Eli, whose mind was made up, shivered at the idea of telling his mother he was leaving for the war.

I should've kept my mouth shut, but I've never been very good at that. "Uncle Eli, where will you go—when will you go—what about . . .?"

I felt Daddy's hand on my knee.

"Mayo, I aim on leaving next week. There's a group of fellows meeting in Hineston and from there we'll travel on to Alexandria to sign up. The Yankees have invaded over along the Missisip', and a big battle's shaping up there. Word is they'll send us to some place called Vicksburg. I figure if I don't help fight 'em there, I'll end up fighting 'em here."

A heavy silence blanketed that corner of West Bay Swamp. Several of the men glanced around the swamp, and Mr. Barney spoke for them all when he said, "The idea of an army marching into our woods is nearly too much to think about."

There was nothing else to say. Even the silent frogs and crickets seemed to be digesting what'd just been said.

All of a sudden, I wished I were home. One of the men said,

"Look, the first faint light's in the east."

It was hard to believe, but we'd been out here all night.

Barney saw it too. "Well boys, it's time to call the dogs, pee on the fire, and go home."

I'm not sure which event ended the hunt—the first light of day, Barney's pronouncement, or Eli's announcement—but no matter, my first foxhunt was over.

The men began blowing their horns and yelling. Within a few minutes, the first of the dogs appeared. Now if dogs could smile, they were smiling. Ben, for the first time that night, spoke directly to me, "Look at 'em. They enjoyed it as much as we did."

Sure enough, the dogs seemed pleased with themselves, and each was greeted by its owner. Barney said, "It's 'cause they've been doing what they were born to do—Yep, doing what they were born to do."

PaPaw turned to Eli, "Son, those dogs were born to hunt. It's what they live for, but I don't believe a man was born to fight and die in a war that ain't his quarrel."

Uncle Eli just stared into the smoldering ashes of the fire, never replying or looking up.

We loaded the wagon, got on our horses, and broke camp, little knowing it would be the last foxhunt for a long time.

For some of the men present that night, it would be the last foxhunt of their lives.

Chapter 11

RIDING home from the hunt, I was tired but exhilarated. I knew I'd taken one more step into manhood. The men had talked openly about "manly things"—war, money, and their personal lives—in my presence.

"Daddy, are you going on that log float?" I asked.

He rode on in silence before saying, "I'm thinking about it. There's a lot of 'ifs,' but if we don't get some salt, we won't be putting up much pork this year."

Salt was an important part of our lives. We used it to preserve meat and for many other daily needs.

His comments about the trip were the opening I was looking for. "If you go, can I go?"

"Son, that ain't a trip for a boy your age."

"But, I ..."

"I said *no*, and I meant *no*."

His firm tone showed he meant it, so I should've left it alone.

"Daddy, if we need money, why don't we just ask Unk for some more of that gold?"

He gave me such a look that a fly wouldn't have landed on him. "Son, I don't want to hear *another* word about those coins and your uncle. *Do you understand?*"

I wondered if he was just tired from the night's hunt, or if I'd struck a nerve.

"Do you understand? I don't ever want to hear about it again!"

"*Yes, Sir.*"

I wasn't brave enough to ask again about the float and coins, but I sure thought about both. In the silence, I began developing plans on both subjects.

My first plan dealt with the mystery of the coins—the log float could wait until later.

The origin of those gold coins was burning a hole in my pocket, or rather in my mind. It wasn't the money itself as much as the mystery of it all. I couldn't figure out how Unk, who herded sheep, could have that much money.

The fact that my parents were the only people who seemed to know added to the intrigue. I was born with a good dose of curiosity. That dose has kept me in trouble for most of my life.

By the time we reached home, my plan had taken shape, but for it to work I'd have to wait for the right time.

We had breakfast and then started our chores. That afternoon, I was tired and told Daddy, "I might go take a little nap."

He handed me a hoe. "No, I don't believe so. Go out there and work with the cabbage and spinach. If a fellow's big enough to hunt all night, he's big enough to work all the next day."

I didn't like what he said but knew his words were true, so I picked up my hoe and went to work.

Two weeks later, I put my plan into action. It started at the breakfast table as I sat watching my mother cooking eggs and bacon. She'd mentioned the day before that Unk had been sick with a bad head cold.

"Momma, I been thinking about going over and spending a few days with Unk. He's had that bad head cold, and I believe a visit from me might make him feel better."

She never took her eyes off the stove. "I guess that'd be all right if you're caught up with your chores for your daddy."

"Yes, Ma'am. I'll check with him."

Before she could say more or ask questions, I rushed out to find Daddy. He was in the barn putting the traces on Dallas for a morning of plowing.

"Daddy, Momma said it'd be a good idea for me to go over

and check on Unk 'cause he's been feeling puny." It wasn't the whole truth, but I'd learned to work this game between my parents.

"If it's fine with your mother, I don't mind. But I want you to take my muzzleloader in case you come across a varmint."

I'd pulled it off. Before they could compare notes and change their minds, I was on my way.

My motive in going was to find out about the gold coins, but I was also happy to see my uncle. He was always my favorite. Though he didn't have a knack for any book learning, the Lord had given him an extra helping of good sense blended with good humor.

He possessed great insight into people, noticing things no one else did. Daddy called him "Doc," and explained why. "He sees things that nobody else can. He's a step above the rest of us, and where I come from, that deserves a title of respect.

"Doc—your Uncle Nathan—has a lot of common sense, and the thing about common sense is that it ain't common."

I was also excited to get out into the woods, free from chores and parents. As Bo and I traipsed through the woods, I shouldered the gun. Word was that Roscoe had returned to greener pastures in West Bay, so I wasn't worried about running into him. I wasn't sure my gun would even slow a bull down, but carrying it made me feel better.

First, I had to find Unk. He traveled about with the sheep, camping under a tarp as the weather dictated it. He was a true wanderer and said that it was due to his Indian blood.

First, I went to his house. Calling it "a house" was an exaggeration—it was a simple lean-to. Being gone most of the time, he didn't see much need for a home or its trappings.

Upon entering, I could see no one had been home recently. I rummaged about the room looking for a key part of my plan. Behind the bed, I found it, slipped it into my bag, and headed out.

For most of the afternoon, I wandered about looking for fresh sheep tracks. I went to several places where he often took the sheep but saw no sign of him or them. Bo kept sniffing around, and I had to call him to keep up with me as he kept chasing squirrels on the edge of the swamp.

I whistled and then shouted, "Come on, Boy. Let's go to the pasture. I bet we'll find him there."

We followed the winding trail to the Big Pasture, an open area with ample grass and a nearby stream. My first sign that we were on the right track was the wisp of smoke I saw from the distance. Next, I heard the bleating of sheep, and knew I'd found him.

Bo ran ahead and greeted Unk. Seeing me, he said, "Well, look who's out on a hike. What are you doing in these here woods?"

"I come to check on you. Momma's been worried about your head cold."

He was hoarse and kept dabbing at his runny nose. "Yep, I ain't felt too good in a week or so, but it ain't no use moaning 'bout it. Sit down here."

He had a good fire going, and I smelled roasted coffee. The sun was setting, and I realized how far I had walked during the day, as well as how famished I was.

He stirred the embers before asking, "Have you et yet?"

"I'm hungry enough to eat a frozen dog."

"That's pretty hungry. Now, I ain't got nothing fancy—but we're having grits and ham for supper. Can you stay?"

"Yes sir, I was hoping to stay with you tonight."

"That's good. I could use the company."

There's nothing like a meal around a campfire with darkness closing in. It makes a man huddle closer to the fire, and the food tastes better. Out in the woods, even the simplest meal is fit for a king, and Unk's grits and ham were no exception. He stirred them together and poured a generous helping of cane syrup on top, before handing me my plate.

Then he poured up steaming cups of coffee for both of us and began his campfire supper ritual. Putting a spoonful of grits to his mouth, he stopped in mock horror, "Wait a minute now, we ain't blessed it."

Doffing his hat, he began, "Now Lord, we thank you for this meal we're fixin' to eat, and I wanna thank you for letting us eat it out in these woods you made. In Jesus' name. Amen."

I'd heard this blessing, or one like it, all of my life, but still loved it. I knew it came from his heart and reminded me that the Lord takes delight in simple things and the words of simple people.

When he prayed, I always felt as if I were eavesdropping in on a conversation with God. When I mentioned this, he said, "Well, that's just what I'm doing—talking with God. Ain't it supposed to be that way?"

"It sure sounds like it."

"Well, let's eat." We ate, lulled by the baaing of the sheep and the soft wind in the pines.

"This is as good a supper as I've ever had, Unk."

This was his cue. Taking a loud slurp of coffee he said, "Yep, I wonder what the poor folks are eating tonight." This always tickled him, and he spilled some of his coffee chuckling at his own joke.

"Well, I know what two of 'em are eating, and it's pretty good," I answered as he continued to chuckle.

He pointed his cup in a northerly direction. "Mayo, there's folks up in New York City or 'Washington, *P.C.*' thinking they've got it good, but they ain't got it near as good as us."

I'd learned long ago that it was no use correcting him on Washington *D.C.* It usually came out as T.C., B.P., or whatever. I also grinned as he talked about these two American cities as if he'd walked their streets many times. This was coming from a man who'd never been over thirty miles from the house he was born in.

"Well, those fellows in them big cities probably feel sorry for folks like us, but I feel sorry for them having to live indoors, locking away their treasures, always afraid somebody's gonna steal 'em." He spooned another helping onto our plates, as he said, "City living ain't for me."

His mention of "treasures" caught my attention and opened the door for the first step in my plan. "Speaking of *treasures*, have you heard about those gold coins lots of folks have found?"

He stopped in mid-bite and looked hard at me. After chewing a while, he answered warily, "Well, I did hear something about it."

"It's something, ain't it?"

"It sure is. Sure is."

He moved the subject quickly back to our national capitol, this time calling it "Washington, V.P.," and began describing the buildings and sights he'd heard about.

As darkness deepened and the crickets and frogs began their mixed chorus, we lay back on a blanket. The cool night was clear, and a sky of bright stars formed a canopy over our heads.

"I don't believe I'll put the tarp up tonight," He said. "The sky's too pretty to be covered up."

Settling down for the night, I said, "Unk, my momma's been worried about your head cold and sent you some medicine for it." I reached into my bag, pulled out a jar of honey, a pinch of sugar, and a small cup.

"She said a good hot toddy'd do you good." I then pulled out the bottle I'd gotten from behind his bed.

"I've got a little whiskey to help that cold."

Unk was surprised, and I couldn't tell if he was pleased or not. "Now son, you know I don't hardly ever drink, but I do believe a good toddy will help me sleep better and clear up this cold."

Just as if I were a bartender in one of those bars in Washington B.P. or New York City, I mixed his drink. After heating the jar of honey in the boiling water left over from supper, I stirred it in.

He then began with the corny joke I'd heard him tell dozens of times. "Mayo, have you heard about where Sugar Creek runs into the Whiskey Chitto River?"

"No, I don't guess I have."

"Well, at the spot where they run together—you know *Sugar* Creek and *Whiskey* Chitto—that spot is called '*Little Toddy*.'" He had emphasized the words so I would catch the joke. I laughed as if I'd never heard it before.

He added, "In the summer when it's hot, they call that spot in the creek, *'Hot Toddy.'* He laughed so hard he went into a coughing fit and was more than glad to take the glass of toddy I handed him.

He downed it, smacking his lips. "I done feel better already."

After a second shot of toddy, he lay back and soon was snoring soundly. On the other side of me, Bo lay sleeping. The snoring of my uncle and dog were in the same rhythm.

After waiting ten or fifteen minutes, I nudged him and he coughed. Unk was famous for talking in his sleep. When he stayed at our house, Colleen and I delighted in slipping in and carrying on a full conversation with him as he slept. He'd answer any question, and we always had fun asking.

That was my plan to solve the mystery of the gold coins. I knew the hot toddy would help put him out as well as completely loosen his tongue.

Kneeling by him, I whispered, "Unk."

There was no answer, so I spoke louder, "Uncle Nathan."

Still no response.

"Wake up, Nathan Dial."

"Huh?" He answered sleepily.

"I need to ask you something."

He turned, eyes still closed. "Go ahead."

I tapped him to ensure he was asleep. Satisfied that he was, I continued. "I want to ask you about the gold coins."

He shivered and I was afraid he was going to wake up, so I waited until he was snoring evenly.

"I need to know how you got those gold coins."

"I took them from that man that was kilt."

"What man?"

"That stranger in the Big Pasture with the bags of money."

We were lying in the middle of that very same pasture, and a chill ran through me.

"I didn't kill him. Amos kilt him as I watched, but I took and hid the money."

I couldn't believe my simple uncle had been part of a robbery and murder. "Where's the money now?"

"I hid it."

"Who else knows about it?"

"Don't nobody know but Eliza . . . and Joe Moore."

I nearly said "Momma and Daddy." Instead I asked, "You mean Joe and Eliza were in on it?"

"Not Joe at first, but my niece Eliza was in on it from the very start. She's the first person I showed where I hid it."

This was too much for my young mind—my mother involved in a murder and the hiding of blood money. I wondered if I was finding out things I'd later wish were unknown, but I couldn't stop now. "Who is Amos?"

"He's the one who actually kilt the stranger, but he's gone. We got rid of him."

I cringed at the thought of another murder to cover the first. Trying to focus my brain, I stammered, "But you've done good with the money helping people."

"Yep, that's what I promised the Lord after it was all over. Now, go to sleep. I don't wanna talk no more."

In spite of peppering him with more questions, he was through answering. His deeper snoring told me that the toddy had taken him farther down the Whiskey Chitto River, and he didn't have the strength to paddle back upstream.

I lay awake under the stars before finally drifting off to sleep. The trouble was that I had more questions than when I started.

They were hard questions with no simple answers.

Chapter 12

TRY as I might, I couldn't learn more about how the coins came into Unk's hands or the part my parents played in this mystery.

About a week later, I learned an important lesson. It had nothing to do with the gold coins, but resulted in the worst whipping of my life.

It all started with our new corncrib. The old crib had taken a licking from the hurricane and was beyond repair, so we built a sturdy new one. As we finished, Momma stepped back and made her classic comment, "It's built 'horse high, bull strong, and pig tight,' and I don't believe no animal or storm can tear it down."

I recalled her use of that term during the hurricane when the rafters of our house were lifting and shingles were blowing off. Thankfully, she'd been right that night.

Now, my daddy, who'd grown up in snakeless Ireland, was scared to death of snakes—not just poisonous ones—but all snakes. I believe a foot-long garter snake put the same fear of the Lord in him as a huge timber rattler.

He loved telling the story of St. Patrick tossing Ireland's snakes off the mountain near his hometown, and laughing as he added, "All of the snakes tossed out of Ireland by the saint landed here in Louisiana."

I didn't inherit that fear of snakes; in fact, I've always been fascinated with them. I grew up in a world where boys caught snakes. Now I wasn't stupid—I was careful with copperheads or cottonmouths, but I wasn't one bit afraid of the harmless ones making up most of our snake population.

I'd learned a great deal about snakes from my Uncle Eli. He was fearless with them and taught me both how to identify and handle them. How ironic after he'd nearly died from that rattler bite as a boy. He'd been bitten twice since then by copperheads with little effect and claimed now to be immune to snake poison.

My Uncle Eli was a whiz at lots of skills and passed lots of his know-how on to me. Among his varied talents was one I admired the most: snake-popping. He'd catch a snake by the tail—most often a chicken snake—and pop the snake like a whip. If snapped with enough force and a tight enough grip on the tail, the snake's head would pop right off.

It was an impressive sight. Eli taught me how to do it, and I was rightfully proud of my newfound skill.

On this fateful day, I was cleaning out the old corncrib and unearthed a three-foot-long chicken snake under the corn shucks. In spite of its normal diet of rats, which we detested, it had a bigger appetite for chicken eggs and biddies, so anytime we found one on our place, we killed it.

Since it was winter, the snake was sluggish and easily caught. Just as I left the crib, holding the snake with both hands, was when fate took over. My Irish daddy came around the barn whistling, carrying a pail of milk in his hand. I thought this was the perfect time to show him my new snake-popping skill, figuring he'd be properly impressed with my brave action.

Laying the chicken snake on the ground, I grasped its tail, and with a mighty whipping action, propelled the snake in an arc. . .

And that's when trouble started. I didn't have as good a grip as I should've, and my whipping motion didn't result in the head popping off—rather it caused the entire chicken snake to fly out of my hands.

In horror, I watched it fly through the air straight for Daddy, who stood frozen with his mouth open. The snake twirled in a long arc like a stretched rubber band, and its downward path landed on Daddy, wrapping itself around his leg.

Momma, who was on the porch and saw it all, later commented, "My man Joe 'got religion' when that snake wrapped around his leg."

The bucket of milk was the first casualty—flying upward ten

feet before coming back to earth, milk spilling in every direction.

But, that wasn't the end of the flying—Daddy got ahold of the snake and flung it across the yard. Once again, like a thrown rope, the poor snake was airborne, finally hitting the barn wall with a loud thump before sliding to the ground.

I should've sprinted for the safety of the woods but could only watch in horror. Daddy was hollering in Irish—which is what he always did when he was mad or scared—and he was a lot of both at the moment. I glanced at the porch for help from my mom, but she stood with her hand over her face, trying to suppress a laughing fit. I heard her sputter, "Ain't no use cryin' over spilt milk."

Looking back, I saw Bo charging the helpless snake. Grasping the snake in his mouth, he shook it violently and tossed it through the air—right back toward Daddy.

At least this time, he had time to duck. It cleared his head by about a foot before landing with a "whomp" in the barnyard.

The next movement in this drama did not bode well for me: Daddy was on the move *toward* me. Collaring me with one hand, he began wearing me out with the other. When his hand started hurting, he picked up a stick and used it until it broke. Finally, he picked up the now empty milk bucket and walloped me loudly on the behind with it. He kept it up a long time, chewing me out the whole time. Who knows what he was saying, since he was still yelling in Irish.

When he stopped, we both looked to the porch, and Momma was gone. Also gone was the snake. It seemed as if its three flights would've dazed or killed it, but evidently it had cleared the premises. Speaking of clearing out, that's what I did—going to the woods until Momma called for supper.

Things were tense around the Moore table as we ate in an uneasy silence. Momma stayed busy bringing in our plates, and each time she went to the kitchen I heard her giggling.

Colleen finally broke the silence. "Daddy, don't be too mad at Mayo. He was just showing you his trick."

Momma burst out laughing, unable to restrain herself any

longer, repeating, "Joe, it ain't no use cryin' over spilt milk—or even flying snakes. . . ." She was laughing so hard, she couldn't continue speaking. Finally, Daddy, who usually was good-humored, began to smile.

That was all the opening she needed. "I've always wanted to see a circus and worried that I'd die without going to one, but today, thanks to you two boys, my dream came true."

He cut his eyes at her, but she kept on. "Well, I don't believe—." Another fit of giggles overtook her. "I don't believe any circus could be better than the show the three of you put on out there."

"The *three* of us?" Daddy asked.

"Yep—the three of you—you, Mayo, and that chicken snake."

"If it'd been wrapped around your leg, it wouldn't have been so funny."

"I now know how St. Patrick tossed those snakes off that mountain—now what was the name of the mountain?" She asked.

"Croagh Patrick—Patrick's mountain."

"I bet St. Patrick slung them just as far as you did."

I wolfed down my meal and excused myself from the table—my behind was still burning, and I figured I'd best lay low.

It was the worst whipping I ever got, but there was an upside to it. It was a long time before we ever found another chicken snake in the corncrib or barn. It seemed they'd all cleared out.

We weren't in Ireland, but evidently no snakes were brave enough to show up at the Moore household after that day. I believe that dizzy, tossed snake spread the word that those folks were crazy.

As he'd promised, Eli continued with his plans to leave for the war. When he made up his mind on something, there was no way to stop him. PaPaw described it as, "That boy's got smoke in his britches."

As predicted, my MaMaw was some kind of upset when he broke the news of his decision. She went through every emotion that week—anger, denial, resentment, crying, but none worked on her son—he'd made up his mind and was going.

The day before he left, he came by our place for a visit. Colleen met him in the yard, and he swung her into his arms. My baby brother Patrick, who dearly loved Eli, crawled to him to be tossed high in the air.

Uncle Eli spent several hours with us, laughing and joking as if he were going off to the fair instead of a war. The talk was light, and he refused to let anyone get too serious.

Then he stood and said, "Well, It's time for me to go." Without another word, he hugged his only sister—my momma—shook Daddy's hand, and said goodbye to us kids.

I went with him up the trail, the wind in the trees the only sound as we quietly walked on the cushion of pine needles.

"How long do you think you'll be gone?"

"I don't rightly know."

"Uncle Eli, is it true that white men with twenty slaves or more don't have to go?"

"I'd heard it's so, but I guess I'll find out for sure."

"That don't make no sense to me."

"It don't to me neither, but a lot don't make no sense in life."

"Why're you going when everybody *but* you thinks it's a mistake?"

"It don't matter what others think. What matters is in a man's heart."

He hesitated, before adding, "By the way, one of your Daddy's Irish sayings helped me make my decision."

"Which one?"

"It's easy for dead fish to follow the tide."

"What's a 'tide?'"

"According to your daddy, in the ocean, the water flows in and out during different times of the day. Just dead things follow the flow—and I ain't dead."

"But are you scared, Uncle Eli?"

He stopped, took a deep breath as he scanned the woods all around us. "I'm sure gonna miss these pines. You know what I don't like, Mayo?"

"What?"

"Leaving before the honeysuckles bloom. It's always been my favorite thing about spring—going down along the creek and catching a whiff of them. There ain't nothing like the smell of honeysuckle. I'd always bring my momma a bouquet of them and put them in the house. She'd come in, smell them, and know I'd been there."

"I'll pick some for you this spring and surprise her."

"You do that. That'll make me and her happy."

He'd avoided my earlier question, so I repeated it. "Are you scared?" He still didn't answer.

"Uncle Eli, two of those Bradford boys from up near Hineston went off to the war and never even made it out of camp. They got the measles and died. Momma said it was 'cause they had them all crowded up where everybody passed along sickness."

I waited a few seconds. "*Are* you—are you scared?"

"Not really. I ain't scared, but I'm not sure I'll be back."

"What do you mean?"

"I had a dream the other night." He winced and stopped.

"What about?"

"It's too real to tell you, but in it everyone was there but me."

I didn't like what I was hearing. "That don't mean a thing."

"Then I heard an owl hooting outside the window. It called in pairs of threes. The old folks always said that meant death was coming to the hearer."

Now I was the one who winced. "You don't believe that stuff, do you?"

"Mayo, I wish I didn't, but I believe it was an omen."

Once again, that word I'd come to despise—omen.

"You'll be back. I just know it."

"I hope so, but I'm not sure. I just hope if I don't make it, it's a Yankee bullet and not no measles or fever. I sure prefer to die with my boots on."

He stopped, looking around as if he thought someone might be eavesdropping.

"Now listen closely Mayo. If I *don't* come back, there's three things I need you to do. Can I depend on you?"

"You know you can."

"Good. Now you can't tell nobody else about the three things."

"I won't."

"Good."

For the next mile of our walk, he instructed me what to do. When he'd finished, he made me repeat his instructions. Satisfied that I understood, he rubbed my head. "Just between you and me, now. Got it?"

"Yes sir." Then I asked something that had been on my mind. " Uncle Eli, if something happens to you, do you think you're right with God?"

He winked at me. "Now that's a right serious question for a fellow to ask, but the answer is yes.

"When I was about your age, I heard a sermon about getting right with God and asking Jesus into my heart. When the preacher asked anyone who wanted to do that to come forward, I stood there grabbing that pew so tight I pinched the sap right out of it." He let that sink in before continuing.

"They sang about thirty verses of the invitation hymn. I still held off and went home miserable. After lunch, I went off in the woods and made an altar out of a stump and did it."

"Did what?"

"Asked Jesus into my heart."

"Did he come in?"

"Sure, he did. Jesus is a man of his word. I asked and he answered." Uncle Eli kicked at a crawdad mound in the road. "Some folks worry about me with my wild ways, but Jesus is in my heart and in control of my life. So don't worry about me, no matter what happens."

"I won't."

"Good."

We said little more after that, walking along, lost in our thoughts.

Finally, he said, "Mayo, you've come far enough. It's getting toward dark, and you'd better head home."

I reluctantly obeyed. Uncle Eli hugged me, saying, "Don't worry 'bout me. I'll be fine." My uncle walked away with those words ringing in my ears. He was the first member of my family drawn into that stupid war.

I wondered if he'd be the last.

In my heart, I knew there'd be more.

Chapter 13

FEBRUARY 1863

A few weeks after Uncle Eli left, nine men gathered at our house to plan the log float. Coming in from a cold rain, they all crowded around our fireplace. The smell of wet leather and boots mixed with the aroma of coffee cooking over the fire.

The nine men were: Barney Bryant, Caleb Johnson, Ben Tyler, Fred Wilson, Pistol Perkins, and his son Dan, Unk, Daddy, and my PaPaw, Willard Clark. Although I wasn't counted, I sat in the corner hanging onto every word.

Pistol, who'd been on log floats, explained, "We'll cut up the fallen pines closest to Cherry Winche Creek. Then we'll use my ox as well as Caleb's team to drag them to the creek—if that's all right with him."

"Fine with me," Caleb quietly said. I kept a mental note that his word count for the day was at three.

"Once there, we'll make a slip or a dump, then build our rafts."

Every eye was on Pistol. Just as his cousin Barney was the master of the foxhunt, Pistol, the only one of our group who knew the first thing about a log float, was the leader.

The inexperience of the other men in the room was evidenced by the slew of questions.

"What's a 'slip'?" Ben asked.

"It's a cleared place on the creek where we can easily slide the logs in during high water. A dump is a cleared bluff on the creek where we can roll the logs into the river."

"How'll we build that raft?"

"When we get the logs in place at the creek, we'll line them up side by side, and use poles to nail them together into rafts of ten or fifteen logs each. Over on the Sabine, they call each raft a 'crib,' and the 'raft' is actually the chain of cribs lashed together to float as a group."

I watched the men's faces as they listened intently. The light from the crackling fireplace, contrasting with the cold gray day, revealed both their excitement and concerns.

PaPaw raised his hand to speak. "Boys, I been a thinking— this trip is a little beyond me, but I'm still in. I'd like to help with the cutting and hauling and I'll do my part, but I'm gonna let my son-in-law here, Joe, take care of my raft."

My heart beat faster as I envisioned riding on PaPaw's raft, but knew it was not to be. That very morning when I'd mentioned to Daddy about my willingness to go, he cut me off. "Mayo, if you ask again, I'm gonna whip you real good. The answer is *no*, and it's going to *stay no*."

So I kept quiet. Fred Wilson said, "It sounds like a good idea, but I'm going to pass on it, too. My wife's due to have a baby this spring and it ain't a good time for me to be gone."

Everyone agreed with Fred's reasoning.

His brother-in-law, Ben Tyler, said, "Why don't you help me with my logs, and we'll work something out."

"Sounds good."

Ben turned to Pistol. "How long will this trip take?"

"A good week or so floating to Lake Charles. The walk home should take a little less than that."

"When will we go?"

"We'll need to get to work now, cutting the logs and getting them to the creek. Then it'll all depend on enough water in the creek to get our raft to the Calcasieu. If there's not an early spring flood, we'll go with the June rise."

The meeting broke up with good spirits buoyed by dreams of better times ahead and pockets crammed full of cash.

As the men filed out, Momma stood with her arm around my daddy. Watching Ben and Fred walking side by side, she said, "I still can't get over having the Tyler and Wilson families under one roof. Back during the feud, they would've tried to kill each other."

"Well, Eliza, you had something to do with it."

"I was just there when it ended."

I listened closely. I'd never been able to get the whole story about the blood feud between the Wilson and Tyler families. There was also the mystery of how the feud ended suddenly one day on Cherry Winche Creek. Momma was there on that day, but was always hesitant talking about it.

Now that the planning was over, the hard work began. Daddy selected a site near the mouth of Cherry Winche to cut and collect our logs. The good thing was that nature had already done much of the hard work. The most dangerous part of logging is cutting down the trees, and the hurricane had already done that for us.

Because hundreds of pines had been downed by the hurricane, it was a matter of selecting the best, fallen trees closest to the creek. Longleaf pines grow on higher ground away from the creek bottoms, so we had to clear a rough trail to the creek.

Pistol and Caleb brought over their oxen and dragged, or skidded, the logs to the sloped creek-side slip, where we nailed sweet gum saplings on top of the logs to form a raft.

The plan was to make up five of these rafts, rope them together in a long chain, and float them downriver with high water.

I watched with awe as the men and oxen struggled to get these huge pine logs in place along the water's edge. The teams, leaning on each other for support, slowly dragged the logs to the creek.

Another part of the process that caught my attention was the building of the largest raft. It was longer than the others, containing the longest and straightest pines. These would fetch more money because of demand for ship's masts.

On this raft, they built a crude lean-to for cooking and getting out of the rain.

None of the men was sure how long the log float would take. This became a constant source of discussion among the men. Pistol said that it'd take a week, but the other men argued from "three days at the most" all the way to "two weeks or better."

Lake Charles was about seventy miles away as the crow flies, but it was only a guess how many miles this would be on the winding Calcasieu. Everyone agreed the float's time would depend on the river's height plus their skill—or lack of it—in guiding the rafts.

That was about all they agreed on. There were all kinds of arguing about the length of the float, route back home, and the needed supplies. Of greatest concern was how long the walk or ride home from Lake Charles would take.

There were two schools of thought concerning the trip home. The Perkins—Pistol and his son Dan—felt we should buy wagons and a team of horses to bring home our supplies. Most of the other men, led by Ben, thought wagons would be a waste of money. It'd be better to buy a few horses and pack mules for the supplies, and walk home.

Next, they branded the logs. PaPaw made a cattle brand with the letters "TM" and imprinted it on each end of the logs. This stood for "Ten Mile." We were now the Ten Mile Logging Company. No lumber baron was ever more proud than this motley group of men as 'TM' was branded on each log. I was just as proud as any of them, being as I considered myself a full partner.

Additionally, Daddy took his double-bit ax and chopped "TM" on the middle of each log length, so there could be no mistaking of ownership when we reached the sawmills.

When the raft was finished and made ready for the trip, I made up my mind—*there was no way they were going without me.*

Walking home the last day of work there, I mentioned the trip to Daddy. He was in a good mood and I felt the timing was perfect. "Say, I believe I could be some good help to y'all."

His answer was quick and direct. "There is *no way* you're going on that trip. You can go later when your legs get longer, but not this time."

I looked down at my twelve-year-old legs, willing them to be longer. As if reading my mind, he said, "There'll be other trips" and winked, "when your legs are longer."

With the work and preparation done, there was only one thing to do—wait. The float couldn't take place until high water came, a factor completely out of our control.

When that high water came, whether from a winter flood, spring storm, or the annual June rise, *we'd* be ready to go.

You'll notice I said "we." I was going—none of them knew it yet, but that didn't matter—I knew it—*and I was going.*

Chapter 14

THE men didn't sit around waiting on high water—idleness was never an option for Ten Mile settlers. Every bit of daylight, other than the Sabbath, was spent trying to stay alive. The storm's destruction—what it did to our late crops and foodstuffs—made times even more difficult. So, we worked hard—and then worked some more.

Every cloudy day filled me with hope it would bring the rain to flood the river and start the trip downriver. The waiting also gave me time to develop my plan of joining the float.

However, when you're waiting, things still happen, and the cold winter weeks of early 1863 brought two events—both sad— that affected my family.

The first event was actually an outgrowth of the log float.

Before the next planning meeting, Momma made my daddy promise to bring up the idea of inviting Silas Merkle to be part of the enterprise. My parents argued back and forth about it until Daddy reluctantly agreed to mention it.

I sat beside him at the meeting and could feel his hesitance as he said, "Uhmm, men, being neighborly is something we all know about. How about us, uh, inviting Silas Merkle to be in on our plan?"

No one said a word. There were no seconds to his motion, and an uneasiness filled the room.

Finally, Ben Tyler said, "I don't trust the man, but I do feel sorry for his family. Maybe we should try to help, 'cause they don't have any way of making a living from what I see."

The men reluctantly agreed and decided to send Daddy and PaPaw to issue an invitation. They were equally hesitant but agreed to go the next day.

I was in the front yard when they returned from their "visit." The disgust on their faces was clear evidence that the visit hadn't gone well. PaPaw hardly ever cussed, but in describing their reception spit out a string of bad words before my momma could stop him.

"Well, Eliza, you'd cuss too if you'd heard the way that nut talked to us." His eyes darkened as he continued, "We went over there to help him, and he ran us off as if we were taking advantage of him."

"What'd his wife say?"

"She jes' stood there looking scared. That woman's got a rough row to hoe."

"We offered to help him get another log raft together," Daddy said. "His reply was 'I don't need you fellows doing nothing for me. We're doing just fine.'"

"Then he motioned toward the door, and we put our hats on and got out of there.

"And I won't be going back. Now, he's a sorry ...." PaPaw added.

Momma interrupted, "*Daddy.*"

"Well, I wouldn't build a doghouse on his grave and...."

"*Daddy.*"

My own daddy came to PaPaw's rescue. "Honey, if you'd been there, you'd understand. Merkle's a bad fellow."

"But you *did* the right thing by going over there and asking him."

PaPaw turned to get in the last word. "He ain't nothing but a bald-faced liar."

"Now, Daddy. . . ."

"Don't 'daddy' me. I wouldn't spit on him if he was *afire.*"

Momma didn't answer her father, just sadly shook her head.

However, it wasn't the last word on Silas Merkle. The very

night after the men's visit, Merkle disappeared.

On the second day after her husband went missing, Sarah Merkle sent the twins to our house for help. We followed them back to their place and entered the lean-to, where we found the poor woman sobbing, "He's been gone since Tuesday, and I've seen neither hide nor hair of him."

My parents peppered her with questions trying to unravel the mystery.

"Did he say he was going anywhere?" Momma asked.

Mrs. Merkle angrily jabbed a finger at Daddy. "No, it was after *you men* came by that he left. Y'all upset him bad, and he just sulked about 'fore he left for the woods. He came back around dark, still upset. During the night, he didn't sleep very good—nothing unusual about that. I heard him rumbling round during the night and morning found him gone, and I ain't seen him since."

Her gaze and words revealed that she felt Daddy was responsible for her husband's disappearance. Momma listened to Sarah Merkle, but her stark gaze rested on Daddy. .

My father had heard enough. "Lady, I'm right sorry Mr. Merkle is missing, but I don't know nothing about it. We came to help—" I could see cheeks glowing red, a sure sign he was getting fired up.

Mrs. Merkle either didn't see it, or didn't care. "But y'all came over here and upset him."

"Lady—" But Daddy stopped. The cold stare of my mother was enough to cool him off, so he turned to me. "Mayo, let's go with the twins and give a look around for clues about Mr. Merkle. We'll let you ladies talk some more."

He stomped out of the stinking lean-to, bumping his head on the low entrance on the way out. In anger, he flung his hat across the yard. "The idea that woman blamed *me*."

Turning to me, he said, "And *your* own mother's on her side."

I knew better than to say anything, so I stayed clear while he cooled off. I saw him go to the twins and begin talking to them. I stayed safely at the edge of the yard juggling pinecones.

In about twenty minutes, Momma came out. She had her chin in the air, not even trying to hide her aggravation. She grabbed Patrick from Colleen and walked ahead without a word. We followed in her wake toward home.

When Daddy told me to drop back with my sister, so he and Momma could talk, I knew trouble was ahead. I obeyed, but still stayed within earshot, not willing to miss one word.

He trotted to catch up with her.

"Joe Moore, I need to ask this one time," Momma said. "Did you and my daddy have *anything* to do with that man's disappearance?"

"Now, Eliza, you know better than that."

"I'm asking for a direct yes or no. I've got to know in my heart." She shifted my baby brother from one arm to another.

"I don't like him, and can't say I'm sad to see him gone, but—"

It was as if she couldn't wait for his answer. "Y'all didn't bushwhack him, did you?" The use of that word caused Daddy to stiffen and made me close the gap by walking faster.

"Eliza, I can't believe you'd think I'd do something that cowardly. If I've got a problem with a man, I'll settle it *face to face*."

His entire face, not just his cheeks, was beet red. She'd hit a nerve in questioning his integrity. He was all *worked* up, and not even her cool stare would *work* to calm him down now.

"To answer your question directly, and once for all—*No*. I didn't kill or hurt that man. You didn't marry no bushwhacker or murderer, and I'm real hurt you'd even think of it. Then accusing your *own* daddy of the same thing—one of the best men in these whole woods—you oughta be ashamed of yourself!"

He was hot and Momma knew better than to rile him up anymore. "Here you are defending a wife-beating man, and the woman who'd probably lie for him in any situation."

His next words were slower and softer. "Let me say this—while that lady was crying on your shoulder, I looked around, asked a few questions, and fit a few pieces of the puzzle together.

"Those twins do a lot of talking, and evidently their daddy talked a lot. Now, a man that's been kidnapped or killed doesn't take a slab of bacon when he leaves."

Momma looked up in astonishment. "What?"

"Yep, they're missing a whole slab."

My own thought was that *old rascal done stole our bacon* **again**.

"And a kidnapped man don't take his gun and horse," Daddy added.

"All that's missing?"

"According to the boys."

"What else?"

"Just before dark, when the chickens came to roost, one of the boys saw him catch three of their frying hens, tie 'em up by the legs, and drape 'em over a limb. Next morning they were gone."

Now, Daddy had her full attention—and mine as well.

"And worst of all, he took their two gold coins when he left."

"He didn't!" Momma's face flushed. "That sorry—"

"Yep, he did. Their mother found them missing from her hiding place. Also, Mr. Merkle dropped hints to the boys that he was 'going off on a little trip.' He told them that if anyone asked them, to say that he'd gone off to join the army.

"Now, he don't impress me as the patriotic type."

It was one of the few times I'd seen my momma speechless. Finally, she stuttered, "Then, what... what *do* you think?"

"I think just like those chickens, he's flown the coop—had enough of this trouble and didn't see things ever getting better, so he left, and I don't expect to see him back. He's done 'gone to Texas.'"

"But his family—"

It was then Daddy got in the final word as he drove the stake deep into my mother's heart, "Not every man chooses to stand by his family in tough times. You need to think about that next time you accuse me of being a bushwhacker."

They walked a good ways before either spoke, and it was Momma who broke the silence.

"I'm sorry I even thought of you harming that man."

"Well, I did think about getting him after how he treated your daddy and me, but I didn't, and I wouldn't."

He turned toward me. "But you need to be careful about what you're saying with your son walking behind you listening to every word."

Momma spun and eyed me. "Boy, what you'd hear?"

"*Hear what?*" I asked innocently.

Knowing I'd heard every word, she snorted, "You're just like *your daddy.*"

She was right, but I don't know if she meant it as a compliment or an insult. As usual, she got in the last word. "You two men—the cone don't fall too far from the pine tree."

With that, she scooped up two large pinecones in the trail and hurled them at both of us.

Neither of us was brave enough to say another word.

Now before you think my mother was a hard woman, let me tell you about her kindness. When she realized that she'd unfairly accused Daddy, she went out of her way to make it up.

The next day he pulled me aside, "It's nearly worth fighting with her when we make up."

"It looks like you're milking it for all it's worth."

"I sure am."

Later that day, she pulled me aside, handing me a package. "Take this to the Merkle home place, and hand this to Sarah Merkle."

It was a bundle of baby clothes, supplies, and some biscuits and bacon wrapped in oilcloth. I hefted it on my shoulder and headed out.

As Bo and I went, an armadillo ran across the road, and Bo took off in hot pursuit. When I hollered for him to stop, I dropped the package.

As it hit the ground, I heard a light metallic click. My curiosity aroused, I stooped, and opened the bag to inspect its contents. There were sewing supplies, a Bible, and another smaller sack. Shaking it, I immediately knew what was in it. The smaller bag caused the noise when I dropped it, and it was the sound of clinking coins. There were two gold coins in the bag—a closer examination ensured that they were two of the four we'd received.

I shook my head as I realized what Momma was sending this poor family.

I bagged it back up and continued. The youngest child, Tabitha, met me at the door, and I believe she was the dirtiest kid I'd ever seen.

"Momma, somebody's here."

Sarah Merkle came to the door. It was a funny feeling placing the package in her hands knowing that it contained half of all the money my folks had. Even as she thanked me, she looked sad.

I turned to leave, more than glad to get away from this depressing homestead.

"Mayo, stop. I want to ask you something."

"Yes'm?" I turned but still kept my distance. I couldn't help but notice how she was cuddling the care package exactly the way I'd seen her with the stolen sack of flour.

"You've never told your folks about that day at your house, have you?"

"No, Ma'am."

"Why not?"

"I'm not real sure. I've started to tell them several times, but . . ."

Her eyes had a kinder look than I'd ever seen. "But what?"

"But I didn't see where it'd do anybody—y'all or us—any good, so I've kept it between the doorpost and me."

"Thank you kindly. I thank you for that."

If she hadn't been holding that sack, I believe she'd have hugged me. I sure didn't want her to, so I quickly said what I'd been taught, "You're right welcome, Ma'am," before stepping away.

Her parting words followed me. "Somehow—some way—I'll make up for the kindness you've shown us. I swear to God I will."

Hastening my pace, I thought, *she'll like our kindness even better when those two coins drop out of that bag.*

From that day forward, the relationship between Sarah Merkle slowly thawed. We shared a secret—just the two of us now that her sorry old man was gone—that gave us common ground. My family had been neighborly, and I've found you never forget the neighbor who helps you in hard times.

Her promise to "make it up to us" rang in my ears as I trotted home. At the time, I wondered what—and how—this poor woman could ever do anything for my family.

I had no idea—no idea at all.

Chapter 15

SILAS Merkle's disappearance was the talk of every homestead along the creek. Folks couldn't get over how he'd just up and disappeared, with many thinking there might be foul play involved.

There were all kinds of stories floating around, but most folks agreed he'd "Gone to Texas." In No Man's Land, "Gone to Texas," meant a person had run off to escape the law or whatever might be after them. They even called it "GTT" as in 'he's done GTT'ed."

It had to do with the history of our area. Before Texas and Louisiana were states with clearly defined borders, men in trouble with the law freely moved back and forth across the Sabine as conditions with the law dictated.

My parents kept what they knew about the disappearance to themselves, but Daddy's words were clear, "The only *foul* play involved is how he took the chickens before he 'flew the coop.'" It was clear he didn't have any patience with a man who'd desert his family.

I'd told you earlier there were *two* things that went missing that winter. Mr. Merkle's vanishing was the first. The second one was even more painful for me, and to be honest, it bothered me a lot more than the man's disappearance.

Hog dogs are born to hunt—as well as born to wander, and my cur dog Bo was no exception. If we didn't keep him tied, it wasn't unusual for him to disappear for a couple of days.

Eventually, he'd show back up, muddy, bloody, or both. Often his paws were raw from the miles he'd traveled. He'd retire to his dusty spot under the front steps, licking his wounds as he recovered from wherever he'd been—and whatever he'd been doing.

One time when Bo returned, Daddy said, "Well, I believe he's been out fighting again."

"What was he fighting?" I said.

"Probably that herd of wild hogs that stay north of the slough."

Another time he studied Bo. "Hmm, he's been off loving. Look at his sly look—I think he's been making the rounds of his girlfriends again."

Bo lay there, seeming to grin at Daddy's comments.

However, about a week after Silas Merkle's disappearance, Bo went missing. On the first and second day, I didn't worry. By the end of the second day, I began to fret. Something just felt wrong. I took Daddy's cow horn, blowing it repeatedly at the edge of the swamp. Normally, a few toots was all it took to bring Bo running.

My pitiful calling brought Momma out on the porch, wiping her hands on her apron. "Boy, give me that thing. I'll show you how it's done."

It embarrassed me—and irritated me—that she could blow it better than me. However, I said nothing—I was worried about Bo, and if her blowing hastened his return, it didn't matter.

For the next hour, I sat on the porch watching for him to show up.

When he didn't appear, I began looking, starting with the neighbors, inquiring if they'd seen Bo. Stopping at the Merkle home, Felix, the meanest of the twins said, "No, we ain't seen your old dog, but Daddy said if he showed up here again, he was gonna shoot him."

I recalled how Mr. Merkle pointed his rifle at Bo on the day of the theft. Picturing that scene, I remembered Miz Girlie's words, "Don't trust no man who don't like dogs."

I was glad this dog-hating man was gone. It didn't matter to me where he'd gone. I was just happy he was gone.

I turned to Felix. "In Ten Mile country, to shoot a man's dog is a serious thing. Even talking about it is fightin' words."

"Well, you better keep your smelly dog away from here or ..."

He stopped, and I'm glad he did. I left, determined to find my dog, a growing knot in my stomach pushing me on.

I broadened my search to the hog wallow near the creek. Blowing the horn from time to time, I waited for Bo to bound out of the swamp.

He didn't bound. There was no sign of my dog.

It was a good walk to the wallow, but I smelled it long before I saw it. Around the wallow were lots of fresh hog signs—muddy holes and dirt smeared on tree trunks.

No hogs were there, and neither was there any sign of Bo. Standing there, I alternated between blowing the horn and hollering, "Hunt 'em up. Bo. Come on, Boy. Hunt 'em up."

The only answer was my echo.

The evening's long shadows reminded me that it was nearing dark, but I wouldn't leave yet. I crossed the shallow creek there, deciding to make a quick round before going home.

Coming up the far bank, I found and followed a small trail of dried blood. It led me straight to Bo, who lay on his side.

I ran, calling his name, but there was no movement. As I knelt down, Bo roused and weakly raised his head. He was alive and that was all that mattered.

My touch brought a low guttural growl from him as he bared his teeth. I'd never seen him act this way before.

Then I saw a dried pool of blood on the leaves. My closer inspection revealed a terrible wound that gaped across his belly. He was lying on his side, covering most of the wound, but the amount of blood was enough to know my dog was hurt bad.

I needed to examine the wound, so I eased closer, talking

softly. 'Here, you go boy. You know I ain't gonna hurt you."

He growled lowly, but I held my ground. Bo might bite me, but I wasn't backing off. Daddy had taught me that even the best dog could turn on you when hurt. He told me to use a soft voice and slow movements in situations like this.

Whether from fatigue or sensing my affection I don't know, but Bo lay his head down. I reached over and patted it reassuredly. He grunted as I attempted to move him, but seemed to sense that I was no threat.

I'd seen enough tusk wounds to know how jagged and irregular a hog cut can be, but nothing prepared me for the terrible gash I saw. He'd been cut across his belly, and his entrails showed. Blood was everywhere, and I wondered how long he'd lain there. Tears ran down my cheeks, "Bo, if I'd known you were hurt, I'd been here sooner."

In spite of his weakened state and pain, his tail softly thumped in the leaves.

"Boy, I ain't sure you're gonna survive this."

It was common for hog dogs to get cut, and I'd seen neighbors sew up dogs from tusk wounds. I'd once held another dog as Daddy sewed its ear back on after it was torn loose in a fight.

However, I knew in my heart that Bo's wounds were too severe for him to survive. I wondered how long he'd lain there without water. Using my hat, I carried water from the creek, which he lapped up weakly.

Only a true dog lover can understand how I felt as I knelt there, feeling the weight of the world on my shoulders. Darkness was falling over the swamp. I swallowed hard, having no idea what to do next.

I only knew one thing—this was *my dog*, and I wasn't leaving him.

Chapter 16

I THOUGHT about picking Bo up to tote home, but any attempt to move him brought a terrible whimpering, and anyway, he weighed too much for me to carry that far.

Leaving him was out of the question. There was *no* way my dog was going to die alone.

In daylight, I would've gone for help, but I wasn't sure I could find my way in the dark. To be honest, I was also scared 'cause of my deep fear of the dark. I still hated to be in the dark by myself.

I talked to Bo, but I was really telling myself, "There ain't nothing out here to be scared of. I'm taking care of you, Bo. Just like you've taken care of me."

I spent the next hour petting him and remembering all the things we'd done together. I especially thought about how Bo had saved my life in the storm as well as when Roscoe chased me. My love for this cur dog was stronger than my fear of the dark, and I didn't feel alone anymore.

I piled a bed of leaves and eased some of them under Bo. I kept bringing him water, and he greeted each return trip with a thumping tail.

I wondered what my family was doing at the house, thinking, *my folks are probably turning flips wondering where I am. I'll have some explaining to do, but I ain't leaving my dog.*

It makes for a long night in the woods with a dying best friend. It was a cool night with the wind blowing softly in the trees. Every noise and movement in the night made me wonder what creatures were wandering around. I snuggled up by Bo, listening to his shallow breathing. Sometimes he seemed to stop breathing, but I'd put my hand on his side and feel his heart beating.

I drifted off to sleep and was awakened by distant calling in the pitch-black night. It was quiet for the next few minutes, and I thought I might have only dreamed of voices. Then I heard it again—a far off yell that sounded like my name.

I reached down for the cow horn and blew it repeatedly. Stopping, I heard nothing—then I heard distant shouts, "Mayo. Mayo."

They were searching for me. Soon, I saw torches bobbing through the woods. As they neared, I hollered, "Over here. I'm all right."

Three torches bobbed through the swamp. My rescuers were coming at a trot.

"I'm all right. It's Bo. Hogs done kilt him." I yelled.

Daddy was the first to get there. He was out of breath, and the flickering torch light revealed the worry on his face. He spoke with a mixture of anger and concern. "Son, what in the world are you doing out here? Your momma is worried to death about—"

But he stopped when he saw Bo. I was ready to explain why I'd stayed, but he'd already seen why. "I'm sorry, Son."

"He ain't gonna make it, is he?"

He knelt and had me hold the pine knot torch while he inspected Bo.

"Easy, Boy. I ain't gonna hurt ye. Let me take a look."

He didn't say another word. He didn't have to—we both knew. In fact, I believe Bo knew it, too.

The other torches arrived, and through tears, I looked up and saw PaPaw and Unk standing above me.

PaPaw, holding his gun, quietly said, "That's the worst hog cut I've ever seen."

Unk kindly put his hand on my shoulder, "There ain't no good way to lose a dog."

I'd held up pretty well until then, but my heavy heart was broken, and now the tears came freely as the four of us stood around my dying dog.

Daddy started hesitantly. "It'd be the uh, kindest…."

I looked up at him through my tears.

"Uh, son, it'd be the kindest—and best thing—to not let him suffer anymore. He's been lying here probably two days like this."

He turned to PaPaw. "Hand me the gun."

I rose in horror. "There ain't no way you're shooting *my* dog."

"But, Son...."

"There ain't *no way*."

I stood directly in front of Bo, pushing between him and them.

Daddy turned to the other men for help and PaPaw said, "Mayo, your dog's suffered enough. It ain't a kindness to let him lay there like that."

"Bo's last moment ain't gonna be a musket blast blowing his head off."

"But..."

"Don't *but* me. Y'all just leave us alone."

I'd never talked to my PaPaw that way. Normally, Daddy would've been swatting me, but he held both his tongue and belt.

It got very quiet around Bo—only the dog's labored breathing and my crying broke the night's silence.

I lay down beside Bo, as if doing so would make them take their torches and leave.

A hand touched my shoulder, and I jerked away, afraid they would drag me off before shooting my dog.

It was Unk, and he was crying.

One of the things I loved about my Redbone kin was the emotion of the men. No one would ever accuse them of being soft or weak, but beneath their tough exterior was a tender heart. A Redbone man might cry at anything—a song at church, a beautiful sunrise, a newborn baby—and even the heartbreak of a boy losing his dog.

Unk leaned down, placing his arm around me. "Mayo, I know how it feels to lose a good dog. I'm sorry. Your daddy and papaw are just trying to help. Don't be mad at 'em. They're just trying to help."

PaPaw knelt beside me, adding, "I tell you what we're gonna do—we'll leave you and Bo right here. I'll be back—but it won't be with a gun. I'll bring a pick ax and shovel, and we'll bury him here—unless you want to bring him home."

I looked up into the kind eyes of my PaPaw as my Daddy said, "I can stay—"

PaPaw raised his hand and cut him off. "It'll be just fine with the two of them."

Turning to me, he repeated, "Do you wanna carry him back or bury him ri't here?"

I stared off into the darkness. My answer was so low they leaned in to hear it.

"We'll bury him here—this'll be *a good place.*"

They handed me one flickering torch before leaving. I watched the two torches recede into the swamp. Soon, it began raining, and the torch sputtered out. Lying in the dark, I put my hand on Bo's chest, felt his heart beating rapidly, then slow, and finally stop.

Bo's suffering was over.

I cried like a baby—but felt strangely warm inside, wondering if I would ever have as good a dog again in my life.

Exhausted, I fell asleep curled up by my dog as a soft rain peppered down through the beech trees.

Daylight awakened me. Bo's stiff body lay beside me. He'd died with a slight smile on his face—a peaceful look a gunshot wouldn't have left, and I was glad I'd stood my ground.

I sat up and looked around the swamp. Seeing movement under a big oak about fifty yards away, I saw PaPaw waving. He slowly got to his feet, shouldered the shovel and pick ax, and came over.

We didn't say much as we dug the grave and buried Bo. Sometimes words aren't needed—especially among fellows who know each other's hearts.

When we finished our job and heaped plenty of dirt on top of the grave to keep the varmints from digging around, PaPaw took his hat off, closed his eyes, and prayed.

"Lord, thank you for a good dog named Bo and letting him and Mayo roam the woods together. All good things—including

good dogs—come from you. And thank you Lord for letting Bo
die doing what he loved—chasing and fighting hogs."

I should've closed my eyes, but didn't. Instead, I watched his
face, eyes closed as he prayed. Suddenly he looked up, smiled, and
winked, "And Lord, if you don't mind, let me and Mayo live like
that too—running with our nose to the ground, living life full to
the end. Amen."

I added an amen as we stood at the foot of the grave of the
best dog I ever had—a hog dog named Bo.

Our walk back home was quiet. Being out in the woods
makes a man ponder, and pondering can't be done with words.

We walked together. I carried the shovel and my PaPaw,
Willard Clark, whistled "Rock of Ages" while shouldering the
pick ax.

Chapter 17

LOSING a beloved dog is a tough thing and takes a while to get over. However, several things helped me in the days after Bo's death.

The first one came from my mother. She understood how I felt about losing Bo due to her easy way with all creatures—especially dogs.

She wasn't as mad at me as I'd expected for staying out in the woods. After hearing Daddy's description, she'd softened. As PaPaw and I straggled in, she fed us a good breakfast and insisted I lie down for a while.

After a few hours, I got up, wandering into the kitchen. She had a cup of coffee and smiled, "Let's go for a walk."

I couldn't, and wouldn't, say no. Walks with her in the pines were one of my favorite things. It's where she taught me so much about nature and what she called "the wisdom of the woods." With all of the chores at home, it didn't happen much, but when it did, I loved it.

Best of all, it was always a time when we would talk.

Momma stuck her head in the door. "Colleen, you keep a good eye on Patrick. We'll be back shortly."

The morning sun was brilliant as it streamed through the tall pines and the lingering fog. The only noise was a pair of crows cawing in the distance.

Momma grasped my hand as we walked. I'd reached the age where I was embarrassed by her gestures, but on this morning, I didn't mind.

"Mayo, losing Bo's a rough go. I'm sorry."

"Yes'm."

"I remember when I lost my first dog as a small girl—it was

a fine gyp named Ringo. When she died, I cried bitter tears for days."

"How'd she die?"

"Old age. My daddy found her dead one morning right by the porch, and I thought it was the end of the world."

I looked into her eyes, but said nothing.

"So I kind of know how you feel. But then again, Ringo died of old age, and Bo's death was a lot harder."

"Yes'm."

"I want to ask you something."

"Yes'm."

Holding my hand tightly, she led me to a log beside the creek. I hadn't even realized we'd left the pines and wandered through the oaks to the creek. Patting the log she said, "Sit here. This here's my spot where I meet with the Lord."

Gazing around at the canopy of greenery, white sandbar, and flowing creek, she smiled. "It's where I come to sit, listen, and let God speak to me. This is a good spot to ask you the question I have for you."

"Yes'm?"

"Here's my question: If you could just ring a bell, and you'd never hurt again in life, would you?"

"What do you mean?"

"If you could choose never to hurt again—not feel deep pain—but in return you'd lose the ability to love things—and people—passionately, would you?"

I was trying to follow her question, but she could tell I was still confused. "Let me put it this way: if you knew you'd never hurt deeply again, but it'd mean giving up your love of things like Bo, these woods, and your family—."

Now I understood her question, but wasn't quite ready to answer. "Let me think on that a while."

Finally, I turned to her. "Momma, I don't like this feeling I got . . . but if that's the price to pay for loving things like dogs—and people, I wouldn't ring the bell. I guess *loving* and *losing* go together."

Momma pondered my answer, nodding her head. "Life is a string of getting—loving—and losing. They go together. God made you—just like me—to love deeply. *Loving deeply* means *hurting deeply.*" She stared off toward the creek. "You can't have the one without the other."

She put her arm around my shoulder, "You've got a lifetime of memories of Bo stored up in your heart. Keep him alive in your heart."

"I will."

We continued talking. It was an unforgettable moment of my life as my mother and I connected our hearts openly and without hurry.

"Mayo, I like looking into your heart. God gave you a tender soul and personality. Don't let life—and the hard knocks of life ever change it.

"I won't."

We both knew this moment was a special one and further words would've clouded the moment. Only the wind up high in the trees broke the silence of the woods.

Finally, she stood and stretched. "Well, there's work to be done back at the house. We'd better get going."

Then she asked, "Would you like another dog?"

My answer was brief. "No Ma'am. I don't want no other dog."

"I understand, Son. But when—and if—you get ready for one, let me know."

We walked back in silence—just my mother and me, hand in hand—and in spite of my loss, it was a happy silence. I still had what mattered most—my family.

On the walk out of the swamp, the thought echoed in my mind. *Getting, loving, and losing.*

Getting, loving, and losing.

I didn't know it then, but there was plenty of all three waiting for us in the coming days.

Chapter 18

MY parents were always good at keeping me busy, and in the weeks after Bo's death, they worked double-time at finding plenty for me to do. Spring began and warmer days meant planting time—our busiest time of the year. After losing much of last year's food in the hurricane, there was a special urgency as we plowed and prepared our fields.

We began with Irish potatoes and snap beans, early season crops that could withstand the frosts of February. Daddy fervently believed in planting Irish potatoes on February 15, or as he called it the "Ides of February."

Once, I recall us planting on that date in the middle of a freezing rain. This year, the fifteenth was clear and mild. As we were putting the potato pieces in the cold ground, the sound of birds singing stopped both of us.

"What's that noise?" Daddy said as he stood up and stretched. "Look, your momma's birds are here."

Two purple martins were flying around the gourd houses. They were Momma's favorite kind of birds, and their yearly arrival was a special day for her.

I ran to the house, dragging her back outside. "Listen, Momma."

She broke into a wide smile when she heard them. "My birds are here. It's a good day."

I think part of the reason she loved martins so much was their mystery. A few—what she called the scouts—would arrive in late winter and stay around a day or so, then disappear. Within a week, the entire colony of dark bluish-purple birds showed up. Their loud singing and acrobatic flying entertained us through the spring and early summer. Momma called them "skeeter-eating" machines, explaining that their diving wasn't for show, but feeding.

The purple martins raised their young in the gourd houses we'd erected, and then in early July they'd disappear until the next year.

As Momma joined us outside, she greeted the birds. "Welcome home. Where have y'all been?" She had several pet theories about where they went, and would often say in the depths of winter, "I wonder where my martins are today?"

The martins chattered as if in reply. Daddy walked up, answering for the birds, "I believe they said they've been to Timbuktu... or was it Katmandu?"

He'd name all kinds of crazy places that he claimed he'd heard about, but I always suspected he made them up.

The martins continued singing what Momma called "their happy song" as she said, "I like the way they grit their teeth when they sing."

"Eliza, I don't believe they've any teeth to grit," Daddy said.

She slapped him on the shoulder, gritting her own teeth at him. "Why don't you go back to Ireland and plant some potatoes there?"

"Well, I might just do that after I plant these. And when I go, I may plant some in Timbuktu, too."

With the birds singing their happy song, we returned to the field where our Irish potatoes awaited us. Thinking of the martins, my dog, and the playful love I saw between my mother and father, the words echoed just like the martin's bubbling song, *getting, loving, and losing.*

March meant warmer weather and putting in the main garden with corn, followed by tomatoes, squash, and all the other garden vegetables. When April arrived and the ground warmed even more, we moved to a new field Daddy'd cleared. It was closer to the creek where he chose to plant our late spring crops of field peas and okra.

I was excited about helping because plowing new ground meant there'd be arrowheads galore. My job was to follow behind the turning plow pulling up roots and pine knots. My real attention, however, was on finding arrowheads.

Three nights later, I heard the rain on the roof. When you farm for a living, the sound of rain means so much: crops will grow; you'll have a day off if the rain is heavy enough, and plowing will follow. However, to me, rain meant one more thing—arrowheads would be uncovered on the newly plowed ground.

That next day is when I found the best arrowhead of my life. Following behind Daddy's plow, I tossed pine knots out of the field, pulling on them until they came loose. As the plow turned the soil, it gave off the rich dirt smell that anyone with farming blood loves. The day was clear and cool, and in spite of the work, I was happy to be here. Other than when Daddy said, "Haw" or "Gee" to Dallas, all was quiet.

I was carrying an armload of knots when I spied a pointed arrowhead on the plowed ground. I dropped my armload and grabbed the arrowhead. It was perfectly leaf-shaped and a deep rich brown. I happily picked it up, holding it tightly in my hand. Its rough edges were sharp against my fingers as I grasped it. I wondered about the man who'd spent hours carefully shaping it.

A man who'd walked and lived along this same creek that I love so dearly.

How long ago did he live? What was his life like?

I heard Daddy: "Hey, get to work."

I held up the arrowhead, and he smiled and waved. I stuffed it in my pocket, picked up my load of knots, and sang my own version of the happy song.

Once planted, a productive garden becomes a matter of keeping the deer out, hoeing the weeds, and waiting for rain. Normally, April and May are wet months in Louisiana, but they weren't in the year 1863. Days were cool and clear, with no sign of rain day after day.

We'd scan the sky each day for any of the weather signs that predicted rain, but no relief appeared. Soon, I overheard my parents' worried talk as the drought deepened, and our crops began to wither. We hauled water to the tomato plants, but it was impossible to water the entire field.

I watched the weather just as closely as they did, but my interest was slightly different. My mind often returned to the log rafts sitting on the bank of Cherry Winche. When the good rains came, and the creeks rose, it would be time for the float down the Calcasieu River.

In spite of my daddy's rebuffs, I still dreamed of the adventures of floating down the big river, visualizing what the city of Lake Charles would be like. I didn't have much to gauge it by, having never been to a city before. I'd heard Daddy describe his experiences in the bustling city of New Orleans, so I knew any river city would be exciting.

Lying in my bed at night, hoping for the sound of rain on the roof, I made my plan and once again told myself, *they may not know it yet, but I'm going on that float.*

Several days later, Unk was at our house with a pronouncement: "It's gonna rain—my ears has been stopped up for two days."

My uncle may not have had all of his senses, but he never missed on the weather. He'd lived outside in the elements and possessed a sixth sense when it came to these things.

That night Daddy pointed out another weather sign. "Look at that moon—there's a halo around it. It'll be raining in twenty-four hours."

"How do you know?"

"I just know. Something to do with the humidity in the air."

Sure enough, it clouded up that night and was raining by

morning. It rained all day and most of the next. Our crops were saved, and the creek was rising.

The next day as we were standing back up some of the field corn blown over by the wind, Daddy said, "Lookee there."

He pointed toward a full rainbow arcing across the southern sky. "That's a fine one, ain't it?"

"It sure is. Now I got a question for you. Do those rainbows in Ireland really stretch to the ground?" I'd heard all of his tales of pots of gold, and leprechauns, and knew of his love for rainbows.

"In my home country, you might see several in a day during the spring rainy season. I remember once watching one from the mountainside that seemed to drop one end right into Clew Bay and the other end into a green field."

He leaned on the stick he was using to tamp down the cornstalks. "Rainbows are one of the things I miss most about home."

"We have 'em here."

"Yep, but compared with the open landscape and weather of Ireland, Louisiana rainbows leave a lot to be desired. They're so infrequent and short-lived. Look at that one." He pointed to the rainbow that already was breaking up and fading.

"Gone so fast."

The day after, I rode with Daddy over to check on the rafts at Cherry Winche Creek.

Pistol Perkins and his son Dan met us on the way. They were excited about the rain as well as the upcoming trip, and asked, "Joe Moore, that was some kind of rain, weren't it?"

"It was."

"It was a toad strangler." Pistol said.

Daddy punched me and whispered, "Watch Dan."

Dan said, "It was raining bull heifers and enough hay to feed 'em."

"It was a stump floater." was his Dad's retort.

Just then is when we arrived at our logs; pointing to them, Dan said, "That rain was a log floater, too."

Not to be outdone, Pistol said, "Rained cats and dogs."

"I saw a mule float by," Dan said seriously.

"I saw a line of animals lining up at a big boat, getting on two by two," Pistol proudly proclaimed.

Daddy leaned down to me, "There ain't nothing better than a Redbone 'lie-out'."

The "animals going in two by two" got Daddy tickled, and he said, "That's pretty good, Pistol. I'll give you this round."

Dan complained, "He always wins."

"I've just had more years to gather sayings," said his daddy.

Daddy leaned in, whispering in my ear. "And more years to work on lying."

Their talk about the rain continued. It had been a true flood, and the result was the muddy creek being out of its banks—with all of our rafts floating, securely tied to nearby trees. We inspected the nearby Calcasieu River and found its level bank high.

"Well, I believe it's time to go," Pistol said.

"If we're ever going to do it, now's the time," Daddy added.

Before leaving, Papaw rode up and inspected the rafts. As we turned and rode home, Daddy talked to PaPaw concerning the care of our crops during his absence. I cringed when he said, "Mr. Willard, Mayo'll help you out on everything while I'm gone."

When they finished discussing it, I asked, "Daddy, you ever done anything like this before?"

He shot a glance at me as if I doubted he was up to it. "No, but Pistol has. Anyway, it don't seem too difficult. We just have to get them out into the Calcasieu, and let the current do the work. I figure we'll know when we get to Lake Charles."

I thought to myself, Ain't **nothing** as simple as it looks.

I'd heard Momma and Daddy discussing a thorny issue about the trip. Gingerly I brought it up. "I heard Momma mention that Mr. Pistol and Dan are kind of allergic to whiskey."

I was riding between my grandpa and daddy, and both

reacted as if they were going to knock me off my horse. Daddy spoke first, "That's the last we'll hear of it. We'll worry about that if—and when—we get to Lake Charles. I doubt if there's any stills on the Calcasieu 'tween here and there."

Changing the subject, I turned to PaPaw and asked, "How'd the Calcasieu River get its name?"

"I've always been told it was an Attakapa Indian word meaning, 'Screaming Eagle.'"

"Is that so?"

"It's what *my* granddaddy said."

I had another question, and it was for Daddy, but I waited until we were nearly home. I cleared my throat. "You know, I sure believe I could be good help for y'all on this float—if—"

He cut me off. "I done told you—when your legs get long enough. There'll be other trips."

That was the end of it as far as he was concerned, so I kept my mouth shut. However, if he could've read my mind to know what I was planning, he'd started whipped me all the way home.

Part II

THE JOURNEY

Chapter 19

MAY 1863

The weather cleared off on Saturday. Enough rain had fallen upstream that the creeks stayed up, so the six men decided to leave on Monday morning.

Other men who'd helped cut and stack the timber would stay behind and share in the money from the sale. Their job was to look out for the families, take care of their places, and keep everyone's crops in good shape.

That Monday there was an air of excitement among the men and their families. Most had never been past Sugartown or Hineston, and this would be a world-class journey for them. My dad, being an immigrant, was the most traveled member of the crew, even though he'd never been on a log float, and as Momma said, "He wouldn't know a sawmill if it hit him in the mouth."

Even though I wasn't going on the float—at least they thought I wasn't—I walked with them to the creek for the launch.

The men going—Daddy, Unk, Pistol Perkins, and his son Dan, as well as Ben Tyler and Caleb Johnson—were accompanied by their families. Several neighbors came along to see the launch. Bart Cooley, one of the local skeptics on this venture, tagged along to the launching point. He'd passed on being part of the float, but hadn't passed on making fun of it. This was his last pre-trip chance to ridicule the adventurers, so he came along.

"I hope you fellows don't miss Lake Charles. If you do, hang a right when you get to the Gulf of Mexico. I've heard there's sawmills in Galveston, Texas."

It was evident he'd looked forward to this day as much as the floaters, and had practiced his sarcasm. Pointing at Pistol, who had a long beard, he said, "Hey Noe, since y'all are floating the Ark down the Calcasieu—where's all your animals?"

"You're just jealous, Bart, 'cause you ain't goin'," Pistol said.

"How are you fellows gonna know when you get there? None of you would know a city from 'Adam's off ox.'" He laughed hard at his own joke and continued a steady stream of banter, until Caleb Johnson spoke up. "That's enough. Now you shut up and go home."

Even Bart was scared of Caleb, so the tormenting stopped.

As they loaded gear on the rafts, I noticed that each man had brought his musket and powder horn. Several of them also wore sidearms. Their guns reminded me that the trip wasn't just a lark—instead there was much unknown and wild country ahead of them.

Fred Wilson, standing beside his pregnant wife, waved and hollered, "Von Boyage, fellows. Von Boyage."

I turned to Daddy who had one foot on the raft. "What'd he say?"

Daddy laughed. "Fred thinks he's Ten Mile's version of Shakespeare. He meant to say 'Bon Voyage.'"

"What's that?"

It's French for "Have a good trip."

The men climbed aboard the five rafts, untied the mooring ropes, and pushed off with long poles. They floated slowly along Cherry Winche toward its junction with the Calcasieu River. We walked along the bank, watching as they eased into the faster current of the river and began the journey southward.

Bessie Tyler yelled at her husband Ben, "How long do you think y'all will be gone?"

He looked back and shrugged. "Don't rightly know."

Truer words have never been spoken.

The spectators watched the rafts disappear down the river before turning to walk home as a group. After we'd walked about a quarter mile, I said, "I forgot my hat back at the creek. Y'all go on, no need to wait for me."

I really had left my hat back at the creek, but not by accident.

Quickly retrieving it as well as a knapsack I'd hidden, I began slipping southward along the river and soon spied the last of the rafts. It was now a matter of staying close enough to keep them in sight, without being discovered.

A hot day of walking through the swamp followed, with mosquitoes buzzing around me every step. Several times, I came to small creeks that I waded or swam. Because the river made such a winding course, I'd cut across the bends and actually be hiding in the woods as the rafts slowly drifted by.

Having a boy's vivid imagination, I fancied myself as an Indian watching these strange explorers coming down my river, totally unaware that a great warrior was stalking them.

My plan was to camp nearby when they stopped for the night. However, it hadn't entered my mind that they might not stop.

As darkness fell, I realized they weren't pulling up for the night. Fear gripped me as I wondered how I'd follow them in the dark. As the nighttime sounds came alive, darkness surrounded me, and I began second-guessing my plan.

It was decision time: I could wait the night out here, abandon my plan and return home tomorrow, making up some believable story before I got home to face my mother's wrath.

Or I could continue with my plan, even though it meant walking through these woods all night, a thought that filled me with dread. But turning back wasn't an option. I'd planned too long to abandon ship now. The waning moon rose about an hour after dark and supplied me with just enough light—and courage—to move ahead.

What followed was a long night of scrambling through briar patches, wading through sloughs, and hoping not to step on a snake or encounter a panther.

I believe I busted through every spider web in Calcasieu swamp. I'd feel spiders on my face and quickly brush them off. Even though they were harmless garden spiders, I was still terrified.

Often I would trip over a muscadine vine or a root and sprawl face first in the wet leaves. However, my die was cast. There was no way out but forward.

The rafters had lit several torches, and the flickers of light helped me to follow them. I lost sight of them when a large slough blocked my path. I got turned around, and panic welled up like a flood in my throat as I wandered aimlessly for about an hour.

Finally, I calmed down, found the Big Dipper and North Star through an open gap in the tree line, and regained my bearings. Soon I was back by the river and stayed along its right bank working my way downstream.

I heard the rafters before I saw them again—and knew it was Dan Perkins, who considered himself a good singer, singing "Old Dan Tucker." His singing and the pine torches kept me oriented.

I followed along to,
"Old Dan Tucker, he got drunk.
Fell in the fire and kicked out a chunk.
Coal of fire got in his shoe,
Oh my, how the ashes flew."

Repeatedly, he sang his song, and the night air carried it as a beacon for me. Daylight came not one moment too soon. My arms and face were scratched and bloody from the briars. I ate the last of the beef jerky I'd brought and re-filled my canteen with creek water.

When I caught up with the floaters, they were stopped. One of the rafts was snagged in the bank. The men were all pushing hard with their poles to back it off into the current. It took about thirty minutes before they budged the heavy raft free and poled it back into the river's channel.

That day was full of walking and then waiting. I'd figured out about the bends and easily stayed ahead of them by cutting across.

On one bend, I was hiding behind a pin oak when a skiff holding Ben and Dan came around a sharp bend. They tied a long rope just above the water's height across the point of the bend, securing it to two stout river birches at the water's edge about fifty feet apart, before hurriedly paddling upstream.

I huddled down, curious to see what would happen next. I heard the rafts approaching as they bumped along, and Dan singing,

"Get out of the way, Ol' Dan Tucker.
You're too late to eat your supper.
Supper's over, and dinner's cooking.
Ol' Dan Tucker just stood there a lookin'
And a lookin'."

I watched closely as the lead raft came into view and floated up against the rope, which pulled taut. As it caught the raft, it eased it around the bend, avoiding the delay that had happened when it snagged. Each raft easily made the turn, and Ben and Dan paddled back, untied the rope, and caught back up with the rafts.

Throughout the day, they repeated this procedure at each sharp bend in the river.

Creeping along all day, I constantly pulled ticks off. I could feel the redbugs working around every joint of my body as well as the stinging of the briar scratches all over my face as I sweated.

I was hot, tired, and hungry before I made my decision: I *was not* staying in the woods tonight—one way or the other, I'm going to be aboard by dark.

Late in the afternoon, they pulled up on my side of the river, lashing the rafts securely before setting up camp.

I figured they were far enough along that Daddy wouldn't— or couldn't—send me home, so it was time. The men were gathered around the fire cooking supper when I walked out of the woods. All movement stopped as they saw me. Unk spoke first, "By Lazurus's grave, it's Mayo."

One of the other men said, "Son, what in tarnation are you doin' here? Is somethin' wrong back home?"

Scared to death, but trying to grin, I said, "I came along to help you fellas."

Unk said, "Son, you look like you got in a fight with a buzz saw and lost. Where'd all those cuts come from?"

"I been squirrel hunting."

They all had a good laugh except one—my daddy. He didn't smile or say a word—just left the campfire, walked over to a nearby pine, and broke off a stout limb.

I knew what was coming, and I'd already counted the cost. As he came toward me, I pulled off my belt and held it out for him.

He ignored the belt, which I dropped at his feet, and began wearing me out with the pine limb. It stung like crazy as he thrashed up and down my backside, but I steeled myself to not move or yell.

He whipped me until the limb finally broke. Tossing it aside, he pulled off his own belt and continued tearing my butt up. The only thing that stopped the whipping was when his britches began to sag.

He stepped back, looking me in the face. I knew I'd embarrassed him by showing up like this, but once again, I'd counted the cost—counting the whipping worth it to be on this trip.

His heavy breathing from anger and exertion was the only sound on the creek bank. No one else dared say a word, until Unk broke the silence. "Like father—like son."

Daddy gave him a hard look, but Unk continued, "Well, Joe—he came by it honest being a stowaway—learnt it from you."

The other men all laughed in agreement, and even Daddy smiled and I saw a mixture of bewilderment, anger, and amusement in his eyes. I believe I even detected a hint of pride from how I'd taken my whipping like a man.

"Son, was it worth it?" he asked.

"Yes sir, I expected it."

"Well, we'll see if it's worth it. There's a lot of this trip left. *We'll see.*"

I thought of Momma's "we'll see" horse/broken leg story. I started to comment, but thought better of it.

Pistol, who'd never taken his eyes off me, cocked his head. "Joe, your boy took more of a whipping from them briars and brambles than anything a pine limb or belt could do."

He motioned me over. "Son, you been sliced up good, and you stood your ground while your daddy dusted your britches real good. If it'd been me, I'd been hopping like a flea on a hot stove."

Sizing me up from head to toe, he asked, "How'd you get here?"

I picked up my belt and put it back on. "I followed y'all along the river since you left."

He put his hand on my shoulder. "That's some of the thickest woods in West Bay. You're lucky a catty-wampus or rattlesnake didn't get you."

Daddy stood behind him, shaking his head.

Unk, who was trying to help me, said, "Another thing, Joe. I jes' believe there is some reason the Lord sent this boy on this trip. 'Fore it's over, maybe we'll understand why."

Daddy pulled me by the collar toward the circle of the fire. "Son, I *hope* the Lord told your momma that He sent you. What is she gonna think has happened to you?"

I had my answer ready. "Sir, I left a note with Colleen explaining my trip, making her promise to give it to Momma today. I don't write too well, and I know Momma don't read too much better, but the letter will explain it."

"All I can say is you'll have a lot more explaining to do when we get home."

I'd counted that cost, too. "I know, but we'll cross that bridge when we git to it."

"There ain't *no* bridges to cross between here and Lake Charles, or on the long walk home," he said.

I had no idea what lay between here and home. If I'd known, I probably would have re-traced my walk back to Ten Mile right then.

Daddy's final words on this were. He looked at my cuts and tattered clothes, shook his head and said, "Well, if you're gonna be dumb, you've gotta be tough."

The men welcomed me one by one, patting me on the back,

offering me a plate of beans and cornbread. It seemed they were making me "one of the guys." I'd done what every one of them would have loved to have tried at my age—slipped off on a real adventure.

This newfound respect showed in the way Dan Perkins handed me my plate, "Here you go, Columbus. You're one of the travelers now." Redbones loved nicknames, and now I had one.

That night Daddy called me something else—he called me a man. "Son, if you're going to be on this float trip and the long walk back, you'll hafta act like a man. I'm gonna treat you like a man, and I wanna see you work and act like one."

"You'll be glad I'm along."

"We'll see. Yep, we'll see."

Chapter 20

FLOATING downriver, I strained my eyes to take in every sight, fully curious about the sights and sounds of the river and nearby swamps. I watched otters playing in the river and spotted deer, turkeys, and bobcats.

On my second day aboard, I saw my first alligator. He was sunning on a log and slid off into the river as we approached, taking any desire I had for swimming with him.

That same afternoon we came to the mouth of the Whiskey Chitto River. I was surprised at how it was larger than the Calcasieu where they converged. With the influx of more water, the river became much wider, and this made it easier for the rafts to maneuver. However, the river's depth made our poles useless away from the banks.

That led to the first major problem of the trip. The men agreed to keep floating through the night, but cloud cover made it difficult to see in the dark. Caleb, out front on his raft, didn't see the bend ahead and couldn't pole around it. His raft crashed into the bank where it lodged tightly under a downed tree.

We tied up our rafts and walked back to where Caleb's raft was jammed into the bank. On land, we became easy bait for the mosquitoes that thickly swarmed around every man.

Pistol studied the stuck raft, scolding Caleb. "Son, couldn't you have kept it out of there?"

"I tried, but the water was too deep to pole, and the momentum just carried me in."

"How bad's it stuck?"

"Pretty snug and high-centered on a sand bar."

We lit our torches and closely studied the predicament. First, the men used their poles as pry bars to no avail. Next, everyone waded in together and tried to push it off.

Pistol directed. "Heave ho, boys. Heave ho."

It didn't even budge.

We started again with all manner of straining and grunting as Pistol said, "On three now—one, two, *three*."

All of this did absolutely no good. Finally, he said, "Let's go to our rafts, get some rest, and look at this problem in daylight. We'll 'lick this calf over again' in the morning."

Everyone agreed to his wisdom, and we returned to our rafts.

Daddy spread a piece of oilcloth on our raft for us to sleep on. The mosquitoes weren't biting too badly out over the water, especially after a nice breeze picked up. It also cleared the clouds, revealing a beautiful star-lit sky. The river gurgled as it flowed over a nearby submerged log, mixing with the din of the frogs and crickets from the swamp.

Staring up into the sky, I found my favorite constellation, "The Hunter," and used a stick to measure its slow movement across the sky. Neither of us could sleep, so I asked, "You think we'll be able to unjam it?"

"I'm not sure anything, other than the next high water, will free that raft."

"What'll we do?"

"If we can't get it loose, we'll just have to leave it."

"Leave Caleb's raft?"

"Yep, not much choice."

I knew this would be a blow to Caleb, who like every man on the trip, was counting on the money this float would bring.

After a few minutes of silence, I asked, "Daddy, are you mad at me for coming along?"

"Yep, but I'm getting over it."

"You can understand, can't you?"

"I can, but you shouldn't have done it. Your momma'll be spitting nails until you get home. One day you'll understand: parents worry about their kids."

"Would you've done the same thing when you were my age?"

"Probably."

"See, you can understand."

"I was a little older than you when I made my journey across the ocean." He leaned up on an elbow, looking sideways into my face. "My trip *evidently* wasn't quite as planned as yours. By the way—how long had you been planning this?"

"Since y'all first mentioned it on the foxhunt."

"That's what I figured."

I decided a change in the conversation was needed. "Tell me again how you decided to get on that ship in Ireland." I'd heard the story many times, but each time he related it, new facts emerged that helped me fit the puzzle of his flight from Ireland together.

He lay back down, staring up at the stars. Downriver, a big bullfrog was croaking. I wasn't sure if Daddy was going to speak or leave the bullfrog to sing solo.

Finally, the bullfrog stopped and he began. "As you know, it was all over that dog I killed. When the police came after me, it was run or die."

"Why'd you choose to get on a boat?"

"Running inland wasn't much of an option. The English were everywhere, and with the famine raging, no one would've taken me in. Westport Harbor—and the sea beyond it—seemed like the best place for escape.

"I arrived there in the dark of night, and a friend took me out to the deep-water harbor where the big ships lay. I swam out to one of them, slipped aboard, and ended up here."

"Was it the only ship there?"

"No, there were several more—seems like three . . . maybe four."

"What made you choose the *Amelia?*"

"I was so scared I don't remember, but it had its sails unfurled, and looked like the quickest way out of trouble."

"Have you ever thought about if you'd chosen another ship?"

Stopping his upwards gaze, he smiled at me. "Boy, you think too much."

Then he continued, "Yep, sometimes I have wondered. If I'd gotten on another ship, I wouldn't be laying here in the middle of the Calcasieu answering your questions. I'd probably be in France, or Italy, or who knows where."

"Do you think it was just luck that you got on the *Amelia?*"

"Like I said—Boy, you think too much." After another pause, he added, "No, I don't think *luck* had anything to do with it. My mother, who died two years before I left Ireland, once told me, 'God has a good plan for you, Joseph. He'll guide you step by step. Step by step.'

"And that's how it's been. Step by step. Like Caleb's raft, I been grounded a few times on my trip, but I do believe God's guided me, step by step."

I had a question: "Daddy, did your momma call you Joseph or Joe?"

"Everyone in Ireland knew me as Joseph."

"But here in Ten Mile, you're called Joe. Why?"

"When I crossed over into No Man's Land back in '49, it was a new start for me, so I got me a new name."

"Is that because you didn't like Joseph?"

"Not a bit. I liked it—that's why it's your middle name. I just shortened mine down to 'Joe.'"

We both lay there for a long time looking up into the dazzling dark sky full of stars.

"Daddy, do they have the same stars in Ireland?"

"Mostly. The North Star's higher in the sky, but other than that it's pretty much the same."

That was the end of our conversation for the night. Two stowaways—father and son—lay on the raft, softly rocked to sleep by the river's current.

A redbird's daybreak singing woke me, and I sat up on a log raft in the Calcasieu River. Daddy was already gone.

It was a good place to be, and I was ready to start another day.

Chapter 21

YOU'VE never seen men work harder than we did trying to free Caleb's raft. We tried every manner of prying, pushing, and wedging, all to no avail. We grunted, strained, prayed, and cussed, but the heavy raft didn't move an inch—it was stuck fast.

Compounding our problem, the river had dropped several inches during the night, grounding the raft even tighter. Everyone sat glumly on the raft. Caleb, who didn't talk much anyway, looked like he was about to cry. Pistol finally said what everyone knew, "We're gonna have to leave her behind."

"I sure could've used that hundred dollars," Caleb said. All of the men ducked their heads. It was a hard blow, but there was no alternative.

Then Unk spoke up, "Caleb, you're gonna be riding with me now, and we'll split whatever I get."

"Unk, I can't do that."

"Yes, you can."

"But it's your money and . . . ."

Unk winked at my daddy. "Oh, what do I need money for? I got way more than I can ever spend."

He grinned and his eyes widened. From my vantage point, his eyes looked like two shining coins. Then he winked again—this time at me. "I'd probably jes' bury it anyway. I'll be just as good off if I split it with you."

None of the men said a word. There was nothing to say because "Unk" Dial had spoken. Walking past me, he stopped. "What're you looking at?"

I whispered, "You really do have money buried, don't you?"

"I don't even know what you're talking about."

As we returned to our raft, Daddy nudged me. "Mayo, don't

ever forget that your Uncle Nathan is one of the best men I know. He's got something I wish I had—a pure heart."

There was nothing to do but return to our rafts, untie them, and continue. Thankfully, the rest of the day was uneventful. All of the men were quieter and much more observant of our location in the river.

The river widened and the current slowed. Pistol commented, "We're closer now to the flatlands and the Gulf. That's why the current's sluggish."

Pistol had proven himself a real character on this trip. An incident that day indicated his colorful way of doing things. He'd fixed up a trotline to drag behind the boat, hoping to snag a few catfish. He'd caught several nice-sized fish during the day that would be our supper. Additionally, he'd caught two large snapping turtles that he'd put in the cook shack, wedging the door where they couldn't get out.

Floating southward, we began encountering "flying fish." They'd jump out of the water a couple of feet high, before flopping back with a splash. Later we learned the river people called them "jumping mullets."

By chance, one of the flying fish landed on Pistol's raft. Quick as a cat, he grabbed it by the tail, slinging it back into the river. "No sir. No sir. If you don't *bite*, you *don't* ride with us."

Drying his hands on his britches legs, Pistol Perkins stood proudly, the captain of all he surveyed.

Daddy said to me, "Son, that fellow right there's a 'Redbone's redbone.'"

After our loss of the raft, the men agreed it was best not to float at night. That evening we found a dry, level spot for camp. Ben, who was a good cook, made a big pot of beans and ham to go with our catfish, and after eating, everyone felt better.

Pistol, sitting by me at supper, asked, "Did you get a look at those alligator-snapping turtles."

"Yes sir." To be honest, I was scared of them. One of them must have weighed fifty pounds. It also exhibited a mean streak, as evidenced by biting off a limb that Ben poked it with.

"Did you know that if one bites you, he'll hold on until it thunders?" Pistol asked.

"Really?"

"That's what I been told all my life."

Pistol nodded toward the cook shack. "Why don't you go over there and find out if it's true?"

"I think I'll just take you at your word."

Caleb, still bothered by the loss of his raft, asked, "Pistol, what'll happen to my raft?"

"High water'll eventually dislodge it, but it also might push it farther into the bank. When the strips rot, the logs'll separate. If any are waterlogged, they'll sink. Yellow pine hardly rots, so I guess they'll be down there on the bottom forever—unless someone pulls them up."

"Why would anyone want to pull up a sunken log?"

Pistol shook his head at the tall trees surrounding our campsite. "I don't know no reason why they would, but there might be a time when all of these trees are gone."

Every man around the fire scoffed. "That'll be the day."

Every man was skeptical but one—Daddy. He quietly said, "It happened in my homeland."

"What happened?"

"Ireland was never as forested as these woods, but a thousand years ago, there were plenty of trees, firewood, and lumber for everyone. Then the English came and over the next several centuries cut our trees down and shipped them out. We have a saying in Ireland, 'The trees of Ireland are in the furniture of England.'"

"You Irish don't care much for them English, do you?" Pistol asked.

Daddy's answer wasn't bitter or with resignation, but stated simply. "We got lots of reason not to."

"Trees are what lured you to our No Man's Land. Ain't that so?" PaPaw asked.

"Yep, I'd never seen big trees or so many trees, even in New Orleans. When I heard about the big pines of western Louisiana,

I had to see for myself."

"Were you disappointed when you saw them?" Dan asked.

"Not one bit. Those endless miles of tall pines caught my heart, and haven't let go yet.

"My original plan was to continue to the wide-open spaces of Texas." He looked at me before speaking his next words. "However, I fell in love with the pines, the wildness, and the freedom of the woods—and stayed, and I still haven't made it to Texas."

The next day we passed another good-sized stream on the west bank. Pistol, using a rough map, said this was probably Barnes Creek, which meant we were about twenty miles north of Lake Charles. He estimated we'd arrive at the sawmills late the next day. Daddy asked, "Twenty river miles or miles as the crow flies?"

Pistol who always had an answer for every question, whether correct or not, said, "Twenty-eight by river, eighteen by air."

The sluggish current slackened the pace of our float. There wasn't much to do but sit back and watch the scenery. The banks were lined with moss-draped cypress trees and often no riverbank defined the river from the surrounding swamps.

Dan, who continued calling me "Columbus," began singing, *"In 1492, Columbus sailed the ocean blue."*

He sang it repeatedly to everyone's annoyance, and soon added his own verse.

"Then in 1863, Columbus sailed the Calcasieu with me."

It was pretty corny, but he enjoyed hearing himself, so we had no choice but to endure it. Caleb, riding with Unk out front, said, "I've got to get away from that singing, before I hafta drown him."

They let their lead raft drift close to the shady east bank. Just as they went under a low hanging willow limb, the hollering began. It sounded as if they were yelling, "Waltz, waltz."

Daddy looked at me. "Are they shouting 'Waltz'?"

"Sounded like it to me."

They were jumping up and down, slinging their arms as if fighting off an invisible foe. Daddy, who loved to dance, said, "It's sure a fast waltz if they're dancing."

We were puzzled as both of them dove into the river. When they came up, we were closest enough to understand Unk's gasping words, "Wasts. Wasts."

I turned to Daddy. "Did he say 'wasts'?"

"I believe they got into a wasp nest."

By now, the second raft, occupied by Pistol and Dan, neared the same limb. Dan's singing stopped abruptly as he and his daddy tried like crazy to steer clear of the limb. It was too late as hundreds of angry wasps awaited their arrival. I heard Pistol hollering, "Abandon ship. Abandon ship."

We laughed as they plunged into the river.

Ben's raft was next, and he hollered, "I can't swim a lick. I'm just gonna hang on." He lay down on his raft, using his hand as a futile paddle to get away from the limb.

He took his hat off and fought them off as the raft went under the limb. Luckily, they had spread out, and there weren't as many to fend off. Seeing the futility of fighting them with his hat, he rolled up in a ball, covering his head.

We could hear his muffled voice praying one sentence, and cussing his lungs out the next.

Ahead of us were three rafts, two of them empty, and one manned by a fellow alternating between swearing and entreating the Lord. Three men were in the water and one—my uncle—was still yelling, "Wasts. Wasts. Watch those wasts."

Now it was our turn. Daddy didn't even try to steer our raft away, instead saying, "Let's get in the water and hang onto the side of our raft."

Trying to forget about alligators, I eased into the water.

As we floated under the limb, Daddy said, "Look at the size of that nest. It's big as a pumpkin." Hundreds of red wasps were on it as well as swarming around. One popped me on the hand and

I yelled. Daddy thought it was real funny until one stung him on the ear. Our yelling and movement attracted a whole wasp patrol on us and he yelled, "Duck under!"

Before I could go under, several stung me, including one right on the end of my nose. I dove under and stayed there until my lungs burned. When I came up, we'd cleared the limb and were out of the cloud of wasps. The other swimmers, now reboarded, seemed to be enjoying our part of the show.

At the next bend, everyone pulled up to lick our wounds and compare notes. Most of the men had dozens of stings. Pistol got his knife out, scraping bark off one of the logs. He dug down into the tree, scooping up pinesap, and daubed it on his stings. Everyone followed his example, except his son Dan, who spit out his chew of tobacco and began daubing it on his stings.

By now the humor of the situation began to sink in. Dan began mocking Unk, "Wast. Wast. Watch out for the wasts."

My uncle smiled, "I was just trying to warn you fellows." This was followed by Daddy mimicking Pistol, "Abandon ship. Abandon ship." as he poked our leader. "When your captain says 'abandon ship,' you know it's a bad situation."

Everyone laughed, and we talked about it for the rest of the float, embellishing every word and sting with each retelling. Soon our encounter even had a name, "The Battle of Wast Bend."

We floated the rest of the day, making sure to stay clear of low-hanging limbs. As darkness came, we tied up at a small island in the river. Due to several alligators we'd seen nearby, as well as the abundance of snakes, everyone stayed on their rafts.

During the night, a thick fog formed, and we awoke the next morning to a different world. It was amazing how different the river and surrounding swamps looked wrapped in the mists. There was an eeriness that made my skin crawl as if we weren't even on the same river that we'd slept on last night.

As we moved about our rafts in the fog, Caleb noticed that Ben was still asleep and attempted to wake him, but couldn't. He yelled for help and we rushed over to find Ben in an addled state with a horribly swollen face, mumbling about having trouble breathing and feeling cold.

Something was seriously wrong with him.

Chapter 22

BEN TYLER had commented right after the wasp attack how bee stings often made him "kind of sick," so we figured that must be the case. However, he wasn't just *kind* of sick. His shallow breathing, swollen face, and slurred speech showed he was bad off.

We knew he needed help, so we quickly shoved off. Pistol's map showed the village of Marion was the first town above Lake Charles, and so reaching it soon became our goal.

After floating an hour or so, we saw a strange looking boat anchored near a cypress grove. Daddy recognized what it was. "That's a houseboat. I saw them on the bayous along the Mississippi and Red Rivers."

We poled over to it, and saw various animal skins stretched on the side of the vessel. A poorly dressed man came out on deck, musket in hand. A woman holding a baby and a small boy joined him.

As we neared, I saw the man raise the rifle and side-cock it. Pistol, waving both hands in the air, said, "Whoa, Fellow. We don't mean you no harm. We need some help," all the while pointing at Ben, who lay beside him.

Neither the man nor woman seemed to understand one word of English, conversing with each other in a strange and animated language. Daddy stepped forward, "I believe they're speaking French and probably don't understand English."

"Can you speak French, Joe?" Pistol asked.

"Not enough to help. I learnt a little on the boat across the Atlantic, but I've heard the kind they speak here is different."

As rafts bumped up against the bank and houseboat, where the man still had his gun aimed at us, Unk stepped forward right up onto the houseboat. The man put his musket against Unk's chest, but the woman lowered his arm, as if she sensed this odd-looking stranger was no danger to anyone.

I knew my uncle didn't speak French, but it looked like he was going to try.

He began speaking the language he knew best, "Unkian."

"My friend—been hurt by wasts." He made a series of buzzing motions and mimicked the wasps stinging. "He's been stung a bunch." He held up all of his fingers twice. "He needs help."

The couple discussed this, as if they understood. The man went to a dugout canoe, untied it, and motioned for us to bring Ben to the boat. We eased Ben in and Unk climbed in. The man pushed off, paddling furiously downstream.

We stood there not sure what to do. Finally, Dan said, "Let's follow them. We can't keep up, but we'll try to figure out where they're heading."

We pushed off and continued our journey. Daddy called back to the woman, "Merci beaucoup." She waved shyly as we pulled away.

"What was that?" I asked.

"Oh, I just used half of my French vocabulary. I *think* it was, 'Thank you very much.'" We lost sight of the canoe in the fog, until we rounded a bend where a bayou came in from the east, and we heard voices as well as footsteps on a wharf. We poled over to the riverbank adjacent to the bayou. After securing the rafts, we tromped in deep mud back toward the voices.

Soon we saw three houses on stilts along the bayou. Several boats, including the canoe Ben had been in, were tied up along a rickety wharf.

Evidently, Ben had been taken to the first house, where people were gathered around the door. As we climbed up on the wharf, Daddy told me to just stay put as he and Pistol went inside. However, I was too curious and slipped to the doorway.

From inside the house, there was loud jabbering in French. Pistol tried to speak, but realized none of them understood. Then from inside the crowded room, I heard a female voice speaking in broken English. Moving so I could see the person, I found myself staring into the face of a girl about my age. My first thought was *She's beautiful.*

She had long dark hair and beautiful dark skin. Her eyes seemed to dance as she struggled to interpret, and her hands were working as hard as her mind and mouth.

Her English was halting and slow, but she was doing a reasonable job of communicating between the two languages in the room.

She asked Pistol, "Your friend is sick from—uh, bee stings?"

"It was wasps."

"Yes." She turned to the others in the room and explained. Repeatedly I heard her use a word, *traiteur.* One man, evidently the leader of this clan, said the word repeatedly as he motioned a younger man out the door. I watched him run to his boat and paddle up the bayou.

I couldn't take my eyes off the girl—especially her eyes. She turned to Pistol. "They gone . . . to get the traiteur." You could see her mind spinning as she grasped for the English word. "The traiteur is a heal . . . healer . . . like a doctor. She will help."

I eased up by Daddy. "Did she say *she*? Is the doctor a woman?"

He was so caught up in what was happening that he forgot his admonition for me to remain on the pier. "It's not a doctor coming; it's some kind of healer. They'll probably make him drink frog pee or something."

"Will it help?"

"I sure hope so."

Unk eased over by the pretty girl. He considered himself a ladies' man and did have a disarming way with women. We'd seen it back at the houseboat and now observed it again.

"What's your name?" He asked.

"Clothilde."

"Clothilde. That's a pretty name. How old are you?"

"I'm fourteen."

I was mentally practicing how she said it, "Clo-teel."

"Have you met my nephew, Mayo?" In a flash, he pulled me toward Clothilde. I could've killed him, but couldn't because I was now standing directly in front of this beautiful girl.

Her eyes met mine. I was at an awkward age and unsure of myself around girls, so I stood smiling stupidly. I couldn't speak a word of French, and at that moment, I'd also forgotten my English.

Fortunately, for my tongue and pride, the boat bringing the healer returned quickly. Everyone crowded in to see the young man helping a bent old woman, dressed completely in black, from the boat. She carried a small burlap sack and was unsteady on her feet. I wondered how old she was.

Old or not, the healer entered the house, taking complete charge of the situation. Giving a few orders in rat-a-tat French, they soon had water boiling and the curtains closed, and she began whispering in Ben's ear.

The old woman turned toward us and said something. Clothilde frowned and said, "Mamma Lapin say she can't help the man with all these people around—everyone out—but him." She pointed at Unk. "You stay."

No one, including any of the rafters, was brave enough to question "Mamma Lapin." Once outside I asked Daddy, "Why'd she pick Unk to stay?"

Shaking his head, he said, "Folks—especially those with gifts—always notice him and single him out." Grinning as he lowered his voice, "Sometimes I wonder if he might be some kind of angel or something. The Lord might've made him a brick shy of a load, but his smarts are of a different kind."

Thinking about angels, the gold coins came to mind. That's what Ten Mile folks had gone to calling whoever left the money, *our angel.*

Daddy grabbed me by the arm, leading me away from the cabin. "Now, don't you wander back into that cabin; that old woman might turn you into a toad or sic the little people on you."

"I ain't interested in the *old* woman."

He smiled. "Yep, I noticed."

"Did you see that girl's eyes?"

"Sure did. Unique, weren't they?" he replied.

"They sure were. In fact, *everything* about her looked pretty unique."

He looked me up and down. "You been drinking that river water, boy?"

I stayed near the door, hoping to catch some of what was going on, but it was impossible.

I'd have to wait until later for Unk's eyewitness account.

Chapter 23

THE traiteur stayed in the cabin a long time with Ben. Periodically, Unk would come out shrugging his shoulders. When asked about the healer, he just shook his head as if he couldn't— or wouldn't—explain what was going on.

I sat on the wharf, hanging my feet into the water. The fog lifted, and we could now watch all kinds of waterfowl flying up and down the bayou. I heard a red-tailed hawk and watched it fly by, a small snake dangling from its mouth. The world around me looked so different from my piney woods, but it was beautiful in its own different way.

I felt movement beside me and was surprised as Clothilde sat down. She put her feet into the water as she rolled her long dress up to her knees.

I felt the touch of her leg against mine, and it gave me that feeling again that caused me to forget how to speak a word. I knew if I tried to form a sentence, something stupid would come out.

She had the liveliest brown eyes I'd ever seen, and they seemed to pierce right into my soul. If someone were to ask me now—as an old man—when I first fell in love, I'd reply that it was while sitting on a wharf near the Calcasieu River when I was thirteen.

"May I practice my English?" she said.

"You can practice whatever you want on me." I felt dumb for saying that, but it made Clothilde smile. She had the softest voice, and her accent was captivating. In fact, *everything* about her was extremely attractive and appealing.

"What kind of name is Clothilde?" I asked.

"It's French. Everyone calls me 'Chloe,' and that's what you can call me, if you wish."

"All right, Chloe. That's what I'll call you."

She smiled broadly. "Your name's Milo?"

"No, it's Mayo. Mayo Joseph Moore."

"What kind of name—is Mayo?"

"It's an Irish name—it's the place where my father came from: County Mayo. But my name—Mayo—is also from a friend of his who drowned in the Mississippi River near New Orleans." I was surprised at how much my tongue was loosening.

She seemed interested. "Tell me more."

Pointing toward Daddy who was standing with the other men, I said, "The sandy-haired one is my father. He came to New Orleans from Ireland and became friends with an Irish family named O'Leary. Their son, Mayo, became his best friend.

"A big flood hit New Orleans and Daddy and Mayo got work where the river levee had busted. An accident happened there, and his friend Mayo drowned. It touched my daddy deeply and led to his leaving the city to come to this part of Louisiana."

"So your name is… uh, special?"

"Daddy says I'm named after a special man *and* a special place and need to honor both by the way I live."

"That's nice, Mayo." I liked the way she said my name. I scooted a little closer to her, and was surprised as she quickly did the same.

Looking around at the swamp and bayou, I said, "Your land is beautiful in a different way."

"What you mean?"

"I love the pines and thick woods of my home, but yours is nice, too. It is beautiful."

I couldn't believe what I said next. "And you are beautiful, Chloe."

She was too dark to blush. "Merci beaucoup."

Switching back to English, she said, "Thank you very much."

"How'd you learn English?"

"I've had some schooling at the convent in Lake Charles. The nuns there helped me with English. One of the nuns, Sister Mary Kay, was Irish. She looked like your father—red hair and skin.

She pointed at my arm. "You don't look Irish."

"It's 'cause I ain't. I'm half Irish and half Redbone."

"What's a 'Redbone'?"

"It's what my momma's people are. Look at the other fellows there—see how they're all dark with Indian features? I got my momma's dark skin, but Daddy says on the inside I'm full-blooded Irish."

I put my hand on hers. Her skin was also dark, but a more delicate shade than mine. "See how dark I am."

"I'm dark, too," Chloe said. "Americans in Charleston made fun of me."

"Where's Charleston?"

She saw my confusion. "Charleston is the old name for Lake Charles."

I kept my hand on hers. "Well, when I get there—whether they call it Lake Charles or Charleston, I'm gonna whip whoever made fun of you." She giggled, gripping my hand tighter, before asking, "Mayo, are you an American?"

"Well, I guess so. Are you?"

"Me? I'm not sure."

"Why not?"

"Well, my heart is French and Creole, and I don't fit in."

"But, you live in America just the same as them, don't you?"

"My family and I are different."

"Like I said, you're beautiful because you're different."

She looked into my eyes. "This war... has it changed your family?"

"Not that I know of. We were poor 'fore it started and we're poor now."

Her mention of the war surprised me. It'd been a source of constant discussion back home, but I hadn't even thought about it on our trip.

Nodding downriver, Chloe said, "No American flag in Lake Charles. They say they're not part of the United States."

I'd never seen a real flag and looked forward to seeing one in Lake Charles. It never entered my mind that the American flag, which I'd seen pictures of, wouldn't be flying there.

"Well, I guess you're right, Chloe. I'm not sure if any of us are Americans. Where I come from, we consider ourselves 'Ten Milers.' That's the area where I live. Our allegiance has always been more to our families and kin than to any government or nation."

"That also true with our Creole people."

"I've got an uncle who's gone off to fight the Yankees, but most Ten Milers couldn't care less about this war. What about your men?"

"None have gone."

I had more questions. Pointing at the small boats tied to the pier, I asked. "What kind of boats are those?"

"We call them 'pirogues.'"

I wanted to know more about the healer, so I asked. "What'd you call the healer?"

"Momma Lapin—lapin means 'rabbit' in French. She's the rabbit woman—She's also a traiteur—a healer. Traiteurs believe their healing ability is a gift from God."

"Do you believe that?"

"Yes."

"What's that word? Tre-toor? "

"Traiteur—healer."

"Why is she wearing black? She's not a witch or a voodoo woman, is she?"

"No. She's a widow. Widows wear *noir*, or black, for a year, but she wearing hers for long years."

We sat talking as the sun set and shadows lengthened across the bayou. It was wonderful sitting by this girl who seemed as sweet as she was beautiful.

The Creole families took care of our every need. Late that afternoon, the healer came out, announcing through Chloe, that Ben was going to be all right. Sure enough, when we crowded in, he was sitting up in a bed, his face still swollen but looking much better.

"Man, we thought you was a goner." Daddy said.

"I was wondering myself. That old lady saved my life."

Ben pulled some bills out of his pocket. "Joe, can we give that lady something?"

Chloe interrupted. "No, no. Against traiteur's rules to take money. Her gift is from God."

The traiteur stated that we must not move Ben until tomorrow, and Chloe's family insisted he stay in their home for the night. Her mother cooked up a big meal and wouldn't take no for an answer on her lodging and invitation for supper.

That night I ate food that I'd never seen and tasting as good as any I've ever eaten. Chloe explained that the delicious thick stew was catfish courtboullion. She pronounced it 'coo-be-ah.' Other meats and dishes were also served. I was enjoying a second helping of one of the meats when she leaned over, "That's snapping turtle."

I pictured the ugly turtles we'd caught on the river. Now, I'm not a picky eater, but it seemed to grow in my mouth. She laughed, "If you don't like that piece, try another. There's seven types of meat in a turtle."

"I believe I'll have to take your word on the other six."

I asked if it was true about a snapping turtle biting until it thundered. She laughed, "I've heard that, but don't know."

As our men went to the rafts for the night, Chloe walked to the end of the wharf with me.

"I've sure enjoyed today." I said.

"So have I, Sha."

"What does 'sha' mean?"

She ducked her head. "It means, uh, 'sweetheart.'"

I'd never kissed a girl until that night. It was my first kiss and probably hers, too. Maybe it was the setting and situation—far from home in a strange land, full from the meal and hospitality we'd received—it all blended into a moment I still hold dear.

And it ended perfectly with a perfect kiss. I can still taste her lips, smell her hair, and feel her hand on my neck. It couldn't have been as good as it seemed, but that's how I still remember it.

As we ended the kiss, she smiled and kissed me again—even

longer. "That's *lagniappe*," she said.

"What's that?"

"A French word for something a little extra."

I've never forgotten that kiss, or the word. It's a good word: *lagniappe*, something extra.

I felt so good that I don't even remember sinking into the mud on the way back to our raft, where Daddy was already stretched out.

"Welcome back, lover boy."

It embarrassed me, and I didn't know what to say, but he let me off the hook. "That was some fine catfish stew, wasn't it?"

"It sure was."

I waited before asking, "Why have these folks been so kind to us?"

"It's 'cause we needed help, and we were in their tribal area, so they helped us."

"What do you mean 'tribal area'?"

"In most areas of the world—well, in rural areas for sure— there's a tribal or family code of taking care of needy strangers. A stranger who comes to you sick, hurt, or needy becomes part of your tribe and under your protection.

"Back home we called it 'kindness to strangers.' I've not traveled to many other places, but I've heard it's part of the culture in places like the Bible lands—hospitality to strangers is freely given, especially if someone's hurt or ill.

"It's what Jesus was showing in the story of the Good Samaritan—a stranger taking care of another stranger."

"Is that kind of what we've done with the Merkles?"

He was silent for a while. "I guess it is. I haven't done too well at it, but your momma—who's the best person I know—has. She's reached out to them.

"Now, I didn't care much for the man, so I haven't done much, but when we get home, I'll do better—if you'll help me."

"I will. I've wondered about something."

"What's that?"

"Is what these people done kind of like our 'evening holler'?"

"I hadn't thought about it, but I guess it is. Neighbors taking care of neighbors."

I waited before I asked the next question.

"Do you think we'll ever see these folks again?"

"These Acadians?"

"Yes."

"Oh, I don't know. You never know in life's journey if you'll cross paths again."

"You think we will?"

He looked at me. "To be honest, probably not."

He knew I was referring to Chloe. His next words were spoken from experience, "Son, time marches on, and it's hard for a fellow to go back. It's a lot easier going down the river than paddling back up it."

"Daddy, will *you* ever go back?"

He knew I meant back to Ireland. He furrowed his brow and looked off before he spoke. "To be honest, probably not. Probably not. Back home we had a saying, 'You can't stand by the same river twice.'"

"What's that mean?"

"Oh, you can go back to the same spot along the river, but it can never be the same. You'll have changed—and so will the river."

Then he smiled. "When my friend back home rowed me out to my stowaway ship that night, his parting words were, 'Ye no come back here?'"

I tried to repeat it with the Irish way brogue he'd used, 'Ye no come back here?'" Then I asked, "What'd you tell him?"

"The same thing I just told you: probably not."

The river lapping against our rafts was the only sound. I thought about Chloe and our time together, knowing for sure it wouldn't—and couldn't—be repeated. If it's possible to be happy and sad at the same time, that's how I felt at that moment.

Daddy's next statement changed the direction of my thoughts. "It's been a trip to remember, ain't it?"

"It sure has—and I wonder what's still to come."

"We'll see. We'll just have to see."

Rocked to sleep by the river's current, I slept hard, without any dreams. Sometimes when you're *living* a dream, nighttime dreams aren't needed.

Chapter 24

WE rose early the next morning and went to check on Ben, who was standing outside waiting for us, looking a heck of a lot better.

"How you feeling, Ben?" Pistol asked.

"I'm feeling strong enough to sit up and take nourishment."

"Well, that's good. Are you ready to go?"

"I am."

We walked back to the houses to say goodbye to our new friends and thank them for their kindness. Chloe was nowhere to be seen. I asked Ben if he'd seen her, and he said, "She and her father left earlier to run their fishing lines."

So, I left without being able to tell her bye, but goodbye in the daylight—surrounded by everyone—would have been anti-climactic to last night's kiss.

We all walked back upstream to our rafts, eager for the last leg of our float. Caleb rode with Ben to steer his raft, and I took his place on Unk's raft.

Unk and I were the last to shove off. We soon drifted past the mouth the bayou and saw the stilted houses through the lingering fog. I squinted closely hoping for one last glimpse of Chloe.

In the distance, I saw the small pirogue approaching the pier by the house. Seeing that it was Chloe and her father, I shouted her name.

She saw me, stood, and waved happily. Soon the river turned and our view was obscured. I could still hear her voice in the distance, but couldn't make out what she was saying, or even if it was French or English.

It soon became quiet again. I turned to Unk who was staring at me. He grinned and said, "Ain't love grand?"

I couldn't help but laugh. "It sure is, Unk. But what would *you* know about it?"

His silly grin broadened. "A lot more than you think I do. I ain't *that* stupid, you know."

I was embarrassed that I'd offended him, but you could hardly hurt his feelings. "I'm sorry if I—"

"No offense taken."

I wanted to hear directly from him about what had happened in that cabin with the healer, so I asked, "What happened with that healing woman?"

He shook his head. "I ain't never seen nothin' like it."

"What do you mean?"

"That woman kept pulling things out of that bag, praying, whispering, and chanting. Within an hour, Ben started getting better and his color started returning. I can't explain it."

I peppered him with questions, but he answered most with, "Just can't explain it."

That day is when the marsh mosquitoes attacked us. They were big, black, and more aggressive than our Ten Mile kind— and they dealt us some misery.

Dan pointed to me and said, "They were so big, I heard one mosquito ask another one about 'Columbus' here: "Should we eat him here, or take him home?"

Everyone laughed and the lying about the ferocity and size of the mosquitoes near where the bayou began. Pistol, with his great knack for exaggeration said, "They were so thick that you could make a quick skeeter scoop with a pint jar and come up with a quart of skeeters."

It all ended when Caleb, who usually never spoke a word, said, "The mosquitoes are so tough here that they'll sting a mule right through the hoof."

"Caleb, you've done surprised me with that. You get first place on this." Pistol said.

"Thank you." It was the last thing Caleb said that day, but he said it with a big smile.

Drifting along, we began to see signs of civilization and knew we were nearing Lake Charles and the end of our river journey. We passed a small village on the east bank. "That's probably Marion," Pistol said. Then later, he pointed to a village on the right bank, "I believe that's what they call Baghdad."

Across the river from Baghdad was a sawmill. We poled over to it, and Pistol went to find out more.

In about thirty minutes, he returned flustered. "This mill don't want our logs. They said so many of the men are off fighting they're not cutting any lumber."

He explained that the village around this mill was called Goosport, and there were several more downstream on Lake Charles itself.

"You don't think we've come all this way and won't be able to sell our logs, do you?" Daddy asked.

Pistol took off his hat and scratched his head. "I sure hope not." Pointing back at the Goosport mill he said, "Those fellows said the Ryan Mill on the Lake was still cutting. Let's go see."

I'll always associate my first visit to Lake Charles with the strong aroma of pinesap. We smelled it long before we saw the lake. When we came to the lake, I was astounded. I'd never seen a large body of water and was equally astounded by the rafts of logs covering the west end of the lake.

Dan shouted, "I believe you could walk to China on those logs!"

From the nearby mill came the steady droning of loud saws. I'd never heard this much noise in my life. It kind of reminded me of the sound of the hurricane—a steady whining noise of destruction.

We tied our rafts along the lake, then Pistol and Dan walked to the sawmill. Daddy and I explored along the lake, amazed at the mass of logs. I noticed he was sniffing the air in a peculiar way. He seemed to detect something besides pinesap—a smell he recognized, but the rest of us didn't. Drawing in a deep breath, he knelt down, dipped up water in his hand, before taking a sip.

He spit it out and began walking up the sandy shore. A light rain was falling as I followed along behind him. He seemed not to notice the rain or me as he stared across the lake. It was the look my momma always called his "homesick look." I didn't know exactly, but something about this lake took him back to Ireland.

I recalled my question from the night before, *Will you ever go back?* As well as his answer of No, *probably, not.*

Whatever was on his mind right now *was* taking him back—not in body, but in his mind.

He walked down the beach as I kept pace.

A large white bird with black-tipped wings circled above us before landing along the shoreline. Its strange call sounded just like, 'hi-yah, hi-yah.'

Daddy watched it run along the shore. When it flew off, he turned and walked back toward me. The rain strengthened, pelting both of us. As he neared, I saw his face was wet and at first, thought it was the rain, but a closer look revealed the streaks of tears.

Quietly he said, "I smelt it in the air and knew this water was salty. I never thought I'd smell the ocean again."

I bent down and tasted the water. It was salty and I spit it out, and then asked, "What was that white bird?"

"It was a sea gull. They're only found near the ocean."

"Are we that close to the Gulf of Mexico?"

"I believe it's around fifty miles, but the tide must bring this salt water in."

We stood a long time in the rain along Lake Charles—my father and I—both of us farther from home than we'd ever been.

Chapter 25

WITHIN an hour or so, the men returned from the sawmill. Two mill workers accompanied them and began "scaling" our rafts. As one carefully measured the lengths and diameters, the other jotted down the figures. They consulted with Pistol before returning to the mill.

"They'll be back shortly with our money." Pistol was grinning broadly. "It's gonna be good."

When the workers came back, they brought an envelope full of money. You should've seen our men's faces when they handed over the wads of cash. I'd never seen "blue backs," or Confederate money before.

"Let me hold one of those," I asked. It felt crisp and even smelled new. I held it up to the sun, studying every detail.

"Look them over good—they probably won't be worth a bucket of warm spit by this time next year," Daddy said.

I watched him help Unk divide his part in half. Unk then walked over to Caleb and held half of it out. "Here's your split, Partner."

"Unk, I can't take that."

"Yes, you can, and you will."

He placed it in Caleb's hand, closing his fingers over the bills. "A deal's a deal."

We heard a small boat coming our way. I'd never seen a steam-powered vessel in my life and watched in fascination as the crew hooked up to our rafts and towed them toward the mill.

As the rafts disappeared along the lakeshore, Daddy repeated Fred Wilson's farewell, "Von Boyage."

Unk said, "What's that mean?"

Before Daddy could elaborate, Ben Tyler, face still swollen from wasp bites, said, "It means 'good riddance.'"

It was late in the day, and we decided that we'd wait to buy our supplies the next day before beginning the walk home. Although Ben was better, he'd been throwing up all day, and we decided he better see a doctor. We roamed the streets until we found a doctor's sign. Pistol, Dan, and Caleb took Ben in.

We had time on our hands waiting so Daddy, Unk, and I decided to explore the city proper. We soon found that time on your hands can be good or bad, but it's usually the latter.

Walking down the street, we soon came to the courthouse, the biggest building I'd ever seen. Lake Charles was the seat of Calcasieu Parish, so this courthouse was the seat of all legal activities for this entire corner of the state.

Daddy took a stick and drew a rough outline of boot-shaped Louisiana in the dirt. "Calcasieu Parish takes up the entire 'heel of the boot.' It goes all the way up to where we live in Rapides Parish."

Even though Lake Charles was a small town, there were more people on the streets and in the courthouse square than we'd see in a year back home.

They made Unk nervous. "If you swung a dead cat in the street, you'd get fur all over everybody. This is too many folks for my liking."

My attention was diverted to the flag flying above the courthouse—it was the first real flag I'd ever seen. It didn't resemble pictures of American flags I'd seen, so I knew it must be a Confederate flag.

The three of us stood staring at the flag. "Is that our flag now, Joe?" Unk asked.

"I guess it is—at least for now."

Just then, an older man walked up to Daddy, "Why ain't you off at the war?"

"I guess 'cause I ain't that mad at nobody."

"You don't have to be mad at somebody to fight in a war."

"It seems like it'd be a good thing to be mad at a man you're trying to kill—and I ain't that mad, at least not yet."

Daddy then added, "This war seems about the same as always: a rich man's *war*, but a poor man's *fight*."

Ignoring these words, the man pointed at Unk and then me. "I can tell that one there ain't right, and your boy's too young, but you're healthy enough to be off fighting for the South." He then pointed down the empty street. "You don't see many other men your age standing around do you? They're off defending our country."

"What country is that?"

He rose to his full height, "The Confederate States of America—it's our country now. Two of my boys are off fighting to protect folks like you and your family. It's your freedom they're fighting for."

Daddy bristled. "Mister, I got about all of the freedom I can stand."

"*You* should be off fighting."

"By the way, what are *we* fighting *for*?" Daddy's face reddened as he said this.

"Freedom from them Yankees trying to tell us what to do and from them taking our slaves."

"Well, Mister, I ain't never *even* known a man who owned somebody else. Do you own any slaves?"

"No... I don't."

"But you're willing for your boys to die fighting to keep another man's slaves?"

The flustered man shook his head before walking off.

Daddy added a parting shot, using his best Irish brogue. "I ain't never owned another man, and no man *owns* me, neither."

Looking back at the flying flag, he said to Unk and me, "Man, I was just getting used to being American, and now they done changed that. I ain't been here long enough to really be mad at the Yankees like that man." Pausing for effect, he said, "I seen about all of this city I want to see."

"Me, too," Unk said.

We wandered down the street near the courthouse looking for a place to eat and to spend some of those Confederate dollars burning a hole in our pockets. Going along the street we came to an eating-place called Farque's Saloon. Hearing music coming from inside as well as smelling the aroma of baking bread, we opened the door. A large cowbell hanging on the door announced our entrance to the crowded room.

My father led the way, with Unk and me right behind. A stout man in a cooking apron who barred our way met us. He spoke to Daddy, "Fellow, *you* can come in, but . . ." Pointing to Unk and then me, "those two aren't welcome."

Daddy moved past the man, who was evidently the owner, as if he didn't see or hear him. The man grabbed him by the arm, swinging him round, and repeating loudly, "Your friends ain't welcome in my place. We don't allow their kind to stink things up."

"Mister, one of them is my son and the other is like my brother. They—and their money—are just as good as anyone else's in here."

The room quietened as the two men stood face to face. Daddy's face was flush, and he was trembling. I'd never seen him this mad and his voice shook, "When you talk down to my son, you're talking down to me."

The owner's face was red too, but it was due to the strong smell of whiskey. Evidently, he didn't just own the place, but sampled its wares, too.

Unk stepped forward and grabbed Daddy by the arm. "Aw come on, Joe. I bet their food ain't no better than their welcome."

As Unk pulled him toward the door, I grabbed his other arm. However, he dug in, and I felt his tensed muscles as we tried to pull him away.

The man sneered. "Get out of here, Irishman, and take your two Ethiopians with you."

Daddy lunged for the man, but Unk now had him in a

bear hug, and we succeeded in dragging him out the door. As it slammed in our face to the cowbell's clanging, we heard loud laughter, and sulked away knowing we were the source of it.

It was my first, but definitely not last, encounter with prejudice.

Unk tried to settle him down. "Joe, it ain't worth fighting about. There'd be twenty of them against you—and me and Mayo ain't much help in a fight."

As we returned to our spot at the lakeshore, Daddy said, "I need a little walk." I watched him go down the shore, kicking at rocks.

While we waited, Unk and I tightened the canvas cover from our cook shack, which we'd strung up for shelter from the rain. I sat on a log staring out onto the lake. Unk sat down by me. "Folks can be plenty mean, can't they, Son?"

"They sure can, and I don't know why."

"Some folks are just that way—especially when they get a belly full of whiskey."

"That man in the apron'd probably be mean whether he was drunk or sober." Staring out at the lake, I still could hear the man's cruel words echo in my mind.

Daddy returned within the hour, not quite as angry as when he'd left. He'd cooled off some, however the hurt was clear on his face as well as in his quiet words. "Mayo, I'm sorry I let that man insult you like that."

"It ain't no big deal," I said. "We didn't want to spend our hard-earned money in there anyhow."

He sat beside me on the log with bowed head, before finally looking up. "When I came to America, I thought I'd left prejudice behind, but I haven't. My time in New Orleans, and then here today, showed that it exists everywhere, among every race.

"Me and my friend Mayo O'Leary—he's the one you're named after—went to apply for a job in New Orleans. Arriving there, we saw a sign in the window: *Irish need not apply*. I picked up a cobblestone and threw it right through the window. Then we ran like heck. "I know what I did wasn't right, but it sure made me feel better."

As he told this story, an idea began bubbling in my brain.

"Daddy, could I borrow that burlap sack there?"

"Sure, but what for?"

"I'm going to get an equalizer."

"A what?"

"An equalizer. You'll see when I get back."

It took about thirty minutes before I returned with the sack, which was wiggling, alive.

"Boy, what you got in there?" Daddy asked as he backed away.

"Not one, but two 'equalizers.'"

I opened the mouth of the sack so he could cautiously peer in. When he looked into the sack, he jumped back. "Whoa, there's a snake in there."

"No, there ain't *a* snake—there's two of 'em."

"What are they?"

"Stinking stump tail moccasins."

"You caught them?"

"Yes sir, I found a forked stick perfect for pinning them down. A nearby small inlet is nearly dry. Snakes are having a feast on the stranded fish, and it was easy to catch these two. Do you wanna go see it for yourself?"

"Nope—I'll take your word for it."

I unveiled my plan. "When it gets dark, I'm going back to the saloon. I'm feeling kind of hungry."

Unk walked up and innocently looked in the sack. "Whoa." He drew back in surprise. "Where're you going with them cottonmouths?"

"We're going back to the saloon. They don't serve Redbones, but we're going to find out if they serve snakes," I said.

Daddy eyed me with a combination of humor, puzzlement, and maybe even pride. When he spoke, it was with a smirk. "Yep, a Redbone is the best friend you can have, and the worst enemy you'd ever want. I believe that man in the apron is fixin' to find out the latter."

When darkness fell, the three of us walked past the

courthouse and neared the saloon, from which loud talking, laughter, and piano music spilled out.

I felt real grown up as they followed me. As we walked past the front door, Daddy spat on the porch and muttered one of his favorite Irish curses, "The death of the kittens to the whole lot of ye."

At the corner, we slipped into the side alley behind the saloon. The sounds were muffled from here, but two high windows were partially open, emitting thin gleams of light.

From one window, we could hear conversation and silverware clinking. In my mind, I visualized the surprise those folks were going to have in just a short while.

A second adjacent window was evidently in the kitchen, from which we could hear the clatter of pans and glasses. I couldn't reach either window, so the men boosted me up to the first one.

It was too good to be true—a card game going on below me. Stacks of chips and money littered the table as six men sat in rapt attention. At an adjacent table, two couples were eating.

"Let me down," I whispered.

Going to the next window, they lifted me. I couldn't see much below, but heard the sound of food sizzling on a stove.

"Hand me my sack." Daddy wouldn't touch it, but Unk passed it up to me. I'd tied the sack where one of the moccasins could be released without the other. I untied it and let the first snake fall to the floor. Snake number one was now in the kitchen.

The men lowered me, and we ran to the other window. As soon as they heaved me up, I emptied the sack. It's a shame I couldn't see what happened as the second snake landed, but the sounds below painted a pretty clear picture.

The snake must have hit right in the middle of the table. I heard a plop followed by the crash of chips, glasses, and silverware. This was followed by a mixture of crashing chairs, hollering, cussing, and the loud report of pistol fire.

I heard a voice. "Quit shooting, you fool. You're gonna hit one of us!"

Another voice hollered, "But it's a snake! Everyone out!"

Daddy grabbed me, dragging me down the alley. Just as we passed the kitchen window, I realized the cook must have been a woman—no man can scream as shrill as what we heard from inside. The screaming was joined by the sounds of metal pots flying and wild yelling. I was pretty sure the yelling was the man in the apron. At least I hoped it was.

We rounded the corner of the saloon and trotted across the street to the courthouse lawn. Loud music was still playing inside the café. Evidently, the fallout from the snakes hadn't reached the front of the establishment yet.

Daddy pulled me back into the shadow of the courthouse, saying, "We ain't leaving 'til we get our money's worth—wait just a little longer—it should be anytime now. Just—about—now."

As if on cue, a blood-curdling scream came from inside the saloon as the door flung open. The music stopped, with a sound as if a mule was walking down the piano keyboard. The sound of glass shattering accompanied the stream of the panicked crowd running out the door. I'll never forget the repeated clanging of the cowbell as the door slammed back and forth during the exodus. In the din, periodic shouts of "Snake" were mixed in with words none of us had learned in church.

My father put his arm around my shoulder. "Evidently they don't serve snakes either."

As patrons ran from the café, we heard more shooting which only hastened the panic of the fleeing crowd. A window shattered, but I couldn't tell whether it was from a stray bullet or flying whiskey bottle.

Finally, we saw what we'd waited for. The man in the apron stood at the door dazed, shouting, "Y'all come back. We done killed the snakes. It's all right—come back."

Daddy leaned over. "Well, we know what'll be on tomorrow's menu at Farque's Saloon."

"I don't think I'll be coming to find out," I said.

"Me neither."

Unk who loved to quote scripture in odd ways at unusual times solemnly said, "The first shall be last, and the last shall be first."

Daddy laughed. "Yep, the tables got turned. 'Top rail done got on top. Top rail on top.'"

As we walked merrily back toward the lake, Unk put the benediction on this evening by singing off key from our spot in the shadows, *"Someone's in the kitchen with Dinah. Someone's in the kitchen I kn-o-o-w. Someone's in the kitchen with Dinah, strumming on the ol' banjo."*

My daddy laughed so hard I thought he was going to bust a gut. You could easily have followed us in the dark on this night I'd never forget.

We retired to the comfort of our canvas shelter. Every time I'd just about get to sleep, Unk would start again,

"Fie, fi, fiddly i o
Fie, fi, fiddly i o
Fie, fi, fiddly i ooooooh
Strumming on the old banjo."

Chapter 26

LATE that night Pistol and Dan returned to the shore, informing us that the doctor wanted to keep Ben overnight, and Caleb stayed with him.

It was obvious from the smell and their speech, that both of the Perkins' had been drinking. They informed us that they were returning for a little nightcap before turning in.

I could sense the alarm in Daddy's voice. "Fellows, y'all better be careful. We're a long ways from home and a 'wast nest' got stirred up over by the courthouse."

They laughed, ignoring him. "Oh, don't worry about us. We ain't going over there anyway, 'cause we done found a gold mine on another street."

We watched them stagger up the shore and disappear toward the few lights of Lake Charles. Daddy's only words before falling asleep were, "They're gonna get 'pig naked drunk' and lose all their money. I'll be surprised if they bring one dollar home with them to Ten Mile."

A bluebird woke me early the next morning. I viewed it as an omen—it was time to go home. Back home, a bluebird outside my window served as my personal alarm clock.

This Lake Charles bluebird told me something—it was time to go home. I was homesick and ready for the piney woods.

The only problem with leaving was that Pistol and Dan were nowhere to be seen. We went into town, finally finding them. They'd evidently been up all night, still a little drunk, and excited.

Seeing me, Dan began singing, "In 1492, ol' Columbus sailed the ocean blue. In 1863, he sailed with me on the Calcasieu."

He was in a good mood, and when he pulled out a huge wad of cash, we understood why.

"Where in the world'd you get that?" Daddy asked.

Unk said, "That's a big enough wad to choke a dog."

"I got into a card game last night and won me a bunch of money. Lookee here." He took his boot off, and flashed another wad he'd hidden there.

Pistol grinned, "And we found some women that helped us spend some of it."

Daddy made a face at me and quickly said, "Well, good for you. Let's go get our supplies, some horses, and get ready to take your money and yourselves back to Ten Mile."

Pistol stepped forward, "Joe, Dan and I been talking. We're thinking about staying a few more days here. This place is kind of growing on us."

"Pistol, now's a good time to head home."

"But Joe, Dan's always been real good at cards." Pistol said proudly. "They thought they were going to skin him at that game, and he skint them instead."

"Well, that's more reason to git out while you're ahead."

However, no manner of talking could keep them from staying, and staying longer wasn't an option for us.

"You sure you fellows'll be all right on your own?" he asked.

"Fine as frog hair split four ways."

"There's a lot of rough country between here and Ten Mile, and they say it's best to travel in a group."

"We'll be fine."

So, our party—the Ten Mile logging company—split up. Everyone shook hands, wishing each other well.

Pistol and Dan's parting words were, "We'll see you back in Ten Mile."

As they walked down the street, Daddy said, "A drunk'll get sober, but a fool just keeps on being a fool." Then he added as if in benediction, "Some folks'll lose a hundred dollars to make a dime. Mark my word—they'll lose it all."

We neared the sight of last night's ruckus at the café. A boy was on the porch sweeping up broken glass. A hand-lettered sign read, "Closed today for repairs."

Unk, who couldn't read, asked what the sign said. After Daddy explained it, my uncle began singing again. *"Fe, fi, fiddle-i-o. Fe, fi, fiddle-i-o. Fee, fi, fiddle-i-ooooh. Strumming on the old banjo."*

Just then, trouble rounded the corner of the side street. There were four men coming toward us. I only recognized one—the saloon owner. When he saw us, he started hollering and cussing, leading the other three men toward us.

As they neared us, I saw a badge on one of the men. The other two trotted along behind them.

Daddy said, "Let me handle this."

The saloon man waved his arms, "That's them, Sheriff. I knowed it was them that did it." He was mad as a Paiute Indian, but I detected something different in the officer. There was a smile trying to break out from under his thick moustache. His whole face seemed to be twitching.

"Sheriff Reid, I know that Irishmen and these two... these two... did it. They put those snakes in the window."

The Sheriff drew himself up. "Fellows, "Pumpkin here is accusing you of putting snakes in his saloon."

Daddy looked at him and then back at Unk, Ben, Caleb, and me. "What makes him think we did something like that?"

"Cause of how mad you left here yesterday."

My father pulled his ace in the hole out, using his thickest Irish brogue. "Sheriff, have you ever known an Irishman to fool with snakes?"

I thought Sheriff Reid was going to bust out laughing. "Can't say I have."

His reaction only further angered the saloonkeeper. "It was probably one of them other fellows."

Daddy moved toward them and pointed at Ben and Caleb. "Those two men were sick and couldn't have been part of it." Then he turned to Unk and me. "I was with these two the whole night and can account for every step they made."

He didn't finish. Nobody asked more.

"I want them arrested Sheriff."

"Pumpkin, I can't arrest them just 'because you think they had the snakes." Once again, the sheriff was trying to stay serious. He winked at the other two men. "And beside I'm not sure what law was broken anyway."

"But, I want them…"

Sheriff Reid had had enough. "Pumpkin, as many people as you've made mad around here, it'd be a long line of suspects down Canal Street who've got a beef with you."

Pumpkin had heard enough and disappeared inside, fuming and carrying on. The door slammed and that bell clanged for a long time.

The sheriff turned to Daddy. "Mister, I'd advise you to clear out before nightfall. Pumpkin has some rough friends who might cause you trouble."

My daddy held his hand up. "Sheriff, we'll be back across the Calcasieu heading home by nightfall. Don't worry about us hanging around. We've 'bout had enough of your town."

"Don't judge Charleston by Pumpkin and his kind."

"We won't."

As the sheriff turned to leave, he stopped and grinned, "Now, I know you boys didn't have anything to do with those snakes in the saloon… but if you ever run across who did it, tell them it was a pretty original idea about those snakes."

Daddy studied the sheriff for a while. "If I meet them, I'll sure tell them. I sure will."

We—I mean Daddy, Unk, Caleb, Ben, and me—spent the rest of the day buying supplies. Ben was much stronger but often had to sit and rest. I'd sit with him as we discussed the trip and the others shopped.

The big decision of the day was whether to buy a wagon for our supplies. The men learned that the roads between here and home were rough and unreliable, so they decided to forgo the wagon and buy horses.

Daddy asked around until he found where the local horse traders were. Arriving there, we saw a wagon with a load of hay and some of the sorriest looking horses I'd ever seen. They were

real nags—Unk called them "First Monday" horses—the kind
you want to get rid of for any price.

The horse trader was Irish—I can't recall his name, but I'll
always remember the lively exchange between him and my daddy.
Two Irishmen trying to make a deal is a sight to behold—as well
as hear. They argued in English and Irish, and may even have
invented a new language during their haggling. Finally, they
shook hands, exchanged money, and we had four horses and a
pack mule for the journey home.

"You think they'll make it home?" Ben asked.

"They'll do," Daddy answered.

"But don't we need five horses? One of us'll have to walk," I
said.

He put his hand on my shoulder. "Yep, and I'm looking at the
walker right now."

"Why can't I ride?"

"Stowaways have to make the best of a bad situation. That
walk will be good for your legs—it'll make them longer." He
winked. "The ankle express has always been a good way to travel."

I knew arguing was useless and watched as he went into a
general store to buy supplies. The main items in short supply back
home were salt, sugar, tobacco, and coffee. Daddy, who loved to
bargain, haggled over every item for the best possible price.

Unk and I sat outside and soon heard some men talking
about a cattle drive crossing the Calcasieu later in the day.
We listened as they discussed the active cattle business on the
Southwestern Prairie. This land, which stretched all the way into
Texas, was prime cattle country untouched by the war so far.

The Rebel army was in bad need of beef, which made for a
good market. General Richard Taylor's Confederate Army was
located in Southern Louisiana about seventy miles east of Lake
Charles.

The men said that a herd of three hundred cattle would ford
the Calcasieu later that day, crossing just north of the sawmills.
Hearing this, I whispered to Unk where I'd be, and scooted off.

At the river, there were hundreds of lowing cattle on the other side. In the distance, mounted cowboys rode back and forth, stirring up clouds of dust. It looked as if I'd arrived just in time as I joined a crowd of thirty or so people who'd come to watch.

We watched one rider wade into the river while several others pushed the herd down the bank. The cattle initially resisted, but soon dozens were swimming, only their heads and horns visible. I'd never seen anything like it and was mesmerized by the sight and sounds.

Riders swam along both flanks to keep the cattle moving toward us. There was all manner of shouting and whistling, but the main sound was the deafening lowing of hundreds of frightened cattle.

They were all in the river now and as they neared, I saw calves swimming beside their mothers. As the lead cattle began coming up the near bank, a cowboy, assisted by two dogs that'd swam over, kept them huddled together as more riders came over.

It was a sight that I'll never forget and I thought, *this is why I came on this trip—to see things like this.*

Some of the cattle were pushed downriver by the current and had to be herded back individually. Several came right through where we sat, scattering our small crowd of onlookers.

I stayed until the other men arrived with our animals loaded down with provisions. By now, the cowboys had gathered up all of the cattle and were moving them eastward away from the river.

"Time to head north." Daddy pointed. "But first we've got to get back across the river."

I hadn't thought about it, but we had to re-cross the Calcasieu to get home. We walked along the river until we came to the ferry that crossed to the village of Baghdad. Its rickety-looking condition didn't inspire much confidence.

"You sure this thing will hold us?" Ben asked. Being a non-swimmer, he was nervous about crossing the river.

"You bet it will," The ferryman answered confidently.

As we led our sorry-looking horses onto the ferry, Daddy said, "A rickety ferry for rickety horses. Somehow it just seems fitting."

I'd been assigned to lead the pack mule. That mule was just

like Ben—didn't care a lick for water, and tried to stay on dry land. It took all of us to push, prod, pull, and drag it onto the ferry.

The ferryman, who smelled as if he hadn't bathed since last Christmas, was ready to talk. "Heading into the Outlaw Strip?"

"It's our home," Daddy answered.

"You fellas better watch out for jayhawkers."

"What's a 'jayhawker'?"

"They're robbers—murderers that roam the roads you'll be traveling. They're just as likely to cut your throat as take your money. Many are army deserters—from both sides—and they prey upon travelers."

"Thanks for the warning. We'll keep a lookout for them."

The man had one final word of advice. "Just don't trust no one. Nobody at all."

Our plan was to cut across the prairie and hit the Confederate Military road. It ran from Niblett's Bluff on the Sabine, veering northeast for over a hundred miles to Alexandria. It passed within a few miles of Ten Mile. Although not the most direct way home, it was probably the best trail with good fords over the streams. We also thought it'd be the safest route.

As the ferry docked on the west side of the river and we went ashore, Caleb said, "We're back on our side of the Calcasieu— back in No Man's Land. I feel better already."

This was as much as he'd said at one time on the entire trip, and Ben commented, "Caleb, you sure are talkative today."

"Yep." That was his final comment for the day.

Being one of the gang now, I added, "I'm ready to cut mud and get back to Ten Mile."

Daddy was ready. "The only thing that's gonna get cut is your butt when your momma gets hold of you."

During all of the recent excitement, I hadn't thought much about my coming day of reckoning. The thought sobered me.

With Pistol and Dan staying behind in Lake Charles, Daddy became the unofficial leader of our expedition. He'd sketched a map from bits of information and laid it out. "The hardest part of this trip probably lies ahead. We've got to stick together and keep our eyes open. You heard what the fellow said about thieves working this area north of here. We'll need to be careful."

Forming a line, we headed northwest to connect with the Military Road that'd take us back to our piney woods homes.

Chapter 27

THE first day of our walk was uneventful. We encountered a few travelers heading toward Lake Charles, who gave us information about the muddy roads awaiting us on the prairie.

On our second day, we began re-entering the pine forests, and we began to feel more at home. Late that afternoon we came to the Military Road. The only problem was that another smaller road angled westward—seemingly straight for our homes.

While I held the horses, the men stood at the fork in the trail carefully discussing our options.

Daddy walked over to a pile of sticks and leaves and knelt beside it. "Come look over here, fellows. It's a 'pattern.'"

"What's that?" Ben asked.

"Look at those sticks, leaves, and pieces of string arranged in an orderly way. It's a patteran—a message of some sort."

"What's a patteran?" Ben repeated.

"Back in Ireland, Gypsies would leave messages in the road for those coming along later. These arrangements of sticks, stones, and leaves communicated information—such as which trail to take."

Daddy looked down each road and then back at the strange display. "I just wish I knew what this meant." He said, poking at the pile.

Finally, he said, "We're taking the wider of the two roads. Even though it looks like it's veering away from home, I believe it's the right one." No one had a better idea, so we went in that direction.

Late that afternoon, after we'd set up camp, is when the trouble happened. Everything was so quiet that we let our guard down. That's what led to the robbers getting the jump on us.

I'd gone out in the bushes to take care of business when I heard loud voices. The sound of shouting signified trouble.

Staying low, I crawled over and saw a scene that chilled me. Four robbers, their guns drawn, surrounded Daddy and the others.

One of them, a short, redheaded fellow was going through our gear and horses, throwing on the ground anything they didn't want. As the biggest man of the group kept his rifle trained, two others went through their pockets, taking the wads of cash from the timber sales. One of them, a fellow in a tattered green shirt, took Unk's money and grinned as he stuffed it in his own boot.

After this, the big man with the rifle ordered them away from the horses, lining the men under a pine. No one needed to tell me what was coming next—these outlaws didn't plan to leave any witnesses. I suddenly knew exactly what a jayhawker was.

I stood frozen in place, not believing what I was seeing.

Daddy stepped out front. "Killing us all ain't gonna put more money in your pockets. Just move on and we'll do the same. We'll call it even—you'll have our money and our horses and we'll have our lives."

The big Jayhawker hit him across the forehead with his gun barrel. Daddy went down as the man smirked, "You won't be standing back up, Irishman. That spot is where you'll die."

I heard the unmistakable click of the gun being cocked, and that's when I ran out of the bushes, and stood in front of Daddy. I didn't say a word—simply because I was too scared. In spite of my deep fear, no one was going to kill my daddy without shooting me first.

It was then that I looked up and into the big man's face. He had different colored eyes—one was a good eye and the other was what we always called an 'evil eye.' That eye, as well as the gun, was trained on me. His smirk widened as he said, 'Well, what have we got here? Any more rabbits like you hiding in those bushes?"

Daddy, recovering from his blow, said, "Leave him be, Mister. He's just a boy. Let him go."

The jayhawker paused. "No Irishman, I ain't gonna shoot your kid."

He spat before turning to one of the younger Jayhawkers. "I'm gonna let my own boy kill him before we take care of the rest of you."

He pushed the teenage boy forward. "Bill, it's time you become a man, and you ain't no man 'til you've killed somebody."

Bill, who looked to be about sixteen, said, "I ain't shooting no unarmed kid."

"You'll do it 'cause I said to."

"But I didn't sign up to kill no child."

"If you're my son, you'll do it. Shoot the boy first—I want the rest of them to see it."

The younger jayhawker hesitated. Suddenly the butt of his father's rifle slammed against his face, collapsing him as if he'd been shot. Blood gushed from an ugly wound on his cheekbone.

One of the other jayhawkers, stepping back out of range of the rifle butt, turned to the older man, "William, you're a hard man. Young Bill here ain't as stone-hearted as you—*at least not yet.*" Pointing to the younger man, he continued, "But you're determined to make him that hard."

The older man's eyes blazed as he leveled his gun at the third one. "I might just hafta kill you too. I'm disgusted with the whole lot of you. Give me their money."

Each robber dutifully handed their loot over to the big man. The fellow in the green shirt gave a wad, but Unk noticed he didn't retrieve the money from his boot.

William, the big jayhawker, then tossed the musket at his son's feet, saying, "I want them killed. You do it—or shoot yourself!"

Still cussing, the older man walked toward the woods, whistled loudly, and shouted, "Bring my horse, Slick." A fifth man appeared from the trees holding the jayhawkers' horses. William walked over, saddled up, and spurred his horse southward, never looking back.

Bill didn't touch the gun but stood up, unholstering his own pistol. The other jayhawkers still had us covered, so running wasn't an option.

Cocking the pistol, he said, "Give me six feet." I knew it was the space he wanted to shoot clearly and keep our blood from splattering him.

The hesitant look in Bill's eyes made me think he might shoot himself, but he pointed the pistol right at my dad's heart. Hesitating, he looked away to see if his father was out of sight. Seeing that he was, he re-aimed the pistol.

He fired in four quick evenly spaced bursts. I'm not sure when I closed my eyes, but I never expected to open them again. However, the only thing that hit me was a falling pine limb, clipped off by one of the slugs.

Bill quickly followed these with two more shots—a total of six shots fired into the pine trees above us.

He never took his eyes off us. Holstering his empty pistol, he picked up the rifle, walked to his horse, mounted up and rode away. The other two robbers, guns still drawn, slowly backed away, got on their horses, and followed the others. They'd tied our horses and mule together, and we watched as they trotted along behind.

We stood there in shock. I felt a strange mixture of emotions—we'd been so close to death, but I'd never felt more alive than at this moment. Even though we'd lost everything—our horses, weapons, cash, and supplies; we had the only thing that mattered—our lives.

Finally, Unk said to my father, "Joe, I told you that boy of yours was meant to be on this trip. He saved our lives when he stepped outta the woods."

Daddy never said a word. It seemed his mind was a million miles away. It was near dark now, but there was no way we were going to stay anywhere near here.

Picking up the few supplies and gear scattered on the ground, we began walking northward. Ben spied a sack of coffee and a smaller one of tobacco, evidently dropped by the robbers. "Well, at least we'll have some luxuries on the ride—I mean walk—

home."

No one laughed at this attempt at humor, and not another word was spoken. We cautiously crept along, afraid any noise behind us might be the returning jayhawkers.

Chapter 28

WITHOUT food, mounts, money, and—most importantly—weapons, we needed help. We were about eighty miles from Ten Mile. That would be a mighty long walk on an empty stomach.

We walked all night along the Military Road. With daylight, we stopped to assess our predicament. Caleb Johnson suggested that we veer west to the Redbone settlement at Bearhead. Folks there were distant kin, and he felt they'd help us. The only other option was walking on, and since that didn't appeal to any of us, we detoured west toward Bearhead Creek.

As we walked, Caleb explained about his kin there. "Years ago, most of our people coming west stopped and settled at Ten Mile, while others headed west to settle along Bearhead Creek."

He pointed down the muddy trail, "Because of the distance and poor roads, there's not been a lot of contact between our group and the Bearhead settlement. I have a great uncle, Smokey Johnson, that we'll try to find. I've never met him, but I believe we'll be welcome under his roof."

Caleb rode out front and seemed to take the lead on this part of our journey. Each mile found him more talkative and even animated. He especially enjoyed talking to me, and I learned a lot about him that day.

However, my daddy became much quieter. He had a bruise the size of a hen's egg above his left eye. What bothered me the most was the look *in* his eyes. His soul had been bruised by what happened yesterday.

I tried to comfort him, but he finally said, "Just be quiet."

I knew to obey.

Trudging along, we passed several homes. The folks there

greeted us suspiciously, offered no help, and were more than
happy for us to move on after giving directions toward Bearhead.

The first Redbone house we stopped at was a typical dogtrot
house with a mud chimney. The man of the house came out,
musket in hand, eyeing us carefully. I could understand it, as we
were a pretty sorry looking hangdog group.

Caleb explained our predicament, ending with, "I'm looking
for my great uncle, Smokey Johnson."

The man lowered his gun. "Any kin of Smokey's is welcome
here. Come on in." Then he stopped and studied my daddy,
before turning to Caleb. "What about this one—he ain't one of
us."

"He's an Irishman who married into our Ten Mile clan. That's
his son right there."

The fellow looked from Daddy to me and back again before
saying to me, "Boy, you don't look Irish."

Unk stepped up, pointed at my daddy, and said, "Fellow,
you better let him in too, or his boy'll put a stump-tail moccasin
through yer window."

The man looked puzzled, and Caleb said, "It's a family joke.
I'll explain later."

We were invited inside the home. The man's name was
Ashworth, and he introduced his wife Alice and their three
children. They listened closely to our story of the float and
our bad luck since then, shaking their heads in wonder at our
adventures.

We insisted on sleeping in the barn, and Mr. Ashworth
finally relented only after putting down fresh hay and supplying
blankets.

The next morning they sent us on our way after a fine country
breakfast. Thanking them from our hearts, we told them we
wouldn't forget their kindness. We had nothing, and that's when
you most appreciate the kindness of strangers. I learned that
someone who helps you when you have nothing to give in return
is truly a friend.

Mr. Ashworth sketched us a map of the trail to Smokey

Johnson's homestead explaining that it was about five miles away. With the map in hand, Caleb led us westward. We were actually moving away from home, instead of closer, but we badly needed supplies and help.

Our arrival at the Johnson home was initially met with skepticism. A woman came out on the porch and initially said, "Ain't no Smokey Johnson living here."

Caleb tried to explain our situation as well as how they were kin, but the woman seemed unmoved. Then the door eased open and an old bent man came out. He was dressed in faded overalls and a straw hat. Watching us closely, he spat a brown stream of tobacco on the ground as he leaned against the porch railing. It was clear he wasn't coming closer.

"What you boys want?"

"Are you Smokey Johnson?" Caleb asked.

The old man spat again. "I'm what's left of him."

I laughed at this and felt Daddy's elbow dig into my ribs.

Caleb said, "I'm your great nephew. My grandpa, Wallis Johnson, was your older brother."

"My brother Wallis was one day older than dirt. He ain't still alive, is he?"

"No sir. Been dead for years."

Smokey Johnson hobbled off the porch and got up in Caleb's face, studying him as if he was a statue or painting. Then he walked all 'round him like you'd inspect a heifer at you're buying.

"Well, you're dark enough to be a Johnson, but I don't know for sure."

Caleb had an ace in the hole card that he chose to play now. "Only a Johnson would know about the reason our family got run out of Carrollton County, Georgia."

Smokey Johnson drew back his fist. "Whoa now. That's enough on th—" but then he stopped. "Son, if you know *that*, you gotta be kin. Tell me what you heard."

I leaned in, ready to learn something about the Johnson family's secrets. However, Caleb carefully whispered it in the old man's ear. I watched Smokey's eyebrows arch and a grin spread across his face. He then whispered into Caleb's ear, and they both laughed loudly. The older man slapped Caleb on the back, before saying, "Welcome cousin. You and your friends are welcome under my roof."

We were treated like long lost relatives, which is what Caleb was. Smokey sent for all of his grown children and their families, and by mid-afternoon a family reunion broke out. We were forced to repeat every step of our float, Lake Charles visit, and the robbery to every arriving family.

My daddy was a special guest with his Irish brogue and fair skin. Most of these folks who lived in this isolated area had never talked with an immigrant. Daddy said he stuck out like 'a red-headed stepchild,' but the Bearhead folks loved him, saying, "Jes keep talking Mister Fellow. We like the way you talk."

The children especially were fascinated with Daddy, and several never got out of his sight the entire visit. I watched a group of five follow him to the outdoor toilet, waiting patiently until he came out.

As we settled down for the night on the floor of the Johnson cabin, I crawled over by Caleb. "Tell me why y'all got run out of Georgia."

This quiet man looked at me. "Now if I tell you, Mayo—"

He never finished because Unk, lying beside me, completed it. "He'd hafta kill you."

I dropped hints the rest of the trip, but knew no more about the secret than I did at the beginning.

The next day, the Johnson clan began gathering things we'd need for the last leg of our journey. They rounded up some horses and saddles, found several old weapons, and gathered food as we made plans for leaving the next day.

That afternoon, a group of Confederate soldiers galloped up to the Johnson homestead. I'd never seen soldiers before and ran out on the porch for a good look.

They were a scruffy looking crew, but I watched their every move. Their leader, a captain from Orange, Texas, said, "Day 'fore yesterday we cornered a group of jayhawkers that'd been robbing

and killing in this area. We'd been hunting them for weeks
and finally got them cornered over on Beckwith Creek. It was
a helluva fight, but we caught them and had a quick trial," He
winked, "and then hung them all and left them a swinging."

He turned to Smokey Johnson. "Sir, one of our men was
wounded in the battle, and we'd appreciate y'all putting us up for
the night."

As they helped the wounded man into the house, the settlers
asked a lot of questions about the war and local happenings. From
the soldier's descriptions of the men they'd hung, we knew they
were our jayhawkers.

Daddy asked, "How many men were there?"

"We hung four of them."

One of the local men asked the soldiers about the exact
location of the battle and subsequent hanging, then said, "That's
about a ten-mile ride. I believe I'm gonna go over there and take
a look for myself." He turned to our group, "Do any of you fellas
wanna go?"

Daddy was the first to reply, "I need to see for myself." As if
he was talking to himself, he repeated, "I just need to see with my
own two eyes."

"Can I go, too?" I asked.

"No, Son. You've seen too much already . . . " Then he
stopped. "No, I take that back. You *have* seen too much, but a
boy needs to see what the end of fellas like them is."

We left with a group of eight men, including Ben and Unk. I
rode doubled up with my daddy. Most of the others were in high
form as if they were going to the circus or a revival meeting, but
Daddy hardly said a word the entire ride over.

My thoughts were about the younger jayhawker, Bill. I'd be
real glad to see his dad swinging from an oak, but the younger
man had spared our lives. The idea of seeing this young man
hanging filled me with dread, and I considered asking Daddy to
let me off the horse so I could walk back.

Before I could ask, we'd arrived. We knew it because of the
buzzards circling and then the stench of death that greeted us as

we came to Beckwith Creek. Hoof prints were everywhere as well as bloody patches on the ground—all evidence of the ferocious battle that had taken place.

The only movement now was the quiet swinging of four bodies hanging grotesquely from a nearby red oak. As we dismounted and walked over, the men who had earlier been so jovial became quiet. The presence of violent death, even when so well deserved, was sobering. We shooed off the buzzards before venturing as close as the smell would allow.

The first one was the redheaded Jayhawker who'd kept his gun on us during the exchange between Bill and his father. Limp hands that hung at his side would never grip a gun again.

Next to him was the fellow who'd rifled our gear. His green shirt was now soaked in dried blood, and I wondered if he'd died from gunshot wounds or hanging.

Unk walked to him and pulled off the man's right boot. The wad of money fell to the ground. Picking it up, he stuffed it in his pocket before saying, "What goes 'round—comes 'round."

The third body was the one I wanted to see—it was the big jayhawker, William. Death had frozen his face for eternity in the same sneer he'd had at the robbery. He'd died just like he lived.

He had several bullet wounds, and I envisioned the shootout that'd led to their capture and his death. It seemed ironic that he'd planned to kill us, but now we were looking at him hanging there dead.

Unk poked his body with a stick and as it swung around, said, "He lived with that hateful look on his face, and he died with it, too. Seems fittin', don't it."

Blowflies were buzzing around, and the stench was terrible. Unk dropped his stick, put his hand over his face, and backed away.

Daddy slowly rubbed the deep bruise on his forehead as he studied the dead man hanging there.

The fourth body faced away from us, slowly swaying in the wind. It appeared to be young Bill. Daddy touched it and the body twisted around.

It wasn't Bill.

"Where's the one they called Bill?" I asked.

"I don't know, but that sure ain't him," Daddy said.

"It sure ain't."

He looked around as if he was searching for another body dangling nearby, but there was none. The only sound was the blowflies, and the only movement came from the impatient buzzards flapping their wings in a nearby tree.

The other men had seen *and* smelled enough and quickly returned to their horses. They weren't treating it like a circus now. The sight of these violent deaths cast a sober pall over the entire group.

Daddy and I stood looking at this fourth dead man. He wasn't Bill—but there was something familiar about him. I studied his bloated face, trying to visualize where I'd seen it before.

As the body twisted around, I saw something—a long jagged scar running the length of his arm. On the next turn of the body, I saw that he was missing the lobe of his ear.

"It's Silas Merkle," I whispered to Daddy.

Gripping my shoulder, he said, "Quiet, Boy."

We stood there for a long time. As I studied his face, it was frozen in the same sneer I'd seen the day I caught him stealing our bacon. Looking at his pursed lips, I remembered his words as he roughed me up. "What are you gonna do now, kid?"

Daddy looked at me puzzledly as I whispered, "You had it coming, Mister."

I knew there was something he wanted to say as he backed away. It took him a while to express it in words and his green eyes had a mixture of fire and sadness. Nodding toward the hanging tree, he said, "It's real simple—you live by the sword, you die by the sword."

Then he walked away, leaving me wondering—was he referring to the bad man William, our former neighbor Silas Merkle, or all of them?

I wasn't sure then, and I'm still not sure.

Before leaving, we looked around for any sign of our gear,

money, or horses, but there was nothing. I've always wondered what happened to it all. Riding away, I took one glance back at the tree thinking our stuff sure didn't help those fellows hanging from the tree near Beckwith Creek.

Daddy was right. They'd lived by the sword, and they'd died by it.

Chapter 29

AS we left Beckwith Creek and headed back to Bearhead, I sat behind Daddy in the saddle of the horse he rode. The other riders were far ahead enough for me to ask, "That was Mr. Merkle, wasn't it?"

"It was."

"I knew it from the ear and that scar on his arm."

"It was him all right. I hate that you seen what you did, but it'll be a reminder of what happens to folks who don't walk the straight and narrow."

"Will we tell Mrs. Merkle what we saw?"

"We won't tell anyone, son."

"Not even, Momma?"

"Nope."

"Why not?"

"What good would telling her do?"

I thought about that and had no answer.

"Mayo, it would only give her a burden to bear. That's why we'll keep it to ourselves."

"Did the other fellows recognize Mr. Merkle?"

"No, they never got close enough to see."

"That ear gave him away."

Daddy agreed. "That bit-off ear was hard to miss, wasn't it?" He smiled weakly. It was the first smile I'd seen since the robbery.

"But won't holding the truth back be lying?" I asked.

He silently thought for a while. As he did, I relived seeing Silas and Sarah Merkle taking the food and bacon from our house. I'd never yet told anyone and wondered if this was the time to come clean. It'd bothered me that I'd been sinning by not being truthful with my parents about what I'd seen.

I'd asked the Lord to forgive me, but I wasn't sure. Maybe this was the time to tell him, but before I could, he said, "Son, when some things happen, it don't do no one any good to mention it. It won't help Mrs. Merkle one bit knowing her man came to a bad end hanging from a rope. Maybe she fancies him riding back up one day. No use destroying hope in her heart."

"But she might be glad he's dead and not coming back."

"Might be, but love's a strange thing, and hope rides along with love. Her man may be deader than last year's bird nest, but we won't kill her hope that he ain't.

"And it won't do a bit of good telling your momma either."

My thought on telling him about the Merkle theft was, *I may tell him about the thieving later, but it ain't gonna be now.*

"I'm ready to drink some cold water out of Ten Mile." He said, "Are you?"

"Yes sir. I been ready." I wanted to encourage Daddy, so I said, "I don't want you being too hard on yourself about the jayhawkers jumping us. It wasn't your fault."

"It was. I should've had us staying more alert. All I did for our group was be a 'Judas Goat.'"

"A what?"

"A Judas Goat. In our Irish sheep culture, it was always a tough day when we'd take sheep to the slaughterhouse. That was one of the main reasons we raised them, but you couldn't help but feel a little attached.

"Most slaughterhouses kept what was commonly called a 'Judas Goat.' The goat was trained to lead the sheep up the ramp into the slaughterhouse. It was something to see that old goat trudging along with ten or twenty baaing sheep behind him. He was leading them right to their deaths, betraying them—a Judas Goat."

He sighed. "That's just what I did for our group: led them right into a death trap."

His pain was obvious, and I didn't know what to say.

"Well, Daddy we made it out alive, and are a lot wiser for it."

"You're right there." With that said, we rode on in silence. I don't know what he was thinking, but I could just imagine that goat doing one job every day of his life: leading those sheep into the killing room at the slaughterhouse.

Our group reached Bearhead at dark. Our visit to the hanging spot delayed our departure for a half day, but it was the closure we Ten-Milers needed to spur us homeward.

We began loading our donated things that night. We had about a fifty-mile ride ahead and were ready to pull out the next morning.

At supper Daddy asked the question that was on my mind too. Leaning over by the Confederate captain, he asked, "Was there a fifth man among those jayhawkers?" The captain laid his spoon down, eying my daddy.

"No, I don't remember one." He turned to the other soldiers. "Boys, we didn't see no one else with those four jayhawkers did we?"

They all agreed that there were only four.

The captain asked, "Why would there be a fifth one?"

"There were four that robbed us, but a fifth one was in the distance holding their horses."

"What'd he look like?"

Daddy glanced my way before answering, "I don't know. He was too far off to see."

The captain made the final word on this subject as he spooned up more potatoes. "I'm sure there were this four."

After the meal, Daddy was busy getting our borrowed horses ready. After finishing, he spent most of the evening talking with the Confederate soldiers. When I ambled over to listen, he shooed me away.

We got up early the next morning and told our new friends goodbye. Smokey Johnson and his family had supplied our every need. We had three horses plus everything we needed to get home. We promised to return the horses and weapons later on. Smokey insisted we not worry about it and refused everything we offered. "I done told *the wife* that we gonna come see y'all. We'll get the horses then."

I asked Daddy, "Why'd he call her 'the wife?'"

"That's just the way they talk."

The soldiers stood on the porch and shook each of our hands. I saw the captain and Daddy engaged in a long conversation in the front yard and wondered what was going on.

As the rest of the men loaded the gear, I watched Unk sneak into the house. I quietly followed and saw him go to the kitchen table, take the lid off the sugar bowl, and put his wad of dollar bills in.

Turning to see me, he put his finger to his lips and walked by me. "Keep that between me and you. If you tell anybody—"

I finished it for him, "You'll have to kill me."

He poked me in the ribs and stepped off the porch.

We started toward home. I was some kind of homesick, and my feet were hurting bad due to several bad blisters. The men took turns riding the horses, but I walked. I finally took my shoes off and went barefooted for the rest of the trip, being extra careful watching for snakes and sharp sticks.

Daddy quoted the 'Irish Walking Prayer' that included this line, "Lord, I'll put them down, if you'll pick them up." It was a prayer I repeated often over those long miles.

About the second day of walking barefooted was when I got a bad case of the ground itch. The soles of my feet were swollen and the itching between my toes was driving me crazy. Unk took a good look that night, saying, "It's not ground itch. It's the 'dew itch.'" This started a comical argument between him and Ben over this diagnosis.

Ben went off in the woods and came back with a handful of sassafras root. He boiled the roots in a pot, and poured me a big cup of sassafras tea. Then he had me soak my feet in the leftover pot juice.

As we sat there, I was finally able to learn more about Ben

Tyler's encounter with the timber people. I asked, "Mr. Ben, ain't nobody in my family been willing to tell about y'all's feud and how it ended."

"Let me ask your dad about it later. If he's all right with it, I'll tell you tonight."

After supper, Ben told Daddy, "Your boy is 'bout driving me crazy about the shooting. Should I tell him?"

"Well, he's shown he's a man, and his legs are long enough. Tell him."

So Ben began, "Mayo, it all started about twenty years ago between my family—the Tylers—and my wife Bessie's family, the Wilsons. Best as I remember, it began over a stolen pig. It's silly how a big fight can start over something so small.

"Clem Wilson, Bessie's older brother supposedly stole one of our woods hogs. When we were at the next church meeting, Clem and my daddy exchanged harsh words, and a fight broke out."

"Right there at church?" I asked as Unk poured more hot water into the pot. I jerked my feet out of the scalding water.

Ben continued, "Yes sir—right on the front steps. From there the trouble spread like wildfire. The Wilson's pine knot pile burned one night followed by our barn burning two nights later. Then a couple of our cows got poisoned.

"The hatred between our families burst into a raging fire that looked to engulf both families. One night during a thunderstorm, one of the Wilson boys' home burned to the ground."

"Did someone in your family do it?"

"As far as I know, they didn't. I believe it was lightning, but passions were so heated that any misfortune on one family was blamed on the other.

"If it'd kept on, somebody would've gotten killed, but that's when the incident on the creek happened."

I shifted on the log. "What incident?"

"The fight at the creek. Your momma's never told you?"

"No sir, she hasn't."

"Well, she was there when the shooting took place."

Ben continued. "As I said, it was just a matter of time 'fore someone got kilt. One day I was deer hunting near Cherry Winche and heard screaming, I ran toward the sound and came upon a chilling sight.

"A big fellow had a knife to the throat of Bessie. Her best friend, Eliza Clark—your momma—was standing there with a stick, ready to fight the man. It was evident the man had bad intentions for both women. Your momma was acting real brave, telling the man to let Bessie go and take her. That's when I hollered out."

"What'd you say?"

"I told the man we had him covered and for him to put down the knife."

"What did you mean *we?*"

"I made him think there were several of us surrounding him. I kind of throwed my voice and made it sound like a conversation."

"Ben, show the boy how you throw your voice," Daddy said.

"Oh, I can't do it as good as I once could."

"Go ahead. Show him."

Finally, Ben Tyler obliged. Cupping his hands, he hooted like an owl and at first it seemed to come from where he sat, but the second hoot came from behind me.

I twisted on my log to look behind me. "Well, I'll be."

Ben grinned and continued. "The fellow had the knife right against Bessie's throat. As he heard the 'voices,' he kept turning in a circle using Bessie as a shield. I waited and when he turned his back, shifting Bessie to the side, I shot.

"They both fell to the ground and Bessie had blood all over her. I thought I'd shot her too, but all of the blood was his'n—I'd shot him clean through the shoulder and he was bleeding like a stuck hog.

"He was one of those timber company bad guys. It was the last time he ever bothered any of our women folk."

"You kilt him?"

"No, I just winged him real good. He got up, holding his shoulder and cussing to beat the band. He left out of there heading for his side of the Calcasieu, and we ain't seen him since."

I could hardly believe this quiet man's story, but Daddy said, "Every word's true. Your momma was there. That day the Tyler-Wilson feud ended, and the romance began between Ben here and Bessie."

Ben grinned. "She'd always had a shine toward me, and I'd always wanted her."

Later, I asked Daddy about the feud and he said, "I've always heard a Ten-Mile feud can only end in one of two ways: one family finally gets enough and moves away, or if an outside force or trouble comes in, it pulls everyone together, and they forget their differences.

"That's kind of what has happened since the storm—people have been so busy trying to survive and help each other out that lots of feuds and pettiness have been forgotten."

I had one more question. "Why have they kept this so quiet over the years?"

"It's real simple. If the law in Alexandria got aholt of this, they'd never believe a Redbone's word over a man from their side of the river—so the less said the better."

"You mean they'd believe a bad man's word over one of our people?"

"That's exactly what I mean. We're looked at different by the outside world. You saw it for yourself in Lake Charles, didn't you?"

He was right. I'd experienced it firsthand.

On our third day out from Bearhead, we stayed at a campground along Hickory Creek.

We built a fire and enjoyed a fine meal from the supplies given us by our Bearhead friends. We were nearing home, and the dark mood of our group lifted some.

Darkness around a campfire loosens up the tongue just like liquor, and when it was just Daddy and I, I'd made up my mind to tell about the Merkle theft. I watched the fire and thought, *when it dies down a little more, I'll tell him.*

Just then, he did a strange thing—he picked up a handful of ashes and tossed them into the wind, and we watched them scatter into the darkness.

Then—out of the blue—he said, "My mind's made up. I'm going."

I wasn't even sure what he was talking about.

"Yep, I'm going—I've got to go."

"Going to what?"

He seemed not to have heard my question. The look on his face—the set of his jaw—even the way he stood—told me what words couldn't.

"I've made up my mind to go off to the war."

I stood up. "Not off to that, Daddy. You *can't* go."

"Yes, I can, and I will."

"Please."

"Son, I ain't going off half-cocked on this. I've thought about it a spell."

Hot tears welled in my eyes. "What made you decide to go?" I couldn't even bear to say the word—'war.' It was like if I didn't say it, it didn't exist.

He looked at me as if he'd not even known I was there—or listening, so I repeated, "I mean what made you decide to go—to go to the war?"

"*Those men.*"

I chewed on that for a moment. "You mean the soldiers?"

"No."

"Then what. . . ."

He interrupted, "The men who ambushed us—them jayhawkers. For me to stay back in my cave at Ten Mile while bad men like that ride about killing and robbing is something I can't bear."

"But Daddy, those men had nothing to do with the war."

"You're wrong. They had *everything* to do with the war. Times like these are what turn bad men like that loose."

I knew better than to say more—it was a time for listening.
Inside, a curious mixture of sadness and anger welled up and
came out as tears. As they rolled down my cheeks, he said,

"My mind's made up. I'm going to join the war."

"But—but what will Momma say?"

He looked up the trail as if he could already feel her
opposition. Nodding his head in that direction, he added, "I
guess we'll just have to walk that part of the trail when we come
to it.

"I could just lay back here in the woods and let it pass on by. I
wish it was that simple, but it ain't."

That was the end of that night's conversation.

Something else started that night and it didn't end, a steady
rain that accompanied us the rest of our trip home. How
appropriate it seemed to walk in the rain and ankle-deep mud—
this kind of summed up the whole trip.

Our mood was somber and silent as we slowly picked our
way, coming to Bundick Creek, one of the larger streams between
us and home. It was rain-swollen and out of its banks where the
Military Road forded it. We backtracked to a nearby farm just
south of the crossing where a family allowed us to stay in their
barn.

The husband was off at war but the woman and her children
showed us kindness. One of the older boys in the family named
Willie, brought us a pan of cornbread, a jar of molasses, and a
jug of fresh milk. We'd built a fire near the barn entrance. He sat
down with us and filled us in on the area.

"We could've got y'all across in a boat tomorrow if you didn't
have horses. As it is, it may take two—three days for the creek to
go down."

Daddy scowled. "We ain't got time to wait that long. Any
other option?"

"Well, you may want to go downstream about five, six miles
to another crossing near Dry Creek."

We were soaked to the bone, and Unk spoke up for all of us.
"I'd like to go anyplace that's *dry*."

So the next morning, we started southward. Willie walked with us for the first couple of miles. He knew the area well, keeping up a steady conversation. "Now when you get to the Dry Creek crossing, you'll follow the narrow road north. Before you reach Sugartown, you'll have to cross the Whiskey Chitto. It's pretty wide, but Harper Crossing is a good place to ford, even in high water. From there, you'll hit the Military Road again, skirt around Sugartown before crossing Sugar Creek, Six Mile, and Ten Mile."

Bidding us goodbye, he headed back home. It'd started raining again, so we trudged on. Reaching the ford, we found Bundick still out of its banks, but the wide plain allowed the water to spread out, resulting in a slower current.

The rain continued in torrents. Unk, water dripping off his hat, said, "I don't see no dry creek here. I believe we'll call it "Wet Creek."

We stripped down, tying our clothes in bundles to the horses. Holding the reins, we swam over. Ben, who didn't swim, was terrified, but Daddy stayed near him, talking him over as he clung to one of the horses.

That was the first of many crossings that day. We crossed a series of unnamed streams before coming to the Whiskey Chitto River. Evidently, there hadn't been as much rain in its drainage area, so the water wasn't as high. In late afternoon we decided to spend the night on the near bank, hoping the river would fall during the night. We set up our tarp and spent a miserable night as the rain blew in all night, soaking us completely.

As we tried to drift off to sleep, I said, "Daddy, I'm ready to see Westport Hill."

He turned in the darkness. "Me, too."

The next morning, we rose early and forded the river. We were getting pretty good at it now; we'd had plenty of practice. Even Ben seemed to lose some of his fear of the water.

I counted that we'd forded eleven good-sized streams since leaving Lake Charles, not including numerous smaller branches and creeks.

We soon were back on the Military Road, but it looked more like a river than a road as each step was made in gumbo mud and standing water. We bypassed Sugartown with only one place on our mind: home. Every step, muddy or not, brought us closer to Ten Mile.

We forded Six Mile and then Ten Mile. I asked about the origin of the creeks' names and Ben said, "From Sugartown, it's six miles to the first creek and ten to the second, so they're Six Mile and Ten Mile Creeks."

Coming to Ten Mile Creek brought out the reality of the situation: our trip had been without profit. Measured by that, it hadn't been a success. Instead, it'd been a dismal failure. That would be hard to explain to our families, and that fact weighed heavily on each man as we silently walked along the last miles on the creek trail toward our homes. All of the work: cutting and dragging the trees, building the rafts, the float, it'd all come to naught.

I knew I'd have a lot of explaining to a mad woman—my momma. I was glad I'd come, but knew there was still a price to be paid for my unannounced absence.

But the heaviest weight was what I knew lay ahead. Every clop of the horse's hooves seemed to say, "War—goin' to war—war."

Whether a cannon would ever fire in Ten Mile or not, the war had come to us. It was taking my daddy away.

Each creek crossing was a reminder that we couldn't ever go back to the way our lives were before the storm, and in my heart, I knew more storms awaited us.

The war, at least for my family, had arrived in No Man's Land.

Chapter 30

JUNE 1863

As we came up the last hill before our house, Daddy said, "Well, Son—you still glad you went?"

I waited before answering. The trip had been a total bust. We'd lost our money, most of our supplies, and nearly our lives, but my answer was sure. "Yes sir, I'm glad I went."

He looked at me and I couldn't figure if his look was pride, puzzlement or both. Regardless, I'd answered honestly, adding, "I'm glad. In fact, I ain't never felt more alive than right now."

"How's that?"

"The trip may have gone bad, but I learned a lot from it."

He grimaced. "So, did I. Yep, so did I." Then he pointed toward the house. "But when your momma gets through with you, you may not be so glad you went."

He wrinkled his eyebrows and nodded down the trail. "I wouldn't be too surprised if she ain't broke your plate and burnt your mattress. You may have to move in with Miz Girlie Perkins."

"Aw, come on. She won't be that mad at me. Besides, I got me a little speech prepared that'll cool her off."

He shook his head. "Son, you're fixin' to find out it ain't easy cooling off a mad Redbone woman. We've been gone nearly two weeks and she's been storing it up for you. The dam's gonna bust when she sees you."

He was right. Everyone was glad to see us back, but my mother was some kind of mad. Even while Colleen was hugging Daddy and she was holding Patrick, she let me have it.

I'd expected it and took it. She'd saved up two weeks of anger that she poured out on my head. I felt sorry for Daddy because he received his fair share of it, too. Although he protested that he had no knowledge of my plan to go, she seemed to think he should've.

When she finally started cooling down, and he told her about our adventures, especially the part about the jayhawkers and how I'd stepped forward and saved their lives, she softened somewhat. But she cornered me and said, "*Mayo Joseph Moore*, promise me you won't go off like that no more. Do—you—understand?"

"Yes ma'am." When she used all three of my names, I knew to answer quickly and crisply.

"I wanna hear the promise from your mouth while I look into your lyin' eyes."

"Momma, you know I won't lie to you."

"Then promise me you won't go off like that again."

"I promise I won't do nothing like that—uh, *without* at least warning you."

I thought she was going to put Patrick down and chase me. I felt bad that I'd worried her, but didn't regret going one bit.

Then I made a big mistake by reciting my rehearsed speech I'd prepared on the walk home. "Momma, it's just like when Jesus got left at the temple at age twelve. He was taking care of his father's business. I was just helping Daddy—and everyone agrees I saved his life."

Her reaction proved my approach was the wrong one. She handed Patrick to Colleen, grabbed the brush broom and came after me. "And I'll show you just how mad *his* momma was when she found him *three days later*."

I went running out the door as her broom loudly swatted my behind.

Daddy was right ahead of me running for cover, too. I ran out of broom-shot to the barn and joined him there.

"She was mad, wasn't she?"

"Your momma was mad, but not as mad as I thought she'd be. I saved your hide by telling her all of the helpful things you did on the trip."

"I don't believe my comparison to Jesus' getting left at the temple was a good idea."

"It didn't go over real well."

"Daddy, I've always wondered about why the Bible don't say nothing about Jesus from age twelve till he's a grown man."

"Me, too." He thought for a second. "Maybe, he was still in hot water over that disappearing for three days."

"Could be. Anyway, thanks for saving my hide with Momma." I turned to him, "But I'm not sure I'll be able to save *your hide* when you tell her you're going off to the war."

"Lord help us." He winced.

"No, Lord help *you.*"

One trait of my daddy was that when he made us his mind, you could mail it to the bank. He could be stubborn to a fault and blamed it on being Irish. *Wherever* he got it, he got a full dose of stubbornness. He liked to call it "grit" but Momma always said, "That's just another word for ornery stubbornness."

He didn't waste any time telling Momma of his plans. They went for a walk on our second day home, and when they returned, I knew he'd broken the news. She was crying, and I could feel the tension as they came in the house.

In the coming weeks, a definite chill was in our home, and it was most evident between my parents. Momma couldn't believe he'd left on this trip completely against the war and come home determined to join it.

She grilled me about it and all I could say was, "Momma, it was our encounter with the jayhawkers that brought it on."

She would shake her head and start crying again. The storm was now inside our house, and hiding under the table wouldn't serve as any protection..

Four days after we arrived home, Pistol and Dan dragged in. Daddy went to see them and came back shaking his head. "They lost it all."

"I knew they would." I said.

"A fool and his money will soon be parted."

"Did they tell you what happened?"

"Pistol had a long complicated story about it all, but I believe Dan lost it gambling."

"All of it?"

"Yep, the logging money, the money he'd won, *and* their supplies."

"You mean they lost their supplies, too?"

"Yep, Son. Said he bet the supplies trying to win back his logging money."

"Can you believe that?"

"They looked pretty sad and worn out."

"Did they have any trouble with jayhawkers on the way home?"

"Pistol said they didn't have a bit of trouble on the way home—said they'd had enough trouble in Lake Charles to last the whole trip home, and if robbers had stopped them, he would of had to write them an I.O.U."

"Was this trip worth it?" I asked.

"We'll see."

He turned to me. "Was it worth it for you? That whipping and all of the work and trouble?"

"I'd do it again in a heartbeat."

"You *truly* are an Irishman in a Redbone body. You've got an Irish heart with a touch of gypsy to boot."

But the good humor between Daddy and me didn't last. Two days later, he and I finished milking in the barn, and he began showing me the things I'd need to take care of when he left.

I felt growing resentment at his leaving us while the excitement over our trip ebbed. "Daddy, it ain't fair for you to go off and fight in that stupid war—leaving us at the mercy of the world.. You've said it before that we ain't got no dog in that fight, and now you're gonna go off and leave us here."

Hot tears poured down my cheeks, and I actually pounded on his chest in my anger. I was out of control and couldn't help it.

He reacted calmly. "Son, I can't stay here and not do my duty—it's that simple. You don't want a coward for a father, do you?"

"I'd rather have a coward for a father alive, than a brave dead one. It's like I've heard you say, 'better to be a live dog than a dead lion..'"

He walked away, choosing not to answer.

I'd been waiting for this chance to unload and willing to pull out all of the stops on changing his mind. "You going off to the war ain't much different than what Silas Merkle did in leaving his family."

I saw him stiffen. I'd said too much, but I couldn't, and wouldn't, take it back.

"Son, don't you ever compare me to *that* man."

"I know just how those twins felt when their daddy left them." I knew I was fighting unfair, but I was desperate.

Daddy lunged toward me and grabbed me by the shirt. His words were sharp and spoken through clenched teeth. "Mayo, I'm a goin.' I don't expect you to *agree with it*, or even *understand it*, but you need to *accept it*. I told you on the trip that I was going to treat you like a man. With me gone, you're going to have to act like one.

"You can whimper about it or accept it. This won't work unless you put your hands on the plow and move ahead. It'll only work if you make it. Do you understand?"

I didn't—or wouldn't—say a word.

"Do you understand?"

I spit out the words angrily. "Yes—sir."

"I've made up my mind. When those jayhawkers held a gun on us, I realized what the world's like out there. I knew I must do my part, and I'm simply carrying out what I know I have to do— it's called duty. To sit back and do nothing is to let that badness creep in and affect all of us.

"It was the same thing back in my home country—outsiders came in and took our freedom. They took our land, and there ain't nothing worse than taking a man's land and his freedom."

He pointed at the woods. "These piney woods have become my land. I can't sit back and let nobody come in and take it and our way of life. I *must* go."

"But, Daddy, you going to that war is leaving us at the mercy of the world."

"I'm doing it for you—not against you."

"Well, I hate you for going."

I'd never talked to my father like this before. Normally, it would have meant a good whipping, but he didn't move a muscle, except to release his grip on my shirt. The hurt in his green eyes was painful to see, but he didn't say another word. He simply turned and walked off into the woods, leaving me to stand there feeling the worst I'd ever felt in my life.

Even though I'd expressed how I felt, I knew I 'd said too much. Speaking hurtful words are like leaving the barn gate open: once the cows are out, it's hard rounding them back up.

Chapter 31

SEVERAL weeks after our return, Unk showed up at our house with an empty tote sack, shovel, and a pickax. He called me to the side. "Mayo, I need your help. Come go with me."

"Where are we going?"

"Can't tell you."

We walked a long ways until we came to the Big Pasture, where I asked, "Unk, does this have anything to do with those coins?"

He hung his head. "I can't find where I buried the coins. I've been going around and digging with no luck."

"You mean, you've lost them?"

"Maybe."

He set the pickax down. "I move them from time to time to hide them from prying eyes, and now I done gone and hid them from myself."

"You don't have any idea?"

"I think they're in one of two places, but I can't remember which one."

We soon arrived at a spot in the pines that was one of the spots. It was easy to see due to the numerous holes and piles of dirt. I counted fourteen spots where he'd dug.

"Is this where they were?"

"I thought so, but I ain't found nothing."

He began pacing off steps from a nearby pine with a scraped spot on the trunk.

"Unk, did you mark that tree?"

"Yep, it's my landmark tree. I skint it with an ax." Pointing across the opening, he said, "See there's the other marked tree. The box should be 'tween 'em."

Most of the holes centered on the space between the trees.
"Come help me."

I took the shovel and began digging. He used his pick ax to probe the holes, hoping for the sound of metal on metal.

But hours of digging revealed nothing.

"Where's the other spot?"

"Not far."

We took our tools, walked to it. Like the previous place, all manner of holes had been dug.

"Do you think someone stole them?"

"I don't think so."

We began digging, once again to no avail.

"How many coins were left?"

"I'm not sure, but it was at least a double handful."

I grabbed the shovel and went back to digging. A double handful of gold coins was a king's ransom in our poor man's woods, and I thought about what we could do with that much money.

But two hours of digging and poking revealed nothing.

"Are you sure they were buried here?"

"I know at one time they were, but I just can't remember.... "

My frustration was mounting. "Come on, you've *got* to remember."

"Well, there might've been another spot."

So we went to another small clearing where he began mumbling and pacing off from several trees. "It might've been here."

"Are you sure?"

"No." We began digging anyway. Soon it looked liked a herd of piney woods rooters had been here. I sat wearily on a mound of dirt and said, 'I don't believe they're here."

"I'm 'fraid you're right. That's enough digging for today."

"Unk, were you in on a killing to get those coins?"

"*No.*"

I stared into his eyes, before saying, "But you told me—" I stopped before revealing his words from that night after the hot toddy.

"I mean I heard—"

He stopped me. "I only saw the man with the money get killed. He was robbed and stabbed by Amos Long right here in this pasture. The traveler had gold coins hidden in the bottom of two bags of corn, and Amos knew about it. When Amos kilt the fellow, he took the money.

"I was hiding in the bushes and followed him to where he hid it. That night I dug it up and moved it. It was blood money and Amos didn't deserve it."

"But you took it—and it belonged to someone else."

"You're right—and if I could've found out who, I'd gladly have returned it. I made a promise to the Lord to find the man's family and return the money, but never found out a thing.

"Anyway, I promised the Lord that if I didn't find the rightful owners, I'd wait a year before touching it."

"Why a year?"

"I don't know. It just felt like what I should do. I had your momma mark the date on her calendar and when a year had passed, I considered it ours."

Unk wasn't the sharpest ax on the woodpile but always had a solid reason for everything he did. I've always believed that was because of his pure heart.

"After a year, I began using those coins to help folks. Do you know Dallas?"

"Our horse?"

"That's him. He's the first thing I bought with the money— got him for your daddy when he was fresh in these woods.

"I've sure enjoyed helping folks these years." He stood among the holes we'd dug futilely. "But honestly, I'm kind of glad the coins are gone. They've been a heavy weight on my heart for nearly fifteen years."

"But they're not gone—you just can't find them."

"As far as I'm concerned, they're gone, and I'm glad."

"Unk, we *need* that money. There—there's so much good that could be done with it. I don't—."

He put his hand on my shoulder. "I'm through looking for them. They're gone. Let's go."

I couldn't believe it, but knew his mind was made up, and when a Ten Miler makes up his mind—be it good or bad—he seldom changes it.

Walking home, he had more to tell. "When I first stole—I mean got it, I buried it in a town ant colony among the ant hills. That was pretty smart, huh?"

"Sure was."

"I've moved them every once in a while. Your parents are the only folks who know about it, but now you do, too." He grinned. "Ordinarily, I'd have to kill you for knowing my secret, but since the money's gone, I'll let you live."

"What happened to Amos, the fellow who took the gold?"

"Well, Amos searched high and low for his money. He never suspected I took it. Later on, he had some trouble—it involved your pa—and after that, he left. We haven't heard from him since."

I shifted. "But I heard you got rid of him."

"Well, I guess you could say that. Preacher Willis and I made him an offer he couldn't refuse."

"What do you mean?"

"Let me just say this: there were three of us in the room when the offer was made. One—Preacher Willis is with the Lord; two—Amos is gone; and—only ol' stupid Unk knows the truth, and I ain't saying."

Approaching home, I realized my uncle had revealed all he was going to tell, but I still had one more question. "What were you going to do with the rest of the coins?"

"If I told you, I'd hafta kill you."

That was the last time he ever mentioned the coins. It seemed not to affect him one bit that they were lost. He was a man at peace with the world and seemed glad to be rid of the heavy responsibility that weighed on his heart.

But me—I couldn't forget the coins. I secretly continued looking for them every chance I had, knowing they were out there somewhere.

Part III

THE WAR

Chapter 32

FALL 1863

In the weeks leading up to Daddy leaving for the war,
conversation was often slight around our supper table. The cloud
of his leaving hung heavy over us. Only Patrick's happy babbling
and Colleen's endless questions, which only received curt answers
from my parents, broke the uneasy silence.

On most nights as I'd climb up to my bed in the rafters, sleep
wouldn't come. At night, with us children asleep, my parents
would talk in bed. They'd wait until they heard the soft sound of
our breathing, then talk or do the kind of things adults do.

I'd learned to mimic the sound of sleeping so they'd think I
was out. They'd discuss the day and events of their lives while I lay
there playing possum, taking in every word.

One night, I especially listened closely to the conversation,
because it was evident things were at a breaking point.

Momma spoke first, "Joe, if you go off and fight in that war,
you might not come back."

"I'll be back."

"I imagine every man that's ever marched off to war fully
intended on coming back, but many didn't."

"But honey, I know I will."

"One of my distant cousins, Wiley Gill, promised his family
he'd be back, and died during the siege at Port Hudson. Just
saying it don't make it so."

In the darkness I could hear them shifting around in bed. I
wondered whether they were embracing or pulling apart. Daddy
said, "I've made up my mind. I'm gonna go. I couldn't live with
myself or face our neighbors if I just stayed here.

"But we can't live without you while you're gone—and especially if you don't come back."

"I plan on coming back, and things will be fine here. Your family'll help look after things. I've talked to both your daddy and Unk, and they'll help out."

"But you'll be gone. I want *you* here."

"Honey, you'll know just what to do. You're a strong woman, and God'll take care of you. Besides, I have great faith in Mayo. He's ready to take care of the place while I'm gone. On our float trip and the walk home, I saw that he's got what it takes."

"But he's just thirteen."

"I know, but he's made of strong stuff, and when the chips are down, he'll come through.

Besides, this will help make a man out of him."

"But he's not ready to be a man. He's still a boy."

"He's sore at me right now—just like you—but I know I can depend on him."

"I'm sore at both of you!" There was a catch in her voice. "He went off on that wild goose chase with y'all, leaving me to worry myself skinny. Now, you're going off on your own wild goose chase—off to that stupid war."

"But, I'll be back."

I could hear the hurt rising in her voice. "Joe, there ain't a soldier in a fresh grave nowhere that didn't plan to come back home."

She began sobbing and the noise of the bed shifting and the ensuing silence told more than human words could say.

No one spoke for several minutes. Finally, Daddy said, "Well, my mind's made up. I'm going."

Momma didn't answer, the only sound being her soft sobbing. Their bed creaked as they turned away from each other. My heart ached as I wondered what the days and weeks ahead would mean for our family. It was the same feeling of dread on that night when the hurricane's winds beat against our house.

Once again, we were being attacked by a strong outside force. Once again, the strength of our home would be tested, not by an oak tree or wind, but by a war that seemed to be tearing our family apart from the inside.

No more words were spoken that night. Only the sounds of my brother and sister's breathing and the far-off honks of geese flying overhead filled my ears.

The other three occupants of the room—my parents and I— each lay there in deep thought. I'm not sure what their thoughts were, but over and over, I heard Daddy's words. *I know I can depend on him to take care of things.*

He evidently had much more confidence in me than I had in myself.

Chapter 33

THE coming weeks were busy. Daddy wanted to brand our new calves before he left, so we rounded them up with the help of PaPaw and his dogs.

One day, taking a break, I sat by PaPaw. "What's your thinking about Daddy going off?"

He stared at me. "And . . . why do you ask?"

"Because I want to know what you think."

"Mayo, a man's gotta do what he has to."

I mulled over his answer, not sure if this was a stamp of approval or simply resignation.

"If I wasn't too old, I'd go myself," he said.

"You would?"

"I'd go."

"Why?"

"I figure we'll either fight them off somewhere—or wait for 'em to come here. I'd go to keep 'em from coming here."

He pulled out a folded Confederate dollar from his pocket. "This dollar won't be worth ten cents a year from now. When the war is over—and it's drawing to a close—Southern money won't help us."

"You don't think we can still win this war?"

"Mayo, this war was over and lost a long time ago. Vicksburg's fallen, and the news from up north is all bad. It's a lost cause."

"Then tell Daddy not to go."

"That's not my job."

He waited for this reply to sink in. PaPaw knew I valued his words highly, so he was careful about what he said. He pulled out a twist of tobacco. Cutting off a plug, he began working on it.

After chewing it for a minute or so, he spat. "You know that's why he's going, don't you?"

"Why?"

"He's going—to protect you, Colleen, and Patrick—to protect all of us. He ain't abandoning you. He's going to protect you."

He sat on a nearby log. "Let me tell you a story. A few years ago, I was over near the Big Pasture the day after a woods fire. The fire must've been hot from how blackened the trunks were on the big pines. As I walked through the area, stumps were still smoking and the charred ground was still warm to the touch.

"I chanced upon an unforgettable sight. In a clearing lay a dead turkey hen, kilt in the fire. It surprised me, because I knew a turkey could fly away from a woods fire.

"So I went over for a look-see, poking the dead bird with my boot.

"Its feathers were scorched, but when I kicked its body over, there were several dead chicks underneath. But there was one more thing: a small chick, chirping weakly, had survived the fire.

"The hen protected her chicks by covering them as the fire swept through. She could've flown, but she didn't."

He shifted his chew around, adding, "That's some good tobacco you boys brought home." I still love the smell of tobacco, something I'll always associate with PaPaw.

"What'd you do about the baby chick?" I asked.

"I scooped it up and put it in my shirt pocket and brought it home. I still got it—it's that big tom I call 'Lucky'."

"That's a good name for him, ain't it?" I laughed.

"It sure is. Now, don't it amaze you how God put it in the heart of an animal to protect its young—even at the expense of its own life?" He paused, letting that question sink in, before reaching out and gently lifting up my chin.

Staring straight into my eyes, in a way I'll never forget, he said, "Son, your daddy's doing the same thing for you, Colleen, and baby Patrick. He's trying to cover you from the fire.

"One day you'll have family of your own, and gladly be willing to take on a fire, a storm, or a bullet for them, and then you'll understand about what your Daddy's doing.

"You'll realize one day—not now, but one day. I know you're mad at him for going off to the war, but in his own way he's trying to do for y'all what that ol' turkey did for her babies—protect them.

"Now you're going to have to be the man of the house with your daddy gone, but you can do it. You got good blood in you. You got the best of both of your parents in you."

As he turned to go, he added, "You'll do jes' fine."

A cold front moved through the next day, pushing with it large formations of southward flying geese.

Working in the field with PaPaw, I watched their low-flying vees come over as he said, "There ain't nothing more lonesome than the call of wild geese."

We stood together, hoes in our hands, watching and listening.

"Mayo, I ain't got no book learning, but I've studied geese all of my life. Watch that lead goose."

He pointed at the lead snow goose at the point of the vee.

"That lead one is cutting the wind for the rest of them. That's why they fly in that formation. It makes it easier for all of the ones behind. God gave them the instinct to fly that way.

"Sometimes the lead goose'll drop back and another one will move up to the point to replace the tired one."

We watched the flock until they were distant dots and their honking faded away, then returned to our hoeing.

It was probably ten minutes before PaPaw spoke again. "Son, your daddy's been the lead goose—out front making it easier for you and your family."

He watched me until he had my full attention. "And your daddy—the lead goose—is stepping out of the way for now. That means you got to step up and take the point."

He patted my shoulder. "And you'll do real good, 'cause you

got good blood in you."

He walked away, leaving me to watch the next flock of geese on my own. I watched until they disappeared into a low cloud, followed by the fading away of their honking.

Chapter 34

THAT night the north wind howled as the temperature dropped. Huddled under the covers, I listened to the steady sound of hundreds of geese passing overhead. My grandfather's words echoed in my heart just as loudly as the honking of the geese.

His two stories—the one about the lead goose as well as the turkey hen—each helped me come to grips—and peace—with my father's decision, and to realize more of what my role would be.

The cold morning made it difficult to get up. I wanted to stay in the warm bed under my heavy layers of quilts, but I climbed down my ladder and ran to the fireplace. Momma was at the stove. Colleen and Patrick were still asleep.

"Where's Daddy?"

"Outside in the barn."

I walked over beside my mother. "Your daddy—PaPaw—can tell a story, can't he?"

"He can. What'd he tell you now?"

"I can't tell you." I acted as if it was a secret, but my real reason was that I knew I'd be bawling if I tried to repeat it.

"Momma..."

"Yes?" She turned from her cooking.

"I'm . . . I'm gonna . . . I promise I'll take good care of you and this place while Daddy's gone."

She put her spoon down and hugged me. "I know you will. I know you will."

The hug embarrassed me, so I headed quickly to the barn. Nearing it, I heard Daddy's whistling.

Walking to the barn, I saw a wild goose in the adjacent rye

grass field. Seeing me, it tried to fly, but couldn't get off the ground.

I went into the barn to find Daddy. "Did you see that goose out there?"

"Been watching him all morning."

"Think we ought to shoot him?"

"No, son, let's leave him be. He's just tired."

"Is he hurt?"

"No, I don't think so—I just believe he's resting."

"That's something, ain't it?"

"It sure is. I believe it's an omen."

"What do you mean?"

"In Ireland, one of our beliefs was that a strange bird's arrival before a journey was a good omen. The bird should be taken as a sign that it was time to go, and the journey would be a safe one."

"Do you believe that?"

Staring out at the goose as it walked in the rye grass, he said, "I'm not sure I do, but I'm choosing to believe it today."

He nodded at the snow goose. "That's my bird, and when it leaves, so will I."

Our presence spooked the goose and it tried to take off, but couldn't muster the strength. I didn't know what to say. Daddy brought many of the old ways and superstitions from Ireland. There were plenty more odd beliefs among our Redbone culture, so I grew up on a mixture of both worlds. I'd never heard the "strange bird" story before, and wondered if he'd just made it up, but it was clear he believed it—at least for today.

And because he believed it, so would I.

"When do you think it'll leave?" I asked with a lump in my throat.

"Probably today. Maybe tomorrow."

He went into the house, leaving me alone at the barn. I ran my hands over the rough boards of its wall. Its coarse texture reminded me of how my soul felt right then.

As I rubbed my hand back and forth, a thin splinter lodged in my palm. As I yelled, the goose lifted its head in alarm. Walking toward it, I said, "You don't have to fear me, Mr. Goose, but I'm fearful of you. When you leave, my daddy's leaving with you."

Digging the splinter out with my knife, I wondered how a splinter in one's heart felt. I believe I knew, and there was no way a knife blade could dig out the pain.

Looking at the house, seeing the smoke curling from the chimney, I knew without going inside that Daddy was gathering his things to leave.

I stood in the cold for a long time, just studying that snow goose. Throughout the entire day's chores, I kept a watch on the goose. It'd gotten comfortable and was now waddling about, eating rye grass.

It was cold again that night. Several times I awoke to hear geese flying over. I slept much better than I had. It seemed I was coming to a peace about Daddy leaving. That didn't mean I liked it. Rather, it simply meant I'd reconciled myself to the fact and was now determined to make the best of it.

As soon as it was light, I ran outside. Just as I'd expected, the rye grass field was empty. The snow goose was gone.

That afternoon Daddy left for Hineston. He would walk from there to Alexandria to be sworn in, and go to some place called Camp Moore near Baton Rouge.

Our extended family walked with him up the Sugartown Road. Finally, they dropped back leaving just Momma, him, and us three children.

Momma, sobbing, said, "This here's far enough, kids." She kissed him a long time, before saying, "Joe, I love you. Be careful." He held Patrick in his arms, then knelt and hugged Colleen, who wouldn't let go of him. He shook my hand and said, "Take care of things, Son."

We turned to walk home, but I broke away, and ran to him. "Can I walk a little farther with you?" I knew it was selfish, but I wanted to be the last one to tell him goodbye.

He looked at me and then at my mother. "As long as you don't pull another Calcasieu River on us."

He smiled, and even Momma, through her tears, laughed, "Go ahead. Just don't go far."

There we were—on the same road I'd walked beside Uncle Eli. Now it was Daddy who was leaving.

He walked slowly as we talked about manly things, and he gave last-minute instructions about the farm. At the next crossroads, he stopped, looking into my eyes.

"I promise I'll be back."

"And I promise to take care of things until you do." I knelt in the dirt, arranging a pile of sticks, leaves, and gravel.

"Mayo, what are you doing?"

"Do you remember what you called a "patteran" at the Military Road crossroads? You said gypsies used them to send messages and find their way. Remember it?"

"Sure I do."

"I'm making one for you, so you'll know which way home is, in case you forget."

"I don't think I'll forget, but thanks anyway."

"This patteran will be waiting for you when you get back."

"Thanks, from one gypsy to another." He pulled me close, his arms around my shoulders. Hugging me, he repeated, "I won't forget my way back home, don't worry none about that."

Then he turned, walked away, and we were both left alone.

I knelt again, finishing the patteran as he disappeared over the hill on his way to Hineston, Alexandria, and the war that awaited him.

Then I got up and hurried home. There was plenty of work to be done.

Chapter 35

FOLKS that lived through the War Between the States still divide life into two segments, *before* the war and *after* the war.

In a way, this war was similar to our hurricane. Its influence so changed parts of our nation that we measured time "before and after the war."

Although the Civil War began up in the Carolinas in 1861, for me it began in the fall of 1863 when my daddy left home.

We remembered the times *before the war* as the good times, but that wasn't completely true. Times were hard back then, too.

It seemed as if our life had been a succession of storms for the last two years. First, the hurricane and now the second storm—that war—was swirling all around us. It'd brought hardship and death to families all across the South—and the North, too—for the last two-and-a-half years. Now, it was our turn in Ten Mile as other families in our area said goodbye to brothers, fathers, and sons.

As the Union army consolidated its hold on the Mississippi River and began inching their way westward across our state, the war became even more personal. The invaders were now in our land.

The war's destruction, at least not yet in our area, wasn't of buildings, trees, and land. It was a destruction of the heart—I guess you would say—the soul. We knew it was coming, but couldn't do one thing about it, and when it came, it affected every part of our lives.

The weeks and months after Daddy left us are still a blur to me. PaPaw and Unk were a great help around our place, but as time went on, they left more and more of the work to me.

I depended on both of them for their *words* of encouragement and guidance even more than their actual *work*. Each one's words helped me in different ways. PaPaw had a story for every situation and knew just what to say as well as how to impart wisdom.

Unk had the ability to make me laugh in any situation. He often said, "Anything you kin laugh at won't kill you." That must've been true because we laughed a lot during that tough time . . . and we didn't die.

From time to time, we'd get a short note from Uncle Eli. He didn't say much, but we read between the lines that the war was also going badly east of the Mississippi.

In addition, the gifts of nature kept me going. I've always believed that a man can stay healthy if he lives and works outside. It's good for the body as well as the mind.

Anytime the ground was wet that winter, I'd slip along the creek to shoot wood ducks. I'd learned to crawl up beside a large stand of pin oaks that towered over the creek. The sound of acorns dropping in the water was a clear reminder that this was prime duck territory.

One day in November, I carefully crawled to the creek bank, pulling my gun alongside me. I saw ripples in the water and knew I was in luck. Easing my gun up from my prone position, I waited until two male wood ducks swam into view together. I fired and about ten ducks jumped off the water. The two I'd seen lay dead on the water.

Thinking of how pleased Momma would be, I began going down the creek bank to retrieve supper. Before I could get there, one of the ducks seemed to be swimming off. I was sure it was dead so its movement startled me.

Then I realized the duck was in the mouth of an otter, and that otter was making half of *our* supper *its* supper. I started reloading the shotgun with powder and shot, but long before I was ready, the otter was gone.

When I got home and told Momma the story, she said, "Well, you supplied supper for two families tonight—ours and the otter's." She and Colleen thought it was real funny.

"I'm going tomorrow and kill that otter."

Momma looked at me sternly. "Now, why would you wanna do that? The otter was just doing what comes naturally. I wouldn't kill no animal over that."

Chewing on the last of the roasted duck, I said, "But it shouldn't have stolen my duck."

The next day my attitude toward the otter had softened somewhat. Colleen wanted to see the otter so I agreed to take her fishing there, knowing there'd be no wood ducks there because of my noisy visit the day before. Gathering our fishing gear, I said to her, "Now don't get your hopes up too much on catching any fish. Look at the cows."

"What do cows have to do with fishing?"

"MaMaw always says that if they're lying down in the daytime, the fish won't bite."

"Why's that?"

"I have no earthly idea."

As we neared the creek, I reminded her, "Now be quiet, Sister, or we won't see the otter."

"I'll try."

After about fifteen minutes of waiting, I saw the otter climb out of the water onto a fallen log. Its rich, brown fur gleamed in the sunlight. It was soon followed by another, smaller otter.

"Mayo, which one got your duck?" Colleen whispered.

"The fatter one, I'm sure."

She giggled and I elbowed her, "Shh."

I noticed how the otters held their heads high out of the water as they swam, using their thick tails as paddles. Everything about their movements was graceful and sleek.

Colleen whispered, "Why do they keep their heads so high out of the water?"

"If their whiskers get wet, they'll drown."

She eyed me seriously, before I grinned at her gullibility. "They're fun to watch, aren't they?"

"They sure are."

The otters climbed onto a mudslide on the creek's far bank, and then the fun began. One after another, they repeatedly slid

231

into the creek with a splash.

We weren't doing any fishing because it was too much fun watching the playfulness of the otters. Then Colleen saw something else and pointed. "What's that?" Easing low, up to the mudslide was a lean, dark-yellow animal.

"It's a bobcat."

I jumped up, grabbed a pine knot, and tossed it at the bobcat. The otters, now alerted to our presence, dove off the bank and under water. The bobcat darted off, its stubby-tailed rump high in the air.

I followed the bubbles in the water as the otters swam upstream, but never saw them resurface. They were gone.

"Was that bobcat going to kill them?" she asked.

"Yep, he was going to have an otter sandwich for lunch."

"I saved them, didn't I?"

I hugged her. "You sure did, Sister. I'm glad you saw it."

When we arrived home from our fishing trip, Colleen told Momma all about the otters. I saw my sister's eyes light up as she described them.

"Colleen, you've got to take me down to see those otters. I've always loved watching them. It was one of my and your daddy's favorite—." She stopped in mid-sentence.

"It was—*it is*—one of my favorite things to do with your daddy—and until he gets back, you'll have to be my otter-watching partner."

There was hope in her voice, but something about how she caught herself in mid-sentence bothered me.

Chapter 36

I DON'T know why country people have always loved scaring their children, but I've heard they do it in every tribe in the world.

I grew up in two cultures—my father's Irish upbringing filled him with stories from his homeland. Momma's Redbone roots gave her a whole different collection of stories and proverbs.

However, one thing both of them liked was to scare kids. I don't understand it, but it was—and is still—part of both cultures.

My parents had taken turns with these nighttime stories. I believe they had a running competition as to who could scare us the most.

Daddy had entertained us with stories of the gypsies, banshees, goblins, and the "little people" of Ireland. These imps, similar to elves, were the source of everything bad that happened to Irishmen. They stole children, gave people the evil eye, and spread all kinds of mischief among the homes and villages. When Daddy crossed the Atlantic from Ireland, he brought the "little people" with him and relished scaring us with stories about them.

I'm surprised I'm brave enough to go outside at night or sleep in the dark as a result of the stories he told. When he left for the war, we missed his stories. Colleen would often say, "I'll be glad when Daddy comes home. I miss his stories."

"I miss everything about him, honey," Momma answered. "But I'm the head storyteller until he gets back." Making sure Patrick was tucked in, she'd crawled up in bed with Colleen for the night's story.

I thought I was too big now for stories, but I still listened in, carefully pretending as if I wasn't interested.

Colleen's favorite story was about the Hobyahs. Here's how Momma'd tell it:

"Once deep in the swamp there lived an old man, his wife, and their tiny daughter."

"What was her name?" my sister would ask.

"Why, if I remember right, it was Colleen."

Also much deeper in the swamp—lived the Hobyahs."

"What'd they look like?"

"Well, they were little green monsters with big red eyes."

"It sounds like how Daddy described those little people to me," I said.

She thumped me. "This is my story. You be quiet now." Then she stared at me. "I thought you were too big for these stories?"

"I am. I'm just trying to keep you straight."

She continued. "Anyway, the Hobyahs would come creeping up each night to the house saying, 'Tear down the house. Tie up the old man. Tie up the old woman, and we'll take the little girl.'"

Colleen's eyes widened, and she'd slide further underneath the quilt. Momma smiled, "But Little Dog Turpie, who belonged to the family, heard the Hobyahs creeping up, and barked and barked and barked, and the Hobyahs ran back to the swamp."

There were numerous variations to the story that Momma would add or change each time. On this night, as the story ended, I barked like a dog. Colleen screamed, "It's the Hobyahs."

Momma put her arm around my sister. "No, it can't be, 'cause Little Dog Turpie ran them away years ago, and they've never been back."

My sister asked, "Can the Hobyahs bother us?"

"No way, this house is protected from them."

"What about those little people?"

"They can't bother us either—they're way across the ocean."

Colleen had one more question. "Are there Hobyahs where Daddy is?"

"No way, Little Dog Turpie ran them way further than that. And besides, Hobyahs don't like the noise of guns."

"I sure miss Daddy."

"So do I. He told me to kiss you every night, so here it is."
She kissed my sister's forehead. "Good night."

We each went to bed to our own dreams—of Colleen's
hobyahs, little people, dogs, family, and the swamps. However,
my dreams were not filled with any of those. I dreamed about
guns firing and wondered where my daddy was tonight.

Chapter 37

IF the hurricane was our first storm and the war our second, the third "storm" that came into our lives was even more personal. To our family, it was also the most destructive.

My brother Patrick, now a year and a half old, got a bad cough, or as Momma called it, the "croup." He caught it right after Christmas, and it hung on through the first of the new year.

Folks today don't understand how serious a baby's sickness was in those days. Momma sat with him and tried the medicines we had as well as several folk remedies to try to get him better.

Patrick didn't get better. Instead, he became much worse.

Then seemingly as quickly as he'd come a year and half ago, he was gone. It was the saddest moment of my life when I came in from chores and Momma quietly said, "Your brother's dead."

I followed her to the bed where he lay. She picked him up, tears flowing down her cheeks. I couldn't believe it and went over to touch him—I then knew it was true.

I wish I could tell you more about that time, but my heart is still too tender, even decades later. I've very seldom talked about it at all. The death of my brother Patrick still weighs heavily on my soul, and just repeating Momma's words, "Your brother's dead," brings tears to my eyes.

After saying those haunting words, she sent me to get help. I ran toward Bessie Tyler's house and got about halfway when I met Bessie carrying a basket on the way to our house.

"Patrick's dead."

The words nearly clung to the top of my mouth as I repeated, "Patrick just died."

"Please, God, no!" She didn't say another word, but dropped her basket, and ran on. I cut through a nearby field on the way to tell my grandparents.

It's still hard for me to talk about the events surrounding my brother's death. It was the darkest time of my life. I cursed silently, wishing Daddy were home. I didn't believe he could've saved Patrick's life, but his presence would have comforted us. If he'd been home, we'd have been a family and handled this dark time together, but he wasn't home.

The rest of that day was busy as we laid out my brother's body at the house for burial. Funerals and burials in those days were quick, so the next morning we went to Oakland Cemetery. PaPaw made a small wooden coffin and placed my brother in it.

We didn't have a preacher then at Occupy Church, so the preacher from Amiable came over to lead the service. It was short and sad. There's only so much that can be said about the death of a child. Standing at the grave of my little brother, Momma, Colleen and I got lots of hugs, and people said all kinds of nice things as they passed by.

They were the kind of things we'd been hearing since the day before—the usual words people say at times like this. I was so broken up that I couldn't even look up, but still recognized most of the voices.

"Now, Eliza, you can't question God. Don't question Him. Just 'cept it as His will."

I heard a cough and a voice whisper behind me, "Bull crap."

The next mourner hugged Momma. "Eliza, God just needed another flower for his bouquet, so he took Patrick."

I heard the cough again and felt an elbow in my back. "Sack of crap." I didn't have to turn to know who it was—it could only be Miz Girlie Perkins.

On the third or fourth cough, she leaned down and whispered, "My soul Son, don't pay no mind to all of that. They mean well, but their theology's way off. We'll talk later."

The stand-in preacher prayed again, and after his "amen," the only sound now was crying. I stood by Momma as she sobbed, but I had no tears. As badly as I wanted to cry, I just couldn't. Everyone else seemed to be crying, and here I was—Patrick's older brother—standing dry-eyed. I needed to weep and felt as if I would explode if I didn't.

PaPaw, tears streaming down his cheeks, nailed the coffin shut, and the men lowered it into the ground.

Watching all of these proceedings, I remembered our visit here a year and half before, right after the storm. It was the very day that Momma went into labor and Patrick was born. So much had happened since that day and most all of it seemed bad.

Then PaPaw stepped forward, picked up a handful of red dirt, and pitched it into the deep hole before saying, "Patrick was a shootin' star. Jes' a shooting star that shone brightly and was gone way too fast."

With that said, he and the other men began covering the grave of my little brother. I watched as the red shovelfuls of dirt covered his final resting place.

I was the last to leave the graveyard. Turning, I went to the cedar tree and broke off a twig. It was the same size as the one Momma grasped on our visit here after the storm.

I recalled her words that day, "The cedar leaves represent eternal life . . . a reminder that this is not the end." I softly laid the cedar twig on the heaped dirt of my brother Patrick's grave, and said, "Goodbye. I'll see you later."

The thing about the death of a child is how it blankets a family with deep grief and a sadness that won't go away. I'd never seen my mother so sad—no one could comfort her. My grandparents stayed with us, trying to keep our place running, but there was a pall of grief in the house that could be felt.

We wrote a letter telling Daddy about Patrick, sending it by a neighbor who was going to the Sugartown Post Office. As I carried it to their house, I turned it over and over in my hand. I wondering how long it'd be before he got it, and how he would handle the news of his youngest son's death, especially so far from home.

I felt sorry for him. At least we'd had the benefit of sharing our grief. In spite of this, I was still mad at him. He should have been here, and he wasn't. I have to admit something else: I was mad at God. I felt as if both of my fathers—my earthly father as well as my heavenly one—had let me down.

One of the things that helped me get through this time was how much work had to be done. Caring for the cows, working the garden, and other chores don't wait because of death or sickness, and being busy was good. PaPaw was right there to help, as was Unk.

The day after Patrick's burial, I helped PaPaw work on a rail fence damaged from a fallen tree. Colleen worked beside us, trying to be helpful.

"Mayo, did you see the stars last night?" PaPaw asked.

"No."

"It was a shootin'-star night. It's been like that for the past three nights."

We worked on silently, with my thoughts on his words at the graveside.

"I'm coming to get you tonight. We're gonna build a friendship fire and watch those fallin' stars."

After supper as darkness fell, PaPaw built a good fire out past the garden. Grabbing an old blanket, he led Colleen and me to the fire.

"PaPaw, why'd you call it a 'friendship fire'?" Colleen asked.

"Because it's a fine place for friends to gather and talk about their cares."

"But, you're not my friend. You're my grandpa."

He laughed. "Yep, I am, but I'm also your friend."

We lay back on the blanket, warmed by the crackling fire, and watched the star-lit sky as day faded away and our eyes adjusted to the darkness.

The fire began to die out, leaving the night around us even blacker. It was a perfect star-watching night.

The three of us lay there staring into the heavens.

"It makes you think of God, don't it?" Colleen asked.

"Everything makes me think of God, Colleen," PaPaw said.

I didn't say a word. My mind was heavy with that burden of sorrow as I lay there dry-eyed.

Then the first shooting star rocketed across the sky and was soon followed by another. Every few minutes another one would speed across the sky. Some were bright and left a trail as they burned out, while others were so faint and fast they were visible for only a second.

"Children, your little brother's up there with God."

"I know it," Colleen said.

"And even though his life was short, it was beautiful. Just like a shootin' star."

"Just like a shootin' star, PaPaw."

My sister drifted off to sleep as we lay there.

"Mayo, you're sure not saying much."

"Ain't much to say."

"But your heart's full, ain't it."

"It sure is." I looked at him, and he was propped up on one elbow looking at me. Feeling as if he was reading my mind, I looked away.

"What's bothering you the most about losing your brother?"

"The fact that I couldn't cry."

"You *couldn't*—or you *can't?*"

"Both. I feel as dry as that dead pine straw under the trees. I want to cry, but ain't got no tears. When Bo died, I cried for days afterwards, and now I can't even cry over the death of my own brother. It's bothering the fire out of me."

We lay silently watching as the periodic falling stars lit up the night. Then PaPaw said, "Son, tears don't always mean sorrow. There's a fellow I grew up with that could turn them on when he needed 'em. If he got caught in a lie—which happened often—

he'd cry something awful. My momma called them 'crocodile tears.'

"Just because you haven't cried don't mean you ain't sorrowful. Them tears will come in time. Just give them time. They'll come."

He looked closely at me before asking, "You're not going to give up on God, are you?"

I looked away—this question was too direct and personal, but grandpas can get away with that. "PaPaw, I ain't concerned about giving up on God. I'm just worried that he's given up on me."

"Now, Mayo," he said in a kind but challenging way, but I wasn't through yet.

"I just feel like God's a million miles away and has forgotten about us."

He let what I'd said soak in, not hurrying his reply.

"I wish I had the words to heal your heart, but I don't. You and the Lord will have to work it out together. And you will." We both lay stretched out under the stars, a wise man and a struggling boy.

The night air cooled and the dew wet the ground, so he picked up Colleen as I folded the blanket. Walking back to the house, he said, "Why don't you build your own friendship fire out here the next couple of nights—just you and the good Lord. I believe out here under these stars is where you'll get some of your questions answered, as well as find those lost tears."

He looked up into the heavens as he said this; we both saw a final shooting star flash across the dark sky.

While I couldn't cry, Momma seemed to cry enough for both of us. In spite of being surrounded by family and friends, she seemed daily to be sinking deeper into grief. One night at supper, still surrounded by my grandparents and her children, she dropped her spoon and said, " I feel like I died when my baby died."

MaMaw got up and put her arm around her. "Eliza, Baby."

"It's like a piece of my heart was cut out when my Patrick died."

"It's gonna be all right." MaMaw said.

"No, it ain't, Momma, it left a hole in my heart. It's an emptiness that I don't think'll ever be filled up." With that said, she left the table, hurrying outside.

I got up to go after her, but MaMaw grabbed my arm. "Leave her be. She'll just have to work out her grief. It takes time. Jes' takes time."

I sat at the table, staring at my food.

"Baby, why don't you help MaMaw clean up?" she asked.

I brought the plates to the wash pan and dumped them in. When I turned around, she was standing with a knife in her hand.

"Mayo, one time I was peeling potatoes with a knife just like this. It slipped and I sliced my hand bad. I couldn't believe I'd done something that stupid and just stared at the cut.

"What surprised me was how it didn't bleed. It was a long deep cut, but bloodless. Then all at once, it began bleeding. The cut took a while to get going, but once it did, it wouldn't stop."

She pulled me beside her, and motioned toward the door my sobbing mother had just slammed. "Your momma's cut is bleeding pretty bad, and you're wondering why yours isn't.

"Your tears'll come. Your heart's cut as deep as anyone's, but it ain't started bleeding yet; but it will."

I looked up into her dark face. "But MaMaw, I cried like a baby when my dog died, and now . . ."

She put her hand on my cheek. "But that was a different kind of cut—*completely* different. Your tears over Patrick will come, and then you won't be able to shut them off."

That night I built my friendship fire and sat by it well into the night. The feeling I had was one of great loss—first I'd lost Bo, then my father, now I'd lost my baby brother, and it seemed on this dark night as if I was also losing my mother.

A dark feeling of choking hopelessness came over me. It

seemed there was nothing I could do to fix my momma's sorrow, and the worst part of it was how helpless I felt.

But two things happened in my heart that night. I lost one thing while gaining another, and I still can't explain either one.

That night I lost my fear of the dark. I don't know how it happened, but it seemed to melt away. Then as I sat around the fire, the tears came, and as MaMaw promised, they didn't stop.

They wouldn't stop. In fact, they didn't stop for a long, long time.

Chapter 38

I'VE always liked cardinals, or as we called them, "redbirds," and their early-morning, happy singing.

However, in the days after my brother's death, it nearly made me mad to hear them singing. One day I picked up a clod of dirt and threw it at a singing redbird. "Shut up. Don't you know my brother died, and there ain't nothing good to sing about?"

The bird flew off, and I felt stupid and helpless over the anger inside me.

That same week the first purple martin scouts arrived. I just knew my mother's favorite birds would help her. I rushed in to tell her and found her still in bed, her face to the wall.

"Momma, your birds are here. There's two martins out there."

She finally acknowledged me. "That's good, Mayo. Maybe later, I'll come see them."

But she didn't. She had no interest in martins or seemingly in anything else. She was in a dark cave that none of us could pull her out of. When I'd go check on her, she'd just turn her back to me, and lie there silently.

For some reason, her deep sorrow made me angry at the martins. Like the redbirds, their joyful chatter and graceful acrobatics reminded me of how happy life *had* been in our house. I was beginning to wonder if they'd ever be like that again.

Miz Girlie Perkins came daily in the weeks after Patrick's death. She helped with the house chores and oversaw my outdoor work. She was a hard taskmaster, but I knew she meant it to be helpful. Just like the martin's singing, her presence irritated me. I just wanted to be left alone, but Miz Girlie wasn't going to allow that.

During these weeks, Momma continued to lie in bed most of

the day, refusing food and conversation. Miz Girlie Perkins, being a no-nonsense kind of person, would arrive and go right to work cleaning up the house. She didn't even ask Momma if she could help. She just went to work.

I closely observed this unique woods woman. She whistled as shrilly and loudly as any man in Ten Mile and was easy to locate by "Rock of Ages" or some other whistled hymn.

Before supper one day, she asked Momma, "Eliza, if you don't mind, I'd like to take Mayo home with me. I've got a day's worth of chores saved up for him."

Before I could protest that I was needed here, Momma weakly said, "Go ahead."

So, I dutifully walked home with Miz Girlie Perkins. Because she was so bluntly honest, I felt I could be the same with her.

"You're not taking me home to work. You just want to talk to me, don't you?"

She never took her eyes off the trail. "After I get through working you, you'll wish we'd just talked. I've got enough chores stored up to keep you busy for a week hand-running."

Then she winked. "I do need your advice on something."

I wondered why this old woman would need any advice from someone my age.

At her house, she didn't even invite me in. Instead, she pointed toward her greens patch. "Now, you git out there and go to hoeing. I need it clean."

When I finished with that job, she had her mule hooked up for me to plow. "I need to get this ground ready for some planting." I wasn't used to her mule, Jen, and the rows I plowed weren't real straight.

As Miz Girlie examined the plowing, she didn't say anything for a long time. Finally she commented, "Well, those rows ain't pretty, but I've always heard you can get more crop from a crooked row than a straight one." Winking at me, she continued, "We'll find out if that's true with your snaky rows."

She couldn't resist one more comment, "Were you following a drunken king snake when you made that last row?"

245

Finished with that poorly done job, I heard the words that any farmhand dreads. "Next, I need you to take this cart and fill it with barnyard. I want to put it on my Irish potato ground."

This old woman had saved every bad job she had just for me. She grinned each time I passed her with a cartful of smelly barnyard fertilizer.

"Don't use that fresh stuff. It'll burn the plants."

Unloading another load of manure, my thought was simple, *I'd like to burn your plants.*

It was evident she was trying to work me down, and I was determined not to show one ounce of fatigue. We had a battle of two strong wills, but by the end of the day, the only thing burnt was me—I was burnt out.

The only benefit of all of my hard work at her place was the cooking. She was known as the best cook in our woods, and I never pushed away from her table disappointed. After the day's work, I was now determined to "eat her down."

I ate several platefuls of ham, cornbread, cabbage, and greens. She kept dishing up more and I kept putting it away. As always, even supper soon became a battle of wills between her and me.

Finally, as she stood with another ladle full of cabbage, I waved her off. "Miz Girlie, I'm as full as the town dog." She winked at me, enjoying her second win of the day. Washing up the dishes, she whistled louder than ever. I was sure it was in celebration of her victory over me.

After cleaning up, she said, "Let's go sit and rock awhile."

It was always one of my favorite things, so, I mentally forgave her for trying to work me down and following it up with "death by cabbage." Our porch conversation was about the woods, farming, and the weather. I waited for her to start preaching to me about my brother's death, but she never brought it up.

The next morning, we started early with work, work, and more work. Late that afternoon, I was cutting stove wood when she came and sat on the rail fence. "That's enough for today. Let's take a little walk."

It was now time for our talk. "Son, you done heard lots of

words these last few weeks since Patrick died. Folks mean it nice and want to help, but they still will say some stupid things. Now, Miz Girlie ain't trying to run your life, but I don't want what they say warping your brain."

I stared straight ahead, but that didn't deter her speech.

"Have you ever heard the story of how I lost my man, George Perkins?"

"Momma's told me a little."

"Well, I'm going to tell you the whole story, so listen up. I got married young. George was eight years older than me. My soul, didn't we have a fine marriage."

The look on her face was softer than I'd ever seen, and suddenly she seemed much younger.

"Lord, didn't I love that man. He was a hard worker and good to me. The only problem was that we couldn't have no children. We tried and tried, but it wouldn't never happen."

"He worked in the woods and one day he didn't come home. Later, a group of men came, and I knew something bad had happened just from the way they walked up. They'd been cutting cypress trees in West Bay Swamp. One fell wrong, and crushed my man George. They said he was dead by the time the limbs quit shaking.

"So, all of a sudden I was alone. Being a widow in these woods without children is hard and lonely. I had to keep up this home place if I was going to survive. I was so sad, just like your Momma is. I had a big hole in my heart like hers.

"That was nearly fifty years ago when George left me, and a day don't go by that I don't think about him."

"Is that hole still in your heart, Miz Girlie?"

"Yep, that hole won't be completely healed till I get to the other side. The hole don't pain me like it did at first, but it's still there.

"During the first weeks after he died, a lot of anger flowed out of that hole. I asked God *why me*? He coulda made that tree fall another way and spared my man.

"Just like those people did about Patrick, folks told me *not* to question God, but I didn't listen to them—I did question him and took my anger and resentment right up to his feet.

"I've always been direct and up front with people, and that's how I chose to go to God. He didn't strike me down."

She turned toward me. "Come with me. I wanna show you something."

A cool breeze blew in the pines, and we soon came to a rough bench under a tall pine.

"This here's my prayer tree. It's my place to meet with God each day, and it was my old momma's place before that."

Patting the tree lovingly as one would an old friend, she continued. "When I first came out here, this prayer tree was a lot straighter and taller. It's kind of taken a lot of knocks over the years—kind of like me."

"How old is it?"

She looked up into its crown. "My soul, I reckon it's a couple of hundred years old. Momma said it was already a grown tree when she was a girl."

She motioned for me to sit beside her on the bench. "Anyway, this tree is where I brought my anger and questions to God after my man was kilt. During that time, it seemed as if I was so far from God, I needed to spell my name for him. Anyway, to be honest with you, I let him have it real good right here on this bench."

"And God didn't strike you dead?"

"Nope. I'm still here and so is the tree. I told God everything on my heart. I told him all about how unfair I thought he'd been to me. Well now—I told it *like it was*. I questioned 'why'?"

"Did you get an answer?"

"Not right then. But as the days passed, I seemed to hear the very voice of Jesus saying, 'I love you. I understand, and I'm on your side.'

"That voice wouldn't go away, and a sense of peace began filling my heart, pushing out that anger. I seemed to hear God say, 'You'll get your answers later, but they may have to wait until the other side.'"

"What other side?"

"Heaven." She scratched in the dirt with a stick. "I'm a lot closer to the other side now, and still don't have them answered completely, but I'm sure I will."

"So you don't think it's wrong to question God?"

"Heck, no. Jesus questioned his Father up on that cross. Listen to what he said, 'My God, My God, why hast thou forsaken me?'

"I don't read none, but those who do have told me there's a question mark at the end of that verse. My soul, if that ain't questioning God, I don't know what is. So, Mayo, take those things well-meaning folks say—and square them up against what the Bible actually says."

She stood signifying that our time at the prayer tree was over. "Now, I ain't no expert, but it seems simple to me—God's in charge, he knows what he's doing, and we gotta trust him."

I'd listened to every word, taking them all into my heart. "Miz Girlie, now I got one question."

"Shoot."

"Why do you say 'my soul' so much?"

She winked. "My soul, do I say that a lot?" She patted her dress down as we stood. "Baby, it's a saying my old momma used, and I been using it all my life. Miz Girlie's too old to change what she says or does."

Darkness slipped up on us, and we walked together out of the woods in the fading light. Miz Girlie grabbed my hand as we walked silently. Sometimes, there's a special bond between friends where words aren't needed.

The next day Miz Girlie sent me to gather pine kindling, saying, "A person can't never have too much pine piled up for the fireplace and cook stove."

My thought was this, you're just making up busy work for

me, but I hooked her mule, Gin, to the drag and headed out to the pines. Following behind us was Pete, Miz Girlie's faithful donkey. Everywhere Gin went, Pete always followed behind, tagging along like a pesky little brother.

Using the ax to splinter off the pine stumps and knots into carrying size, I piled the slip high and hauled two loads to the barn.

As I neared the barn with the third load, the mule, braying frantically, began running. Most of the pine slid off the drag as Gin sprinted away. I heard a noise behind me and looked to see what the problem was.

Trotting toward me was a big bull, and I immediately recognized Roscoe—no introduction needed. Gin flipped the now empty drag over in her hurry toward the barn, and I made tracks for the rail fence in front of the house.

Pete, braying loudly, was right on the mule's tail.

The bull was snorting and pawing as he closed the ground between the fence and me. I hurdled it and the bull came to a skidding stop, now turning his full attention on the mule.

Gin turned and bared her teeth at Roscoe, braying loudly. Pete was doing his best to stay behind the mule for protection.

Right then is when Gin, still pulling the empty drag, charged through the open gate and into the barn, with Roscoe lumbering along right on her heels. They quickly came out the other end scattering chickens, geese, as well as Miz Girlie's two barn cats.

This commotion brought Miz Girlie out on the porch, and I heard her holler, "My soul. It's that bad bull."

She disappeared back into the house, and before the door shut, her goat Fred pushed his way in, not wanting any part of this bull.

Miz Girlie returned, holding an old musket rifle. It had been the prize possession of her late husband and hung in honor above the fireplace. Gun in hand, she left the fence's protection, walking toward the barn right into the bull's path.

"Roscoe, you done made your last mistake leaving your stompin' grounds and coming on Miz Girlie's place." There was

defiance in her voice. "I don't care one bit that you're the bull of
these woods—you done come on the place of the bell cow."

Hearing her voice, Roscoe stopped tormenting Gin and
turned toward her.

I yelled, "Miz Girlie, get back."

But she continued forward, scolding him the whole time. If I
hadn't been so scared, it would've been funny. When Roscoe got
within about twenty feet, he stopped, pawing the ground. That
was his final mistake.

Quick as lightning, the rifle came up to her shoulder. Miz
Girlie, her feet set and her shooting eye down the barrel, fired.

The blast of the gun knocked her back, but that wasn't the
main sight—it was Roscoe, who weighed probably nearly a ton,
going down. Her head shot was perfectly placed and dropped the
bull instantly.

I waited before climbing over the barn fence for a closer
inspection. His front legs were quivering, but his days of
terrorizing the woods of No Man's Land were over, and the
woman who'd ended his life stood cradling her rifle.

Kneeling beside the bull and examining the hole between his
eyes, I whistled. "Miz Girlie, that was a good shot."

"He got what was coming to him."

"Yes ma'am, I guess he did."

"Yep, that bull of the woods got his comeuppance in the yard
of the bell cow." She was openly proud of herself.

"Miz Girlie, you *are* the bell cow of Ten Mile. Can't nobody
match you."

I shouldn't have done it, but couldn't resist. Nudging my
boot against the dead bull's nose, I whispered, "I told you from
that leaning tree that *I'd* get the last word in and *shoot you*, but I
was wrong. You got done in by an old woman—you oughta be
ashamed of yourself. An old woman kilt the baddest bull in all of
the woods."

I guess it was just the muscles twitching, but Roscoe jerked,
issuing one last grunt. I didn't stop running until I got to the
barn. Neither Roscoe nor I laughed, but Miz Girlie, still holding

her rifle, chuckled enough for all three of us.

She couldn't resist one last comment. She walked beside the fallen bull and said, "Babe, you were West Bay bred and West Bay fed, but now you're *Ten Mile dead*."

She motioned to me, "Stay right here till I get back." She went to the barn, returning shortly with a handsaw.

"Mayo, do you have a blowing horn?"

"No ma'am."

"Well, you're fixin' to, compliments of ol' Roscoe." Taking hold of one of the bull's horns, she sawed it off. The grating sound of the saw against solid bone made a chill run down my spine. Holding up the horn, she said, "This one's mine." She handed the saw to me. "If you want a cow horn, you'll have to cut your own, mister."

Well, I wanted a cow horn—especially one from Roscoe. It took me a while to cut off the other horn.

"You need some help, baby?" She asked in a syrupy voice intended to rile me.

"I ain't no baby, and I don't need no help."

When I finished, she took my horn, holding both of them aloft. Where a bad bull stood snorting twenty minutes ago, a dead one now lay. Walking by the bull, Miz Girlie gave her benediction, "My, how the mighty have fallen."

She was in high form and winked at me. "You've heard of taking the bull *by* the horns. We done took the horns *from* the bull."

The only trouble with killing a two-thousand-pound bull in your front yard is what to do with it.

I gave my idea first. "We could butcher it."

"Way too tough."

"We could just let the dogs eat it."

"Too much trouble. It'd take a month of Sundays for the dogs to finish him off."

"What about burning it?"

"Too close to the house. We'd never rid of the burning smell."

I shrugged my shoulders. "Well, if we leave him out here, it's going to smell pretty bad in a day or two."

She ignored me, instead unhooking the drag from Gin, and leading the mule over. Gin wanted nothing to do with Roscoe, dead or alive. Despite her kicking and braying, we tied her trace chains around the bull. However, even in Gin's frantic attempts to get away, the bull didn't budge one inch.

"That's a lot of dead weight to move," she said.

I laughed, knowing she didn't realize she'd used a pun. "Can we bury him?" I asked.

"We'd have to dig a big hole nearly to Chiner to get him in."

"Chiner?"

"Yep, Chiner—that country on the other side of the earth."

After studying our problem from several angles, she announced, "Oh, let's go in and eat. Maybe tomorrow he'll be gone."

But he was still there the next morning, right where he'd fallen. When I left for home the day after, Roscoe lay there like a small mountain, but it was a mountain that was growing—he'd swelled and gave off a terrible odor. I asked Miz Girlie what she was going to do, and she shrugged, "My soul, I don't rightly know."

I told Momma about it, and she made me repeat the whole story several times. For the first time since Patrick's death, I saw a slight smile crease her face.

The next day when PaPaw came by, I reenacted the bull shooting for him. He made me repeat over and over Miz Girlie's words, "Roscoe, this here's Miz Girlie's place and you may think you're the bull of these woods, but you done come on the place of the bell cow."

Each time, he hooted. One of his pastimes was picking on Miz Girlie, and he realized this episode would supply fodder for years to come.

He wanted to see it for himself, so I walked with him to her place. It'd been four days since the bull's death, and we saw buzzards circling near the house. The stench greeted us long before we reached the barn.

Miz Girlie, a bandana covering her mouth and nose, was coming up from the barn with a pail of milk. We met her at the porch and PaPaw began, "Girlie Girl, I'd thought you were an outlaw if I hadn't known better."

She pulled her mask down and said, "That bull's getting pretty ripe, ain't it?"

"It's past ripe, if you ask me," he answered.

She winked at me. "But, he won't be bothering us again, will he?"

Before I could answer, PaPaw waved his hand in front of his face. "Well, he's *still* bothering me a lot. That smell is *some* kind of bad."

He turned to her. "What are you gonna do about that bull?"

She pointed at the buzzards in the nearby trees. "My soul—I guess we'll let the buzzards pick him clean and bury what's left."

"You're gonna have a long time of wearing that rag over your face before that happens. I've got an idea—."

"Well, let's hear it."

"Let me see if Barney Bryant can help you out."

"How so?"

PaPaw scratched his head. "Let me talk to him first."

The next day Barney arrived with his team of oxen, followed by a small group of onlookers. Word had spread about the bull, and they'd come to see the show. I'd arrived early and was standing by Miz Girlie as she watched the approaching throng.

"If I'd known this was the circus, we'd charged admission and sold jerky." She said through clenched teeth.

"I don't believe you'd sell much jerky with that smell," I said, holding my nose.

Barney loved helping folks and was tickled to show off his team of oxen. As he backed the team up, he said, "Well, I've hauled a lot of things with my team, but never a dead bull."

He gave instructions, and ropes were tied around Roscoe. The oxen, leaning on each other, slowly began to drag the bull—at least most of it. It'd decayed enough that some of it was left in the original spot, as well as along the route the oxen dragged the bull.

Moving the bull only intensified the terrible odor, and most of the onlookers, holding their noses, sprinted away. Then, disturbing the body unleashed a storm of blowflies that settled over the remaining spectators and sent them scurrying.

I was standing by Miz Girlie as she whispered, "It just like that plague of flies in 'Moses' Egypt.'"

Finally, Roscoe—or what was left of him—was deposited past the garden at the edge of the woods. We set fire to the carcass by piling up dead limbs and pine knots. It burned all night, and the stench could be smelled all the way to her house.

When the fire petered out the next day, the buzzards, crows, and dogs took care of what was left. Miz Girlie said, "I won't never say a bad word about a buzzard again—they saved my sanity."

The coming years brought unusually good crops to Miz Girlie's garden. The tallest and thickest corn was always down the middle of the field—right where the bull had been dragged.

Miz Girlie called it "Roscoe's patch" and bragged about how that bull ended up being useful to her after all. I sat with my feet under her table for many a meal during those years, but it was a long time before I had the stomach to eat an ear of corn from that field.

Chapter 39

IT'S always odd how the Lord sends comfort in our grief to meet our need.

About a week after my encounter with the bull, I was working in our field and heard the deep baying of a hound. I stopped hoeing as the barking neared. Out of the woods, a short hound bounded toward me. I'm a sucker for any dog, and I knelt to pet it and got licked right in the face.

Looking around, I said, "Now who are you, and where'd you come from?"

It was a healthy looking dog and obviously not a stray. I also recognized the breed as a basset hound. We'd seen one in Lake Charles and all made fun of its long body, short legs, and floppy ears.

This same breed of dog I'd ridiculed was now licking my face. As it playfully climbed up on me, I said, "Hey, you're so ugly— you're plumb purty."

My backhanded compliment only made it lick my face more as I got a close up look into its droopy and sad eyes.

"How can you act so happy when you've got such sad eyes?"

The hound's tail was beating non-stop on the ground, but the eyes didn't change one bit. They were sad and red-rimmed as if he'd been crying.

"Hey, did you lose your little brother, too?"

Of course, there was no answer, but it just made me feel better to ask.

I realized how long it'd been since I talked to a dog—the night Bo died was the last time I'd had anything to do with any dog.

I set my hoe down. "What's your name, fella?"

It was then I was startled by a cow horn's blast at the wood's edge.

Standing, I called out, "Who's out there?"

Another blast was followed by laughter as Unk stepped from behind a tree.

"Whatta you think about that there dog?"

I scratched his ears and repeated, "He's so ugly, he's purty."

"And he's yours."

"Uncle Nathan."

"Yep, he's yours."

"Not really."

"Yes sir."

"Where'd you get 'im?"

"I stole him."

"Come on."

"I traded him."

"For what?"

"I can't say. If I tell you, I'll hafta kill you."

He pointed at the dog. "Looks like he'll trip over them ears if he runs fast."

"But I like him, anyway. You sure he's mine?"

"Sure enough, he's yours."

After Bo's death, I'd sworn not to have another dog, saying, "That was the best dog I'll ever have, and I ain't gonna try and replace him." I'd stuck by this even as family and neighbors tried to match me up with new dogs.

Miz Girlie wanted to give me a pup that was kin to Bo, but I sure didn't want a dog that would remind me of the one I'd lost.

However, this hound licking on my face, didn't remind me of Bo at all—it was completely different from any dog I'd ever had with its odd body and ridiculously long ears.

No one could have gotten away with this except my uncle. He knew the right time and the right dog. I told him, "You played dirty with me letting that dog just wander up and lick all over me. You know I have a weakness for dogs."

I decided to call him "Fella."

He was a special gift from God to comfort me in my sorrow and walk beside me in the rough days ahead. As Fella settled in at our place, he became everyone's favorite. This hound was quickly adopted by my mother—or maybe Fella adopted her. Regardless, Fella followed her everywhere, often sitting by the kitchen door waiting for a bone or any scraps.

On the many days when Momma wouldn't even get out of bed, Fella lay by the door whining. It was as if he'd appointed himself as her guardian.

She referred to him as "your dog," but it was clear we had dual ownership. One afternoon I watched as she peeled potatoes, talking with him. I believe the dog's sad but intelligent eyes were what bonded them together. It was as if this dog understood the sorrow in her heart.

Some people say they don't believe in miracles, but they're just not observant. Miracles occur all around us everyday, but we miss them. Miz Girlie always said it this way, "Most folks is too busy picking huckleberries to notice God all around them. They ain't payin' attention, so they miss the miracles."

As I watched Fella with Momma, I didn't know it then, but I was really watching a miracle—the miracle of a sorrowful woman's heart coming alive again—a miracle that seemingly featured one step backward for every step forward, but a real miracle nonetheless.

Chapter 40

THE spring after my brother's death was made even more difficult by the failure of our crops. We were in the midst of a long drought and watched most of our crops wither and die. This, and a shortage of everything due to the war, made life extra hard.

It was during this time that I came to realize the value of my basset hound, Fella. With him trailing, no rabbit was safe. Momma rationed gunpowder and shot each day. At first, I'd often miss and come home empty-handed, but soon I learned how to lead a rabbit, and began bringing home at least two most days. It helped feed us during these cold months. We survived that bitter winter, in part thanks to Fella's nose and my gun. However, we soon grew weary of eating rabbit. MaMaw said we ate enough rabbit that year that our ears grew longer and we started craving lettuce.

During warmer weather, we couldn't eat the rabbits due to their meat being infested with wolf worms, so instead I shot squirrels. Once again, I had a two- or three-shot limit, so I chose my shots carefully. Momma's people called squirrel meat, "limb bacon," and I kept us well supplied with it.

It was a hard time, made harder still by the ongoing sadness of my mother. Even on days she got out of bed, she wouldn't go outside. It was as if our cabin were her cave, and she planned to hibernate in it until the pain went away.

I wasn't sure her sadness was *ever* going away. It'd been several months since Patrick's death, and she didn't seem one bit better.

One afternoon I came in from chores, and she wasn't in the house. I asked Colleen, "Where's Momma?"

"She went outside." It scared me because I had a fear of her disappearing or hurting herself. I'd heard stories of folks deep in depression doing crazy things. I searched all over our place as well as the barn and outbuildings. I called for Fella, but he was nowhere to be seen either.

I knew that wherever my mother was, my dog was, too. We'd had a rain the day before, so I went down the road looking for tracks, but saw none. I went back, crossed the yard, and looked down the creek trail. I found footprints, and hurriedly followed them toward the creek.

Arriving there, a sight ahead stopped me in my tracks—it was Momma sitting on a log, with Fella beside her. I heard her crying but couldn't understand her words.

She was sitting at the place she always described as "where I come to meet God."

If she was meeting with God right then, she was sure giving him a piece of her mind. Her sobs were angry sobs—the cries of a person pouring out her soul. It hurt my ears—and my heart—to hear the anguished way she was wailing.

But I knew to leave her alone. I wanted to go sit by her and comfort her—this was my mother and she was in great pain—but knew she must face this part of the journey alone.

So I slipped behind a tree and watched as she rocked back and forth on the log. It was nearly dark when I eased back up the trail. I could still see her silhouette rocking back and forth, crying.

When she came in later, she didn't say much and went straight to bed. I listened as her breathing became soft and even. I thought that maybe the worst of this is over. Maybe she'd gotten it off her chest at the creek.

However, the next day she stayed in bed all day. My hopes of her improvement faded, and it was the worst day of all. I felt as if she'd lost her faith in God, and I could feel mine slipping, too.

However, two angels saved us during this time of need, and I'll tell you about them one at a time.

The first angel was Uncle Nathan. Unk became even dearer to our family during the war years, especially during those dark days after Patrick's death. He was mysterious in many ways—always coming and going, with folks never quite knowing what he was doing or where he'd been. I guess he was the closest thing to a gypsy we had in our woods.

He'd be gone a couple of weeks and then just show up again. When I'd ask him where he'd been, the tall tales would begin.

"I was off with the little people. They said to tell you they're coming for you tonight."

Or, "I been to New Orleans . . .," or "I been at the hoot owl singing convention."

However, as our food supplies ran low after the winter and the spring drought of 1864, he began arriving daily with food. I never knew where he got it, but he managed to scrape some up and bring it by.

As summer came around, he appeared everyday with okra. He'd planted a patch that survived the drought. If you know anything about okra, you know it is prolific—it needs cutting daily and will make pods until the first good frost.

From June until November, we ate okra most days. Unk said, "I've et so much boiled okra this year that I can't keep my socks up." Personally, I was never so glad to see a killing frost finally come and end the okra harvest. To this day, I don't eat it much, simply because of how much I ate during that lean year.

With winter, food continued to be in short supply, but Unk continued to take care of our needs. Whether it was a woods hog, ducks from the creek, a bag of flour, or corn meal, he always seemed to find a way to provide for us.

He taught me how to pick poke salad, a plant that grows wild in the open fields. A type of green, also called pokeweed, it can be cooked and eaten like turnip greens. Unk showed me where a large patch of it grew, and sang as we picked,

"Poke salad is my bread and butter.
I eat it every day,
If you don't wash your poke salad,
It'll send you to an early grave."

We filled two tote sacks with it and walked toward the house.

Unk told me, "That song's true. You got to carefully wash it three times before eating it."

"Why's that?"

"I don't rightly know—I've always heard it's got some kind of poison on it."

He winked. "My mother always said if you eat it after a frost, it'll molest you."

"What do you mean 'molest' you?"

"It'll make you *death-finitely* sick."

I started to correct him, but quickly thought better of it.

At the house, I drew well water as he skinned the leaves. We washed the poke salad repeatedly, and after cooking it, it wasn't half-bad. From that day on, I'd pick a mess of it a couple of times every week.

So in spite of the hard times, we scavenged around and found enough to eat. However, there was still a problem—my mother didn't and wouldn't eat much. She said even the smell of food made her sick and would often go sit on the porch during mealtime. Her weight continued to drop and it worried all of us.

I told you *two* angels saved us—the first being my uncle. The second angel came from an unusual place—the Merkle household . . . and that angel's name was Sarah Merkle.

The first day Mrs. Merkle showed up, I was surprised. She'd never been inside our house—other than the time she was stealing from us.

She stood there as out of sorts as I was. "I've come—I've come to see your momma. Is she here?"

"Yes'm." I led her into our house.

Momma was in bed. She sat up and tried to be friendly. "Come on in. You've never been inside my house, have you?"

The look on Sarah's face was a mixture of fear and embarrassment. She answered Momma, but her eyes were on me. "No, Eliza. I haven't, but I've always wanted to."

"Well, you're here now. Have a seat."

As she brushed by me she said, "Thank you, Mayo." I thought it was 'cause I was holding the door, but her look told me it was more than that.

Keeping "our secret" had won me a friend, and I knew I'd done the right thing not revealing the theft.

"Mayo, you go on out. Mrs. Merkle and I are gonna visit." As I left, I noticed Momma's sunken eyes and paleness changed as she welcomed this neighbor into our house.

It was the first of many visits from this strange woman. Colleen and I would be shooed out of the house, and even when I tried to listen through the front door, I couldn't make out their softly spoken conversations.

As these visits became daily, my mother would perk up when her new friend came, and I saw a change was also taking place in Sarah Merkle. It was the change that self-respect and being needed always brings to a person.

This was evidenced one day as she left. "Mayo, your mother's getting better, but remember it takes time to come out of the darkness."

I nodded.

"And your mother's helped me as much as I've helped her."

"You *have* helped her."

"Mayo, I've learned to like *giving* at this house much better than *taking*. I feel right better about myself."

"I'm glad you do."

"I'll always be obliged for you keeping that secret."

"It was the right thing to do."

"And I thank you."

That began a pattern of our visiting daily as she left our place. I'd walk with her part of the way home as Momma watched from the porch. Like me, Momma came to see a totally different woman from the person we'd all earlier misjudged.

One day, Sarah Merkle stopped me in the yard. "Mayo, I can't describe to you what losing a child does to a woman. You've got to continue to be patient with your mother."

"I will."

I saw her eyes moisten. "It's like *you die* when a baby you birthed dies. You saw it with your Momma, and I went through

263

the same thing. It puts your heart—your soul—into a darkness from which you feel you'll never escape.

"But it does get better. Now, I won't say the pain goes away, but it does get better as the light slowly returns. It happened with me—and now it's going on in your mother's heart. She's slowly returning to the light."

She put her hand on my shoulder before leaving. "Whenever we go through something ourselves, God wants us to pass it on to others who are hurting. That's what I'm doing—I'm just passing it on to your momma. And the more I pass it on, the more my own pain—not just losing my baby, but so much more—lessens."

She stopped and said, "Listen."

I heard crows in the distance and the ever-present arguing of blue jays in our orchard.

"Mayo, do you hear them?"

"Hear what?" Then I heard them—a pair of mourning doves whispering to each other over by the edge of the swamp. Over and over their lonely call echoed. I've always considered a dove's cooing one of the saddest sounds in the world.

"Hear those mourning doves?" She asked.

"Now I hear them."

"That's what your Momma and me are—two mourning doves. We've lost husbands and babies and understand each other."

I wanted to blurt out, *Momma's husband—my daddy—is coming back, but your man ain't.*

But I didn't; instead I said, "Thanks for helping. You're always welcome here."

With that she left, and I watched her disappear into the woods. I stood amazed at the transformation I saw in this woman who formerly seemed so hard, cold, and distant. I'd never heard her refer to God before, and today she talked of him as a close friend.

I turned toward the house and saw Momma standing in the doorway, watching her new friend leave. I knew then that healing was taking place in both of their hearts. Earlier, I'd complained about our misfortune in having the Merkle family settle near us, but I never said—nor thought it—again.

I silently thanked God that I'd kept *two* secrets—not just the thieving incident, but also the bad end of Silas Merkle, the husband of this woman who was rescuing my mother from her dark prison.

I'd never told a soul about Merkle swinging slowly from a rope near Bearhead. Waving at Momma, I wondered if Daddy told her about how Silas Merkle met his sad end. I don't believe he did 'cause Momma never mentioned it.

Returning to the barn, I heard only the sound of the mourning doves coupled with the soft singing of my mother as she swept the porch.

Chapter 41

I'M a believer that God is the ultimate healer and uses all kinds of ways for healing. With my mother's great love of the bird world, it shouldn't have surprised me how he used a loud mockingbird to help her.

Momma still had her good days and bad ones, and we never knew when we woke up which one it would be. I learned to cherish the good ones and tolerate the bad.

As I brought in a load of stove wood, she sat at the kitchen table. "Mayo, sit here a spell."

"Yes ma'am. How'd you sleep, Momma?"

"Terrible. I'm still having those bad nightmares that wake me up."

"I'm sorry."

"Last night when I'd been up an hour or so, I went out on the porch. It was black dark without any moon. As I sat there rocking, a mockingbird began singing. In spite of it being after midnight with everyone else asleep, it sang its heart out.

"God kind of spoke to me, reminding me that I can sing in the dark, too. I've sure wondered if He'd given up on me, but last night I realized he hadn't."

"That's good, Momma."

She pulled me over to her. "I know my being sick has been harder on you than anyone else, but we're gonna get through it. Do you believe that?"

"I sure hope so."

"You just hang in there. We'll lean on each other as we lean on the Lord."

Outside the room, that same mockingbird began singing its unique assortment of sounds, clicks, and calls.

Momma nodded. "See there. It's singing now in the sunlight, but last night it sang in the dark, too. That's what I'm trying to do."

She looked out the door and said, "Oh here comes my friend, Sarah, with her kids." Her face beamed and I thought *anything* that makes her happy, makes me happy, too—even if it's a visit from the entire Merkle clan.

One of the results of my mother and Sarah Merkle's blooming friendship was that I spent more time with the twins. While Colleen watched the young Merkle daughter, Tabitha, the boys and I were free to wander once I'd done my chores.

It'd gotten where I could tolerate the twins. They were some kind of bad, but funny as all get out, and extremely curious about everything.

On one visit, Festus said, "I'm sorry about your brother. I know how it feels."

"You do?" I asked.

"Remember how we lost our baby when we were passing through."

"I remember."

Festus spoke up. "It still hurts to think about it, don't it Felix?"

Felix wouldn't answer his brother, but nodded painfully.

Festus continued, "We also know how it feels to lose your daddy."

I shot back. "I ain't lost my daddy!"

"Neither have we," he said.

I started to say more, but didn't.

When the Merkle twins visited, my job was to keep them from tearing up our house and yard. Momma said, "Take those boys off somewhere in the woods or something. Keep 'em away from the house and barn. I believe they could tear up a new wagon with a piece of switch grass."

On their previous visit, they'd broken two plates, messed up the bucket in our well, and rode down a young redbud tree Momma had planted. Her pre-visit instructions to me were clear.

"Take 'em to the wilderness where they can't do so much harm."

I knew my marching orders and dutifully met them at the gate with a welcome. "Hey guys, let's go fishing."

Their mother dismissed them happily with, "You boys, do what Mayo tells you to do and watch out for snakes."

The last warning was timely because both brothers had been snake-bitten in the last year. Fortunately, both were bitten by small ground rattlers and were only sick for a few days.

On the way to the creek, they re-lived the snakebites. Felix, or "Lucky" as he was known, said, "I saw a toad hop down a hole, and when I reached in there and grabbed him, I got aholt of a ground rattler—or I guess you could say that it got aholt of me, right on my hand.

"After the excitement over my bite eased up, we dug down the hole and found him. He was about two foot long. He won't bite nobody again."

The other brother, Fess, had been bitten only about two weeks ago. In fact, his right hand and arm were still discolored, with a scab where his mother had cut the fang mark to drain the poison.

"Mine was a little different. I was moving stove wood when another ground rattler bit me. He was bigger than Lucky's snake, but only got me with one fang." He held up his arm and showed the grotesque purple and red streaks on it.

It was evident that they were real proud of their twin bites. I asked, "Do you fellows do everything together?"

They answered in unison, "Everything."

We neared the creek and found a good spot on the bank. I used the end of my cane pole to poke around for snakes among the roots.

"What're you doing?"

"I'm making sure I don't become a triplet in y'all's snake-bite club."

We caught a few fish, but they couldn't be still or quiet enough to do much serious fishing.

One of the brothers said, "I hear splashing and laughing up the creek."

Sure enough, I heard it too.

"What do you think it is?" he asked.

"I don't know. Let's go see." I should've known better, but I laid down my pole and followed the sound.

Going upstream, the splashing mingled with voices, and became louder. We eased along and cut across a bend before crawling up on a bluff bank. There below us in the creek was a man and woman neck deep in the water.

They had no idea anyone was watching. In their own way, the couple reminded me of the otters I'd watched near here, except in this case, it wasn't a bobcat slipping up, but three curious boys.

One twin was on either side of me. One whispered, "Who are they?"

I didn't recognize the man but the woman was the young Cole widow. Her husband had died, and she lived by herself on Ten Mile. Her first name was Frances.

The other brother said, "Hey, their clothes are hanging on a limb there."

Looking at the sand bar, I also saw a pair of boots, a half-empty whiskey bottle, and a gun belt with a pistol.

"They ain't got nothin' on," Fess said.

"They ain't wearing nothing but their 'Outward Adam,'" his brother added. Seeing my confusion, he whispered, "They're naked."

Fess corrected him. "No, they're *buck* naked."

Lucky jabbed him. "There ain't no difference 'tween 'naked' and 'buck naked.'"

'Yep, there is." Pointing at the empty boots on the sand bar. "You can be naked and have your boots on, but if you're 'buck naked' you ain't got *nothin'* on."

Lucky repeated, "Just got their 'Outward Adam' on."

Personally I was much more interested in Widow Cole's Outward *Eve* and hoped she'd come out of that deep water soon. I was pretty sure she wasn't wearing any fig leaves. With these thoughts in mind, I didn't see the twin nearest the sandbar—I believe it was Lucky—began crawling along the bluff bank toward the clothes.

All I could do was watch—any noise would give us away. With cat-like quickness, he made his way on his all fours to the sand bar. It reminded me of the bobcat's approach to the otters.

The joyous couple—Mrs. Cole and her male friend—were enjoying the water too much to notice anyway.

Lucky, shielded from their view by a river birch, quickly removed the clothes from the limb. He picked up the whiskey bottle, grinning back at us before setting it down. To my relief, he left the gun alone.

Just as silently as he'd made it down, he crawled back to us on the bluff bank, his hands full of clothes—mostly women's things. Proud of his haul, he gleefully showed us each item.

His brother, Fess, who'd been left out of the festivities so far, couldn't stand it, so he gave his loud wolf howl followed by a shrill, "Hey, I see y'all."

That's when all heck broke loose. Widow Cole, much to my delight, was just wading out of the deep water, but the wolf call put her back into deep water screaming like a panther.

Her friend was also caught off guard, but he didn't head toward deep water. Instead, he splashed toward the sandbar, cussing loudly as he grabbed his pistol.

I knew I should run before he got there, but couldn't move. However, the twins, who evidently had more experience in mischief like this, were up and running.

I joined them, only looking back long enough to see the man buckling on his gun belt before pulling his pistol. The sight of a naked man with only a gun belt on would have been funny if I hadn't heard the gunfire.

I never looked back as he hollered, "Hey, bring our clothes back!"

The twins were running ahead waving the woman's clothes above their heads as if they were Indians and these were scalps.

"Whoohooo—Yes siree, we got us a prize," one of the twins hollered.

They stopped when we got to the edge of the swamp. We

knew that man wasn't going to chase us too far in his condition. Panting for air, I couldn't stop laughing even as I calculated how many licks with a pine knot club it'd take to kill those two twins.

"Well, what're we gonna do now?" one of them asked.

"We ought to take those clothes back toward the creek, leave them, and clear out," was my answer.

"All right, Mayo, *you* take them." Lucky threw the bundle of clothes at me.

I dropped them. "There ain't no way I'm going back down there."

"Well, neither are we."

So we took the clothes with us and the boys volunteered to hide them at their house. I gladly agreed—not wanting anything to do with the contraband. They headed home, and I agreed to wait along the tree line for their return, watching carefully in case our swimming friends appeared.

Eventually, the twins returned and we walked on to my house. There we found our mothers happily visiting, obviously enjoying themselves. Sarah Merkle was just finishing a cup of coffee. "How was fishing?" she asked.

"It was fun. We caught several small ones and two great big ones," Lucky answered.

"We threw them back in 'cause we didn't want to clean them," the other boy added. My mother, who tolerated no waste, gave me the evil eye, as I shook my head.

When the Merkle clan finally left, Momma and Colleen waved goodbye from the porch, and the questioning began with, "Colleen, go play outside."

As soon as my sister disappeared, Momma turned to me, "All right now, what really went on?"

"I ain't keeping those boys no more."

"You will if I say so."

"I don't care if it harelips the Pope, I ain't doing it."

She didn't tolerate any lip and stood to her feet.

"Momma, I don't care if it harelips *the world*. I'm through keeping them."

She never tolerated any sass and started toward me.

I put my hand up in defense. "Just wait, Momma. Let me tell you what happened, and you'll understand why." There was no use to lie—no story that I made up could've matched what really happened. So I told her, detail by detail.

Her only comments were, "No way . . . not really . . . *Frances Cole?* . . . Git out of here."

Finally, as I ended my story, she came around the kitchen table. "Mayo Joseph Moore, if you're lying to me. . . ."

"Momma, why would I make up a lie that wild?"

"I guess you got a point." With that, she really got tickled and soon tears were running down her cheeks. "Are you *sure* it was Frances Cole?"

"Yes Ma'am. It was her. You know how she has that birthmark on the back of her neck."

This was true, but not what Momma wanted to hear. "Boy, what are you doing noticing that mark on her neck?"

"Well, we sit behind her in church, and it's hard to miss."

She jabbed me. "Well, what else was hard to miss?"

"Nothing. Honest. She was shoulder deep in water the whole time."

At supper that evening, Momma would periodically look at me and burst out laughing. Her behavior mystified Colleen. "Momma, what's so funny?"

This only made her laugh harder until she choked on the cornbread she was eating. With tears running down her face and cornbread crumbs flying out with each cough, she left the table.

Colleen turned to me, "Why's Momma crying?"

"She ain't crying. She's just tickled—that's laughter."

Holding her fork in mid-air, my sister said, "It's good to hear her laugh again, ain't it?"

"It sure is," I agreed.

272

Fella's barking that night didn't surprise me as I'd expected company. Our house was the closest one to the creek and that poor naked cowboy had to get help from somewhere. Momma and I already'd rehearsed how we'd handle it.

I heard a horse snort as I went out into the darkened yard, cradling our shotgun. Hiding behind the chimney, I said, "Who goes there?"

The horse snorted again and a male voice spoke, "A friend just needing a little help."

My voice was changing and I tried to speak as deep as I could, but it came out as a nervous squeak. "What are you doing, coming up on our place this time of night?"

"I'm harmless, just need a little help."

"What do you need?"

"Two sets of clothes."

"What?"

"You heard me—two sets of clothes. Me and my partner got jumped down on the creek, and the thieves took everything we had, including our clothes."

I knew my mother was standing behind the door and was glad she wasn't beside me. In spite of my fear, I nearly busted a gut when the man said, 'my partner.'

"What size are you, Mister?"

"About normal size."

"What about your partner?"

"A little smaller."

I could actually hear my mother's giggles by the window. Steeling myself, I took a deep breath. "All right, mister, I'll be right back with some clothes. You stay where you're at and keep both hands where I can see 'em."

I couldn't even see him in the dark but wanted him to think I could. I eased through the back door and grabbed the pile of daddy's clothes we'd prepared. Momma was still by the front door, rifle in her hand, but I didn't even go near her. I was too nervous as well as afraid she'd get me tickled.

Back at the chimney, I called out. "I've got your clothes. We're going to do this real nice and slow. My momma and brother both got a gun on you, so don't try nothin'."

"Just want them clothes, and I'll leave you be."

"Fair enough. I'm putting them on the gate. Give me some room, then get them, and be on your way."

I set the clothes down, ran back beside the porch, and squatted down. I was wearing dark clothes and knew he couldn't see me.

I heard him dismount from the horse and walk over to the gate. There was just enough light to see his pale body clad only in a hat, cowboy boots, and a gun belt.

I suppressed a laugh remembering the Merkle twins arguing over "naked" and "buck naked." This man was no longer buck naked, but he was definitely naked. With his care package in hand, the man carefully remounted his horse. I couldn't resist it. "Where's your partner, Mister?"

"She—I mean, *he's* back at our camp." He continued, "By the way, son. You weren't around the creek any today, were you?" It was asked innocently, but had a hard edge to it.

Before I could answer, Momma called out, "No sir, he was here building fences all day long."

The man said, "Well, I thank you kindly." I heard his horse snort as he turned and rode away.

"You're welcome," we both answered.

I'm not sure how long Momma and I laughed—it was well into the night before we stopped reliving every word of our encounter with the man.

The next day found her still chuckling, saying she was actually sore from how hard she'd laughed. I was reminded that laughter is the best medicine of all. Later, I found that verse in Proverbs that says, "A merry heart doeth good like medicine."

My mother was getting her merry heart back, and I was so happy about it that I put off killing the two Merkle twins for their prank. I'd give them a reprieve because their mother was helping mine, and their mischief had made her laugh again.

I could forgive them—at least for now.

Chapter 42

IT wasn't one single thing that brought my mother out of the darkness, and it didn't happen in one fell swoop. However, I'm still convinced it was a miracle. Earlier, it'd seemed she had gone so far into the blackness of her soul that no return was possible.

Now different things—mostly small—signaled that she was coming back out of her cave. It wasn't all at once, and it wasn't without some steps sliding backward.

One of these steps forward occurred one morning when I awoke and saw she wasn't in her bed. Panicked, I ran outside and found her on the porch sipping a cup of coffee.

"Mayo, those martins sure are singing pretty today. Come sit by me and listen."

And that's just what I did.

Another sign of Momma's recovery was how Sarah Merkle no longer came to our house daily—instead, Momma went to her house for some of the visits. Another sure sign of her returning health was a renewed love of the outdoors. She spent less time indoors and more out in the sunshine.

Often I would walk with her to the Merkle place. We'd talk about the woods and listen to the birds. Coming back on a cool morning with Colleen walking between us, I asked, "Do you think Mr. Merkle will ever come back?"

She looked at me trying to read my question, as I studied her face. "Why do you ask?"

"I was just wondering," I asked.

"Well, do you think he'll return?"

I saw the lasting image of him swinging from the rope. "No Ma'am, I don't think he's coming back."

"In spite of the hardships, I think she's better off without him," Momma said.

"I think so, too."

We were quiet the rest of the way. As I watched her, I still wasn't sure if she knew the truth about Silas Merkle's death. I'd had given one of Unk's gold coins to know what she was thinking.

They say revenge is a dish best served cold. I'd been planning to repay the Merkle twins for the trouble they'd caused with the clothes and the swimmers. I carefully laid the groundwork during one of our visits at their place.

"Boys, have ya'll heard there's another wild bull roaming these woods?"

"Really?" The twins had a deep fascination and fear of wild bulls and made me repeat my adventures with Roscoe on nearly every visit. As I'd tell my story, I made bellowing and snorting sounds as the boys stood wide-eyed.

I buttered the twins up good. "Yep. It's a light-colored bull they're calling the 'Grey Ghost.' It gored a man over on Steep Gully and has been seen near the crossroads."

For the next couple of weeks, they grilled me about the Grey Ghost. I laid it on thick and heavy. It was nearly time for revenge. One cool afternoon, I went to the Merkle home. Felix was outside and I asked him. "Hey, I'm going over to the Big Pasture. You wanna go?"

He looked at me. "What about that Grey Ghost?"

"He ain't around no more. They claim he's back in the Hog Wallow country."

"You sure?"

"I'm positive."

"Don't we need a gun?"

"Nah, we'll be fine. Get your brother and let's go."

He came back with Festus, and we were off. I set off at a brisk pace and the boys fell in behind. I'd glance back at them and nearly laugh as I saw them looking carefully behind us about every tenth step. No wild bull was going to get them—at least not from behind.

We arrived at the edge of the pasture and walked to the middle of the opening. The sun was setting behind the pines and our timing was perfect.

"You sure that bull ain't been around here?"

"Well, I'm pretty sure."

"Pretty sure?"

"Well, if he shows up, we'll just outrun him."

"Outrun him?"

"Well, what I mean is this—I don't have to be able to outrun the bull, I've just got to be able to outrun *one* of you."

The amazing thing about these identical twins was how they expressed emotions simultaneously. As if they'd rehearsed together, they both had a wild-eyed look and glanced in unison across the open field, as if calculating how far it was home.

Just then is when we heard it. A loud long bellow followed by another.

"What was that?"

"What was what?" I calmly asked.

"That noise. It sounded like a—like a *bull.*"

The twins scanned the field in every direction for any sign of the ghost.

The next bellow was even louder, and they grabbed each other. "Where's it at?"

They were shaking with fear. I nearly felt sorry for them, but got past that emotion when I recalled how funny they'd thought it was when the naked cowboy was shooting at me.

Revenge is sweet, I thought as I called out, "It's getting closer, listen." The bellowing was nearer and the twins' heads seemed to be spinning like owls as they tried to find the source. Right then I hollered, "Look out, it's the ghost—run for your life!"

And that's just what those baby dolls did. They were headed for the house. I thought they'd at least look back to see how I was faring, but they never did. Remembering my "slowest man gets gored" story, each was sprinting to stay ahead of the other.

I stood there, enjoying every moment of it.

The sound of the bull bellowing was now directly overhead and I glanced up. "Thanks for your help. I really appreciate it."

The two nighthawks above me twirled and soared in their evening courtship. I watched them fly up high, before cupping their wings and suddenly diving for several hundred feet. The loud "whoosh" of this speedy dive gave the nighthawks their local name, "bullbats."

They were neither a bat nor a bull, but they sure scared the heck out of the Merkle twins. It was a long time before the boys would even leave their yard. I never had the heart to tell them the truth.

That saying is correct—revenge *is* a dish best served cold.

As you can see, the war years, although hard years, were also full of memorable events that I still hold dear. The best part of this time for me was being treated more and more like a grown man. I relished this and worked even harder to keep our place looking good for Daddy's return. To hear him say I'd kept the place up like a man was the only reward I wanted.

The older men who'd not gone off to war included me more and more in their activities. One morning, PaPaw came by and with one searching look I knew what today was—the pine kindling strips in his overall's back pockets told me it was burning day.

Toward the end of winter before the grass turned green, the men of the community always burned the woods, to their grazing livestock. The men believed the new tender grass that came up after the fire was better for their livestock.

The weather was just right that day—a light wind out of the north with low humidity. We met up with Barney Bryant and three other men, and after comparing notes, the men started setting fires using the kindling for torches. As soon as the torches touched the tall dead grass, it blazed up and quickly spread.

Soon, a long line of flames was moving southward through the pines. It was my first time to be in on the burning, and I listened to every word between the men.

"Barney, you did let those families over near the big pasture know we'd be burning toward them, didn't you?" PaPaw asked.

"Yep. They're starting some backfires so the flames won't get too close to their homes."

Sure enough, a glance in that direction showed smoke. PaPaw said, "Mayo, a pine straw fire burns with a light gray color—see that?" He pointed to the ash-colored smoke in the sky.

I asked, "What about those black streaks I see?"

"That's where a dead rich-lighter pine is burning."

We set fires all afternoon that spread and were still burning after sunset. Making my way toward the edge of the fire, I saw the outline of two men silhouetted against the flames.

Easing along the charred ground, I recognized the men as PaPaw and Barney. It was obvious they didn't see my approach. Neither heard very well, so they spoke loudly, allowing me to hear every word.

Barney, the louder of the two, said, "Willard, after that bad fire of '51, things changed a lot didn't they?"

"Sure did."

"I've always heard you were part of the crew that took care of the timber men that tried to burn us out."

"I was there."

"Did y'all kill them all?"

I leaned in closer, heart pounding, not sure if I wanted to hear what was said next.

"Barney, we didn't kill any of them. We just made them think we would—and could. Ben Tyler shot that bad one earlier, and a couple of them got winged when we hunted them down, but we didn't kill them."

"I've heard different," Barney said.

"Well, you can hear a lot of things 'round here. The ones

I saw weren't dead, they were sprinting to get back across the Calcasieu and out of No Man's Land—and dead men don't run that fast."

"They don't, do they?"

That was the end of that conversation. Changing the subject, PaPaw said, "Barney, there ain't much better than burning the woods, is there?"

"You're right, Willard. In fact, my two favorite things in the world are burning the woods and sex."

I ducked behind the pine, listening closely. PaPaw laughed as Barney continued, "In fact, if I had to choose between the two, I'd have to think about it a while, because sex is—"

PaPaw's laughter drowned out his words.

Then Mr. Barney coughed and slapped PaPaw on the shoulder, "Now which one would you choose if a brisk north wind was blowing?"

"Oh, that'd make it easy. I'd—"

That was when *I* got choked. I coughed, both men turned, and PaPaw said, "Who goes there?"

"It's just me—Mayo. I was letting y'all know I was coming up."

"What'd you hear, Boy?" Barney asked sharply.

"Not much."

"What?"

"Mr. Barney, I just heard you say, 'that you'd hate to have to choose between burning the woods and goin' to *Texas*.'"

Both men looked startled, before breaking out into loud laughter.

"Are you sure that's *what* you heard?" Barney asked as he wiped away tears.

"Sounded like it to me."

"Didn't hear nothing else 'fore that?"

"Not *a word*."

Soon the day's burning was over as darkness deepened over Ten Mile. We walked past a line of fire burning slowly through the pine straw. All three of us smelled like smoke and our faces were smudged. It'd been a good day—a burning day.

As we walked home, the older men talked about famous fires of the past. I was consumed with another thought. If that other thing Barney mentioned—sex—is better than burning the woods, it must be some kind of good.

When Barney turned down his side trail, we waved goodbye and I couldn't resist hollering, "See you later, Mr. Barney, when you get back from *Texas*."

PaPaw elbowed me. "Say—Boy, you better watch yerself."

I was ready. "No, old man—you better watch *yourself*."

Although our faces were blackened with soot, our grins were visible even in the black dark of a Ten Mile night.

As Momma continued improving, she spent more time outside working with Colleen and me. I loved the lessons she'd share from nature. Her people had a special connection to the woods around them.

One day, she and Colleen met me at the garden where I was hoeing. Momma said, "Let's go over past the Big Pasture and take a look at something I been wondering about."

I was more than happy to stop. She grasped my hand and began talking about how proud she was of me. Although it kind of embarrassed me, I loved hearing—and needed—every word she said.

We walked to where we'd burned the woods last month. The hot fire had killed the underbrush and small trees. Young sweet gums, oaks, and small longleaf pines all were dead, with their leaves or needles burned off.

Momma walked over to where a stand of year-old pines, ranging from ground level to several feet high, had been killed by the hot fire. Pointing out a small pine she said, "See that one—it's what's called the 'grassy stage.' It looks more like a tuft of grass than a tree."

Colleen leaned down and pulled the dead needles off the tree. "Momma, it's a shame that fire kilt these pines."

She looked directly into my sister's eyes. "Baby, these pines may look dead, but they ain't. They're as alive as you and me. You jes' wait and see." Instead of telling us more, she winked. "We'll come back out here in a few weeks, and then I'll tell you the rest of the story.

I didn't think much more about the pines. There were too many other things on my mind and too much work to do, but Momma didn't forget. A month later she said, "You remember those 'dead pines' we looked at?"

"Yes'm, I remember them."

"Let's go check on 'em."

We walked to the edge of the field where the small pines were. New grass was coming up, but much of the ground and small trees were still blackened. We walked over to where the grassy pines were, and I couldn't believe what I saw. "Momma, those burnt trees are green again at the top."

The small trunks had shed their burned straw and new bright green growth was protruding upwards. "Son, a hot fire'll kill oaks and most trees, but something about a longleaf pine protects it. My daddy says they got thicker bark and their deep taproot can't be kilt by a fire. Nobody really knows—we just know that the fire doesn't kill 'em. It just frees the tree to grow taller.

"In fact a longleaf won't grow tall if the area around isn't burned regularly. It'll just sit there in that short stage." She knelt and touched the nearest green pine. "This tree will never be confined to the ground no more. It'll grow up, tall and strong."

She stood, put her hands on my shoulder, and looked deep into my eyes. "Mayo, the wisdom of these woods is here to teach us. Since that hurricane, we ain't had nothing but *storms,* or I guess you could say we've had *fires.* Those fires have burnt our family pretty badly. You've been in the fire along with us, but those fires have made—and are making—a strong man out of you. I'm proud of you." She kissed me right on the cheek, before saying, "The fires haven't killed us. They've just made us stronger—in fact, I wonder if we're 'fireproof'."

She sighed and wiped her face with her apron. "I just wish the Lord would give us a break from any more fires. I feel like we've had our share."

"We sure have, Momma. We sure have."

Chapter 43

AS 1864 went by, all of the news from the war was bad. It was evident that the war was winding down.

During this year there was fighting all over Louisiana—at Pleasant Hill and Mansfield and along the Red River. During this time, in what is now called the Red River campaign, the sorry Yankees burned the city of Alexandria. Ben Tyler visited there after the fire and told a sad story of the stark desolation of our area's largest city. People now lived in tents and portions of burned-out buildings, trying to hang on and survive.

But in Ten Mile—our part of No Man's Land—the Federals hadn't penetrated. We were far enough from cities and rivers to be of little value. PaPaw summed it up well, saying, "All we got here are pine bergs and panthers. They're looking for cotton and slaves. They'll leave us alone."

We got a letter from Daddy saying that he was in the fighting up in north Louisiana. He told about his unit, what they ate, and how much he missed us. His handwriting on the letter's last paragraph was shakier and tighter. "Am saddened to hear of Patrick's death. Words cannot express my sorrow at the news and sadness at not being with you."

Momma left his letter on the shelf. I read it carefully over and over—especially the last part. There was a smudge mark on the last sentence, and I wasn't sure whether it was a fingerprint or a tear stain. Each reading of the letter convinced me of the latter.

Each reading of Daddy's letter also melted the resentment I'd held toward him. His pain at being apart from us, especially during this sorrowful time after Patrick's death, was evident in both his words and handwriting.

At night, Momma would pray and ask the Lord to give him

the horse sense to keep his head down and gallop away from danger.

In spite of the war's nearness, one area tradition continued without interruption—feuding.

Daddy's statement that "A Redbone is the best friend you could ever want, but the worst enemy you'll ever have," rang true on both extremes.

Redbone feuds could go on for years. Then again, they could end abruptly, just as quickly as they started. One of these battles took place in the "Hog Wallow" area northwest of our settlement. It was an ongoing feud between an old man named T.B. Pruitt and a newer settler by the name of Walker. As with many blood feuds, it began with livestock.

Walker moved in by himself not far from Six Mile Creek. He had trouble with woods cows getting into his garden and finally, out of patience, he shot one with buckshot. When told this was open range for cattle and he needed to fence his garden, Walker said, "It's my land and I don't have to fence it. Y'all just keep your cows off my land."

Old Man Pruitt's cows were the main culprits that kept getting on Walker's land. When he shot another one, Pruitt had enough and sent word that he was going to "get the new settler."

The new settler didn't wait for the threat to come to pass. He went to the Pruitt homestead, gun in hand. He wasn't trying to sneak up; instead he walked right up the path. Hearing the dogs barking, Pruitt grabbed his pistol and met his neighbor on the porch.

Because one of them died, the whole story was never known. Evidently, the old man raised his gun to fire, and Walker shot, hitting the pistol and jamming it.

Walker's second shot—and the ones that followed—didn't miss, leaving the old man dead, his jammed pistol lying beside him on the blood-soaked porch.

Realizing he was now a marked man, Walker wisely hit the road. Pruitt's large family threatened revenge. That night Walker's place—a small log house, barn, and corncrib—all burned.

According to Unk, Walker fled west for the safety of the Sabine and Texas beyond it. But, he never made it—two Pruitt men caught up with him at a campsite on Burr's Ferry just east of the Sabine. It was there that the feud ended. Two men were now dead and two families deeply affected.

I tell this to remind you of how violent an area the No Man's Land could be. Everything could be going fine, but then a spark—a wandering cow, a stolen pig, or a simple insult—could start a firestorm of vengeance.

Unk came by our house not long after the Hog Wallow killing and announced, "There's another feud building up, and it's right up at the church."

We went to Occupy Church, located on the banks of Ten Mile. During the war years, we were mostly without a preacher and only met sporadically. News of a feud at our church brought my mother from the kitchen.

"A feud at *our* church?"

"There sure is, and you know how these can get out of hand."

Only a few years before at another local church, a man was stabbed to death on the church steps for insulting the assailant's mother. Our area was such a mixture—of peace and violence, piety and revenge—and even churches weren't immune to it. Because folks came together at church, many times ongoing problems came with them.

I'd heard the story of a circuit-riding preacher who'd taken firearms out of the hands of two men at church. The fellows were having trouble over a common love interest. He'd boldly called both men down, took their pistols, made them come forward and repent. Those present said it wasn't a boring service at all.

So, Unk's declaration of trouble at Occupy Church fully got our attention, so Momma asked, "What kind of trouble, Unk?"

"Well, you know Occupy is the only building around with glass windows."

"Go on." My mother was anxious to hear more.

"Well, the trouble is evidently over the windows. It's caused some fighting."

I saw the corner of Unk's mouth twitch and wondered where this was going.

"Between who?" Momma was anxious to hear more.

"Mr. Red ain't getting along real well with the windows."

"Mr. Red who?"

"Mr. Redbird."

"Who?"

"Well, Mr. Redbird—a cardinal—has discovered those windows and is fighting real bad with that other redbird behind the glass."

Colleen and I were now laughing at the story, but Momma turned and went into the house as my uncle continued, "I'm telling the truth. That redbird—you know how territorial they are—has been fighting its reflection in the glass. He does it all day long. Done broke one window. I believe he's going to have a bent beak before it's over. Yep, it's a real feud and. . . ."

That's as far as my uncle got because Momma came out with a dishpan of dirty water and tossed it right in his face, adding, "Speaking of feuds. I might just start one *with you* for telling a tale like that."

Unk, soapy water dripping off his face, replied, "I just thought you'd like the news about it."

"Get out of here and go watch your redbird," she scolded him.

He jumped off the porch, but we knew he'd be back for supper.

I went inside where Momma was angrily snapping beans. She huffed, "The idea of him telling that story like it was a real feud. A redbird fighting its image in the window—makes about as much sense as that stupid war."

Finally, she grinned, "But I do believe we'll go over this afternoon and see that redbird for ourselves."

I've always liked underdogs. I guess it was the way I was raised, and because of that I'm partial to the "underdog bird."

That's what we called these birds back then. I know today that their correct name is "kingbird." You may not know them by name, but you've seen them—they're the small birds you'll see chasing off crows and hawks.

It still tickles me to see a large bird on the run as this tiny bird dives repeatedly behind it. I've even seen them put an owl on the run. If that owl's talons got aholt of the smaller bird, it'd kill it instantly, but the kingbird's speed and agility keep it safe.

The kingbird, or "bee martin" as it's called by some, is extremely territorial and jealously guards its area from any intruder—be it bird, cat, dog, or sometimes during nesting season, humans. Many old timers called it the "butcher bird" because of how it'd catch lizards and impale them on thorns or barbed wire.

I guess that is why years after this Civil War was over, we Southerners are still reliving it. We were the underdog bird, fighting off the confounded invaders of our homeland. But in spite of early victories and early hope, the size of the owl or hawk and its claws and beak were deadly.

As 1865 began, we all knew the large bird—the Union—had the South in its claws. It was just a matter of time before the war ended. As my mother often said during the war years, "It was a lost cause from the start."

Lost cause or not, I just hoped they'd end it soon and my daddy would still be alive to come home.

Watching all of these scenes from nature—kingbirds, geese, turkeys, otters—I came to be a deep believer in what Momma called "the wisdom of the woods." She'd taught me so much of the lore of the piney woods and how God designed it to work together.

But the best lesson she'd taught was one I observed. I'd seen my mother's faith shaken like a ship on the ocean. I'd seen her heart shredded and her joy taken away. She'd taken life's shots, been knocked down, and yet got back up. It reminded me of a saying Daddy always used, "Fall seven times, get up eight."

I looked at Momma, realizing what a strong woman she was. Her battles over these past weeks hadn't shown her as weak, they only revealed how deep her taproot was.

Just like the pines she loved, she was deep-rooted, in spite of the storm. She'd bent, seemingly broken, only to snap back upright and stand tall.

I now believed what I'd heard her say, "You become stronger in the broken places."

Chapter 44

IN spite of dreaming about my daddy and thinking about him constantly, I found it difficult to talk about him. I couldn't control my emotions when someone mentioned his name, and I avoided any conversations about him. It wasn't that I'd forgotten him. In fact, he was on my mind every minute of the day.

In his latest letter, Daddy mentioned a "slight leg wound" he'd received. We discussed for days what "slight" meant.

We hadn't heard from him since. The silence of the intervening weeks and months—the uncertainty of the unknown—drove us crazy.

Uncle Eli seldom wrote. Last we'd heard, he was near Opelousas. I kept his short letter under my bed and often thought of him and our last conversation before he left. I prayed daily that God would keep both my daddy and him safe.

Chapter 45

SPRING came late in 1865, and the lingering cold weather fit the mood in my heart. We hadn't heard from Daddy in a long time, and I was worried.

As April melted into May, we got word the war had finally ended. General Lee had surrendered up in Virginia, and that was the final blow. Just about the time the huckleberries ripened, the long line of tired soldiers began passing along the Sugartown Road.

The sight of limping, bedraggled men shuffling along was a clear sign that we'd lost. Many days Momma and I stood along the road listening for word of Daddy. Watching the men go by, she said, "They look whipped, don't they?" She called their daily procession, "The Scarecrow Parade." Her term described them well. They were thin, dressed in tattered uniforms, with sunken faces, most passing by as quietly as any scarecrows I'd ever seen.

Momma insisted that we supply clean water for the passing men, adding, "Honey, I hope folks along whatever road your daddy is walking home on extend some kindness to him. It's the least we can do for these sad men."

As they went by on their way home to Lake Charles, Orange, or back to their farms along the Sabine or Neches, we asked for information about Daddy. None of them knew anything about his regiment. We offered them water and any food we could spare, which they quietly accepted before continuing on.

Since Daddy left a year and half ago, I'd faithfully kept the patteran at the crossroads, checking on it every few days and after rains. I'd added some mussel shells, string, and pebbles to the sticks and leaves.

One day in mid-May, I was chopping firewood along the

Sugartown Road when I saw a group of six travelers coming. As they neared, I scanned for my dad, but he wasn't among them. Two of the six carried the visible wounds of war—one had lost an arm, another had a bandaged head. All of them had looks clearly indicating they'd seen more than a human should.

They stopped, and I dipped each of them water before asking, "Any of you fellows ever run across an Irishman named Joe Moore?" Their answer was the same as always, shaking their heads as if in thought of the many men they'd fought alongside, and then replying, "No, son."

It was humbling how appreciative these men were of the slightest kindness. Their faces revealed that any act of compassion was even more welcome than the water.

As the six men drank and made small talk, I realized why their faces seemed familiar. Each had the same shell-shocked look I'd seen on faces in the days after the hurricane. It was a hollow-eyed stare of someone who'd survived a great storm—a look of fear that left a peculiar mark on the face of a man or woman.

I'd seen it on the face of Sarah Merkle when we visited her after the storm—a look of sheer desperation and dread. She'd worn it on her face, but it came from deep inside her—down in her heart and soul.

These soldiers had that same look. They'd been in the storm—not overnight like us, but for months, even years. They'd lived with the daily uncertainty as to whether their next breath might be their last, not from a crashing oak, but from a Union Minie ball or cannon shell.

I called it the "storm survivor's stare."

As the six of them staggered out of sight, I wondered what their lives would be like from now on. I also wondered the same thing about our South as all kinds of rumors were flying, about how the victors would treat us.

In spite of seeing the results of the war among these men, my young mind never considered the fact that my daddy would be one of the changed ones. When he arrived home, he'd be wearing that irrepressible smile, reminding me that everything would be all right. I believed nothing could take away that smile—not even a war.

However, I wondered how many of these returning scarecrows had left with that same grin and lost it somewhere on one of the battlefields where so many of their friends and fellow soldiers lay.

I thought of how many other boys or girls just like me were waiting at the gatepost or road for their daddy, poppa, or pa to come home. I realized this lonely waiting wasn't just happening in Ten Mile, or No Man's Land, or just in the South, but was being played out all over our nation.

Daily gazing into their faces, I wondered what my dad would look like, and be like, when he finally came home.

If he came home—that was the question tormenting me daily.

Many men weren't coming home, and even those who did were changed—wounded in spirit, never to be the same.

Would my dad, whom I loved and missed beyond words, be wounded in spirit? This thought burned in me as I left the roadside and returned to chopping wood.

Leaning for a breather on my ax handle, I saw a lone straggler come over the hill along the road. The men who'd just left said they had friends dragging up the rear, and this was probably one of them.

The man was gaunt and limped slightly. Since he was probably with the men who'd just passed, I knew he wouldn't know my daddy. I figured he could dip his own water from the roadside bucket, so I turned back to chopping.

Then I remembered Momma's admonition to show kindness to *every* traveler, so I stopped and walked toward the road. The man, his back to me, stopped at the bucket and drank two dipperfuls before I got there.

His hat was pulled down low on his head as if he wanted to hide. I thought about walking away, leaving him to fend for himself. He hadn't seen me yet, and I could easily blend back into the woods.

But I didn't.

Easing closer, I called out softly so as not to startle him. "Sir,

I've got some cornbread in my pocket, would you like some?"

His upturned face revealed a shaggy, sandy beard below sad eyes. His words were hoarse as he pointed toward our place. "Sure looks like a good place."

"It is, Sir...It..."

That was when I realized it was him—my daddy, Joe Moore. I was shocked at his appearance—he'd lost so much weight, his face pale and gaunt, and he limped. However, a closer look revealed the green eyes that always defined my daddy.

In addition, what he said—*a good place*—revealed much more about our future than any others words could express. It was said in the way that only a resolute Irishman could say it.

Daddy was home—and in spite of whatever the war might have done to him, in spite of the storms we'd been through these past few years—a hurricane, sickness, death, robbery, and a cruel war—this *was* a good place to be.

I ran to him. "I want to hear you say it again."

"Say what?"

"What kind of place this is—"

He hugged me tightly.

"This here's a good place—it's our home."

Our arms around each other, we slowly trudged up the trail toward our cabin. Before we got in sight of the house, he stopped, looking me up and down. "Son, you've become a man while I was gone."

I didn't reply—I couldn't because of the soft sobbing that was pouring out of me. Finally, catching my breath, I said, "I ain't much of a man the way I'm crying."

"Son, crying doesn't keep no one from being a man."

"I hope not, 'cause I've done plenty of it."

"Me, too," he said.

Changing the subject, I asked, "Did you see your patteran back at the crossroads?"

"Sure did, and I expected to—you said you'd keep it marked."

The evening sunlight shone through the tall pines, spotlighting us as we walked. I gripped his hand—scared to let go lest this only be a dream.

He held my hand just as tightly, slowly limping up the hill he'd named Westport.

When he sighted the cabin, he dropped his pack and stopped. Putting his hands to his mouth, he began the loudest—and most welcome—version of his evening holler I'd ever heard.

His owl call echoed off the surrounding woods. "Hoo hoo-hoo hoo, hoo hoo-hoo hoawww."

I'd waited so long to hear it again.

My vision was so blurred from tears I couldn't see clearly to the house, but I heard my mother screaming for joy joined by Colleen's, "Daddy, Daddy!"

The light through the pines coupled with their hollering made me wonder about the future generations who'd live in these Louisiana piney woods. What would their lives be like? Would their lives be much different from the lives of this family on a hill called Westport?

I knew that, like us, I knew they'd face strong storms of many kinds—that's one of the constants of this crazy thing called living. But I prayed they'd eventually find the same deep strength we found here—a strength discovered in the land of the pines—the strength of faith, family, and the woods.

The strength still found in a good place.

Epilogue: Reconstruction

The years after the war—"Reconstruction"—were hard on folks in all of Louisiana. In some ways, we're still getting over the scars of that time here.

However, the turmoil and violence that marked Reconstruction in the rest of the state didn't touch us in No Man's Land. We'd been ignored before the war, during the war, and the years after 1865 were no different.

Times had always been hard in the piney woods, where we were familiar with trials and trouble. So, the years after the war, with its many more storms, neither surprised nor stopped us.

However, the word *reconstruction* has somewhat of a different meaning for me, because that is exactly what happened with our family. *We were reconstructed.* There was a lot to get over, get past, and move on toward the future. Our personal reconstruction involved plenty of rebuilding from the events that had torn us down. Momma always said it this way, "Those hard war years sure tore us down." She'd wink. "But they didn't tear us apart. We just got up and rebuilt."

That's what my parents did—they rebuilt. Evidently, when they'd made that vow of "for better or worse" back in 1851, they'd meant it. No storm life threw at them could break them. More children were born into our home, and the sounds of laughter filled our house again in Ten Mile.

Throughout the years when asked about the bad times during the war, my daddy would simply say, "It was. There was no other option."

As they aged and finally each of them died, I fully realized that was what they'd given me—they'd passed on the things that really mattered, and among them was a belief in grit, togetherness, and perseverance.

I left Ten Mile and became the first in my family to be educated, but I still reflect on the fact that the best education I received was at the foot and side of my parents and Westport kin.

To my knowledge, no one ever knew about the source of the gold except my parents and me, and that's how Uncle Nathan "Unk" Dial wanted it.

Unk lived to a ripe old age, dying in the first year of the twentieth century. Folks said there were more people at his funeral than any other held in Ten Mile. That shows how much he influenced lives during his long rich life.

I've spent over half a century digging and poking around the Big Pasture looking for his buried treasure, hoping to find that last "double handful" of gold eagles. I haven't found them yet, but know they're out there somewhere.

Then there was the Merkle family. They were our neighbors and that is exactly what they became—neighbors. My mother always introduced Mrs. Merkle as, "My dear friend, Sarah, who brought me out of my time of darkness, and whose name I bless."

I never told Mrs. Merkle or the twins how her husband died on the short end of a rope. Some things are better left unsaid, and that was one of them.

Amazingly, her children all turned out well. The twins grew up into fine men. They started with a shaky foundation, but both finished well. Their sister, Tabitha, still lives in Ten Mile. As far as I know, she and my sister Colleen are the only people in this entire story, except me, who're still alive. Either one of them can attest to the truth of most of what I've told you.

Speaking of telling, I never told my parents of how Silas and Sarah Merkle stole from us after the storm. Once again, some things don't merit repeating. Unless Mrs. Merkle confessed to anyone—which I rather doubt—this is the first time it's ever been told.

I've been looking for two people since 1863—a girl named Clothilde and a boy named Bill.

I never saw Clothilde—or as I knew her, "Chloe," again, but that beautiful Creole girl lives on in my memory. In my heart, she's never aged nor changed. Years later, I went back to their bayou and found nothing but rotten piers. The few people living nearby didn't know what happened to the Creoles who'd once lived there.

Standing in a boat where the bayou runs into the wide Calcasieu, I wondered if I'd only dreamed of meeting her here. I realized then, as I still do, that I still carried a torch for her but it wasn't meant to be. In a way, it was good I couldn't find her—it would have only broken the spell that's lasted a lifetime.

There's a second person I've looked for, but never found. His name was Bill, the jayhawker's son who saved our lives. I would've liked to have met him again to say thanks for sparing our lives. Often, I've seen men resembling my mental image of Bill, but none was he. I wonder if he's even alive, but I know this, I'm *alive* because of the mercy he showed us that day on the trail, and I'll be forever grateful for that.

Uncle Eli never returned from the war. We got a letter from one of his commanders in Mississippi telling us that he'd died in a minor skirmish right before the end of the war. He wrote, "Eli Clark was brave and every inch a soldier. He died instantly leading a brave charge that every soldier who survived it will always remember. You can be proud of him."

We already were proud of him, and didn't need a letter or medal to make it so. I was just glad it was a Yankee bullet, and not some accident or sickness, which ended his life. His wish was to "die with his boots on," and evidently that's exactly what happened.

I've been over to north Mississippi several times searching for his grave but never had any more success than in digging for the coins. I still have the captain's letter and a lifetime of memories of my Uncle Eli. In my heart, he's still riding up at the foxhunt campfire, scaring us to death, laughing, hooting, and living life to the fullest.

I carefully completed the three things I'd promised Uncle Eli

I'd do if he didn't return. I've never told a soul what they were—that was part of our deal. Maybe soon, before my life ends, I'll tell someone. The problem is if I tell anyone, as Unk always said, 'I'd have to kill 'em.'"

I've kept objects related to my family and this story. I still have most of them: a dried cedar twig from a cemetery, a stick from a patteran, that old sturdy table under which we rode out the hurricane, a worn Gold Eagle coin, and a weathered cypress shingle.

These objects are important to me for only one reason: they connect me back to my family during this unforgettable time. They're reminders of the good place where I grew up.

The most important things I have from that time cannot be held in my hands. They are the lessons, memories, and strength all safely stored in my heart.

Now that's my story of the series of storms that battered us beginning in 1862.

It's my story—the story of growing up in the piney woods of Louisiana's No Man's Land—a good place to live.

A good place to be.

Coming Soon
As The Crow Flies
The next installment in The Westport Series.

It's now 1881 in No Man's Land. Joe and Eliza are busy with their lives while running a general store in Westport. However, tension between encroaching outsiders and the isolated Ten Milers creates trouble that thrusts the Moore family into the middle.

Being neutral is not an option as tempers rise and violence erupts. Especially affected is the youngest Moore son, Dan. His entire life and future is torn asunder on Christmas Eve 1881 when what will be known as "The Westport Fight" breaks out.

Lives end and families are split. Lifelong friendships are cut, and no is affected more than the Moore family.

And no one in that family suffers more than their youngest son Dan and his girlfriend Lucy.

From the opening line, it's clear this book is about change and conflict:

"As the crow flies, it's only about twenty miles from Ten Mile to Sugartown, but after what became known as "The Westport Fight" it might as well have been a million."

This distance is especially painful for two families, especially for a young couple in love.

To Dan Moore, it seems ironic that the battle called "The Westport Fight" began on Christmas Eve. Instead of celebrating the birth the "Prince of Peace's" birthday, an armed conflict breaks out that changes everything about his life and future.

It was a time and event that forever changed the destinies of everyone involved.

Especially two families.

Especially a young couple in love.

This is their story.

The story of a teenager named Dan Moore and a girl named Lucy Robinson.

Acknowledgements

So many folks have helped on this labor of love called *A Good Place*. I couldn't do what I do without my family. It all starts with my precious wife DeDe who encourages, edits, and gives me stability. Each one of my sons and their sweet wives are a part of my writing team. Thanks Clay, Robin, Clint, Amanda, Terry, and Sara.

My mother, Mary Iles, and sister, Colleen Iles Glaser, are avid fiction readers and offered timely advice and input. My uncle, Bill Iles, is a lifelong source of encouragement in my life. I'm honored that his painting, "Upper Field Pines" graces the cover of *A Good Place*.

I have a wonderful team of editors who make my writing so much better: Melinda Shirley, Dempsey Parden Jr., Jackie Dees Domingue, Paul Conant, and Frank and Weeda O'Connell.

Special thanks to Mark and Kari Miller. Like me, Mark is a great-great-great-grandson of Joe and Eliza Moore. Mark and Kari are invaluable to my writing.

This book was birthed at a writers' meeting in the home of author Diann Mills. Diann mentors a group of emerging writers known as "Ripplers." I'm especially grateful for four members who helped: Danny Woodall, Debbie Gail Smith, Lisa Buffaloe, and CeCe Benningfield.

I'm appreciative of my agent Terry Burns at Hartline Literary as well as the other encouraging writers who are his clients.

All serious authors are surrounded by a nurturing group, and for me this is the Bayou Writers Guild in Lake Charles, Louisiana.

So many others have helped in large and small ways. Among them are Roberta and Jessica Ciccarelli, Joe Pool, Nola Mae Ross, Dean Burns, Debra Tyler, Mandi Q. Eastwood, Joe McNeill, Joe Chaney, Alda Clark, Haley Laird, Kathleen Y'Barbo, Dee and Wallace Jones, Mike Chapman, Enola Gay Mellen, Peggy Weldon Renfrow, Sue White, J.T. and Auty Platt, Joan Powell Friend, Aurora Wilber, Tim and Kym Couch, Connie Richard, Tegan Sager, Nicholas Casanova, Rose Manuel, Martha Lou Roberts, and Michele Davis.

Technical support and design came from my webmaster Will Johnston, Thomas Umstaddt, Chad Smith, and Marty Bee.

In addition to my many outdoor writing locations, I'm grateful to my special friends, James and Shannon Newsom, for the use of their cabin. Thanks also to friends at two places I love dearly, Dry Creek Camp and Piney Woods Camp.

All listed above, plus many more, have helped bring *A Good Place* to fruition. Their help was invaluable, and any mistakes or omissions are mine.

A final reminder: The reason I write is to glorify God and encourage people. My wish is that this book as well as anything else I write will always accomplish those goals.

Curt Iles with his faithful writing partner, Ivory, at The Old House in Dry Creek, Louisiana. Built circa 1892 on land homesteaded by Curt's great-great grandparents.

Curt is an eighth-generation native of Louisiana's unique "No Man's Land." He and his wife DeDe, are parents of three sons and three grandsons.

He is a full-time author and speaker who enjoys traveling, hiking, and making new friends. Curt is a popular speaker delighting audiences with stories from his books.

Iles is a graduate of Louisiana College and McNeese State University. Prior to becoming a full-time author, he served as a teacher/coach, school administrator, and youth camp director.

An independently-published author, his previous six books have sold a cumulative 20,000 copies. To learn more about Creekbank Stories and the writing/speaking ministry of Curt Iles, visit www.creekbank.net.

For comments, suggestions, and corrections for future editions, contact us at curtiles@aol.com.

Curt Iles is represented by Terry Burns of Hartline Literary Agency at www.hartlineliterary.com.

Also by the author:

The Wayfaring Stranger (2007) The novel that begins the love story between Joe and Eliza.
ISBN 978-0-9705236-9-6

The Mockingbird's Song (2007) Essays of Encouragement for Overcoming Depression. The book that is helping readers world-wide.
ISBN 0-9705236-4-5

Hearts across the Water (2005) Stories of hope from 2005's three major natural disasters, Hurricanes Katrina, Rita and the Asian tsunami. Written from Curt's involvement in all three events.
ISBN 0-9705236-3-7

Wind in the Pines (2004) More stories from the heart and pen of Curt Iles. Contains reader favorites, "A Father's Love" and "Burned, Yet Blessed" plus more.
ISBN 0-97505236-1-0

The Old House (2002) Come sit on the front porch of The Old House where the view is always good and the breeze is cool. Thirty-eight stories of love, friendship, and family, including "Dead End Road."
ISBN 1-4033-5227-5

Stories from the Creekbank Stories (2000) Come to the creekbank for these stories of the beauty of the woods, nature, and good people. Curt's first book is still a favorite of readers everywhere.
ISBN 0-759-69895-3

A Good Place (2009)
ISBN 978-0-9705236-9-3

How to order your copies:
All books are $15.00 each including tax.
$5.00 Shipping/handling per order.
-Order direct through www.creekbank.net
-Order through any of the contacts below.
-Order at www.amazon.com
Contact information
Creekbank Stories
PO Box 332 Dry Creek, LA 70637
Toll Free 1 866 520 1947
curtiles@aol.com
Visit The Creekbank at social networks
Facebook, Twitter, and MySpace.

Book Clubs and Libraries

To schedule Curt for your book club (via telephone/internet or a personal visit) contact us at curtiles@aol.com. Book Discussion Guide, Special Features, and more at www. creekbank.net.

LaVergne, TN USA
16 October 2009
161110LV00006B/1/P